W9-AOF-962

A BOUND HEART

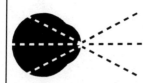 This Large Print Book carries the
Seal of Approval of N.A.V.H.

A Bound Heart

Laura Frantz

THORNDIKE PRESS
A part of Gale, a Cengage Company

GALE
A Cengage Company

Farmington Hills, Mich • San Francisco • New York • Waterville, Maine
Meriden, Conn • Mason, Ohio • Chicago

Copyright © 2019 by Laura Frantz.
Scripture quotations, whether quoted or paraphrased by the characters, are taken from the KIng James Version of the Bible.
Thorndike Press, a part of Gale, a Cengage Company.

LIBRARY OF CONGRESS CIP DATA ON FILE.
CATALOGUING IN PUBLICATION FOR THIS BOOK
IS AVAILABLE FROM THE LIBRARY OF CONGRESS

ISBN-13: 978-1-4328-5981-7 (hardcover)

Published in 2019 by arrangement with Revell Books, a division of Baker Publishing Group

Printed in Mexico
1 2 3 4 5 6 7 23 22 21 20 19

Dedicated to my sixth
great-grandfather,
George Hume of Wedderburn Castle,
Berwickshire, Scotland

SCOTS GLOSSARY

addlepated — mixed-up
aflocht — troubled
Alba — ancient term for the kingdom of the Scots
auld — old
Auld Reekie — Edinburgh
Auld Toun — old-town Edinburgh
bairn — child
bannocks — oatcakes
bethankit — God be thanked
blether — gossip
bonny — pretty
brae — hill
Braiste Lathurna — the brooch of Lorn
braw — handsome
Buik — Bible
canna — cannot
couldna — could not
da — dad
didna — did not
dinna — do not

7

doesna — does not

douce — sweet, lovely

dunderheed — fool

fash — worry, vex

gaol — jail

ghaist — ghost

gruamach — sulky, moody

haeddre — Scottish heather

hasna — has not

haud yer wheest — hold your tongue

hoot! — pshaw!

howdie — midwife

hungert — hungry

ill-scrappit — rude, bitter

ill-trickit — wicked, dangerous

isna — is not

jings — gosh

kelpie — water fairy

ken — know, understand

kirk — church

laird — landowner ranking below a baron and above a gentleman in Scottish order of precedence

leine — shirt

loch — lake

loosome — delightful

michty me — goodness gracious!

Moonbroch — ring around the moon

neeps and tatties — turnips and potatoes

och! — oh!

peely-wally — sick
ruadh — red
sennight — week
sgian dubh — black dagger
shooglie — shaky
shouldna — should not
slàinte — (to your) health
smirr — sprinkle
sonsie — pleasing, pretty
sporran — leather pouch
stayed lass — spinster
tapsalteerie — topsy-turvy, upside down
tolbooth — courthouse, jail
unchancie — dangerous, risky
wasna — was not
wheest — quiet, hush, to hold one's tongue
willna — will not
wouldna — would not

1

Nae man can tether time or tide.

Robert Burns

Isle of Kerrera, Scotland, 1752

As the sun slid from the sky, Lark pressed her back into the pockmarked cliff on the island's west shore. The sea stretched before her like an indigo coverlet, a great many foam-flecked waves tossing gannets about. A south wind tore at her unbound hair, waving it like a crimson flag, as crimson as the fine cloth she'd seen smuggled ashore the previous night. These free-trading times were steeped in danger. Countless moonlit liaisons and trysts. Sand-filled shoes and sleepless nights. How oft she'd prayed an end to it all.

On this breathless May eve, the only aggravation was the sting of tiny midges as night closed in — and the thickset Jillian Brody as she bumped into Lark and nearly sent her off the cliff's edge.

"Look smart, aye? There's tax men about."

"I pray not," Lark breathed, craning her neck to take in the sweeping coastal headland that could only be called majestic. She wouldn't tell Jillian she was more addlepated about the handsome captain of the *Merry Lass* than the chancy smuggling run, and that she braved the midnight hour to gain but a glimpse of him or his ship.

"Yer not out here for the same reasons as the rest o' us." Jillian managed to stand akimbo, hands fisted on her ample hips despite the path's ribbon-like lip. "What's this I hear about ye refusin' to help bring in the haul?"

"My conscience smote me," Lark told her. "I canna be in the business of stealing even if it betters the poor."

"Hoot!" Jillian spat the word out as the night wind began a queer keening, lifting the edges of their plaid shawls. "Yer fellow islanders are not so high and mighty. Be off wi' ye then."

The dismissal, though said in spite, was gladly heeded. Lark turned and hastened away, stepping ably along the path though 'twas nearing midnight. Darkness didn't fall till late, which left precious little time for the free traders to do their work in the

12

smothering safety of night.

Tense, she climbed upwards, casting a glance over her shoulder at the beach now and again. But this long, miserly eve brought no goods ashore, nor a handsome captain home again, and so she entered the wee cottage no bigger than a cowshed, its humble stone her home since birth. Only she and her granny fussed with the peat fire and kept a-simmer the kettle of porridge or soup, which always seemed to taste of smoke. She washed up before donning a worn nightgown, then all but fell into the box bed, exhausted.

Early the next morn she trudged through the mist to Kerrera Castle. Glad she was to have gotten even a snatch of sleep.

Once on castle grounds she quashed the urge to steal into the walled garden and drink from the spring that bubbled forth in a stony corner. Like ice the water was, even in the heat of summer. Most servants weren't allowed in the formal garden. Kerrera's mistress did not like the help to be seen. Her fragile constitution could not bear it. The glorious bower was reserved for Lady Isla and Kerrera's infrequent guests.

Bypassing humble beds of herbs in the kitchen garden, Lark came to the beloved bee garden. Here she could stay content forever. Against one ivy-clad bricked wall were numerous bee skeps. Made of thick coils of straw, they were fashioned into golden domes, a wee door at the bottom of each. Even now their inhabitants hummed a lively tune, already at work among enticing calendula and borage, awaiting a feast of bee balm and snapdragons and cosmos in summer. Come August she would take a hive or two into the heather, making the coveted heather honey of which the laird was so fond.

Her gaze swung to the bee bath she'd created years before, a chipped, shallow dish for fresh water. Beach pebbles were scattered about for the busy creatures to perch on while drinking lest they drown. Their droning seemed to intensify with her coming. The bees sensed her, their singing rising and falling as she moved among them. They did not favor everyone, merely tolerating the head housekeeper yet circling the maids benignly. But they stung Cook in a fury. The laird of Kerrera Castle moved calmly and respectfully in their midst, much like Lark, both of them spared the piercing pain. She'd always wondered about their reaction to Lady Isla. But the laird's wife rarely ventured near the bee skeps.

Seeing all was well, at least in the gardens,

Lark turned toward the castle.

"There ye be, Lark."

Was she tardy? Mistress Baird, the stern housekeeper, never greeted her, only made her feel guilty. In the bowels of the castle came the liberating chime of the case clock in the servants' hall.

Not late. On time.

From her chatelaine, Mistress Baird removed the key to the stillroom. Lark took it, murmuring thanks, and turned to go. She took the crushed-shell path to the small stone building attached to the castle's orangery, which had been damaged in a storm, a few panes of glass broken. The few awakening plants within were seeking summer, showy bright blossoms adorning one glassy corner.

The stillroom door creaked open. The scent of damp, cold stone and pungent peppermint embraced her, a reminder of yesterday's tasks. She reached for an apron dangling on a hook, tied it around her waist, and set to work.

Out the back door she soon went into the kitchen garden, mindful of her mission. The basket on her arm overflowed with herbs before she returned inside again, consulting the receipt book open on a near table though she knew the tincture by heart.

"Good morning to ye, Lark." The laird stood in the open doorway, startling her. He was in finely tailored Edinburgh garments, his hands caught behind his back.

Seldom did he come here. She hadn't seen him for a fortnight or better. He was mostly in Edinburgh at the courts of law. Once the distance had chafed. Now she was schooled to its pain. Close as twin lambs they'd once been, beginning when her mother was wet nurse to his. Only back then she'd not known he was a MacLeish, laird of Kerrera Castle. For all she knew he was one of the servants' children. A ruddy-cheeked, sable-haired barrel of a lad. Nor had he known she was merely a servant's daughter. Together they'd been weaned then toddled about before running together over the braes like unbridled colts.

Seeing him now, she nearly dropped her basket. "Yer lairdship —"

"Be done with that, Lark."

Sunlight spilled into the space between them. And an unseen wall of reserve. She would not — could not — call him Magnus ever again.

"We arrived late last night. I sent word ahead to ye. Did ye not receive it? About the needed tonic?"

"Nay." She sensed his distress. His stoicism did not fool her. His very presence bespoke something dire.

"To Hades with the post," he said with no small exasperation.

"Dinna fash yerself," she said as in days of old, hating that he seemed so vexed.

He looked skyward, his somberness unchanging. "There's to be no heir for Kerrera."

Her soul went still. Not again. What could she say to this? Six losses. 'Twas the reason the mistress was so gruamach. Kerrera desperately needed a babe, an heir. But no remedy or tincture could be had if one's womb was closed, Granny said.

"The doctors have sent Lady Isla here to recuperate. Beyond the stench and noise of the city."

Her hands nearly shook as she blended the herbs at hand. What a predicament! 'Twas no secret the mistress didn't care for the western islands. She found Kerrera uncivilized. Remote. A hue and a cry from her Edinburgh roots. Yet the doctors had sent her back.

The laird ran a hand through unkempt hair, gaze fixed on the sea that gleamed more gold than blue as morning bloomed beyond the castle walls. "What would ye advise?"

"Something calming." Her gaze lifted to the crocks and jugs on a shelf overhead as her thoughts swirled and grappled for answers. "Chamomile. Lavender oil. Lemon balm."

"How soon can ye ready a tonic?"

"Some things canna be rushed," she said. "Ye dinna want a false remedy. Besides, I've more than one tincture in mind." She bent a knee before she brushed past him, leaving the stillroom for a forgotten herb.

"I have faith in ye, Lark," he told her as she reentered the stillroom. "Mayhap more than in the Edinburgh physics."

"Yer faith is misplaced, mayhap." She met his azure eyes for a moment longer than she should have, if only to delve the depths of his pain. "Prayer is oft the best remedy. But this shall help in the meantime." She handed him a small glass bottle. "Have her ladyship's maid steep this in the hottest water, then wait a quarter of an hour before drinking it down."

"What does it do?"

"Rests her ladyship's womb." She flushed, hands busy with the next task. 'Twas awkward discussing such matters, but she forged ahead. "Returns her courses."

He was looking at her expectantly, no hint of embarrassment about him. But clearly flummoxed. Even disappointed. Did he think she could produce a child?

His gaze shifted. Studying the concoction in hand, he merely said absently before leaving, "Bethankit."

She mulled his bad news the rest of the afternoon, her reverie interrupted when she shut the stillroom door for the day and heard a rustling close behind her. She startled, her heartbeat calming at the sound of an unrefined yet familiar voice behind the hedge.

"Prepare for tonight. The *Merry Lass* is expected. When ye return to yer croft, stretch a bedsheet over yer peat stack once ye get the confirmation of landing. If the coast is clear I'll shine the light. But beware. There's talk the tax men are about."

Another smuggling run? "I canna —"

"Wheest! So the blether I hear is true then? Ye'll not help? The captain is dependin' on ye!"

Lark sighed, torn between bowing out or doing her part as a fellow islander. The least she could do was spread a simple sheet, aye?

Lord, forgive me.

Giving the news bearer a reluctant "aye," she took the path down the cliff. The mere mention of excise men was enough to stop her cold.

"The *Merry Lass* will be bringin' a load of salt, ye say?"

"Nay, Granny, I didna say. We can only hope."

"God be praised if so!"

Together they sat at their small table, partaking of nettle kail and the last oatcakes slathered with crowdie, before a smoke-stained window. The view was wide and jaw-dropping, even to Granny who'd lived there the longest. Perched on a cliffside, their humble croft seemed in Kerrera Castle's shadow. The castle was above them, the crown jewel of the coast with its splendid pink harled stone and profusion of towers and turrets, a sea marker for ships coming ashore.

"Who's the captain of the *Merry Lass*?" Granny asked.

Lark's stomach somersaulted. "Captain MacPherson . . . Rory MacPherson."

"Och! Mad Dirk's lad?"

"Aye, Granny, all grown up."

"Reckon he'll spare us a sack of salt?"

Lark swallowed another bite of supper, used to her grandmother's repeated questions. "The whole village is in need of such if we're to make it through another long winter."

"The laird willna let us starve." Granny poured tea with a steady hand that belied her age. The steam whitened the air between them, the aroma laden with guilt. Smuggled Irish tea it was, like the smuggled salt to come. "The last lugger brought only whisky. We have no need o' that but for medicine — or to befuddle the excise men."

Salt, on the other hand, was a necessity for preserving the fish to sustain them. And none could afford salt — or tea — since the Crown taxed both nigh to death.

Granny took a sip. "How are matters at the castle?"

'Twas the one query Lark had no heart to answer. "Lady Isla has lost another babe."

"God bless her." Granny's dark eyes narrowed to apple seeds. "The laird too."

"Is there nothing to help beget an heir?"

A faraway look came into Granny's eyes. Lark waited for some remembrance to kindle. In her day, Granny had been the stillroom mistress like Lark's mother had been the wet nurse. "My feeble mind has too many dark corners. I canna ken much."

"Well, if ye ever do . . ." Lark kept her eyes on her tea, wishing babies were as easily gotten as salt.

Where was the *Merry Lass* this twilight eve? Even if she looked hard, the ship eluded her. Painted black with dark sails, the sloop was nearly invisible on a moonless night. For now, the sun rode the western sea like an orb of fire, casting tendrils of light across their empty bowls and full cups.

'Twas calm. Warm. Lark's gaze sought the expanse of beach where the first tubmen were gathering to bring in the cargo. Soon the sand would teem with horses and carts, island women armed with cudgels and pitchforks to accompany the goods inland.

But before the *Merry Lass* put on all sails and headed straight for them, lookouts must be posted. Then Lark would stretch a bedsheet over their peat stack while someone else onshore shone the light.

The immense sea cave boasted only a few ankers of brandy to one side and empty, shadowed sleeping platforms at the back. As midnight deepened, cold water licked Lark's bare feet and teased the toes of the captain's boots. With the incoming tide, there was precious little time to talk. 'Twas always the way of it. No time. Little talk. Great disappointment.

"So, lass, what have ye need of? Be quick to ask." Dressed in long boots, trews, and a striped jersey, Rory MacPherson had the look of a pirate, pistol and cutlass at hand. He made light of the tax men by calling them names, but the wariness remained. "I'll see no treasure fall into the hands of the Philistines, aye?"

She smiled, Rory's grin infectious. Tonight, the excise men had been outwitted by the free traders once again. The haul had been a roaring success. Forty chests of tea. Thirty mats of leaf tobacco. Eighty ankers of brandy. Two casks of figs and sweet licorice. A great quantity of salt. Oats.

"Salt and oats." Lark imagined Granny's glee. "Molasses, mayhap."

"Aye." Could he sense her delight? Her reluctance? She swung like a pendulum between the two. She nearly said *tea* but feared appearing greedy.

"Tea?" he stated with vigor as if sensing her longing. "A few bricks or a chest?"

"I canna haul a chest —"

"I can. I'm on my way to the Thistle. Ye take the rest."

Weighted down they were. But she was strong and fleet of foot, oft taking the craggy path in the dark by the lights of Kerrera Castle. Soon the tide would wash away their footprints and return the *Merry Lass* to sea, the braw captain along with it.

For now, breathless, her shawl slipping, Lark followed him up the cliff, the elation of a full larder eaten away by the coming separation. Rory never stayed long. Though he stood hale and hearty, surefooted in his upward climb while dislodging a stone now and again, he would soon be gone, a ghostly memory. It seemed she lost another piece of him whenever he left, till the essence of him was no more substantial than the mist that hovered over the water.

She'd felt that way about the laird when he'd wed. Such a part of her life he'd been till Isla had turned his head. Rory had taken to the sea soon after, and she felt rent in two by both losses. While these men made their way in the world, she stayed the same, bound to croft and castle.

She looked up, the sound of the thundering surf in her ears. Tonight Kerrera Castle shone bright as a lantern just above. She glanced down quickly, then took her eyes off the path — off Rory's broad back laden with the tea chest — to rest her eyes on the castle's largest window.

There in sharp relief stood the laird, Magnus MacLeish, looking down at them. She resisted the impulse to throw up a hand. His tall silhouette was more familiar than the captain's sturdy shadow in front of her. She looked a tad too long. Her foot slipped. Pain seared her turned ankle. Noisy pebbles scattered like buckshot, causing Rory to turn around.

The castle's cellars sometimes held cargo secreted away when the threat of excise men made it too risky to move the goods inland. But tonight, with no hazard at hand, they walked free and cargo laden. Breathing hard, she stood taller when they crested the cliff and left the trail, favoring her turned ankle.

"Ye still with me, lass?"

She shifted her burden, the leather straps digging into her back. "Indeed."

"Indeed?" He cast the mocking word over his shoulder. "Why so fancy? Are ye getting above yer raising when a simple *aye* will do?"

She went hot, glad the darkness hid her flush. 'Twas a word she'd heard the mistress say in her crisp, aristocratic tones. Ever since, *aye* seemed too common, like dirt — much like the ancient croft ahead, turned a beguiling white in the moonlight but still simple. Unadorned.

Once there, Rory released the tea chest and Lark gave up her own burdens. Granny cracked open the door, her smile wide despite her missing teeth. "Such as ye give, such will ye get."

Rory gave a little bow at her hard-won words, to which Granny's cackling laugh was short-lived. Only during a run did Granny seem to forget her dislike of the captain.

Lark looked about for any lurking shadows as rain began spattering down, promising Rory a wet walk to the Thistle. Granny began taking the goods inside one by one to secret away in a hole beneath a hearthstone while Lark faced the captain. "I thank ye."

"Is that all ye'll give me?" he returned.

Used to his teasing, she sweetened her goodbye with a curtsy, but the merry singing of Granny's teakettle did little to banish Lark's melancholy as Rory began backing away from her, hat in hand.

"Someday ye must tell me of yer travels. If the French ladies are as comely as they say. How green Ireland is," she called after him, her voice falling away in the damp dark.

Small wonder he wanted to be away. The Thistle did more than wet his whistle. She'd heard tales of him charming the tavern wenches there with satin ribbons and bits of lace from foreign ports. He'd not given her such fripperies, naught but salt and tea and oats, a fact that held the appeal of curdled milk.

But her own charms were few. She had no power to hold him. No ale with which to entice him. He was less inclined to talk than the laird of late. But even if he'd paid her attention, her spirit stayed unsettled. All this smuggling — ill-gotten goods — squeezed the very life out of her.

Granny hovered in the croft's open door, as if chaperoning their parting. "Take thy tea, Lark."

And so she did.

2

Oats. A grain, which in England is generally given to horses, but in Scotland supports the people.

Samuel Johnson

Magnus moved about the castle's unlit corridors, the taper he carried a-dance in Kerrera's draft. 'Twas chill for May, and the prior winter had been long and lean. The village children who'd perished from disease and want of nourishment over the cold months were never far from his thoughts, as marked as the crosses that shadowed their graves in the kirkyard. His view from his study window took in those wind-beaten crosses. They and his own desire for a child melded into a lasting melancholy he prayed warmer weather would mend.

How different it would be if childish laughter echoed in Kerrera's halls. Six bairns lost in as many years. What he would give to have his half-dozen ringing his table and overflowing the nursery. On the heels of this wistful thought came the crushing reality that Kerrera would stay empty and echoing.

His bride was weak. Not in strength of will. Her pedigree and even the jut of her jaw bespoke a far from congenial partnership. But she was barren. Unable to carry a child. If only such calamities could be foreseen ahead of contracts and commitments. "Till death do us part" now held an onerous ring. But he would honor his vows, the covenant they'd made, and keep praying for miracles.

He passed Isla's door, treading lightly so as not to disturb her, his collie at his side, the nuzzle of the dog's damp nose a comfort.

His wife's bedchamber was partly ajar, her voice leaking out. "Magnus?"

He motioned for Nonesuch to stay in the hall before entering, aware his fading candle was mostly melted. No matter. Her sumptuous room — gold themed with London's finest furnishings — glowed with no less than a dozen tapers in candelabras. Tonight, despite the late hour, a book lay open on her lap, more volumes on her bedside table. She read her days away and sometimes her nights till dark circles rimmed her eyes. Kerrera's library seemed more hers than his. He was a man of action, managing his tenants and holdings with little time for the printed page other than Scripture.

"Isla." He stood at the foot of the immense bed he shared less and less, its curtains half closed. A fire in the hearth warmed his backside but failed to make its way to the castle's cold corners. Her lady's maid was busy doing whatever ladies' maids did.

"I cannot sleep." Abandoning her book, she stroked the twin pugs on either side of her. "I must have more of the stillroom's tincture. From the bees' mistress."

"Lark's remedy?"

Isla all but bristled, and he rued the stubbornness that kept him naming the servants if for no other reason than it nettled his wife. Never did she call the servants by anything other than their standing in relation to her. That nettled *him*.

"The stillroom maid, yes."

"Did yer own maid not give ye the tincture this morn?" he asked.

"Indeed. But 'tis all gone, she gave me so little. Can you not send for the lass now? Rouse her?"

"Nay." His mind skipped back an hour to

midnight when he'd last seen Lark on the cliff's path with her burden. She was no doubt abed, having taken tea with her granny like the three of them had oft done in his youth. They'd sipped the hot brew while the stillroom's former mistress spun stories of Kerrera's glory days when his father and grandfather, former lairds, were alive. "In the morn she'll return to the still-room. Bide yer time till then."

Isla made a face. Arguing was pointless. His nay was nay. "Have her make me a gen-erous quantity. I shan't be without again."

He bade her good night, starting for the sitting room that adjoined their two bed-chambers, but stopped cold at her next words.

"My maid tells me the free traders were on the beach tonight before the turn of the tide. Is that true?"

"Tonight, aye." Why did she ask? He rarely mentioned what happened after dark, though sometimes he himself disappeared. "The haul went well. All the cargo is on its way inland."

"Last time a great quantity of goods was stashed in the kirk."

"An unsuspecting location," he replied.

"Reverend Blackaby is more sot than saint!"

"We all have our besetting sins," Magnus said quietly.

Isla settled back on the bank of feather pillows, twisting her flaxen braid with agitated hands. "Rather *he* dangle from a noose than the laird of Kerrera Castle."

He waved a hand at the draped windows. "No gallows are in sight."

"Don't make light of such. Betimes the castle cellars are as full as the kirk. Ye turn a blind eye to the dubious goings-on —"

"The cellars last held salt. Oats. The staples of life. Would ye wish the deaths of more bairns? More aged? More disease from lack of nourishment?" His voice rose in thunder, his stub of candle held high. " 'Tis a small risk to incur when we dinna go begging bread."

She looked away from him, bristling. Her ever-present maid seemed to be taking a long time to return the jewels her mistress had worn at dinner to their case. Eavesdropping again?

"Good night," he said, thinking of the double portion of smuggled goods the reverend had sent to the crofts of the bereaved this very eve. But did it fill the hole in their hearts? Return their kindred? Nay.

With a shrill whistle, he called for his collie, then pushed open the door to his own turreted room, the tapestry walls holding the fire's heat. He stood before the snapping hearth, feeding the remaining taper to the flames. The wind was rising, forcing a dark plume of smoke into the ancient chamber. He never minded. 'Twas the scent of simpler times. Boyhood. More carefree days on Kerrera.

In Gaelic, he gave vent to his angst beneath his breath. " 'Tis better to dwell in the wilderness than with a contentious and angry woman."

The thorny Scripture was followed by a far sweeter one. *Husbands, love your wives.*

"Ready to retire, sir?" Brown, his manservant, appeared with his Bible and a dram of the water o' life. Both were bracing but a curious combination, truly.

Brown disappeared, and Magnus sat down in his favorite chair, feet to the fire, as a blast of wind forced more than smoke into the masculine chamber. 'Twas long past midnight. Full dark. He opened to the Psalms, reading in Gaelic the holy words he'd read most every night of his married life.

Lo, children are an heritage of the Lord: and the fruit of the womb is his reward. As

arrows are in the hand of a mighty man;
so are children of the youth. Happy is the
man that hath his quiver full of them.

A half measure of comfrey. A pinch of
lemon balm. A palm full of mint. What
needed gathering next? When would the
next need arise? Growing up in the castle
by Granny's side had taught her much. Lark
knew by heart the helping herbs and those
with poison in their bite. Some were like
gentle friends, others she need be chary of.
She had within her power to heal or hurt.
'Twas not a task she took lightly.

Queen of the stillroom and bees she was,
or so the laird once said. He'd come upon
her in the castle's bee garden one day, a
daisy chain crowning her, bees ringing her.
The slant of the sun had turned her golden
from the tip of her flaming head to her bare
feet, he'd said. She had no memory of that
long-ago moment, but Magnus had not forgotten.

Now, the day after the *Merry Lass*'s landing, her hands worked with mortar and
pestle, grinding dried rosemary to mere
ashes. Its pungent scent was like the sweet-
est perfume. Queen of the stillroom and
bees, indeed.

"Are you at work?"

Lark turned. 'Twas Rhona, the mistress's maid. Inwardly Lark recoiled like she would at an adder. Rhona never looked at her directly. Like Isla, she looked everywhere else as if she could not lower herself to meet a servant eye to eye.

In turn, Lark was curt, always glad to bring their hasty meetings to an end. "What is yer need?"

Frowning, Rhona moved inside. " 'Tis not mine but milady's. She desires a wine tincture . . . something stronger."

"Stronger?" Lark questioned. "I am pondering a remedy, something to truly help. Not spirits."

Coming to the table, a slab of coastal oak that served as a work counter, Rhona surveyed the gathered herbs. "What are you concocting?"

"Help for rheumatism. Auld Abel, the gardener —"

"The gardener? 'Tis your mistress that needs attention." Rhona folded her arms. "Have you something for more than sleep? Have you nothing for her womb?"

Six babes lost. Lark bit her lip. *Ye are asking for the moon.* "Aye. Prayer."

"Are you implying my mistress is not devout?"

"I ken little of yer mistress's habits as she

keeps herself closeted so."

"She is not well enough to leave her bedchamber, except to dine with the laird."

Lark continued her mashing and mixing. "Get her on her feet. Take a thimbleful of whisky with her porridge. Saddle her mare and ride along the beach. Stroll about the garden beneath the spring sun."

A grunt of disgust. "Is that what you islanders do? 'Tis so . . . common."

"Lying abed makes one weak."

"So you've no herbs? No help? You are the stillroom's mistress. Do you not value your place?"

Lark fell silent as Mistress Baird's tall form darkened the doorway. "Yer mistress is ringing for ye, Rhona. She doesna like to be kept waiting."

Finished with her mixing, Lark began to bag the tonic for rheumatism as Rhona disappeared without a word before the housekeeper's rebuke. Watching her go, Lark felt a stab of pity. For all her bristling, Rhona seemed naught but the worst sort of servant, subject to Isla's moods and whims, rarely out of her mistress's sight.

Mistress Baird came nearer and raised a sleeve, revealing a pale arm that had been reddened with rash before. "The salve ye gave me is quite effective."

Lark smiled. " 'Tis naught but oil, oats, and sea salt." She could take little credit for nature's gifts. "I'll gladly make more should ye need it."

"I doubt I shall." Passing into a small anteroom, Mistress Baird was joined by Cook to take stock of the pantry for the coming ball.

"One gill of brandy for the laird's cake," Cook said, tallying items on paper. "A quantity of dried currants and raisins as well."

"Dinna forget rosewater and essence of lemon," Mistress Baird replied. "And ample cinnamon."

"Aye, aye. The mistress is wanting a confection of her own," Cook added, sounding vexed. "She's forever wanting a great many things."

Their talk dwindled to disgruntled whispers. Lark's mind spun back six years prior when Isla had arrived at Kerrera's gates. All the servants had lined the drive that autumn day to greet the castle's new mistress, each holding something that bespoke their service. Cook fisted a beater. The grooms sported horseshoes and riding whips. The butler, a small silver salver. The maids, feather dusters.

Lark herself held a bouquet of fragrant

lavender, representing refinement, grace, and elegance, all of which she hoped her new mistress would be or bring from far-away Edinburgh. The simple nosegay's stems were tied with silk ribbon from her mother's dower chest. When she'd held it out to the laird's bride as she passed, Isla had not taken it but turned aside, silken skirts swirling.

"Never ye mind," Granny consoled Lark later. "She mightn't have seen it. Just think what a spectacle awaited her — an army of servants and an auld castle. 'Twas her first time on the island, ye ken."

Truly, mayhap Lark's hopes had been too high in assuming the lofty lady would take her humble offering. 'Twas Magnus who had reached out and plucked it from Lark's hand at the last. It had assuaged her some-what, though the memory was still sore.

"We'll be needing yer help for the ball, Lark." Cook stood at table's end, a long list in hand. "Fiona is out with her sick bairn, and Archie is in Oban for his father's wake."

Shorthanded again. "Granny can help too if ye like. In the kitchen, at least."

Cook turned contemplative. "We're ex-pecting no less than a hundred. The Great Hall's being readied as we speak. 'Twill be quite a feast. The laird's ordered sweetmeats and provisions from Glasgow."

Lark's heart lifted. Twice a year came the tenants' ball. Betimes it seemed the only occasion the people felt full. Relieved of their labors. Though the ball was for the laird's servants, his tenants, and the like, she didn't mind helping as she was one of them. The joy it brought was worth the extra work. She would dress in her best. Mayhap step a reel or jig. There'd be small gifts for each, a compliment or two. The laird would oversee it all.

Would the captain come?

Rory MacPherson was a fine dancer. Not so fine as Magnus but less ticklish than the laird. With Rory, there was no chasm to cross, no title other than captain. No lady to call his own. Hope took root. Was he still at the Thistle?

Mistress Baird and Cook left the stillroom to make the most of the fortnight before the ball. As for Lark, time enough to ready a gown. Mend her hose and garters. Carry her shoes to the cobbler. Decide how to dress her wayward hair. School her disappointment if the captain did not come.

And ponder the best tonic for Lady Isla.

3

My heart is sore — I dare not tell, my heart is sore for somebody.

Robert Burns

The wind shifted south the next day, delaying departure, carrying the reek of seaweed and salt water. Rory lowered himself between two pieces of driftwood onto the sun-warmed sand, hat covering his eyes. At his back lay the sea town of Balliemore, the Thistle its only tavern, the few cottages of brown stone and slate sprinkled about the sole muddy, beleaguered street.

Beyond the sweep of harbor with its battered fishing boats was a huge rock leading to a high promontory, Kerrera Castle atop it. Once there had been a second castle, Gylen, the stronghold of Clan MacDougall. Now it was crumbled gray stone on the southwest tip of the island, besieged and burnt. All that remained were tall tales and

40

one weather-beaten wall.

And Lark.

He never looked at the castle's remains without thinking of Lark. 'Twas a favorite haunt of theirs in childhood, particularly hers, and he wondered anew if the stories were true. Her father had been a MacDougall, scion of a high and mighty clan, till time and misfortune turned them common. Yet somehow the tie between the MacDougalls and the MacLeishes remained. Enough for Rory to notice Lark's few privileges, on account of the laird's grandmother being kin to the MacDougalls. Or some such blether.

For years Lark had been schooled with the laird before he'd left for university in Edinburgh, neither of them much bigger than a wee haddock back then. She'd had her own mare in the stables. Been welcomed into the castle proper. Even the MacDougall croft lay in a secluded hollow leading to Kerrera Castle, a bit larger than those in the village but still earthy. Lark's family had long been in service, be it the stillroom or nursery, though her mother's people were naught but fisherfolk.

Rory was most interested in the missing Brooch of Lorn, which had been in possession of Lark's clan when the castle burned.

How he and Magnus and Lark had dug for it in the castle's rubble once upon a time! Till dirt stained their knees and hands nearly beyond washing off, their expectations at fever pitch. He still tasted the fascination of it now. A hard history, those MacDougalls and the Covenanter Wars. The brooch was once the treasure of Robert the Bruce himself. He'd forfeited it when ambushed by the onerous MacDougalls, who'd pulled off his cloak and the brooch along with it. If only such a treasure could be found. If so, Rory's free-trading days would end.

He slept, then was awakened by two boisterous lads digging nearby for sand eels. Rousing, he sat up, the rush of the tide smothering their childish voices. The *Merry Lass* lay at anchor, in the next cove, sails furled. Waiting. Wary.

Spirits had been high and talk plentiful at the Thistle, more about the laird's losses than the threat of the excise men. News from the castle trickled down into the village like a waterfall from a loch.

Six bairns. Six heirs. The laird MacLeish was esteemed far and wide, even fishing and shepherding alongside the common folk through the seasons, though more oft atop his horse, his stallion a black streak across

42

the sandy beach. Betimes he even graced the Thistle, though when he entered through the low door, nearly scraping his sooty head on the lintel, the drone of voices dwindled in respect and more than one hat was doffed.

Used to be that Rory thought all the laird touched turned to gold — fields and livestock and business dealings aplenty — though he seemed cursed personally. A sister and mother both dead of the pox within a fortnight's reach. And his powerful father fallen in battle. And now a barren if bonny bride.

"Hoot! Why's a ship's captain, king o' the largest haul the island's e'er seen, lying low like a sand eel?"

Rory chuckled, putting on his hat to better see Jillian Brody through the sun's glare. Bare of foot, she walked the beach, hands full of briny treasure.

"Yer half mermaid, ye are," he told her.

She laughed, robust as a man, with none of Lark's gentle graces. Jillian was a mere scullery maid, the envy of no one, and no doubt on her way to the castle.

"What have ye this morn?" he asked, eyeing her bulging pockets.

"Well, it ain't the Brooch of Lorn," she flung back at him, reminding him of what was said about her.

Jillian had the gift of second sight. Taking a peek into islanders' minds. Smiling slyly, she produced a particularly loosome shell from her pocket for his admiration. The wind carried a whiff of her and he wanted to curl his nose. Instead, he simply studied her, emptying his mind of all ignoble thoughts.

"Where were ye last night when they had need of ye?" Of late there'd been a woeful shortage of tubmen to manage the hefty haul.

"Tidying the castle afore the coming tenants' ball."

He expelled a breath that was half epithet. That had been the buzz at the Thistle too. "Will yer da play his fiddle?"

"Oh aye," she replied, bending to snag another shell from the sand. "What's yer pleasure?"

"Lord Glynlyon's Reel. Or Jacky Stewarts. But like as not I'll be in Ireland."

"A shame, truly. There's no grander time to be at the castle than May."

"Wheest! Ye make it sound fetching." Tempted he was. Might he delay the next sailing given this landing had been so lucrative? Delay the danger? Outfox the Philistines? Indulge in a bit of dancing and such?

Yet Ireland was like a siren'scall.

"Éire?" Jillian wrinkled her snub nose. "Who's to dance with Lark if not ye?"

At this he wanted to throw back his head and laugh at the sheer lunacy of such. Lark never lacked for partners.

"Yer away too much, ye ken." Jillian's face fell. "What's to keep a braw lad from stealin' her away?"

"Let it be said I'm not inclined to settle down. The *Merry Lass* is my mistress."

"And a cold, hard one, to be sure." She snorted. "Yer a fool, Rory MacPherson. And her of noble birth. Word is Lark's turned her back on free tradin'. Refuses to lend a fair hand any longer."

He shrugged. "All the more reason to set my sights no higher."

"Ye best stop dallying with the tavern wenches."

He dug deep in his own pocket and extracted a gold guinea. "Yer in need of a new frock. For the ball."

She took it, biting it in disbelief. "Yer no lowly sailor."

"Just one wanting to spread cheer after a lean winter. And take a wash, aye? So some man can get downwind of ye?"

"No man be wantin' a scullery maid."

"If ye shine up, they just might."

Her laugh was no less merry. "Yer a broad-hearted man, Captain, despite yer wandering ways."

Lark lifted the trunk lid, smelling dust and dried lavender. 'Twas her mother's dower chest, the contents so removed from croft life that they rarely saw the light of day. But Lark knew each intimately. And though she'd once vowed to save her mother's marrying dress for her own marrying day, it now seemed naught but woolgathering.

"Och!" Granny said from behind her. "Yer messing with Rosemary's heart things."

Lark felt a qualm. "Does it make ye melancholy, Granny?"

"One step from heaven that I am, and seeing her again, nay." With that she turned from their cramped bedchamber and put the kettle on for tea.

Gently Lark shook out the gown, which cried for a good ironing. A good airing. At least Mama had been twin to Lark in size on her wedding day.

Beneath the gown was a pair of silk hose and garters, yellowed with age. A scrimshawed fan with a trompe l'oeil design had captivated her since childhood. There was even a choker of freshwater pearls, not milky-hued but tinged pink like the climbing roses in the castle garden.

She sat back and hugged her knees, overcome with a burst of pleasure. Surely no castle was as magnificent as Kerrera lit up at night. Not even Edinburgh could boast anything grander, could it?

"Take thy tea, Lark," Granny called as the kettle ceased singing.

Her thoughts veered to Magnus and Rory. Thanks to the captain, the entire croft smelt of the finest forbidden tea to be had, the same that graced royalty's table, or so he said. Its fragrance seemed to elevate their humble surroundings, giving the cracked cups and horn spoons a special polish. She took a slightly less guilty sip, knowing half the tea in England was said to be smuggled.

"Enough tea to last till Hogmanay or better," Granny crowed, eyeing the hearthstone beneath which their stash was buried. She took a drink from her saucer, declaring it divine.

Lark's gaze wandered to the wrinkled gown spread across the bed. "I'm afraid to take a hot iron to such auld fabric. Suppose it melts before my very eyes?"

"Leave it to me. 'Twas I who ironed it on yer mother's wedding day. And again on the day of yer christening."

The subtle mention of babes shifted

47

Lark's thoughts again. "Have ye truly no memory of some remedy to help Lady Isla?"

Granny heaved a sigh, her silvery eyes clouded. "Like as not when I go up to help at the castle on the morrow, 'twill return to me."

" 'Twould be a gesture of goodwill to make a gift of such to the mistress before the ball."

"Aye," Granny said, relishing another long sip. "We'll pray so."

4

Be happy while you're living, for you're a long time dead.

Scottish proverb

Magnus walked along the cliff's edge to the ruins of Gylen Castle as the Sabbath dawned. Nature seemed to have reversed itself, teasing them with the blues and greens of spring before returning them to the silvery white of winter. Through the mist of May came the pealing of the kirk bell in the village.

His absence in church would be felt now that he'd returned home — sure to set a dozen tongues wagging — but in truth he was more at worship outside kirk walls where the grandeur of sea and sky and headlands took his breath away. Even if he was a stray sheep far from the fold.

He sat on an outcropping of cold feudal stone, Nonesuch at his side, glad there was no wind. Patient he was, and that patience was soon rewarded. Slowly the fog began to lift. But not his fog of spirit. Nor his circumstances.

Squinting into the endless indigo sea, he saw a few fishing boats riding the water's calm surface. The view before him never changed, the beauty had by all, whether rich or poor. And the poor ruled on Kerrera. He himself had never suffered want. He only suffered secondhand, feeling the lack of others and wanting to relieve it. The villagers — especially the fisherfolk — regarded him as if he was some sort of savior. But he was quick to remind them he did not walk on water and the miracle of the loaves and fishes was well beyond his ken.

Father, do Ye care about the tenants' ball and the goods slow to arrive from Glasgow? The moods and whims of my wife? The sick-to-death bairn of a tenant farmer? The smuggled goods in kirk? My own relentless discontent?

Forgive me, Father, was always quick to follow his every honest prayer. *Ye care in ways I canna ken. Ye defy the box I've built for Ye in my mind.*

Reaching out a hand to stroke Nonesuch's fur, he cast a glance at Gylen's sole castle wall, the lancet windows tall and arched and still beautiful. Once he'd written a bit of verse about Lark's kinfolk, but of late life left little time for poetry.

He blinked, adjusting to the sun's strengthening glare. Through the haze he saw a figure, shawl about her shoulders, basket in hand. Nonesuch sat up and took notice, her plumy tail swishing in welcome.

"Ye growl at all but Lark," Magnus murmured as she drew nearer.

She was out early on so chill a morn. Likely on the way to Kerrera's southernmost tip to visit the few kin she had there. Other than the Sabbath, she seldom wandered far from castle or croft.

Her lips were moving. Was she praying? Singing? She had a loosome voice. She looked . . . cheerful.

"And what would the laird be doing in enemy territory?" she asked as she caught sight of him.

" 'Tis more peaceful here than at Kerrera, enemy territory or no." He gave a grin. "No ponderous party preparations. No business begging to be dealt with." He eyed her basket.

"Just oatcake fresh from the bake oven."

"Yer granny's?"

"None other." She lifted a coarse linen cloth and gave him what was surely the biggest of the batch along with a ready smile. "Ye can have two if ye like." She unearthed another for Nonesuch.

" 'Tis a frightful waste as she hardly tastes it," Magnus exclaimed before devouring his own. "Mayhap 'tis the reason she ne'er growls at ye."

"But ye still do."

His collar heated. "Ye dinna seem to mind."

"I'm used to it, raised alongside ye. The laird can do as he likes. 'Tis us simple folk who have to mind our manners."

"I'm sorry, lass." He meant it. Circumstances oft turned him terse. And made a rare bannock all the better.

"How is her ladyship?"

"The same."

"I'm pondering a remedy. I've not forgotten. Granny is thinking on it too."

"She's missing Edinburgh." And already packing to return there. He'd lost count of all the trunks his wife owned. But in six years' time he'd gotten used to all the comings and goings, the massive preparations and leave-takings between their Edinburgh townhouse and the castle. 'Twas no secret Isla loathed island life. "We'll likely depart after the ball."

"She'll be well enough to attend, I hope."

"I'll make no promises."

"And I'll ask no more questions." With a little dip of both her head and her knees, she went on her way again, Nonesuch following, the bannock basket an outright temptation.

He wanted to do the same. Fall into step behind her. Listen to her simple singing. Canting his gaze away, he returned his attention to the sea and let the sun seep into his winter-weary bones.

In time, Nonesuch returned, tail still a-wag, eyes bright. Lark had that effect, be it on man or beast. She made both better than they were, better than she'd found them.

Despite her warlike MacDougall roots.

"Tell me about yer gown," Catriona said wistfully. "I've no such finery of my own, especially big with a bairn as I am."

Lark studied her comely cousin, who was expecting another child and was all round and rosy. "Ye dinna need any trappings, yer so bonny." Though Lark did wish she had some colorful cloth to counter Catriona's paleness and drape her wide girth. "Mother's gown is auld. Granny's set to press it, though I fear 'twill fall to pieces."

"And the color?"

"Blue brocade. Bonaventure blue."

"To match yer eyes. But no heirloom brooch, sadly. Just yer family pearls? What about yer shoes?"

Lark extended one naked foot beneath a flounced petticoat. "I'd best go barefoot as I'm missing a heel, and no time to see the cobbler."

Catriona smiled. "Best go barefoot, aye, so ye willna tower over the laddies."

Lark drew herself up, shoulders back, striking a regal pose as she'd seen Isla do. Isla was tall like the laird and owned a finesse and queenly carriage unknown to the islander women. She only lacked a crown. Lark had long wondered what it was that had caught Magnus's eye. Surely this was it.

"Mayhap hunch yer shoulders. No man wants a lass so tall."

"Captain MacPherson is taller," Lark mused.

"Hoot!" Catriona chuckled. "Not so tall as the laird. He's got Norse blood, I tell ye."

Magnus was immense. Viking-like. And with such queer blue eyes, more silver in a certain light. "His hair was the color o' milk as a lad before it went dark."

"But Saundra's stayed fair as flax."

They grew quiet, lost in the sorrowful memory. Lark's longing for Magnus's sister never left. She'd been as fairy-like as Magnus was formidable. And far sweeter of temper. Her untimely death had sent the island spinning. Left Lark spinning still.

"No more mourning," Catriona said, patting her great roundness. " 'Tis time for births and balls, not wakes."

Lark's spirits soared. More than one tenants' ball had kindled a romantic match. Laboring hard as the islanders did, courtship was hard-won and frolics few and far between.

"I'd best get back to Granny." A last look at her bannock basket returned her thoughts to Magnus and Nonesuch. And the dangling remedy for Lady Isla.

"Till the ball then, cousin."

Over the next week, Cook and Lark gathered the needed herbs from the kitchen garden to season the fowl and mutton and other manifold dishes being prepared for the coming fete. A palpable excitement seemed to thread the island, making people merrier. Or was it just her own?

So intent was she on her task she hardly noticed Cook pause at the garden wall. At the clatter of a coach, Lark joined her.

Through the swirling mist of midmorning came a small army of servants bearing trunks of all shapes and sizes. Someone seemed bent on leaving Kerrera forever.

Isla?

"I canna believe it." Cook pursed her lips in contemplation. "And there goes the high and mighty Rhona with her. Good riddance!"

Lark's eyes widened at Cook's outburst. Usually curt, she was in rare form this morn.

"Edinburgh bound?" Lark whispered.

"Aye. Where else? And on the very eve of the ball."

Oh, Magnus. Did he know? When she'd last seen him at the ruins he'd said he and Isla were to leave after the fete.

"And the laird's gone to Balliemore, none the wiser, likely." At that, Cook stalked out of the garden and into the castle, leaving Lark alone with her burgeoning basket.

Try as she might, Lark couldn't tear her gaze from Isla as she got into the coach. The sky-blue feather atop her hat was nearly crushed as she cleared the door and disappeared inside, Rhona right behind, each of them carrying a twin pug. They seemed in a great hurry, perhaps on account of Magnus's imminent return?

Chewing on a piece of mint, Lark found it sour. Isla's departure would cause a scandal ricocheting from one end of the island to the other. Any sympathy given her latest loss would be stripped away, her leaving considered a slight. To the laird. His tenants. The entire isle.

How would he explain his wife's absence? Knowing Magnus, he would not.

As the coach rolled down the drive and turned east at the gate, Granny emerged from the stillroom to Lark's hasty explanation.

"Gone, ye say?" Her tone was as grievous as Lark felt. "But I've just been concocting what might help her. Stinging nettle. Red clover and red raspberry. A bit o' dandelion too."

"I've already tried them, Granny." The lament in Lark's tone had more to do with Magnus's dismay than Isla's condition. At least she'd done what she could while Isla was in residence. Half a dozen tonics had been dispensed, but Isla declared them of no use.

"Oat straw . . . black cohosh . . ." Granny went away mumbling, her tread slowed by rheumatism.

Lark gave an exasperated poke to her basket. Rosemary. Thyme. A favorite, sage, could not be had so early except in the orangery. Magnus had talked of rebuilding the damaged hothouse on the castle's south side between the kitchen and formal garden. She and Cook supported him whole-heartedly, but Isla protested the expense, dust, and noise. Mayhap the project was not timely. Isla's leaving certainly wasn't.

The fading of the coach wheels gave way to the sight of the laird riding the beach. A fierce tug-of-war began. Should she mind her work and stay out of the MacLeishes' personal affairs? Or should she run down to the water and tell Magnus the news so that he might go after Isla? Reason with her?

"Yer as downcast as I've ever seen ye."

She whirled, stunned to see the captain peering at her over the garden wall. He removed his hat, the strong coastal wind rif-fling his longish hair. Expression aggravated, he batted at a bee bedeviling him.

"What brings ye to the garden?" she asked as nonchalantly as she could, bending to pick a sprig of parsley.

"A meeting with the laird. The *Merry Lass* is in need of repairs before the next run."

Repairs the laird would help fund, no doubt. Setting aside her basket, she joined him at the wall and pointed. "His lairdship is down there."

Rory's gaze swiveled to the long stretch of beach. Magnus was already riding from sight around a rocky bend. "Och, I just might give up sailing if I had such a horse."

" 'Tis far safer, riding," she chided. "No Philistines in pursuit."

He cracked a wry smile. "Next they'll be taxing saddles and bridles and whatnot. Hide and watch."

She made a face. "Surely not." Leaning into the sun-warmed wall, she pondered a bold question. "Are ye coming to the ball? Or off to Éire as I've heard?"

He grimaced. "Jillian's mouth's a mite big." A sly wink. "If I stay on, will ye dance with me?"

"Hide and watch," she echoed. With a half smile, she returned to her work just as Cook appeared, no less agitated.

"Supposing this means the ball will be canceled." Raising her fists, face red as a Glasgow apple, Cook stared at Lark as if waiting for her to confirm or deny it. "I've worked my hands to the bone preparing and have enough to feed six generations of islanders. Will it all come to naught?"

Rory stared at Lark in question, obviously unaware of Isla's leaving.

Lark opened her mouth to explain when Granny reappeared. "Yer in need of some mint tea, Margaret. Shall we?" Taking her old friend by the elbow, Granny steered Cook back into the kitchen, leaving Lark alone with the captain again.

"No ball?" he queried.

Lark shrugged. "The mistress just left for Edinburgh." At his scowl she added, "Ye canna blame her for not feeling like a frolic. She's gone to seek a physic, likely."

His scowl held. "Seems like a physic can be had as readily after the ball as before."

True enough. So far the physics had not helped Isla, nor the island midwives. Nor Lark. She longed to endear Kerrera to the mistress in some way. Turn round Isla's dim view of them.

She met his hard gaze, trying to soften her own dislike by being kindly and bringing Isla into every conversation if she could. "Mayhap she needs the comfort of her family in the city."

"Mayhap she needs to think of someone besides Isla." At that, the captain returned his hat to his head and took the path to the stables, the crunch of shells beneath his boots.

Sighing, Lark felt in need of some mint tea herself. Reclaiming her basket, she entered the castle kitchen, where Granny was attempting to mollify Cook as she put the finishing touches on a grand dessert, a towering confection of sweetmeats.

Jillian, the sole scullery maid, gave a tart greeting as two kitchen girls scurried hither and yon under Cook's watchful eye and a footman polished silver in a corner. Lark eyed the copper pots and pans suspended from iron hooks over the immense worktable. The stone room was cavernous and cold but replete with every Scottish staple and delicacy, the mingled aromas heady. Stomach growling, Lark took a mincemeat tart when Cook gestured to the tea tray.

"Ye might as well have one now that the mistress has fled," Cook said. "They'll not keep."

Would the ball go on?

A bit defeated, they sat in the servants' hall at one end of the long table nearest the hearth, just Lark, Granny, and Cook entwined in a rare idle moment.

With the harsh light from the tall window falling over her, Cook looked worn to a frazzle, shoulders bowed. "Michty me! I'm too auld for dramatics. The laird likes things nice and smooth. But his lady — she errs on the theatrical side."

"She's young yet," Granny replied. "Give her time."

Lark held her tongue, wondering about

Magnus's reaction. Somehow she sensed he was unaware of Isla's leaving. 'Twas Magnus who always accompanied his wife and ferried her across to the mainland half a mile distant. Rarely did he remain at the castle without her.

As she thought it, the butler came in, expression downcast. "Ye've heard news of the mistress?"

"Oh aye. Wretched timing!" Cook replied with a sweep of her hand. "But I'll not throw all this bounty into the sea, nor work myself to the bone for naught."

Lark swallowed hard to stifle a chuckle. Cook's bulk was far from bony. Of all the islanders, she was the thickest. But never trust a malinky lang legs of a cook, she said.

"Ye'd best tell Brown," Granny said of Magnus's manservant. "Who will tell the laird."

With a nod, the butler withdrew and Cook huffed a sigh, her teacup drained dry. "The musicians are set to arrive from the mainland, which means a half dozen more mouths to feed."

Musicians among tenants were plenty, but Magnus wanted them not to entertain but to be entertained, for this night at least. And he spared no expense doing it, securing the best bow hands to be had among fiddlers from Oban.

"What more needs to be done?" Lark asked Cook as she pushed away from the table.

"Flower arranging. A great many blooms arrived from Glasgow's hothouses in the forenoon. Take Annie if ye need help, though I can hardly spare any kitchen maids."

"No need. Where are the vases?"

"In the storeroom. The best silver will do. None o' that tawdry pewter or glass."

Lark nodded. The quantity of blooms dictated the needed vases. Best take a look in the Great Hall first. She trod lightly, used to tiptoeing around Isla. But now, with the mistress on the way to Edinburgh, she grew bold. She even dared set foot in the stairwell where the massive cedar staircase climbed to elegant heights.

Odd how a person's presence or absence changed the mood of a place. When Isla and her retinue left for the city, the castle was like a flower in bloom. The remaining servants talked and laughed more freely, doors were left open, the mood turned festive.

Lark listened to the staccato tap of her own footfall across the marble foyer of the Great Hall, past oil portraits and Flemish tapestries on paneled oak walls that hadn't altered in the last century, to the waiting blooms.

The chill of the two-storied hall kept the flowers fresh, and there were armfuls of them in such varied hues she nearly gasped. Bending low, she breathed in their honeyed scent, the roses foremost — armfuls of scarlet roses the very color of British red-coated soldiers. Isla's favorite flower, Lark remembered with a pang.

"I recall yer preference being lavender."

She turned, finding Magnus behind her, arms crossed. And looking far more at ease than she expected. "Lavender, aye. Practical as well as bonny. If only roses grew as readily. Cook asked for help arranging these . . ." She was babbling, caught in the maelstrom of the moment.

"Ye heard about Isla."

"I saw her leave myself. I'm terribly sorry."

"The ball is to go on regardless."

She smiled, but there was sadness in it. "Glad I am of that."

" 'Tis her loss, not ours."

She pondered this. His tone held no bitterness, just regret. By shunning the island and its people when she might embrace them, Isla did lose. And her absence, while igniting gossip, would be mourned by no one Lark knew.

"Granny and I are at work on another, better remedy," she said, but there was more hope than truth in it. "When the mistress returns . . ."

"If she returns."

The flowers were forgotten. Lark simply stared at him, detecting a shattering shift in their circumstances.

"She might be done with Kerrera for good. Edinburgh has her heart."

"Auld Reekie?" Her calm fled. How could a stinking, smoke-filled city compare? Even so, one's heart should cling to people, not places. "But this is her home. Ye are her husband . . ."

He was looking at her like he'd done since boyhood — with obstinacy and admiration — yet reminding her of her place. "Have a care, Lark."

"There's the rub, Magnus. I do care. And 'tis she who should be standing here arranging flowers for an occasion that means so much to ye."

"Ye canna blame her entirely. 'Twas rash what I did, marrying her with little thought as to how island life would suit her. Mayhap I should leave Kerrera for good and go to the city too."

To Edinburgh? For keeps? In her angst,

she clutched a stem too tightly, a thorn drawing blood. A stray drop stained her apron, crimson on creamy linen.

"Here, Lark." He took the rose, his calm almost harder to bear than his temper, as if he'd thought it all out and the tenants' ball would be his last. "Ye've ne'er been to Edinburgh. The city has its charms."

He looked about the long, polished hall empty of all but banquet tables at the outer edges. The butler and footmen came in, bearing silver and place cards for the table settings of the more prominent islanders who'd feast on the raised dais at the hall's far end.

Without another word she fled, trying to master her emotions. Once in the storeroom she selected the best vases, chin still a-tremble, the excitement of the fete tarnished and seeming frivolous in light of Isla's leaving.

The castle needed a child. A family. But would a child change Isla? She did not seem meant to be a mother either in temperament or in body. There was no cure for being barren and selfish to the bone save Christ.

5

My thoughts and I were of another world.
Ben Jonson

"Best don a smile with yer fine frock," Granny told her.

Together they trudged up the cliffside path to the castle in the long mid-May twilight. Fists full of pressed brocade, Lark tried to iron out her tangled thoughts. She'd not spoil Granny's glee by sharing the burden Magnus's words had wrought. His imminent departure for Edinburgh — mayhap for good — would dampen the festive night.

"Look at that, will ye?" Granny crowed as if she'd never seen the castle lit up so in all her fourscore years.

Lark looked. Softened. Surely there was no grander sight than Kerrera with its doors open wide in welcome, light illuminating every crevice and corner.

They were not alone in making their way to the ball. Behind and before them trod islanders in their Sabbath best. Over brae and hillock they came till a long line snaked at the castle's main entrance. For once the air was windless, yet it still carried and married a great many aromas — smoke and candle wax and roses, roasted meat and baked bread.

Overhead rose a full moon, perfect for romantic trysts in the formal garden, the fountain at its heart. The head gardener had torn and trimmed and readied every awakening bed, even scrubbing the stubborn moss off stone benches and statuaries. 'Twas the one night the tenants were allowed in.

Mayhap she and the captain could take a turn there. Mayhap she could convince him to use the *Merry Lass* for honest gain and give up smuggling for good.

" 'Tis time to leave yer spinsterhood behind, aye?" Granny's whisper was warm on her ear as Rory came into view. "Set yer sights on a more noble lad."

Passing beneath the castle's lintel he was a striking sight, shed of his sailing garb and battered hat. In a proper weskit and coat and breeches fit for the drawing room, he looked more gentleman than ship's captain.

"His whiskers need trimming," Granny said in the next breath. "He has the look of a pirate, he does."

"That he is. No sense pretending otherwise." Lark waved a hand at Catriona and her wee family just ahead of them. "Glad I am the island's small and the moon full to guide everyone home."

" 'Twill be no home-going till dawn."

"Oh? Shall ye stay all night, Granny?"

"Dancing and feasting and such, aye, for as long as my auld eyes stay open. With the mistress away, the frolic might go longer."

They hastened into the castle's stony foyer and through the door to the Great Hall, now crowded with a great many islanders of all stations and occupations. Overhead hung two Venetian lanterns, the massive brass chandeliers casting a glow like fairy dust over the assemblage.

Cook stood by a long table where dishes were being laid out by footmen, her expression watchful. Lark's gaze rose to the minstrel's gallery where musicians were tuning their fiddles before her focus shifted to the laird. At once he took her breath away — for all the wrong reasons.

Entering by the far hall door that led to the cedar staircase and his private chambers, he nearly brought the Great Hall's hubbub to a halt.

Oh Magnus, have a care.

Kilted, his plaid a magnificent loch blue and heather purple, he looked like a bonny prince. Lark knew the sentiment behind it. 'Twas in honor of his father, the previous laird, killed in the Jacobite Rising of '45. Astonishment melded to admiration, both her own and others'. Lark could feel it. See it in myriad faces. She was torn between awe and fear.

The British king had outlawed all forms of such dress after Culloden, the penalties severe. Magnus wore it in protest — that she understood. But he'd only done so on the anniversary of his father's death. Till now.

Her gaze cut across the crowd to the entrances. What if some authority should walk in? Fear shuddered through her. Six months' imprisonment for the first offense. Seven years' transportation for the second. Thus far he'd escaped punishment. Though Magnus was beloved by most of Kerrera's residents, might some bear him a mindless grudge and rejoice to see him brought low?

The feasting began, but Lark had little appetite. She sipped cider and kept to the shadows, glancing about furtively in case one of the king's men appeared.

In time Catriona sought her out, her gown hardly disguising her girth. "How bonny ye look in yer blue brocade, cousin. But why so downcast?"

" 'Tis a right terrible risk to be kilted on such a night as this."

"Hoot! The king's Dress Act can go to Hades! Why quibble about a piece o' cloth? Besides, the laird has posted lookouts. He's no fool. Did ye not see auld Archie and young Reginald? Both kilted and proud!"

Still, Lark sent up a silent prayer. *Lord, please. He's a good man who bears a heavy burden. He means no trouble with his dress. His every thought is keeping Kerrera well and safe. Let no one pass this way with harm in mind.*

"Will ye do me the honor, Mistress Mac-Dougall?" The captain stood before her with a little bow.

Charmed, she set aside her qualms as he led her onto the marble floor amid a melee of swirling, sweating dancers. One Scots reel gave way to another till the laird's favorite, the boisterous "Strip the Willow," was struck.

The opening note was drawn out expectantly. 'Twas the tune the laird usually danced with Isla. Reserved for her alone as the castle's mistress. But Isla was not here.

Would he bow out? Let someone else lead?

Lark stood by the oriole window, wishing Isla back, knowing this was an awkward moment. Those who didn't know Isla had left for Edinburgh were looking about, realizing something was amiss.

And Magnus?

Before she'd caught her breath from the reel she'd stepped with Rory, the laird stood before her. In Gaelic, he asked her to dance. She schooled her shock, aware of a great many eyes upon them. At last she curtsied, heartened to see a flash of gratitude warm his stoic face.

She kept her eyes down, stepping the reel as smartly as she could. Magnus was a braw dancer. Moreover, he enjoyed dancing. She could feel that as well. Had she not learned to dance in this marbled hall as a girl of eight? Was he thinking it too? Like a lady, a true MacDougall, as if Gylen Castle lay not in ruins. Once upon a time Lark had spun and stepped and crushed toes till she learned these dances right and proper. Oh, to return to innocent days of old before barren brides and shipwrecked dreams, gnawing hunger and sleepless nights.

The music had them circling and gliding and spinning, testing their skill and surefootedness. Beneath it all pulsed a sweetness, an excitement that she danced with the handsomest man on Kerrera, mayhap in all the islands. Once she looked up at him, and his eyes were every bit as warm and lively as the music when they met hers. Her heart turned over. Oh, what a joy it was to be wanted. Chosen. If only for a dance. The delight of it cascaded over her, from her beribboned head to her soles. She was out of breath, all a-tingle.

Their hands met, parted, as did their steps. She dared another glance at him. This was their moment, their dance, though she found herself wishing for the slower strathspey reel instead if only to draw the fleeting moment out a wee bit longer.

After this she'd escape to the garden for air, to collect herself, to stay out of the eye of any who thought she might think herself above her humble station.

Rory swallowed his surprise and the last of his ale as Lark partnered with the laird. Magnus was in fine form tonight, kilted and taking his pick of the beautiful lasses. Rory's gaze swept the crush of merrymakers, knowing just who among them were the tale bearers, the foremost gossips. Isla's absence was questionable enough. Did Magnus have to choose Lark in her wake? Why not partner with Granny or some old crone above any tongue wagging?

But he could not blame the laird. Lark *was* the bonniest. She was like her name — openhearted and brimming with life and spirit. And beloved.

The music ended on a triumphant note, with Lark curtseying prettily to the laird. Rory tried to put down the queer twisting inside him. It rose unbidden, tainting his enjoyment of the moment. He half wished for a ruckus to be raised — that the rashly kilted laird would be found out. Or that Isla would reappear, her own jealousy erupting, the ball coming to an early end.

He'd seen Isla explode in most unladylike fashion over a lamed horse and muddied skirt. It was said she snapped at the servants if they were seconds late with a cup of tea. Rhona was also regarded with suspicion. Servants were loyal and close-lipped about those they liked but not those ill-favored.

Another dance commenced so he picked Jillian, cleaned up and in a passable frock. The laird was not dancing now but mingling and talking and threading his way through the swelling throng, goblet in hand.

He seemed uncommonly merry with his wife away, deepening Rory's uneasy twist. He and Magnus had never been at odds.

What was there to quibble about now? Magnus had even agreed to repair the *Merry Lass*.

Still . . .

He looked about for Lark. Had she left? Earlier he'd seen her in a quieter corner, talking and laughing with fellow islanders.

"She's in the garden," Jillian said slyly above the noise.

His smile of thanks was wry. Leave it to Jillian to read him. He elbowed his way to a far door, hoping the garden was easily found. Nay. A labyrinth of candlelit corridors lay before him, but soon an attentive footman steered him right.

He stepped into moonlit darkness. Beyond the garden wall stretched silvery sea, far more his home than a haughty castle. He stood near a trellis getting his bearings. The trickle of a fountain. Doves cooing. The scent of emerging flowers. These sated his senses and swept away the customary brine and reek of fish he was so used to.

Lark sat on a low stone bench beyond the fountain, hands in her lap. He took a seat beside her, a bit off-kilter without his hat. When nervous, he liked to set it a-twirl in his hands. He reached instead for a near climbing rose, the buds yet unopened.

"Yer missing the sea," she said quietly.

Would she read him like Jillian? "Betimes I want to get beyond these islands. See the colonies."

"America?"

"Aye. There's no castles there. No crofts. Imagine it. Mostly log dwellings. Few fine houses."

"Indians."

He nodded. " 'Twould be a sight, aye? Well worth a two-month crossing."

"If ye survived it." The pragmatic Lark weighed in. He far preferred the Lark of fancy. "Why wander?" she questioned. "Many live and die here on Kerrera, never even setting foot on the mainland."

"And ye? What's yer pleasure?"

She smiled. "The sea, 'tis so fickle. If we did get there . . ." She hesitated.

He liked that she said *we.* "Yer remembering yer da," he said, bowing his head slightly in respect.

"Aye, always." She took the rose from him, bringing it to her nose. "What would we do there? In America, I mean."

"Get a piece of ground to call our own." His *our* implied an intimacy he was unsure of. "Men make their own way in America, by their wits. No lairds or Philistines to speak of."

"It sounds strange. Hard."

"No harder than here. Mayhap freer."

"Ye can be freer here if ye abandon yer smuggling."

"Hoot! My smuggling keeps the island afloat." He gave a shake of his head. "I've no wish to talk such foolishness. At least till I hie to America."

"Are there cities there like Auld Reekie?"

"None the likes of Edinburgh though a few have grand names. Philadelphia. New York. Boston. There's a colony called Carolina to the north, a Scots stronghold near the sea."

She looked at him, eyes alive with interest. Or was it dread?

"Mighty rivers and woods as far as the eye can behold. Cape Fear is where I'd settle."

"Cape Fear?" She drew back a bit. "Sounds frightful."

He chuckled. "I dinna ken why it's called that."

"Ye'd best be finding out."

"And if I do?"

She looked away. "I'll not leave Granny."

"Mayhap she'd want ye to go."

"I'm all she has left."

"Let the laird look after her."

"That's cold, Captain." She used her sternest tone.

"Granny's served his family well all these years. So have ye. But yer granny's come to her earthly end nearly."

She abandoned the sore subject. "How d'ye ken so much about America?"

"I leave Kerrera. And learn."

She sighed. 'Twas hard for her to see beyond this rocky island, confined to croft and castle, he knew. Even so, she did not share his wanderlust. That he knew too. There was a mystifying contentment about Lark that defied hunger and uncertainty and want. Kerrera was her home and had ever been. Whatever it handed her was her accepted lot, even the loss of her kin's mighty title and lands.

He heaved a sigh. "Ye and I are spring lambs no longer."

"Five and twenty. Some call me a stayed lass, a spinster. Yet I look into the glass and expect to see a wee lass."

"The Buik says our days are but a breath," he said in a rare nod to Scripture. "A vapor."

"Too short to spend sailing to fearsome parts." At that, she stood. The very moment he'd been about to take her hand. "Best be inside. We dinna want to stir gossip."

No more than ye did with the laird, he did not say.

6

In his company, I am grieved to the soul by a thousand tender recollections.

Jane Austen

By dusk the next day tongues were worn out wagging. Even as the castle decorations were taken down, those too ill and infirm to weather the tenants' ball were stuffed full of morsels they'd missed. Who danced with whom. Who drained the punch bowl. The number of delicacies to be had. The quality of the musicians. The lateness of the hour. Who the laird had chosen for the first reel. Why the mistress of Kerrera Castle was missing. Even the Thistle was abuzz. Jillian had told Lark so.

Never mind that Magnus had danced with every willing woman present as he did every tenants' ball. That he'd led out with Lark was tantalizing enough.

"Where no wood is, the fire goeth out,"

Granny muttered as she hung the kettle over the hearth's flame.

Lark mulled this to solace herself all the long afternoon as she savored the Sabbath after kirk, staying near the warm hearth and drinking several cups of fragrant tea as rain slashed sideways in the rising wind, clouds marring her magnificent view.

In the adjoining bedchamber Granny snored softly. Lark's only company besides Tibby the cat was the book the captain had lent her, the title onerous. *Travels into Several Remote Nations of the World. In Four Parts. By Lemuel Gulliver. First a Surgeon, and Then a Captain of Several Ships.*

Gotten from Ireland? Rory had the wanderlust, no doubt, like Mr. Gulliver. She purposed to read one chapter, the cat warming her lap. But the book did not hold her, and her thoughts ran back and forth between the Thistle where the captain lodged and the castle.

What did Magnus do on a day with the mistress away?

Granny snorted, stirring awake. Her cobwebbed mind seemed on the verge of some remedy for Isla. But what? Lark had thought of everything, had even raided the castle library for apothecary books. She'd best have some answer when Isla returned, especially if the Edinburgh physics did not help her.

From where she sat in the rocking chair by the hearth, she had no view of the castle, but its shadow seemed to fall over her. It now seemed to blanket Magnus, who'd once been unlined and carefree. Since his father's death — and then his mother's and sister's — his joie de vivre had leached out of him by degrees. They'd all hoped his marriage would spell new life. Lark was not the only islander who longed to see Kerrera Castle restored, a true family seat again.

Truly, any gossip about her and the laird was laughable and would soon fizzle. Magnus was the brother she did not have, their shared history and love of the island's tumultuous beauty lashing them together. His leaving on the verge of manhood seemed a little death, snatched from her life as he'd been. She stroked Tibby's fur, traveling backwards through long corridors of dusty memories. Away a year or better in a succession of longer and longer absences, he'd left a boy but somehow returned a man with little warning, the wall between them ever widening. She felt it but was powerless to stop it or cross it, though it rent her heart.

Once he'd written her a letter. But she'd had no ink to pen a reply nor coin to post

81

it, and so it lay unanswered. Later, she'd cobbled together enough coin to pen more. But he'd never written another. She'd saved it, the ink faded from the passage of lonesome years though the fine flourish of his script remained. Now she reached for the Bible and opened it to Ecclesiastes, where the letter lay pressed between the pages. Her eyes focused on the blurred words, but truly there was no call to read it, for she knew it by heart.

Dear Lark,

Because the time seems very long since I first left Kerrera, I finally write. With you continually in mind, I remain half there, in the salt spray and wind, not the smoke and soot of the city with its myriad wynds and closes.

Before I sleep and when I wake, I set you on Kerrera's cliff edge in my mind's eye, the sea at your back, waiting for me as you used to. Then and only then can I shut out the strange smells and sounds of Edinburgh and close the onerous distance.

You once said you would never leave the isle. Would that I had not left it too. I long to be free as you, with no title or ties to weight me. If so, I would return and find you waiting, and together we would make a different sort of life.

Yours entire,
Magnus

The letter lay open in her lap. Still a thorn. Still capable of piercing her heart. Folding it up, she allowed herself a final remembrance, mulling the day Magnus had told her he was to take a bride. 'Twas April of her nineteenth year, the hard, hungry winter giving way to a fragile spring. Had fate arranged for him to find her on that very cliff's edge he wrote about, the sea at her back? Recovering from a fever, she'd paused as she crested the cliff's top, still weak and a bit winded from her climb. 'Twas all she could do to stay standing in the face of the wind. And then his shattering words.

Above the kestrels and crashing waves he'd called to her. "Lark."

She turned, disbelief and delight turning her girlish again. So long he'd been away this last time, months crowded with two wakes, three births, and a good many missed holidays. A whole year lay between them, full of the unspoken and unshared.

He stood apart, arms crossed, Nonesuch by his side, the cape he wore furling and unfurling like an indigo flag. Edinburgh had turned him a stranger. In that instant she felt a wild, everlasting hatred for the city.

"Magnus?" The question held heartache. Could it be him? Aye, but not the Magnus she knew and loved — the young laird, the lad he'd been.

"I've come home to announce my impending nuptials." A sudden gust nearly flung his unwelcome words away.

She took a step closer. "Yer to wed?"

"Aye. An Edinburgh lass." He did not smile. Why, when even the basest fisherfolk announced such news with joy?

She looked to her battered shoes, trying to take it in. Why was she fashed? Truly, no one on the island was his equal. No woman worthy.

Yet a town-bred lass?

"The daughter of an auld friend of my father who is Lord Ordinary of the Court of Session. Isla Erskine-Shand."

The proud name seemed a comeuppance to the simple *Lark*. At once she knew all his schooling in law had come to this. He was a rising advocate — a barrister — not only laird of Kerrera Island. 'Twas said that when in court or chambers he wore fine robes and a powdered wig. She'd never seen such, but it sounded high and mighty. But 'twas more than this, truly. Such a father-in-law would protect him, protect Kerrera from English revenge over the Jacobite cause. When lairds and clansmen were being imprisoned and tried for their Scottish loyalties, such a marriage might give him immunity. Was that why he was to marry, now that he'd just come out of mourning?

She looked up then, half afraid of what she'd find if she met his gaze. But he was staring past her to the sea, the jut of his jaw signaling determination. Or resignation.

She swallowed hard and dredged up polite words she had no wish to say. "I'm pleased for ye both." And then, weak-kneed and half-fevered still, she set her own jaw, dangerously close to tears. She'd always tried never to tell a lie, but she just had.

"I wanted ye to be the first to ken."

First? Was it an honor? Still he did not look at her. Her own gaze strayed to the basket on her arm, brimming with bannocks.

"Feel free to speak of it," he finished, knowing that if she told but one person it would be all over the island by sunset.

She gave a nod, wanting a swift end to this excruciating reunion. Though she'd widened her stance to fight off lightheadedness, she swayed. His hands shot out to steady her. She'd not realized he was standing so close.

The warmth of his touch seemed to burn her. "What ails ye, Lark?"

"The tail end of a fever." Before he could respond in sympathy or otherwise, she changed course. "Will ye and yer bride live at the castle?"

"Aye." His hands fell away. "We wed the first of June in Edinburgh. After our honeymoon we'll come here."

Honeymoon. How lovely the sound. All the emotion behind it. If she was a bride she'd want to spend it on Kerrera, tucked away in some sunny cove, just she and her groom . . .

Her skin grew hotter. "My work awaits." She sidestepped him, gaze on the rocky ground.

"Lark . . ."

Unwillingly, she turned around, but not before dashing a tear away. Seeing her so, he seemed to think better of saying anything at all, and so he turned away a second before she did. 'Twas the last time she spoke to him untethered.

7

Lost time is never found again.
Benjamin Franklin

The castle stillroom was blessedly quiet at midday as May inched on. The coming calendar change had been all the buzz, replacing the stale gossip from the tenants' ball. Word had just reached the island that come September, no longer would their year begin in March but in January. King George seemed to think he could rearrange time to suit him, and now with Parliament's blessing, all British subjects must adjust to a year unlike any other and the loss of eleven days in September.

Finished with the noon meal in the servants' hall, Lark returned to the rose lotion she was making, spying the remedy Granny had given her. The small, blown-glass bottle bore a parchment label marked "Fertility Herbs."

One long whiff gave rise to a few ingredients. Plantain seeds to prevent miscarriage. Milk thistle. Licorice root. Raspberry leaf. Returning the stopper, she breathed in ginger and goldenseal.

A potent tonic.

Lark opened a cupboard and set the bottle in a cool, dark corner. When Isla returned, this might aid her. *Bethankit,* she said as much to the Almighty as Granny. A weight seemed to slide off her to have something in hand at last. But what if Granny erred? Slipped in something harmful unintentionally? Her mind was growing more muddled. Recently she had put salt instead of sugar in their tea.

Shaking off the worry, Lark looked through the open window at the sun spilling into the sea. It drew her out into the kitchen garden to weed the parsley bed, and her hands were soon stained a rich brown, the sun warming her shoulders like a shawl.

Summer was at hand. A sennight had passed since the tenants' ball, and island life seemed sleepy again. Lark's heirloom gown was returned to the trunk. The *Merry Lass* had put out to sea with nary a fare-thee-well from its handsome captain. Granny's rheumatism flared with the change of seasons. No murmur was heard of Isla's return. Or the laird's leaving.

As for Magnus, he went about as usual, donning the garb of an islander and carrying on as he'd done in days of old before he'd wed, Nonesuch at his side whether he was on foot or horseback. He was especially fond of tending his large flock of sheep. Lark oft saw him carrying a struggling lamb or minding a ewe though his farm managers were never far. He stayed connected to the land, to his people, in this way. Islanders who wouldn't dare approach him in his Court of Session attire did not hesitate when he wore common dress.

"A word with ye, Lark." Jillian had left the kitchen and stood over her, her considerable bulk blocking the sun. "From the captain."

Sitting back on her heels, Lark ceased weeding. "All right."

"He's set to land in Cinnamon Cove two nights hence and needs ye to signal him from Gylen's ruins with a flash."

Cinnamon Cove was a favored landing with Gylen Castle, an ideal vantage point, sitting so high on its cliffside perch. And packing her father's old flintlock pistol for the desired beckoning blue light was easy enough. But nay, she could not.

She looked Jillian in the eye. "I told ye I

dinna want any more to do with such."

"And why not?"

"I dinna feel easy about it. Something about all this secrecy and darkness jars sourly with my need to walk uprightly."

"Hoot! Yer righteous, ye are!" Jillian's voice was scathing. "I'm needed with the tubmen to fetch and carry the haul. Jack Blaylock is going to light a fire on the heath near the mill to foil any Philistines about. The captain believes there's a spy among us."

Lark settled on her backside with a little thud, her thin petticoats a dismal cushion. "Someone on the island?"

"Aye. Likely Balliemore."

"All the more reason to say nay."

Jillian glowered. "The captain'll be sore wi' ye, Lark MacDougall." She began moving away as Cook's voice rose in the background, calling her back to the kitchen. "Ye'll regret it, ye will."

The captain stood on the quarterdeck of the *Merry Lass,* watching grimy wharfmen on the Isle of Man load cargo. Fifty matts leaf tobacco. Twenty small casks sweet liquorice and prunes. A dozen hampers earthenware. Three casks molasses and black pepper. Twenty firkins soap. Twenty-two reams writing paper. One hundred bars iron.

He kept a close eye on a bale of silk and card of lace. For Lark. The dress she'd worn to the ball was an embarrassment of wrinkles and worn cloth. An antique. Though he knew she prized it as an heirloom, her beauty called for something newer. Finer. If she was a true MacDougall she should dress the part. She wasn't in ruins. Gylen Castle was.

He threw a word to his quartermaster. "Stash the cloth and lace in my cabin."

The memory of Lark in the garden, so close on the bench beside him, was molasses sweet. She'd hung on his every word about America despite her reluctance, giving rise to the hope he might somehow woo her away from the island. 'Twas mostly Granny that held her. But if the old crone was to pass . . .

He shook off the base thought. Lark's clan was aggravatingly long lived, Granny at least. He might well reach midlife before Granny passed. Mayhap those tonics and potions of hers were to blame. The truth was, he gave Granny wide berth. He did not fancy the old woman, nor she him. 'Twas Magnus who shone in her eyes. No matter how Rory had tried, there was simply no way into Granny's good graces when the laird was near.

"Almost ready, Captain," a mate called.

By midafternoon they'd left the premises of the smuggling company Ross, Black, and Christian. This day the *Merry Lass* was part of a smuggling fleet, one of a dozen ships, heavily laden and steering for southwest Scotland to land their cargoes at various points. Rory's crew was so skilled that within a quarter of an hour the ship's cargo could be unloaded and the waiting tubmen would whisk it away to the horses the islanders had lent for transport. Speed was of the essence in avoiding the tax men.

He took out a spyglass and studied the churlish water and clumps of craggy islands off Britain's west coast, alert for English revenue cutters. Customs officers had the power to board and search all vessels at will. Though thus far Magnus's influence secured immunity from prosecution near Kerrera, it did not extend this far south to the *Merry Lass* and crew, at least in these waters.

"All hands shorten sail." He gave the order before sliding back the hatch and climbing down the ladder to the companionway. First door to the right opened to his quarters, a low-ceilinged affair that nearly left him scraping his head. His hammock swung a bit as the ship tilted, the groan of timber and shriek of the rigging like cantankerous old friends.

Mindful of Lark, he opened the bale of cloth and examined the finely worked Brussels lace atop it, fit to adorn a wedding dress. Would she like such fripperies? Daft he was. What woman wouldn't? He'd seen Isla wear lesser quality. Somehow the thought gave him pleasure.

'Twould be a personal thank-ye for her signaling them ashore from Gylen's ruins. If the Philistines were about, the *Merry Lass* would wait offshore till fishing boats could ferry the goods, as was oft done beneath a moonless sky, before the authorities could reach them.

Now there was the added threat of a spy. Had Jillian warned Lark as he'd instructed? To be more wary? The stakes were indeed high, the risk of discovery great. Would Lark, suddenly distancing herself from the whole business of free trading, refuse to take part? He well knew why, her Christian sentiments aside.

The penalty for smuggling was death.

Gylen Castle by day was a different creature completely. Lark liked to pretend it was more than crumbled stone and she herself more than a common crofter. Up the crumbling steps she oft went in broad daylight to the first floor, where a fireplace survived along with the ancient chimney and bread ovens in one blackened wall. Though the castle was roofless, its carvings above the sole oriel window were still beautiful and enduring. Little remained of her family's stronghold but the unparalleled view.

By night the castle assumed an eerie unfamiliarity. Tonight she stood a bit paralyzed in the dark, gaze swiveling from the sea landward. Nary a sliver of light. She missed the magic of moonlight shining on pale stone. The chasing away of shadows. Positioned by a castle window, she leaned into the cold opening and waited. 'Twas long past midnight, and all was black as the earl of Hades' waistcoat, as Granny said. She'd come here to make a stand not only against smuggling for herself but against the island's children taking part.

What's more, smuggling seemed especially wrong on the Sabbath. *Thou shalt not steal.* This and a certain Proverb followed her here, nipping at her with convicting claws. *Men do not despise a thief, if he steal to satisfy his soul when he is hungry. But if he be found, he shall restore sevenfold; he shall give all the substance of his house.*

All her life she'd believed their free trading was to sustain their very lives. She knew the awful hollowness of hunger, had seen its ugly work in the gravesites of islanders too weakened by want to fight disease. The laird did what he could to relieve them, but only the king himself could maintain so many for so long. Smuggling seemed a godsend, a practical answer. Were the king's ministers not thieves, taxing the people so? Even the American colonies rebelled against unjust taxes, so the captain told her. Still . . .

A quarter of an hour brought a village lad, so young and full of promise. He jumped at the sound of her voice. "Brodie, 'tis ye?"

"Jings! Ye look like Gylen's ghaist!" he exclaimed, backing up at the sight of her, pistol in hand. "The light needs flashing."

"I've come to talk ye out of it. To warn ye to return home."

He studied her soberly, his cowlick accenting his youth. "Why d'ye?"

" 'Tis wrong. And the danger's too great. There's said to be a spy about, so signaling is especially chancy."

He pondered this, appearing more alarmed. At last he handed her the weapon. "But the captain'll be all aflocht!"

She nearly sighed. Truly, the captain in his anger was nearly as fearsome as the laird.

Together they looked to the sea. The pistol in her hand grew heavy. The night gave no hint of a vessel, either friend or foe. But the *Merry Lass* was indeed out there somewhere. Any minute now would come the flash from the mill signaling the coast was clear, then the expected charging of the pan with powder and pulling of the trigger. The resulting blue light was unmistakable on shore. But tonight there would be no light.

'Twas so calm. Nary a breath of wind. This was why she heard someone else approach. Her blood froze. The spy? Standing in front of Brodie, she faced the sound, hating the taste of fear.

"Lark." The bottomless voice left her weak-kneed with relief. Magnus?

"Why have ye come?"

"To send ye home where ye belong." Though it was dark she read his consternation. He fairly bristled with it. "What risks ye take on such a night. What's come o'er ye?"

She sought to explain. "I —"

"No more, Lark." Closing the distance between them, he put out a hand. "I'll not have word of ye in gaol alongside the captain, aye?"

"Ye misunderstand me. Brodie was set to signal but I talked him out of it."

"And d'ye think the excise men and sheriff would believe such blether? Armed with a pistol, yer as guilty as the ground ye stand on." He took the weapon and thrust it into his waistband. "No more free trading for the both of ye."

Chastised as a child she felt. And near tears at his tongue lashing.

In moments they scattered in three directions. Would this be how he left it between them? With cross words? Would he now ride off to Edinburgh, never to return?

"Make haste," Magnus said over his shoulder.

She grappled for her bearings, staying away from the cliff's rain-slicked ledge to take an inland path that led the long way to Kerrera Castle and her croft. Even in the darkness she knew it by heart. Halfway home she began to make sense of the meagerest silhouettes, thanks to a bonfire above the beach. The *Merry Lass* had finally run aground despite the missing blue light. Now the sand teemed with people and carts and horses, all working to unload the goods and spirit them away.

Thieves, all?

Lord, forgive us.

Lark awoke to a gown of lustrous yellow

and a card of lace that was like seafoam. The captain of the *Merry Lass* was gone but had left a gift. Was he not angry with her then?

Granny clucked over the gift with a kind of awed disapproval. "A lass like yerself canna wear such finery. Ye'll draw the tax men like bees to the blossom. And they'll not rest till they have yer story. What can the captain be thinking? Besides, yellow makes ye look sallow. 'Tis not the color for ye, and the captain should ken such. Hide it, we will."

Beneath the hearthstone it went, but before Lark felt any loss there came a knock at the door. A footman from the castle?

"I've a note from the laird. He bids ye answer by morn."

Slowly, Lark broke the seal bearing the MacLeish crest, an angelic being in a praying posture. The note was addressed to them both. She read the words aloud, voice rising in surprise. "Your presence is required in Edinburgh. Details to come. We depart week after next."

They looked at each other, disbelieving. Edinburgh? Auld Reekie? Years ago Granny had set foot on the mainland, but Lark, never. They faced a ferry crossing. A long coach ride. She was pitched between dread and expectation. Did Magnus hope to remove them from any trouble between smugglers and authorities by taking them to the city?

"There's no saying nay to the laird," Granny murmured, going to assess the state of their laundry. "I suspect this has something to do with Lady Isla."

At once any high feeling left her. Of course. What else? Had Isla summoned them? Unlikely. But if so, they'd best bring the fertility herbs from the stillroom and anything else that might be of merit. Yet wouldn't so great a city with all its physics mock their wildcrafting, their herbs and simples?

"How far, Granny?"

"A good hundred miles by my reckoning."

" 'Twill be more than a day's journey then."

"Aye."

" 'Twill be arduous for yer auld bones." Lark looked at her with alarm. " 'Tis a hard thing he asks of ye."

"Och! I'm merely decoration! Ye canna be traveling alone with the laird. Now *that* would set tongues afire!" Granny smiled so widely she revealed all her missing teeth. "Mayhap Edinburgh is to my liking. I've heard tell of the castle and such. 'Twould be a fine thing to lay eyes on before I die."

"What is it all about, d'ye think?"

Granny took the summons from her hands. "We'll soon find out."

8

Edina! Scotia's darling seat!

Robert Burns

On the rare occasions Lark traveled by
coach, she became queasy from the pitching and swaying, and today was no exception. The world outside seemed to be wearing a winter's cloak, draping the island and
mainland in shades of gray. A stiff wind
shook the coach, never allowing a moment's
ease. With the weather so chancy, the
coach's shutters stayed shut and the airless
interior, though very fine, escaped her appreciation.

Magnus sat across from them, eyeing Lark
as she extracted gingerroot from her purse
and commenced chewing. "We'll come by
an inn shortly," he said as if to cheer her.

And so they did, but not before she'd lost
her midday meal of cheese and oat cake and
they'd covered countless leagues. Never had

she been so glad to set foot on muddy ground. The sun was setting as she looked up at the colorful sign swinging in an inland wind. The Osprey Coaching Inn. The Thistle seemed bedraggled in contrast, mere shirt-tail kin.

"I've secured the best rooms for ye," Magnus said. They followed an apron-clad maid up polished steps to untold wonders while Magnus remained below for a pipe and tankard of ale.

Lark suppressed a gasp as a door flung open. The timid maid was eyeing them as if trying to reconcile two commoners with such genteel accommodations. "His laird-ship's called for tea. 'Twill be here shortly."

Into the bower of brocade and beeswax and paneling they went, Granny's cackle overriding Lark's own sigh of delight.

Tea was brought with a platter of sweet-meats that settled Lark's uneasy stomach. Feet to a crackling fire — made of coal, not peat — they enjoyed copious cups of hyson that rivaled any that the free traders smuggled ashore.

"Can it be that in all my years I've never once left the island?" Lark's gaze traveled the length of the room, savoring every richly appointed detail. She and Granny would share a bed as they always did, but 'twas a big bed, a box bed, with brocade curtains to guard against any chill. "Being a lady, even for a day, suits my fancy," she admitted, stirring both cream and sugar into her tea.

"Once yer stomach settles, aye. Bethankit we're not ship bound."

Lark shuddered. "The captain talked of the American colonies. He wants to go there."

"Then let him go with all the other lunatics and convicts. 'Tis no fate for a lass such as yerself." The firm line of Granny's mouth declared she had no more to say on the subject. "Best hie to bed as we rise early, the laird says."

Lark could give no objection to that.

"Yer room was to yer satisfaction, I hope," Magnus said as he handed them into the coach the next morn.

Granny's nod punctuated Lark's effusive thanks. But truth be told, neither of them had gotten much sleep. Though lush, the bed was strange, the feather mattress swallowing them in its downy embrace. There was all manner of sounds in the street — talk and sated laughter, not the relentless rush of the sea and a clean coastal wind. Lark lay awake wondering if they'd indeed locked the door as the footfall of noisy guests in the hall kept up a steady rhythm.

Within two miles, Granny's snore was muted by the clatter of coach wheels. Magnus opened the shutter nearest Lark, letting in the early summer air. A smirr of rain gave way to sun, turning every leaf and blade of grass glistening.

"A farthing for yer thoughts, Lark," Magnus said, eyeing her from the opposite seat.

"A gold guinea for yers," she returned, gaze fixed on a distant manor house that rivaled Kerrera Castle.

He chuckled and removed his hat, laying it on the upholstered leather seat. "Have ye ne'er left the island?"

" 'Tis obvious then?"

"Aye. I ken yer missing yer bees."

"I ken what I have missed beyond those bee skeps . . . and count it as very little." She smiled and returned her attention to him. "A simple life suits me."

"Yet ye have MacDougall blood."

"Once upon a time. And now I've traded the castle for the croft."

"Uncomplainingly so. Yet I ken ye appreciate a bit o' finery."

His words seemed laden with meaning. She nearly squirmed. Did he know of Rory's gift? "Betimes I'm guilty of coveting a comely gown or hair ribbon — or yer library. But it doesna stray much beyond that." She looked to her lap, glad she'd worn her second-best dress. The soft green was the color of moss and paired well with her plaid shawl. She'd used a bit of the lace the captain had given her to trim her sleeves and bodice, though his gift of fine cloth remained hidden at the croft.

"Where did ye come by yer lace?"

A faint tingle turned into a full flush. "From a certain captain of a fast sloop."

"The *Merry Lass,* no doubt."

Alarm doused her. "Is it too much?"

"Nay. It becomes ye, though I wonder about the sentiment behind it when a chest of tea would do."

Their eyes met. Held. Was he . . . displeased?

"I have tea besides," she confessed.

" 'Tis easy to be generous with smuggled goods," he mused, buttoning the top button of his greatcoat against the damp. "I've no quarrel with the captain except for his reputation."

Drinking and wenching? The ladylike part of her wouldn't allow for such plain speaking. "People change. Better themselves."

"Many die as they lived."

He was in a rare, reflective mood. They'd not spoken so freely for years. It cast her back to former days that had a golden mist about them. Before Edinburgh. Before his barrister life.

"Ye need to be away from the island and anything unchancie there. Not even to cover a peat stack nor shine a light."

She let loose a sigh. Somehow the captain's latest gifts seemed more bribe. A bid to sway her and return her to smuggling. "The captain was so fashed when I refused to help —"

"The captain answers to me." He'd switched into laird and barrister again, not her childhood friend. Not the Magnus of old. "He's not to ask yer involvement ever, nor complain of yer refusal."

His stern tone roused Granny just for an instant, and then her head lolled onto her chest once more. Lark stroked the lace of her sleeve, wishing she could peek inside Magnus's finely tuned mind. He was so like his father that the previous laird leapt to memory with unusual force. 'Twas hard to believe such a man had fallen in battle. Not one larger than life.

"I've always had reservations about yer involvement," he told her. When she opened her mouth to agree, he cut in. "Though most of Kerrera's women are part and parcel of the trade, 'tis doubly dangerous with a spy unaccounted for." His gaze bore into her. "Promise me."

She took a deep breath to quell her rising queasiness, despite the pinch of her stays. "I promise. But what of ye?"

He rubbed his bristled jaw with a leather glove. "I feel called to forsake it as well. The Almighty wants us clean — holy — in all our parts. Ever since I heard George Whitefield preach in Glasgow, I've been struck by the light he brought."

"Are ye now a member of the Holy Club?" she teased, seeking to dispel the dark mood of before. "Alongside Mr. Wesley and others?"

He chuckled. The coach took a sharp bend in the road with a lurch that nearly launched Lark from her seat into his lap. It came to her in that instant just why he forbade her involvement with any smuggling. Because of Isla. Because Lark might, as mistress of the stillroom, be of help in some way.

Were they not hurtling toward Edinburgh for that very thing?

"You've come." Isla gestured to a settee in the parlor of the MacLeishes' Edinburgh townhouse.

They'd arrived but an hour before, and Lark had the impression Isla wanted them in and out of Edinburgh as quickly as possible. Magnus had disappeared altogether once the housekeeper had led them to their bedchamber. His sudden, unexplained absence upended her. Likewise, Granny had been kept from this meeting, was even now upstairs napping, and so Lark faced the laird's wife alone.

"Allow me to introduce my physician, the renowned Scottish surgeon, Dr. John Hunter," Isla said. " 'Tis he who summoned you." *Not I,* she seemed to say.

A slight, tidy-looking gentleman rose from a chair and gave a little bow. "You are Mistress MacDougall of Kerrera," he said, making it sound like a most dignified title. "Keeper of the castle stillroom."

"Like my grandmother before me, aye."

"Quite lovely you are. And quite young," he said with warm enthusiasm. "I was expecting neither."

The mischievous light in his eyes set her at ease. If he was fire, Isla was ice. She regarded Lark with no warmth, but if she had, Lark would have been doubly upended.

"Perhaps we can combine our skills and treat my patient successfully. Allow me to explain just what I do. Are you familiar with the term *accoucheur*?"

Though she'd been schooled in French,

the word rolled off Lark like water. "Nay."

"It simply means a physician specializing in obstetrics. A male sort of midwife, if you will."

A male howdie? She worked to stay stoic when she wanted to laugh. What would the island's midwife think of that? Men were kept from such matters, at least on Kerrera.

"Please, be seated. What is in your kit there?"

"The herbs and simples of the castle's stillroom," Lark answered.

"Excellent. May I see them?"

"So what kept ye all afternoon?" Granny asked as Lark entered the townhouse bedchamber.

"I returned to the schoolroom and learnt all about male midwifery."

"Hoot!" Granny looked more dismayed than shocked. "Since when were men let in the birthing room?"

"City-bred doctors, mayhap. Isla seems to favor it." Lark went on to explain all she'd found out and in turn what she'd told the doctor. To his credit, Dr. Hunter seemed genuinely interested in what she had to say and was not altogether ignorant of wildcrafting. "He believes we must meld the Almighty's natural remedies with more scientific methods."

"What's that ye say?"

"Bring the bounty God has given us in nature into the medical rooms. We clashed on but one matter. Dr. Hunter feels barren women must partake of bed rest and forsake all activity. I say they should walk or ride about freely and live wholeheartedly."

"And Isla? What did she say?"

"Very little. She mostly sat with her pugs and listened."

"And the laird?"

"He came in at the last." Lark sat by the window, wishing it would open to more than iron gates and a congested street. "He sided with me on living naturally but respects the doctor. He's arranged to take us about the city day after tomorrow once we've rested."

"Has he now?" Granny seemed pleased. "I've always wanted to see Auld Toun."

"I've brought hartshorn to mask the smell. Mayhap I'll stay behind and let ye and the laird go."

"And insult his hospitality?"

Truly, Lark had no desire to see any more of Edinburgh than she had from this soot-stained window. But for Granny she put on an expectant face. "Till our outing, then."

9

Piled deep and massy, close and high;
mine own romantic town.

Sir Walter Scott

Magnus hoped for sun and got rain, but it
in no way dampened Granny's glee. As for
Lark, she was unusually quiet, taking in the
filthy, early June streets and tottering tenements with a canny eye, hartshorn in hand.

"There's talk of a new town," he told
them, the words wrapped in an apology. "A
more genteel section with parks and town-
houses. Safer. Cleaner. The city planners
are already calling it the Athens of the
North."

"Well, I'll not live to see it, but Lark
might." From her carriage seat, Granny
regarded her surroundings with a lively
curiosity. "Now where is that coffeehouse
ye speak of in this great sea of need?"

He smiled, telling the coachman to turn

onto a side street. A wayward cow and gaggle of geese barred their way, and several dirty, barefoot children ran after them, begging. He emptied his pockets of coin if only to ease the telling empathy in Lark's face. He was used to turning a blind eye. But Lark . . . She reached out to them, extending her fingers toward these dirty urchins who craved all sorts of attention. The simple gesture cut him to the quick. Had he grown callous to city life?

The carriage slowed before a respectable coffeehouse, frequented by physics and barristers and open to gentlewomen as well. At Lark's wide-eyed look, he sent the carriage back to the townhouse and offered both women his arm. "Edinburgh is better seen on foot. Besides, the townhouse isna far."

He had to remind himself she'd not been off the island, had never seen a village bigger than Balliemore. Nor had she much considered the novelty of a meal beyond the croft or castle kitchen.

Her voice rose in amazement as she read from the bill of fare. "Potato pudding under a leg of mutton larded with strips of Seville orange peel."

"The best food is the simplest," Granny put in, not giving the offerings a second glance since she did not know her letters.

"I'll have the mutton pie ye mention."

Before the meal was served, two fellow barristers approached their table, clearly curious about the company Magnus was keeping.

"Fancy seeing you in the presence of two lovely ladies other than your wife," one said. "I hope Lady Isla is well."

"Friends from Kerrera," Magnus returned, making introductions. "Her ladyship is well, aye."

The younger of the two men kept his eyes on Lark. Truly, with Lark adorned in the lace the captain had given her, her bright hair subdued beneath a ruffled cap, she seemed more a lady about town than a maid of the islands. She nodded demurely at both gentlemen with a polite, self-effacing smile, giving no indication she was anything but a landed MacDougall.

"There's one more place I'd like to take ye," Magnus said as they left the coffeehouse.

"Where else can that possibly be?" Granny asked. "We've been down the crag and back, from Holyrood Palace to the castle, with all the hawkers and merchants in between."

"A bookseller," he told them. "On the same street as the townhouse."

Lark smiled, surely understanding his

intent. She loved books but seldom had access to anything but the castle library, and then only on rare occasions.

Once inside the expansive shop with its heavy scent of ink and leather, he knew he'd not erred.

"Never in my life did I imagine a place with so many books." Her gloveless fingers trailed over countless spines, her lips sounding out titles, her whole countenance alight.

Granny sat on a Windsor chair near the entry, watching them. Dozing. At last Lark settled on a burgundy book of verse. She was partial to poetry, or had been in the schoolroom. Their tutor had often pitted them against each other in memorization.

Standing in the pale light of a window, she held the book aloft, indigo eyes a-dance. "Thomas Blacklock."

"The blind poet?"

She blew the dust off the cover and hugged it to her chest. Her words were more whisper as she recited the godly poem. "O come, and o'er my bosom reign. Expand my heart, inflame each vein." Her voice trailed away in invitation. "Though ev'ry action mine . . ."

He took it up without missing a beat. "Each low, each selfish with control; with all thy essence warm my soul, and make me wholly thine." He caught the glint of emotion in her gaze before she looked away. It knotted his own throat and left him staring unseeing at the wall of books in front of them.

" 'Tis yers," he told her. She'd been about to return it to the shelf. "To keep."

"Mine?" The word warbled on her tongue.

This poetry of old had struck a chord with them both. He simply nodded, missing the island — the old days — so acutely he didn't trust himself to speak. For a moment time seemed suspended and then gave way to its sweet fleetingness.

She finally said, "Bethankit," her happiness his.

After Edinburgh, the chill of the sea seemed colder, the sky bluer, the island's headlands more majestic. Lark returned to the still-room with new appreciation, her book of verse tucked in her pocket. On the flyleaf she'd written the date of their bookshop visit, *8 June, 1752.*

Privately, her thoughts took another turn. *Lord, let me never see Edinburgh again.*

One visit was enough. Nay, one visit was too much. It wasn't just the grime or the filth or the misery she'd seen on the faces of the children who'd run after their carriage, or the tattered, staggering lot of those befuddled by drink in shadowed corners. Mostly it was what she hadn't seen but sensed within the walls of the MacLeish townhouse. The doctor's quiet befuddlement. Isla's brooding presence. Magnus's restlessness. Her own conflicted feelings.

Magnus and Isla had not yet returned to the castle, and so Lark watched for them as the next fortnight unfolded. Watched, too, for the captain till Jillian arrived at her door the next Sabbath.

"The captain's waiting for ye in the cave. Says he needs to speak with ye posthaste."

Lark thanked her and Jillian went on her way. With Granny napping and in no need of explanation, Lark donned her shawl and slipped out. Where was the *Merry Lass*? Likely the captain wanted to plan the next landing of cargo. 'Twas time once and for all, backed by Magnus's stern words, for her to bow out.

The wind tore at her as she descended the steep path to the beach, Kerrera Castle at her back. By the time she reached softer sand, her carefully wound braid had unraveled, whipping coppery strands in her face. Bending, she took off her shoes to walk more quickly, the mouth of the cave a good quarter mile or more.

The captain had planned their tryst well with the tide out. Last time she'd come this way, two revenue officers were nearby with their long probes, searching for hidden contraband in the sand. When danger from the tax men was highest, the captain resurrected the old tale that inspired fear. Once he'd hung a lantern about the neck of a black ram, mimicking the ghost dog of Kerrera with its devilish eyes and fatal bite. Those who crossed Auld Mort's path were said to die within a twelve-month.

As a child, she'd felt the hair on her neck rise at the legend, and it did again now, making her look over her shoulder. Behind her bounded Nonesuch, a parcel of lonesomeness with the laird away. As she had grown up with the collie, it attached itself to her when Magnus was gone too long, sleeping at their very doorstep.

"Come along, Nonesuch. Yer master should be home shortly."

Today with the weather so squally and it being the Sabbath, no one was about. She walked past several smaller caves seldom used to cache goods, as they filled with water at high tide.

"So we've company." The captain's voice issued from the back of the cave, a discordant note in it. "Kerrera's cur."

Apparently sensing his displeasure, None-such slunk to one side of the cavern and lay down beside an open pit.

"He's an agreeable companion," she shot back at him, prepared for a confrontation. "Far more so than Auld Mort."

He chuckled, taking a seat on an upturned tub. "Yer well?" At her nod, he fixed his eye on the mouth of the cave. "The land crew will be here soon. We've found our spy."

She stayed standing. "Who?"

"The club-footed farmer, Kerr. Smells a reward, likely. We'll soon see him whipped."

"But he's lamed —"

"And dangerous." He spat into the sand. "Would ye rather we poison his sheep or set fire to his hayrick?"

"None of it," she returned vehemently.

"What's this I hear about ye hieing to Auld Reekie?"

"For a wee bit. On account of Isla."

"Yer at her beck and call now too?"

Lark stiffened. "What means ye?"

"First the laird, then the mistress."

"I do what I can." Hurt by the accusation in his tone, she sunk a hand into her pocket, caressing the book of verse. "I wore the lace ye gave me. 'Tis fit for town."

"Aye, that it is. What about the fancy yellow cloth?"

" 'Tis best to keep hidden, Granny said."

He made a face. "What came of yer visit?"

"The physic has all in hand." She felt disloyal discussing such matters. " 'Tis none o' yer business, truly."

He faced her, cupping her chin in his work-worn hand. "Dinna growl at me, Lark. We've precious little time. Sweet talk is what I'm after. And this." He pressed against her, the butt of his pistol in his waistband as jarring as his kiss.

Rum. Tobacco. Need and impatience. His mouth moved over hers possessively, his arms pinning her on either side as his hands rested against the cave's damp wall.

Her first kiss. But not how she'd imagined it. Not soft and lingering, delightful and tender. Just raw and wild as a contrary sea wind. And yet, for all its tumult, it affected her no more than a kiss on the cheek by an uncle or brother. Not a lover. Nor did she return it. Did the captain even notice — or care?

Nonesuch gave a growl and Lark started. The captain stepped back and took the pistol from his belt. Together they looked toward the noisome sea. The cave's entrance soon filled with a half dozen tubmen and lookouts. She knew and liked most of them, fellow islanders like herself, all loyal to the laird. To a man they doffed their hats upon seeing her, a courtesy that offset the captain's churlishness.

He climbed atop a rock. "We've three hundred ankers of brandy to beach, all still aboard the *Merry Lass* since the Philistines have been alerted by the spy. The plan is to waylay the tax men at the Thistle with the finest of spirits till we see the cargo well down the Smuggler's Road."

The men nodded, asking a few questions at will. Lark listened, retreating to where Nonesuch lay and sinking down into the sand, glad to be out of the battering wind.

"No flashes of pistols nor covering peat stacks nor lighting clifftop fires. I'll come into Black Cave at the stroke of midnight if all's calm on both land and sea." The captain's decisive gaze landed on Lark as she sat stroking the collie's damp coat. "With the laird away, 'tis left to Lark to keep the castle's stable doors unlocked. We're in need of the laird's carriage horses."

She stiffened, trying to stay atop her guilty feelings. *He who steals must steal no longer.* Following that were Magnus's own forbidding words. Yet keeping the stable door open seemed such a small thing, like the flash of blue light. No doubt the laird's horses were needed. Magnus had not minded before.

But . . .

Was it any wonder she felt so addlepated?

The meeting ended. The crew departed to inform their cohorts of the chosen time and place.

"Needs be I bow out of this," she said to the captain, her words nearly snuffed by the encroaching surf.

"Needs be?" He jumped down from his rocky perch.

She had his full attention. But how to explain her change of heart to a man who never cleared the lintel of kirk? "Is smuggling not robbery? Does it not cheat the king and every soul in the nation?"

He crossed both his arms and his boots. "Ye seem to have no quarrel with yer pretties."

She flushed, no longer mindful of the cave's chill. "Fair enough. 'Tis yer three hundred ankers of brandy that concerns me. Since I've been to the Cowgate in Edinburgh and seen folk weaving about like blind men because of drink —"

"So 'tis the quality of cargo, aye?"

"If oats or molasses, even tea, 'tis more understandable. I've known enough hunger to welcome that. But the others — the unnecessaries. The Lyon silks and laces. The spirits."

To her surprise, he shrugged and crossed the distance between them and sank down beside her, back to the wall, pistol on the sand. "There's a remedy, ye ken. We can quit all this. Bid goodbye to the damp caves and midnight dangers, the unlocked stables and lost sleep."

"Go to America, ye mean."

"Ye've weathered Auld Reekie."

"The hundred miles to Edinburgh is a mere walk compared to an ocean voyage."

"Ye lack spirit, Lark. Vision." He took her hand, her slender fingers swallowed in his callused palm. "Think of what awaits."

"Cape Fear."

"Aye, so named by an early explorer who found the coast tricky to navigate. 'Tis all."

So he'd learned that, at least. His taking her hand somehow seemed to pull her nearer his plan. Off this beloved beach into the unknown. The untried. From a distance, the captain seemed intriguing and exciting. Up close he was dangerous. All that was good within her balked.

She pulled free, scrambling to her feet and rousing a sleeping Nonesuch. "I'd best be away. Granny will wonder what's become of me." At the cave's mouth, she turned back. "I canna do as ye bid. Not even something as simple as leaving the stables open one last time."

He crossed his arms, staying stoic, further addling her.

"Stay safe, aye?" she said as she turned away.

She had, at last, quit this ill-trickit business, if not him.

10

He is happiest, be he king or peasant, who
finds peace in his home.
Johann Wolfgang von Goethe

Magnus entered the castle foyer, Isla close
behind with a pug in arm, Rhona trailing
her with another. Footmen fanned out
behind them, shouldering two trunks more
than when she'd left. His wife's indulgent
parents never let her go without extra baggage. Soon they'd need a separate wagon to
haul it all.

She climbed the stairs with her maid after
greeting Mistress Baird. "Please send supper to my room. Dr. Hunter has ordered
bed rest."

"Very well, mistress." The housekeeper
sent Magnus a tight smile before he turned
into the study. "Welcome back, sir."

Magnus paused in the doorway, entirely
focused on the cask in his path. "Some eau-

de-vie?" he quipped. "The carriage horses are lathered this morning, I take it."

" 'Twould seem so. The beach was quite busy into the wee small hours." She approached from behind. "Would ye care to eat alone in the dining room tonight?"

"Nay. My study will suffice." He unclasped his cloak, weary of rich Edinburgh fare. "Something simple. Oatcakes. Cheese. Whatever Cook has on hand."

"Very well, sir. I'll see it arranged."

He went to stand by the largest window, arguably the best view of any in the castle save his turret bedchamber. From here he had full command of the formal garden and beyond it the sea and countless leagues of coastline. If he leaned to his left, he could almost scale the wall and see into the kitchen garden and the stillroom beyond, its door open.

Lark was still at work, likely, as it was just two o'clock. Still time enough for him to ride about the island and learn of anything that had transpired in his absence. A gladness he'd never felt in the city swept through him like a headwind. Clearing his mind. Filling his soul. *Home.*

Half an hour later after he'd sampled the cask the captain had left him, he sought the stables, bypassing the stillroom. Lark was singing as she often did, once saying it sweetened and dignified her work. Low and melodic, her voice snuck out and halted him on the shell path.

He took a step back, toward her domain. But he had nothing to say to her, truly. Nothing other than hearsay. Jillian had told a housemaid who'd told his manservant that the captain was talking of taking Lark to the colonies. The dismay he'd felt upon learning it cut to the bone. But why wouldn't he want to be done with the islands' foremost smuggler, if not Lark? She was a free woman. Free to wed whom she pleased. Even an unprincipled ship's captain.

Her singing ended. He heard a cupboard open and close. As he'd recently seen her, entertained her and Granny in the city, he had no cause to seek her out except to inquire if the rumor about America was true.

Other than the pleasure he always felt in her company.

Thy word have I hid in mine heart, that I might not sin against thee.

A strong check in his spirit sent him on his way again. Yet the tug to tarry remained.

"My mistress said you're to read Dr.

Hunter's instructions at once." Rhona handed Lark a sealed paper.

The doctor's writing hand was much like him. Forceful. Exacting. Bold. He gave detailed instructions for Isla's new health regimen: Complete bed rest. A strong cup of nettle tea upon arising, sweetened with a little island honey. A steam inhalation of various herbs. No sweetmeats. Fresh curd cheese and fish daily. Two cups of cold fertility tonic at bedtime, consisting of burdock root, milk thistle, and raspberry leaf. No less than ten hours' sleep.

Would he make an invalid of her?

"Well?" Rhona said, arms crossed.

"Well . . . what?" Lark returned with a rare flash of fire.

"You'll need to provide me the prescribed herbs."

"And I will, once I've finished my task." Lark waved a hand at the crowded worktable. A large bowl, a sack of salt, and a great many dried flowers and herbs left little room for Rhona's request. "Return in an hour's time and ye shall have what ye seek."

Rhona cast a wary eye about. "What is that horrible smell?"

"Valerian root. 'Tis helpful for sleep."

The lady's maid covered her nose with a handkerchief and hastened away.

Mindful of Rhona's order, Lark hurried her task as best she could. At last she had a great quantity of leaves and petals preserved in sea salt for a fragrant potpourri that even Isla liked. Well within the promised hour, Lark cleared the table and set about honoring the doctor's wishes. Mayhap she should petition Providence again for a miracle too.

Half the island was his dominion, and the other half belonged to those who paid rent in exported corn. Tethering his mount to a hitch rail at one end of Balliemore near the Thistle, Magnus walked the length and breadth of the village, engaging the few shopkeepers and tradesmen and learning the latest news and needs.

A blacksmith was coveted. He'd fetch one from the mainland. The annual visit of the tailor was overdue. Could he hasten his coming? The island physic feared the smallpox had again reared its ugly head. Just last spring he'd inoculated fifty-three of the islanders at the laird's insistence, at two shillings sixpence a head. Should he inoculate the rest? Aye, without hesitation.

Magnus had had the pox long ago. Had Isla? No scars marred her skin. Why did he not know that for certain? Because she'd been in Edinburgh during the outbreak and he'd thought it best not to worry her. Why did he feel less cumbersome gauging the health of villagers than he did his own wife?

Removing his wet hat and thumping it against the door frame to remove the worst of the damp, he entered the Thistle with its customary stink of spirits and taint of fish. On this ill-scrappit day, the taproom was full, the captain occupying his usual corner seat. Magnus had heard the revenue men had been this way, tipped off by a supposed spy. Plying them with spirits had kept them away from the last lucrative haul that left his horses so spent. The captain's smug smile seemed confirmation that all was well, or at least calm, the weather notwithstanding.

As he was seldom at the Thistle, no seat was familiar, and he wished himself back in his book-lined study, boots up on a leather stool. Betimes the tavern left him wanting a bath in the nearest loch.

"Ho, yer lairdship!" Several voices rang out, and Magnus nodded a greeting, intent on the captain's corner.

An extra chair was brought along with a pint of ale.

"So what brings ye?" the captain asked.

"News of the run."

"Three hundred ankers sent inland."

"Minus the one in my study."

"Aye. The Philistines are off the island and the spy's been dealt with. We merely lashed him at Lark's request."

"She requested ye lash him?" Magnus queried, eyebrow raised.

"Nay." The captain laughed and called for another pint. "She requested we do nothing, lamed as he is. But ye well ken some punishment must be dealt. The man has earned a few stripes for loose lips."

Magnus took a long drink of the heady brew. The knowledge sat like gravel in his gut. As laird, he was concerned foremost with every islander's well-being, yet here he sat listening to news of a lashing that was more likely vengeful beating.

" 'Tis Lark that most concerns me," Magnus said.

The captain's smugness shifted to concern. "She's well?"

"Aye." Magnus still felt the warmth of her singing in the stillroom. He cut to the chase. "I dinna want her involved in any more free trading."

"Nay? I asked her to leave yer stable doors unlocked this last time. But she refused."

"As she should."

"Given they're yer stables and yer horses, I think it matters little. I'll not forget how ye were caught violating the Dress Act a twelve-month ago. No fine was forthcoming. Ye walked away."

"Free trading isna looked on so kindly as being kilted. Ye'll likely hang."

The captain shrugged. "I'll take my chances."

"Then leave Lark out of it." Magnus underscored his words with a direct gaze that the captain did not hold.

Eyes averted, the captain swallowed more ale. "They wouldna hang a woman."

"They would indeed. I've seen it done in Edinburgh's Grassmarket." It had been a public spectacle of which he wanted no part. Though the woman was unknown to him, he'd felt sick to his boots.

"We're to sail for the Isle of Man once the weather clears." The captain recovered his good humor. "East India and Dutch goods. Virginia tobacco — fine pigtail and coarse roll. Spanish brandy from Barcelona."

"I'd rather leave the spirits alone. 'Tis a form of slavery. Besides, there's talk in Edinburgh of sending more cruisers into the channel to target the Isle of Man's smugglers who load cargo there."

The captain leaned back in his chair. "As I said, I'll take my chances."

"Then do so without Lark," Magnus restated in parting.

11

I do not want people to be agreeable, as it saves me the trouble of liking them.

Jane Austen

"You've received a summons from the mistress." Rhona seemed none too pleased with the unusual message delivered below stairs, which simply caught Lark by surprise.

Wiping her hands on her apron, Lark left the stillroom and followed Isla's lady's maid into the castle by way of the garden door beneath the laird's study window. Magnus stood looking down at them, book in hand and expression unreadable, or mayhap her glance at him was too fleeting to register his mood.

The gloom of the castle was in stark contrast to the outright gaiety of the sunlit garden. Or was it because of who was in residence? Lark shook off the thought, only to have it resurface as she climbed the servants' stair to Isla's chambers. Behind them a door shut. In seconds a catapulting, furry creature nearly buckled her knees as Nonesuch came bounding from behind, Magnus in her wake.

With a quiet reprimand to the collie, he took the hall to his turret room, further befuddling Lark. Something was afoot. Today the castle seemed especially weighty, even unfriendly, the servants coming and going with downcast eyes and light feet.

A sharp rap by Rhona announced their arrival at the bedchamber door. The immense room was even darker than the hall, drapes drawn, a single, smoking candle lit. Lark felt an odd revulsion at the stale air tainted with . . . laudanum tincture?

"At last. How long does it take you to climb those stairs?" Isla questioned with less fire than before.

Lark stifled a hasty retort, her gaze swinging from the rumpled bed where Isla usually reclined to a settee beneath a window, her new resting place, a pug in her lap. Lark had an overwhelming urge to push back the drapes and throw open the windows. Instead she fixed her attention on a small glass bottle at Isla's right. But 'twas Isla's next words that most dismayed her.

"My sleep is fitful so I summoned Dr. Burns."

The island's foremost bamboozler? "Burns . . ." Lark would not even call him a physic. "He lacks training. Dr. Hunter is far more able."

"But he is not here, is he? I need relief. Not even your herbs will do." Isla stroked the sleeping pug. "Don't stand there looking at me like that. You remind me of Magnus, all fire and brimstone."

Rhona passed into the dressing room, tending to some task, and Lark approached the table bearing the strange bottle. "Ye must give the herbs I distilled room to work," she said, voice soft. "They're far better for ye than this." Picking up the tincture, a blend of opium in wine, she held it aloft, gauging the contents in the feeble light. Fresh alarm took hold. Had the bottle been full? 'Twas now nearly empty.

"Are the contents not made from poppies?" Isla asked. "You have the very same in the kitchen garden, am I right? Bright red ones."

"Those are common poppies, not medicinal ones."

"Then what of this talk about opium tea Cook mentions?"

Lark nearly sighed. Cook spoke too freely

oftentimes. " 'Tis sometimes given to counter the most persistent aches and pains. Cook's rheumatism and the like."

"Well then. What benefits Cook shall surely be of benefit to me."

Lark studied the bottle. "How much of this have ye taken?"

Isla lifted thin shoulders and yawned. "Enough to make me deliciously drowsy."

"What does yer husband say to this?" Lark set the tincture down, unwilling to be in the middle of a family fray yet increasingly concerned for all involved.

Into the prolonged silence came an unexpected answer. "Her husband has sent Dr. Burns away, and his dangerous remedies along with him but for this, which was hidden from me." Passing behind Lark, Magnus retrieved the tincture, examining it with a critical eye.

"Dr. Burns has brought me more relief than Dr. Hunter or your stillroom altogether." Isla's voice rose like a wave before cresting. "Would you deny me my one comfort?"

"There is comfort to be had beyond this bottle." Going to a window, Magnus thrust the drapes open. The sunlight pushing back the darkness was so profound Isla winced. " 'Tis now July, Kerrera's kindest month.

Why not ride or walk about? See to needs in the village? Enjoy the garden I had planted for yer wedding gift?"

Isla looked aghast at his outburst. Used to his moods, Lark stood perfectly still as a small war waged around her.

Isla folded her arms. "Dr. Hunter prescribed complete bed rest."

"Even bed rest must have an end." He handed Lark the bottle. "Lock it in the still-room. Throw it in the sea. Whatever ye will." Turning back to Isla, he issued a final ultimatum. "I expect ye to be dressed and in the dining room for dinner at eight o'clock, as we're expecting guests."

"Guests!" She flung the word at him like a curse. "I am in no mood to entertain!"

"Have yer maid prop ye up then." He cast a baleful eye about the shadowy room. "Where is she?"

"Here, sir."

Lark had never seen Rhona so meek. Head bowed, she stood in the doorway as if awaiting execution. Even Lark felt a qualm. Isla was in no condition to be at table, propped up or otherwise. She gave him a rare warning glance.

Magnus seemed unmoved. "If yer mistress isna ready to dine at the appointed hour, I'll see ye Edinburgh bound come morning." To Lark, he said, "We'll misuse ye no longer. Return to the stillroom and whatever it was ye were doing there before ye were needlessly interrupted."

With a nod, Lark fled the bedchamber, fire to her heels. Nonesuch sat in the hallway, thumping her plumy tail in adoration. It was for her master she waited, as if sensing his disquiet.

Still clutching the bottle, Lark hurried out of the castle past footmen and maids and through a maze of corridors. She did not stop till she stood on the cliffside, the sheer drop making her head spin. Not a foot away was two hundred feet of air and churning surf. She hurled the bottle over the precipice and into the salty spray, wanting to do the same with Magnus's heated displeasure and Isla's predicament and the captain's maddening talk of America.

She returned to the sanctuary of the walled, sun-warmed kitchen garden but saw all that was wrong with it too. A midge-ridden bed of kale. A rhododendron broken in the last windstorm. A rusted garden gate in need of fixing. Damsel bugs in the struggling vegetables. 'Twas a woefully fallen world. She tried to return to her fermenting, but it seemed as sour as their circumstances.

She pulled a commonplace book from a stillroom cupboard, then sought a secluded garden bench amid the bees and began searching, turning pages, the sun warming her bent head. Receipts of all sorts were penned in her hand, many told to her by her granny.

Lord, the right remedy. Please.

One was marked *womb.* Milk thistle. Raspberry leaf. Goldenseal. Was this what Granny had given her and she'd placed in a cupboard? She retrieved the bottle and uncorked it, again breathing in the scent and spilling some of the mixture on a snowy linen cloth.

The ingredients lined up with the book's receipt save one unidentifiable addition. Try as she might, Lark couldn't discern it, and this was what kept the bottle cupboard bound. Till she determined just what it was, she could not share it. And Granny, sadly, could not remember.

Magnus eyed Isla through the golden wink of candlelight. Seated to his right, she was trying her best to be polite to their guests. But failing. Her slender hand with its silver fork trembled, at least to his steady observation. 'Twas clear she had no appetite. Her troubled gaze held a glassiness he found especially troubling. The lingering effects of opium tincture?

The only saving grace was the high spirits of their guests, so sated with food and drink — and themselves — they seemed oblivious to his wife's fragile state. Watching her, he felt a strange thawing. For once the hard, crusted shell of his heart regarding Isla cracked enough to allow empathy in. How must it feel to be barren? To listen to conversation about guests' children around this crowded table without comment? Though childlessness carried little of the scorn of the Old Testament, the burden was heavy to bear. And though he'd not belittled Isla himself, his silence had oftentimes been harsh.

Had he not despised her in his heart?

Husbands, love your wives, and be not bitter against them.

Regrettably, theirs was no love match, though few were among the gentry. Pondering it, he brought an end to the lengthy supper, and when plates were whisked away, the ladies retired to the adjoining sitting room while the gentlemen lingered in the dining room to take up less genteel topics and their smoking pipes. Through the adjoining door he could see Isla seated on a settee, looking a bit more composed, Rhona near at hand. If nothing else, he wanted to shield Isla from the inflammatory talk of the blustering laird from Mull.

"I'd always rather deal with sheep than people," Hugh Sinclair said. "The crofters and cottars must go. I've just given notice of eviction to forty-five families."

Forty-five? Some two hundred souls? Magnus felt the news like a blow. "Are ye not being rash with so many?" he questioned quietly. "Denying them the right to labor and live out their lives honestly and independently on the land of their forefathers?"

"Aye, at my everlasting expense," Sinclair all but growled. "My plan is to convert these small crofts into larger, more profitable farms."

"Sheep farms? What of the very young and the very auld tenants?"

"Let them apply to the Relief Committee. Or emigrate. Canada and the Americas are wide open."

"Last I heard, a great many crofters and cottars who were turned out fell victim to cholera aboard ship or were left to die on foreign shores."

" 'Tis their choice to sail or no. They can always stay on in the cities instead. Glasgow. Edinburgh. Aberdeen." Sinclair took a drink of brandy with one hand and then a long draw on his pipe with the other. "Mark my word, ye'll one day do the same. There's far more profit to be made clearing these tenants than ye'll find maintaining them on this rocky isle of yers. How many inhabit Kerrera?"

Magnus hesitated, aware of the equally heated side conversations of the other gentlemen swirling around them. "At last count, three hundred twenty-six souls."

"A small isle, to be sure. If not for Kerrera's meager crops, ye'd be in considerable debt, so I've heard."

"Dinna believe hearsay," Magnus replied. "Fishing is our mainstay — and sheep. Both are steady."

"What about all that free trading the western isles are guilty of? The dragoons are out in greater numbers, and some of the revenue men are going about in disguise."

"I'm now cautioning the islanders against any free trading in hopes to turn the tide against it, but 'tis a long-standing tradition amongst generations all over Britain, like it or not."

" 'Tis smuggle or starve, that I understand. But free trading is a perilous occupation for all involved. Another reason to be rid of those islanders and thus the worry they cause ye."

Magnus digested this without comment, and talk turned to more mundane matters. When the men rejoined the ladies, Isla seemed more herself, waving the lace fan he'd given her for her name day and speaking of a coming fete in Edinburgh.

For early July, the drawing room was close, the dampness beneath his collar telling. Aside from the tenants' balls, they rarely entertained, saving most of their socializing for Edinburgh. This was an obligatory evening, hosting local lairds to discuss local matters.

The clock struck midnight. He stood by a window once the guests retired to their rooms, Isla among them. Through the sooty blackness of night shone a tiny light from Lark's croft. He looked beyond that to the beach, scouring every rocky outcropping and sandbar.

Another landing by the captain was imminent, so he'd heard. Did MacPherson know of the increased presence of dragoons and tax men? Mayhap it didn't matter. The captain showed a callous indifference to danger. Did his life matter so little? Would he heed Magnus's warning about Lark being left out of it?

Her light nettled him, as if it was a beacon of sorts, a piece of the coming haul's dangerous puzzle. Leaving the drawing room, he spoke a word to his valet that he'd soon return before he trod the path to the lighted croft.

A soft but distinct rap at the door gained him entry. Granny sat by the window, a cup of tea before her. She seemed not at all surprised by the late hour or his appearing, her toothless smile welcoming. "Come in, laddie, and have a wee rest. My rheumatism is keeping me awake." Her gaze ran up and down him. "Yer dressed proud as Bonnie Prince Charlie himself."

"Guests," he said simply, casting a discreet glance about the tiny dwelling place. No Lark?

"She's gone out with the howdie. 'Tis her cousin's time."

Relief and disappointment pummeled him. Relief she was not a part of the coming debacle on the beach. Disappointment she was not here, eyes a-glitter, taking tea as in days of old.

"Sit ye down."

He sat just as Granny got up, none too quickly, and served him the steaming brew in a chipped ceramic mug once used by Lark's father. The tiny cracks in the salt glaze bespoke time and constant use. The handle was large enough to fit four fingers through. Lachlan MacDougall had been burly. Braw. Before the sea had taken him and not given him back.

Granny surveyed him with a canny eye. "Yer wearing the look ye used to as a lad when something was troubling ye."

"Yer eyesight's keen."

"Hardly. Betimes I sense things. What weighs ye down so, m'laird? The state of her ladyship and no heir?"

"Always." All that was left of his line was he himself. Was it any wonder he wanted a child? The castle remained empty while a simple croft on Kerrera's south shore was bursting with bairns, and Lark had gone to welcome another. He swallowed some tea, finding it more satisfying than all the heavy supper on crested china that had come before. "But this is different. 'Tis something I canna name. A darkness. A foreboding."

Usually if he felt it, he could pinpoint its source. But not this time. Not this hovering, malevolent blackness as if they were all on the verge of some unseen calamity. Some soul-shattering change.

"Yer roots go down so deep on Kerrera, 'tis no wonder ye have a sort of sense about things. I well remember me Lachlan."

He set down his mug, numbed by the recollection as she continued speaking of

Lark's father.

"The eve of his dying ye sat here just as ye are right now, looking twice as grieved, yet naught had happened yet. No news brought."

Twelve years it had been. Granny was right. The foreboding had been much the same. Inexplicable. Intense. A violent storm, one of the worst in the island's history, had come out of nowhere and wreaked untold havoc. He'd felt that strange foreboding again before the death of his father in battle, his mother and sister soon after.

Even as he thought it, the queer restlessness, that ugly dread thickened, ushering in a timely, little understood Scripture. *For we wrestle not against flesh and blood, but against principalities, against powers, against the rulers of the darkness of this world.*

Granny was looking at him like he was Reverend Blackaby in kirk. "There's naught to be done but storm heaven with prayer," she said.

He bent his head, needing little prodding. The words were hard-won if heartfelt. "O Almighty Lord, who art a most strong tower to all them that put their trust in Thee. Be now and evermore our defense . . ."

12

Were it not for hope the heart would break.
Scottish proverb

Lark smiled as the long-awaited bairn made his entry into the rain-washed July day. "Bethankit," she murmured as much to the Almighty as the howdie who'd washed and bundled the wee lad and passed him to her waiting arms. Bending her head, she breathed in the ineffable newness of him while the midwife tended to a jubilant Catriona.

The two-day ordeal had been an exercise in patience, though Lark's part in the process had been small. She'd simply obeyed the howdie's bossing her about.

"Keep yer legs and arms uncrossed, mind ye, and unlock all the doors and windows," she'd said at Catriona's first pangs. "Needs be the babe has no hindrance entering the world."

Lark nearly balked at her insistence that the small mirror be covered up and every bottle and container in the croft be left open. Island superstitions were very much alive though Lark now looked askance at such. Had her brief time in Edinburgh with Dr. Hunter made her a skeptic? Not entirely. She couldn't quite imagine a male midwife or physic, Edinburgh trained or no.

To banish the fairies, Lark had given Catriona the customary tonic of rowan berries. Though Lark had her doubts about fairies too, she firmly believed the potent berries lessened the pains of birth.

"Welcome, little stranger," she said, rocking the babe in her arms and spying his father, Kenneth, looking in the window.

His bearded face was awash with pleasure, gaze riveted to the bundle she held. Her own smile was so wide she nearly forgot the tooth that had been troubling her. Once home she'd tend to it. For now, joy sang through her, despite the previous long, sleepless night or the fact she'd be late for the stillroom. Thankfully, Magnus never minded. He was a kindly laird, the needs of the islanders foremost. Once at the castle, she'd give an accounting.

Lord, help me with that.

Dread sashayed through her, so at odds

with the jubilant moment. She'd soon stand before him and share the date and babe's forename and surname, if not the birth's details, and he'd enter it into a ledger.

Infant, Duncan. 5 July, 1752.

A gift would follow to Catriona and Kenneth, usually silver coin. She knew Magnus so well she'd see behind his forced smile.

"We'll be having our oats now," the howdie said, going to the hearth where a kettle hissed.

Lark placed the newborn in Catriona's arms. "A braw lad to go with yer other lad and lassie."

"I dinna favor an empty cradle for long. A house, no matter how humble, is made better with bairns." She eyed Lark. "Even a castle."

"Oh aye," Lark said as Kenneth entered with an iron-nailed cradle of stout oak. "I'll fetch Annie and Murdo home again when yer ready."

Lark didn't want to miss that first meeting with brother and sister. Though Annie was but two and Murdo three, both were bonny and bright and had long anticipated a brother or sister.

"We'll soon carry him to kirk for his christening," Kenneth said, setting the

cradle near the warm hearth before returning outside to bring in a new chaff mattress.

Lark lingered as long as she could. With
the howdie staying on, there was little need
of her, and so at suppertime she began the
winding walk back to croft and castle,
through heavy mist that left a sheen upon
her skin.

Never had her thoughts been so full, her
heart newly pained by the castle's lack. Seeing her cousin's family so content only
drove the longing deeper. If a miracle did
happen and a babe was born for Kerrera,
all the island would rejoice. But knowing
Isla, Dr. Hunter would be at hand, and he
shunned howdies. And no doubt Lark
would hear of the birth secondhand. Would
miss the triumph and joy on Isla's face as it
had been on Catriona's. Would not be privy
to Magnus's deep pride and delight. She
always felt outside the circle looking in, and
never so much so as in these private moments that changed a life so remarkably.
Though she'd accepted it as the way of
things since childhood, it in no way lessened
the wistful feeling.

On such a joyous day, it seemed the sun
should shine, the sea be blue glass. Should
she go to Magnus straightaway? All she
wanted was to dose her sore tooth with

clove oil, then fall down in the cozy familiarity of her box bed and go to sleep. Till the cock crowed and returned her to the stillroom once again.

If the night had been clear she would have seen the castle's lights, the wink of Balliemore in the distance. As it was, she only heard voices. Strident, panicked voices.

Pulling her plaid closer about her shoulders, she hastened her step as a dozen misfortunes presented themselves. Toward the headland the mist lifted, rising like a filmy, tattered curtain. Half a dozen men gathered at the cliff's edge that jutted beyond the castle's lit facade, peering over its precarious rim. A lantern swung from a man's hand. The sheriff? He sometimes ferried over from the mainland when a rare crime had been committed.

Aye, the sheriff, his burly silhouette unmistakable. Mistress Baird, the housekeeper, stood behind him with several white-faced maids, including a distraught Rhona. And Magnus — he was far too close to the cliff's edge — grief and disbelief sketched across his face. His manservant, Brown, shadowed him.

Had someone fallen? Or — *Lord, nay* — jumped?

A cry from Rhona confirmed something

dire. The lady's maid's arm extended Lark's way, her finger pointing. At once, two of the sheriff's men came toward Lark, hemming her in as if certain she'd run the other way. Their cold hands encircled her bare wrists, sending another chill through her.

" 'Tis the stillroom mistress, I tell you! She mixed the tonic. Left it for my mistress to drink and then fall to her death —"

"Silence!" Magnus swung round, features as angry as they were sorrowful. "I'll not have ye leap to conclusions. Where were ye when yer mistress was raiding the stillroom? Tell me that!" To the men holding Lark, he said, "Unhand her. There'll be no blame laid till the facts come clear."

Granny's tonic. Lark had never meant to use it, not till she'd determined the contents. Would Granny be blamed?

The hard hands fell away though the men stayed on either side of her. She swayed, the fatigue of a sleepless night and too little to eat cutting into her. Pressing her shoes into soggy ground, she tried to make sense of the scene, but her thoughts were slow to catch up.

Isla? Gone? Her little pug dogs stood precariously near the drop, their throaty barks shifting to mournful howls. The sound joined sourly with Rhona's sobbing, sending prickles up Lark's arms and down her neck. She drew in a deep, shuddering breath, trying to make sense of the macabre scene, willing her pulsing heart to return to its regular rhythm.

Just out of sight was home, the croft behind a rocky outcropping on the path below. And Granny. Was she well? Lark inhaled the damp air, but it seemed to freeze in her lungs. Her gaze swiveled to the sea, her shocked senses conjuring up Isla's lifeless form as the waves gathered her into a foamy embrace.

"Go home, Lark." Magnus stood before her, the rising wind pulling at his coattails, face grim and tone insistent.

She forced a few words past her tight throat. " 'Tis terrible, this." With that, she left, avoiding Rhona and the last of servants, the sheriff, and all who gathered.

Down the hill she went. One push at the croft door and she all but fell into Granny's arms, sobbing out Isla's story.

The castle's Great Hall seemed more courtroom. As dawn streamed through the mullioned windows the next morn, the sheriff finished questioning the servants, Lark last. She took the chair the sheriff offered, Magnus to one side.

"Where have you been these two days past?" the sheriff began.

"To a lying-in at my cousin's," she replied, eyes downcast.

"What sort of relationship did you have with the dead?"

Magnus winced. *Deceased,* mayhap. Or even *former mistress.* But the sheriff was not one to mince words.

"I ken her little, being mostly in the still-room."

"Yet the tonic her maid claims she drank was your doing, was it not?"

"I didna give her the tonic. 'Twas kept in a cupboard."

Aye, Lark. Dinna let him hem ye in. Magnus crossed his arms, cheering her on silently.

"Why was it kept in the cupboard? 'Twas labeled 'Fertility Herbs,' aye?"

"Labeled so, aye, but I dinna ken the ingredients —"

"What do you mean, you dinna ken such? You —"

"No badgering, Sheriff." Magnus kept his voice smooth, but his innards churned. "It matters little who made the tonic when it was not dispensed."

The sheriff bristled, perhaps cross from a lost night's sleep. "Very well, m'lord. Can you show me the cupboard in question, then?"

They traded the Great Hall for the still-room, which seemed strange and melancholy since Isla had been the last one in it. Lark seemed to work to contain her shock, clasping her unsteady hands together as they stepped into the room Mistress Baird always locked at day's end. Several cupboards were open, herbs and various stores spilled onto the floor. Isla's doing?

"Is the stillroom door kept open?" The probing question was meant for Lark, but Magnus could not stay silent.

"Cook told ye she had Mistress Baird open it as she needed some ingredients. 'Twas forgotten and left unlocked. Last time I checked, forgetfulness was no crime."

Rhona had not given a reasonable explanation as to why her mistress had been left alone for an extended time, especially since Magnus had advised her to be vigilant. The last Magnus had seen of Isla she had been sleeping. 'Twas the lady's maid's negligence, no doubt.

"Do you handle medicinals — herbs and simples — that would be considered poisonous, Miss MacDougall?"

"I do," Lark said, looking the sheriff in the eye. "Even the humble rowan berry is dangerous till stewed or frozen, and then 'tis of benefit. I take care, sir, to make sure naught is ill-used."

"How long have you been the stillroom's mistress?"

"Since I was one and twenty, though I learnt from my grandmother from the time I was wee. She was the stillroom mistress before me."

The sheriff looked to Magnus as if for confirmation.

"Lark grew up at the castle, being schooled with my sister and myself," Magnus told him. "Her mother was also in service."

"And your father?" the sheriff inquired.

"A fisherman," Lark answered. "Drowned at sea."

"Fisherman . . ." The sheriff closed a cupboard and stepped over a broken crock. "*And* free trader, no doubt."

Magnus's resistance roared, but he stayed silent. He was still flummoxed that the sheriff had already been on Kerrera at the time of Isla's death, waiting at the Thistle, passing the time by talking to villagers about any sea activity. Tipped off by another spy, likely.

"Did you know that the mistress of Kerrera had a penchant for laudanum?" the sheriff asked, righting a broom.

"Aye."

"Did you ken she'd been given that by the island's doctor?"

"Burns had given her such, aye. But he's no doctor," Lark said in rare judgment. "Not like the mistress's physic in Edinburgh."

"Did she seem much affected by it when you last saw her?"

"By the laudanum? She seemed" — Lark darted a look at Magnus — "tired . . . more out of sorts."

"Out of sorts? Like she'd been taking too much?"

"Mayhap. Best ask her lady's maid. I was seldom with her mistress."

"Her maid claims she used all the laudanum, then went looking for more in the stillroom." He withdrew a bottle from his pocket. "This was empty and found on the cliffside, and the stillroom door was left open."

"I am sorry to hear it."

"Seems to me if you'd been here or the door had been locked, none of this would have happened." His tone laid blame, and Lark flushed.

Magnus kicked aside a jagged piece of broken crockery. "The damage done within these walls bespeaks desperation. My wife, God rest her, isna here to tell the tale. A great many things have combined to dig the hole we now find ourselves in. Lark's absence. My housekeeper's and cook's forgetfulness. The lady's maid's negligence. My own trip to Balliemore about a business matter. And though it may sound harsh, ye can lay the most blame at my wife's door. No one forced her to ransack the stillroom or walk too close to the cliff's edge."

The words, spoken in an even tone, still had the force of a fist. A closed door. Magnus MacLeish was done with the matter even if the sheriff was not.

"You're excused," the sheriff said to Lark.

With a nod, she went out, and the two men faced each other in the courtyard beyond the stillroom.

"You said your wife's relatives are on their way?" the sheriff asked.

"Aye. I sent word to them in Edinburgh during the night."

"There's to be a burial of sorts though no body?"

"I'm not privy yet to her family's plans. 'Twill be in Edinburgh, if anywhere." Isla hadn't wanted to be buried on Kerrera. She'd told Magnus that on more than one occasion. He'd reconciled himself to it, though at the time it had grated.

"I'll meet with them when the time comes," the sheriff said, turning away.

Kerrera was plunged into mourning. All the clocks were stopped, the entire household clothed in sable. All letters were sealed with black wax and penned on paper edged in black. The Balliemore bellman was heard proclaiming the shocking news of Isla's death about the tiny town.

'Twas not customary for the husband to attend the funeral of his wife. Magnus would remain behind closed doors at the castle. But would there even be a funeral?

'Twas a mournful death, much like being lost at sea. No grave. No gravestone.

"Her folks have come," Jillian told Lark as she visited on the Sabbath after Isla's passing. "I doubt they'll stay long. Her mother hasna lowered her nose once since their carriage first came through the castle gates. And her da — always a pipe in hand. I can smell it clear to the kitchen."

"I feel for them, losing their only child," Lark said quietly. 'Twas unnatural, truly, parting with one so young, so full of possibility. Their own bloodline was at an end.

"The laird has closed the stillroom," Jillian told her. "Yer to keep to the croft with yer granny."

Once Jillian had gone on her way, Granny asked Lark, "Why, d'ye suppose?" They huddled near the hearth where a peat fire held off the chill of a long rain that felt more like November than July. "Ye dinna think all this has turned Magnus against us?"

Lark rubbed her pounding temple, trying not to take Granny's words to heart. "The sheriff's still about. Wanting to stitch together what happened. I ken the laird wants us out of his way."

"Glad I'll be once the sheriff's gone back to the mainland."

"Jillian said the captain is overdue for another run."

"Well, he'd best hold off with the sheriff near."

"Does he ken, d'ye think, about Isla, being gone on his ship for a sennight or better?"

Granny studied Lark through narrowed eyes. "Who's counting?"

Lark flushed. "He's been away long enough to make me wonder. I didna say I missed him."

"D'ye?"

Lark shrugged hunched shoulders, her shawl slipping a bit. "I canna decide. He makes me tapsalteerie."

"Mercy! Sounds like love to me."

"But would a man stay gone so long if so?"

"A seafaring man, mayhap." Granny sighed. "Yer prospects are so few here on Kerrera. But the captain seems wrong for ye somehow."

Lark knew why. Would she marry a man who might be away more than at home? Whose every delay might spell disaster? Who *stole*?

Granny's expression clouded. "Well, my mind's not so much on the captain as the laird."

"Because of his ongoing misfortune?"

"Aye. He's lost everyone he holds dear. No parents. No sister. No wife. No bairns."

"Granny, he'll come through it well enough. Magnus isna one to be cast down for long."

"Aye, he's young yet. Braw. He'll likely wed again in time. And all this trouble will seem naught but a bad dream."

"So I hope," Lark murmured. But first, mourning.

'Twas odd being absent from the stillroom. She missed it yet was disturbed knowing Isla had been in it prior to her death. Would it always hold that taint?

Lord, help us. Heal Magnus's heart in his

time of grief. Comfort Isla's mother and father in their heartache. Return the castle to a peaceful, productive place. Thy will be done.

She kept busy with her handwork as one day bled into the next, the summer rain never ceasing. There was a comfort in knitting the wool, the pleasurable softness of lanolin on her hands, and feeling the heat of the peat fire through her skirt.

'Twas nearly ten o'clock on a Friday night. Granny's own knitting pooled in her lap as her eyes closed, her chin to her chest. Lark nodded off as well, her body and thoughts less tense than they'd been in the days since Isla's death, but only by a hair.

When the knock sounded on the door, 'twas loud as a gunshot. Granny startled and Lark set her knitting aside before cracking open the door. The sheriff stood before her, rain dripping from his hat brim, bookended by two of his men.

At once her angst spiked. He wore no smile nor gave a greeting. His tone was gruff, just as it had been in the stillroom that day. "You're being taken into custody, Lark MacDougall, for the death of Isla MacLeish."

Behind her, Granny exploded in a string of Gaelic, nearly as upending as the shackles now weighting Lark's wrists. Like a physical blow their charge was, knocking the wind clean out of her. Ire-laced words sprang to mind, but cold disbelief choked her.

Granny was clutching at her shawl as if refusing to be separated. Lark wanted to reach out to her, embrace her, but her bound wrists prevented such.

"Pray," Lark told her, the single, all but choked word breathless. There was no time for more. The men ushered her out, none too gently, leaving Granny standing in the open doorway, wailing.

'Twas late. Lark was weary and addle-pated in the extreme. But not guilty. Guilty, mayhap, for failing to feel deep remorse for Isla, at least the personal, heartfelt kind. 'Twas Magnus she grieved for. But she had never wished Isla ill.

So why the shackles? Why the terrifying night march across the island? Why the bumpy ferry ride across the Firth of Lorn to the mainland, the salt spray on her heated cheeks? She had on her simple plaid shawl but couldn't stop shivering, more from shock than the damp.

One hope buoyed her.

Magnus would soon set things right.

13

Proud people breed sad sorrows for themselves.

Emily Brontë

The cell was small, a bit of soiled straw on
the floor. Never before had Lark been inside
a gaol. Tolbooths were for thieves and
vagrants and those deprived of their reason.
'Twas cold as winter here, a great many
unsavory smells in the drafty air. The clank
of the gaoler's key as he locked her in
knocked the edge off her disbelief. Two men
gaped at her from behind bars across the
way while a third slept, snoring. Two cells
were empty but equally rank.

Panic turned her queasy. Her fingers
curled into fists, sharp against her cold
palms as she tried to piece together the little
that had been told her.

*"You are being held as accessory to the
death of the laird's wife."*

How was that possible when she had been at the other end of the island? Her jumbled thoughts veered to Catriona and the babe. She'd planned to visit them again on the morrow, excited to see their sonsie faces. By now all knew of her predicament. Except, perhaps, the captain, away as he'd been.

God in heaven, help Thou me.

The landing was near perfect. A moonless night. An easy glide into a secluded cove on Kerrera's western shore. Rory's crew was nearly crowing at the cargo's quality. Silks and satins. Tobacco. Madeira. Salt and spices.

Rory stood on deck, elation and anxiety at war inside him. A bit weak-kneed from a fever that had kept him on the Isle of Man till now, he rested callused palms on the ship's gunwale as the tubmen swarmed forward to land the cargo.

Reaching into a pocket, he fingered the prize he'd brought for Lark. Gotten from a silversmith in exchange for his finest cask of brandy. He hoped she wouldn't ask about that. She disdained spirits, even whisky, except for medicinal use.

His gaze roved the craggy coastline, alert for any light or motion. All at once a flash of musket fire flared in the darkness, the ping of bullet lead after. He swore as his lead tubman pitched forward into the shallow water, dropping a cask.

"Enemy in sight!" someone shouted.

And then — utter mayhem. The orderly landing unraveled, cargo abandoned, men scattering like ship's rats.

He looked up again at the cliff's dark face, into the glare of a dozen torches and the stony expressions of the sheriff and his men.

With a step back, he turned and took the smooth deck at a run, then dived over the gunwale with a satisfying splash.

Every jangle of keys set her teeth on edge, her spirits rising in false expectation. Would Magnus come? He had such clout, was well respected. The few petty crimes on Kerrera had never made it to the mainland and were soon resolved with his influence.

But none carried the weight of this.

Shivering, feeling the trail of an insect across her bare arm, she sat upright on the bedstraw. A commotion — even a scuffle — was just outside the entry door. An angry shout swept the last of sleep's cobwebs from her mind as much as the yellow slant of lantern light.

A shackled man was brought in, a hood covering his head much like that of a prisoner facing the gallows. Into the cell beside her he went, denying her another look at him, the slam of the cell door jolting.

She returned to her bedding, wide awake. Eventually the new prisoner settled. But the combined snores of the men rivaled her hunger pangs, keeping her awake. Her panic had faded to prayers, and now prayerlessness took hold. Was the Lord with her here, in the moldy dark? Her prayers seemed to rise no farther than the gaol ceiling.

Why couldn't she recall how long she'd been here? The sameness of the cell robbed all recall. No window foretold daylight or dark. Her own internal clock was broken.

"Lark?" She was dreaming, surely. Jillian hovered beyond the iron bars, forehead scrunched in dismay, clad in a soiled frock and what appeared to be the captain's hat.

Lark came upright, grappling for firm footing.

"I dinna ken who to talk to first," Jillian said, gaze swinging from Lark's cell to the one beside it.

"Quit talking in riddles," came a recognizable, aggravated voice.

The captain?

Lark shut her eyes as their plight came clear.

"Who would ken the both of ye would

land side by side in gaol?" Jillian uttered with a sly cackle. " 'Twas meant for ye to be together, truly."

A pause. "Lark, be ye here?"

"Sadly so," she answered the captain. Such small words for the overarching terror she felt. Even now their plight knocked the wind from her and left her voice wheezy and wavering, her body drained by weariness.

He swore and she flinched, though she felt like swearing too. And sobbing. She merely bit her lip, worrying the sore spot she'd made there above the tooth that had been troubling her.

"What in the name of heaven brings ye here?" His voice was nearer now, as if he was at the adjoining wall of their cell. "Why are ye not on Kerrera?"

Lark leaned in, voice failing her as her throat smarted and her eyes stung.

Jillian's whispered words carried the lingering shock of it. "She's here because Isla flung herself off the castle cliff and her folks be wantin' someone to blame."

Lord, nay. So she was the scapegoat?

"Where is the laird?" the captain said, as calmly as if he believed Magnus's appearing meant their cell door would swing open.

"Wearin' sable," Jillian said, frowning.

"And playin' host to her ladyship's folks at the castle."

Lark stiffened, imagining it. What a mournful task 'twould be to host Isla's distraught kin. "How's Granny?"

"She sent ye some bannocks, but the guard got them first. She says not to fear. The Almighty has all in hand."

"What happened with the *Merry Lass*?" Lark asked the captain, crossing her arms to hug close what little warmth she could. "Why are ye here?"

"Seems the sheriff got wind of our landing."

Never had the captain been caught. Some said he had an uncanny ability to avoid detection, eluding the law again and again. "I pray the court is lenient."

"I'm most concerned about the *Merry Lass.*"

"Jings!" Jillian exclaimed. "Yer life is worth more than a floating tub."

"She's all I have," the captain shot back. "Humble as it is."

"Well, she's been seized by the Philistines. 'Twill be quite a feat for the laird to free both ye and yer boat."

"But not God," the captain said in a rare burst of righteousness.

Lark listened, beset by the same needling

questions. Could the captain count on the Almighty to help him and fellow free traders if what they were doing — dealing in smuggled goods — was ungodly? Was it wrong even when they, the people, were being crushed by corrupt taxes? Which was the lesser evil?

"As for ye," Jillian said, glancing at the gaol door and then at Lark, "yer plight is not so simple. If the laird is to help ye, 'twould seem he's betraying his own wife."

Lark went numb. The truth of Jillian's shrewd words cut to the quick.

"What's more, there's said to be both judge and jury brought in from Edinburgh."

Lark looked hard at her. Hearsay?

"Amazing what a few bannocks can gain from gut-greedy guards," Jillian continued with a smirk. "And the promise of more news besides."

Lark sank down on her haunches, light-headed.

The captain scoffed. "Meaning the court's been bought by Isla's father, the high and mighty Lord Ordinary of the Court of Session."

"Aye, something like that. Ye'll not have long to wait till yer trial. The hawkers and peddlers will soon be screaming the news, selling broadsides for a ha'penny in Auld

Reekie."

Lark had read the more reputable *Edinburgh Evening Courant* while visiting the city, marveling at the wealth of news within. No doubt Isla's demise would see print. Somehow it seemed to make the charge more binding. Her very name would be linked to so tragic a circumstance in bold, black ink.

"And they're not sayin' it's self-harm neither on Isla's part. Only that ye poisoned her to death —"

"Haud yer wheest!" The captain's voice rose strong as a coastal wind. "Dinna come again unless ye bring more than ill news, aye?"

With a lift of her chin, Jillian turned on her heel and left them. Silence ensued, broken by a fellow prisoner's racking cough.

"Here ye be, Lark." The captain's voice was a caress, though all she felt was a callused, sea-worn hand reaching through the bars.

Dangling from his fingers was a . . . necklace?

"Ye canna see them but they're a warm, rich red shot through with pink. Coral, ye ken." The pride in his tone shifted. " 'Tis not the Brooch of Lorn — *Braiste Lathurna* — but quality nonetheless."

She brought the gift nearer, holding the beads to her bodice next to her heart. He'd meant this for her in a calmer, more settled season, mayhap with a heartfelt declaration attached. Awe bloomed as she felt what might be a carved silver clasp, a far cry from the simple ribbon tie of her mother's necklace.

"Bethankit, Rory." 'Twas the only gift she could give him, to say his given name for the very first time, abandoning *Captain* altogether.

His voice grew hoarse. "Ye ken what's said about coral. That it has properties to ward off sickness. Offer protection at sea."

"Aye." Coral was worn by both children and adults, though she'd never seen it in hand with its reds and pinks. Orange was far more common. Yet all coral was known to be fragile. Brittle. As fragile and brittle as she herself felt.

"Ye can wear it proud, like the MacDougall ye are."

Wear them in gaol? To be taken by the bannock-greedy guards?

"To conquer or die, aye?" he insisted at her silence. Her clan's motto, oft murmured by Granny, caused a deeper pang. In times of hunger or sickness, Granny spoke the words to strengthen them both, much as she did Scripture.

But Lark could not echo them now.

Once again cast in mourning, the castle would not grant him a moment's respite. Everywhere he turned brought a blacker memory. First his kindred. Now his wife. When he opened his eyes of a morn, 'twas hard to grasp solid ground as one grief slid into the next, shadowing, almost stalking him.

Every death had been so different, thus the resulting sorrow different. And now Isla. What had brought her so low? One too many miscarriages? A fondness for opium? Both, no doubt, but by no hand except her own.

Not Lark's.

What might he have done as a husband to stop the darkness from overtaking her? He'd seen it, felt it, as their fragile bond eroded. He'd been out riding, visiting a tenant who had not paid rent in more than a twelvemonth. If he'd just stayed at the castle and not gone into the Thistle on his way home to inquire about some missing sheep . . . if he'd just returned home and not let Isla's fits and starts keep him away . . . she might still be living.

He stared into the candlelight, fork idle in

his hand. Cook had thoughtfully prepared his favorite dishes. Roast turkey stuffed with sausage. Neeps and tatties. His study desk served as a table. Beneath his chair was Nonesuch, head resting on her paws, alert to her master's slightest movement or mood.

"Here ye be," Magnus murmured, moving an untouched turkey leg from his plate to the stone floor.

Since Isla's parents had come and gone their sorrowful way, he'd kept to the castle, mainly his study, sinking himself in Scripture, walling himself off from the world. A cluster of verses from Jeremiah soon lodged in his brain like a pebble in his boot, one foremost.

Stand ye in the ways, and see, and ask for the old paths, where is the good way, and walk therein, and ye shall find rest for your souls.

He felt driven to act, to take some course, some path. But which? His foremost concern was Lark.

Two nights prior he'd taken the muddy, meandering cliffside trail to the croft she shared with Granny to see how the old woman fared. She sat knitting by the fire much as she'd always done, yet she was such a lonesome spectacle his eyes watered. Lark's absence was profound here in so small a place.

"Be ye in need of anything?" he'd asked from the doorway, hands fisted behind his back. "Anything at all?"

"Ye well ken what I'm in need of," she returned calmly, motioning him inside out of the weather.

Mute, he took Lark's seat at the table as there were few chairs in so tiny an abode.

"But ye canna bring me Lark. Yer in mourning," Granny said, intent on her handwork. "And ye canna be traipsing to the mainland and meddling in legal matters involving yer wife, God rest her."

"But I can do something."

"Ye can pray."

"That I'm doing."

"Betimes 'tis enough."

He looked to the peat fire smoking in the downpour. Would this strange summer's rain never end? "Word is she's being moved to Glasgow for trial."

Granny regarded him now with something akin to suspicion. "Why Glasgow?"

"The procurator Fiscal has sent the case to Edinburgh's Crown office and recommends prosecution there. This has moved beyond the local sheriff's jurisdiction. She's to be indicted for" — the words hung in his throat — "the crime of manslaughter." He could see the legal details baffled Granny, so he tried plain speaking. "She'll be examined by a judge and members of the jury. In felony cases there's no defense barrister, none to speak in her behalf."

The lack of a defense had always troubled him, but never so much as now. His chief worry was what Isla's parents were doing behind the scenes, and that worry of a witness, Rhona. The fury he'd felt upon reading the latest copy of the *Edinburgh Evening Courant,* which he'd prayed to a simmer, now returned full boil.

Nary a word was said about Isla leaping to her death. Just that she'd been poisoned. All suspicion was cast on Lark. The broadside's phrasing was blatantly misleading. Clearly Isla's parents did not want their name besmirched by the death of a daughter from self-harm.

"What of the captain?" Granny asked, never ceasing her knitting.

"I've no word of him except he's to be tried in Oban's local court."

"Better for him, aye?"

"Not necessarily," he replied.

"I should like to go to Glasgow."

"I'd advise against it." He was sounding like the barrister he was. The trip to Edinburgh had gone hard on her. She'd come down with the ague on their return. Glasgow might well finish her.

"Then I'll continue to pray that the Lord's will be done," she said, her wrinkled face touched with a resigned sorrow. "His ways are too mysterious to ken. Even for an auld woman who's watched His workings for a lifetime."

He went away, pondering it. What was the Lord's will? Would the Almighty rescue and restore Lark to Kerrera?

He returned to the castle reluctantly under a moonless sky. When had it ceased to be a home, a haven, and become little more than a mausoleum instead?

As if sensing his disquiet, Nonesuch turned into the castle garden. At full flower in mid-July, its fragrance intensified at night. It bespoke neglect and begged harvesting. Lark was never so happy as in the midsummer blooming. And her bees — they seemed to sense her leaving. Or was it only his own sense of loss imposed on them? In the drenching rain they kept to their skeps, awaiting fair weather and Lark's return.

The stillroom faced him. A sodden climbing rose framed the closed oak door. His right hand gripped the knob while his left fingered the stillroom key. A dozen different scents assailed him as the door swung open.

Lavender. Hartshorn. Roses.

Lark.

Standing in the doorway he fought a gaping emptiness. For years Lark had adorned the stillroom, singing her simple songs, whispering to the bees, and making a dance of her work. Without her the place seemed . . . haunted. His melancholy widened to a blistering ache.

Setting his shoulder against the timbered door frame, he felt another lick of guilt.

Losing Isla was bearable.

Losing Lark was not.

14

A friend in court is worth more than crown in the purse.

Scottish proverb

A sennight dragged by. Lark kept time by the captain, whose remarkable memory for detail, honed aboard ship in the midst of a changeless sea, stayed strong despite their windowless, dank cells. His constant company cheered her, though their fellow prisoners, privy to their every exchange, squelched any true companionship.

Jillian did not return, nor did anyone else from Kerrera come. Lark's high hopes to see Magnus dwindled. Were they being denied visitors?

Deprived of a bath, she was glad none could see her, not even the captain. They'd gotten into the habit of keeping to their adjoining cell wall so they could talk. Her thankfulness for his presence knew no bounds.

How she longed to be sunk into her work, to feel the weight of the mortar and pestle, to hear the gentle buzz of bees and breathe in the garden's special fragrance at mid-summer. Her former life, at times so mundane, now seemed altogether winsome and delightful. How desperately she missed her island. The castle. The sea. Her simple tasks.

Magnus.

"The laird hasna come," the captain said, echoing her private thoughts.

"D'ye truly expect him, mourning as he is?" she said softly.

"I would expect him to stand by those still living, aye."

She heard a harsh laugh. "Ye'll not be living ere long. Yer trial is set to begin, I heard the gaoler say." The prisoner across the way peered at them, having been brought in the night before. "Ye well ken the penalty for free trading."

Lark shrank back from the bars. Sitting on the straw, she gathered her soiled shawl about her.

"One has to be found guilty first," the captain replied.

"Aye. But ye were caught red-handed, 'tis said. I'd be praying for mercy if I were ye."

Lark heard the creak of the bars as the captain shifted. "Since yer throwing stones, what brings ye here?"

"Sheep thief."

"Pillory. Whipping. Mayhap hanging then."

The man grunted. "First offense. Likely a fine. But the lass there . . ." Lark felt his probing eyes on her, though hers were fastened on the straw-strewn floor. "She's here for murder —"

"Nay." The captain cut him off. "She has naught to do with it."

Nothing more was said. A pouring rain strengthened, a hundred tiny hammers on the leaking roof. Supper consisted of soggy hardtack taken from the gaoler's grimy hand. Ship's rations, the captain said. Mindful of her ever-loosening dress, Lark ate without complaint, falling asleep even as the cold deepened.

By morn, she would be gone.

Lark's trial was at hand. Though she'd been to Edinburgh and counted it more friend, Glasgow was an unkempt stranger. Once a small merchant town, 'twas known for its fine weaving of linen and woolen cloth as much as its polluted drinking water from the River Clyde. Controlled by the Tobacco

Lords who made their fortunes trading with the American colonies, which named city streets *Virginia* and built palatial houses, it boasted a thriving shipbuilding industry. The sight of so many masts and sails drove home the captain's absence.

Atop the wagon used to transport criminals, she winced at the feeble sunlight after being so long indoors. Tottering stone tenements looked precarious as child's blocks throughout the dirty, crowded city. Child beggars stared and ran after her as if knowing she secreted the lovely coral beads in her pocket. Overcome with the stench of the city, Lark covered her nose with her shawl.

The reek of her cell was worse. Here in Glasgow's crowded tolbooth, she was treated like any other prisoner awaiting trial. Dozens of cases were heard each day, some in mere minutes, though few carried the weight of hers.

"Ye'll not have long now," said the gaoler who made his nightly rounds, holding a lantern aloft. "Else ye'll get gaol distemper."

The dreadful words settled over her as he moved on, darkness enveloping her cell. Never had she felt so humiliated. Her skin crawled and itched. She seemed to move in a cloud of filth. Would it not be easier for them to condemn her given she now looked the part? Shame flushed her face as dozens of probing eyes roamed every unkempt inch of her when the gaoler passed by a final time. Not one familiar face did she see. Nor did she understand how the proceedings would play out.

Magnus would know all the details, the legalities. But the laird was not here. Were Granny's fearful murmurings true? Had he turned his back on them?

As she was led out of her cell the next forenoon, she bent her head and murmured a silent prayer.

Once she set foot in the courtroom, the tumultuous hubbub ceased. Herbs and scented flowers were sprinkled about the cavernous chamber. To fight disease? Or simply staunch the smell of unwashed prisoners?

Thirteen strangers she guessed were jurors were grouped at the front of the room. A pockmarked official held the dittany sheets, the thick ream of court papers. He read — nay, shouted — the charge against her. "The prisoner, Lark MacDougall, spinster, is indicted for the crime of manslaughter."

Shouts and curses erupted from the gallery, followed by the judge's gavel pounding. How she longed for someone to leap to her defense, shout *nay*. Beneath her soiled bodice her heart thudded so loudly she had trouble drawing breath.

"Your name, miss?" This from a stone-faced, bewigged gentleman she took for the court clerk. No matter that they'd just announced it. They would have her speak before this terrifying assemblage. "Your age and occupation?"

She hated that her voice shook. She stammered out her answer. Next the name of the victim was read. A sharp cry rent the courtroom. Lark's gaze swung to a veiled woman in sable. Rhona. Would they call Isla's lady's maid as a witness? She was regarding Lark as if she was the worst sort of criminal.

Lord, nay, please.

The proceedings started on a precarious foot. Benumbed, Lark fisted the ends of her shawl in her lap to keep from keeling over on the hard bench as the questions rattled on.

"So you're saying there was ill feeling between the stillroom mistress and your own?" the prosecution asked Rhona.

"Oh aye," Rhona replied, dabbing at her eyes with a handkerchief. "Many a time I did plead with Mistress MacDougall for some remedy to help my mistress."

"What malady do you speak of?"

"A bodily female complaint. She'd lost six babes, ye see."

A murmur of dismay washed over the chamber.

"And Mistress MacDougall was unwilling to help, thus causing enmity between the deceased and Mistress MacDougall?"

"My mistress was nigh driven mad because of it."

"Would you say this was the reason your mistress went to the stillroom the day of her death, seeking such a remedy?"

Rhona's dark veil swayed as she nodded. "Indeed. My mistress was the gentlest, most obliging creature. She was so afraid of Mistress MacDougall that she had to sneak into the stillroom when the woman was out to try to find the help she needed."

"And instead of finding help, she discovered this particular bottle?"

A green glass vial was held aloft. Granny's mysterious concoction, labeled "Fertility Herbs."

Nodding, Rhona cleared her throat, voice pitching higher. "That's naught but poison, left there in plain sight to harm my mistress."

"And Mistress MacDougall is the one who concocted this tincture, this poison?"

"Indeed she did. My mistress is not to blame for taking it. Desperate she was. Mistress MacDougall knew it too. Killed my mistress as sure as if she'd run a dagger through her."

Such venom. Such blame. Lark's jaw ached from clamping her mouth shut.

"And so, finding no help, your former mistress drank the contents?" the man intoned.

"She did just that, sir. What was she to do otherwise, given the promise of the bottle's label?"

"And where were you when this tragic incident occurred?"

"Going about my duties inside her dressing room, sir."

"At what point did you realize your mistress was not in her bedchamber?"

"The supper hour, sir. Near about eight o'clock."

"Where was the laird?"

"Detained in Balliemore on business, sir."

"And so, realizing your mistress was missing, you went in search of her?"

"That I did, sir. Found her by the castle cliff, out of her mind from drinking the poison. She was standing too near the edge, she was, her back to the sea. Her legs were unsteady. I could see her sway a bit, so I called for her to come into the castle."

"And her response?"

"She was crying, you see."

"And?"

"I reached out my hands to her, but she stepped back as if forgetting just where she stood. And then —" A half sob. "She fell back, off the edge. It happened quick as lightning. If she'd not drunk the poison the stillroom mistress meant for her —"

"That is all, Miss Gilliam. For now, we'll examine another witness."

Lark held her breath as Dr. Hunter appeared. He gave a long, scholarly explanation of Isla's inability to carry a child and her resulting melancholy. He regarded Lark with a kind of distant pity as he stepped down.

"All rise," the bailiff said.

At this, the entire courtroom got to their feet as if the king himself was present. 'Twas Isla's father, from Edinburgh's Court of Session. Lark was cast back to the rare times he'd visited the castle when she'd seen him from a distance. Now, clad in unrelieved black, he was a daunting presence. Isla's mother, too grief-stricken and too highborn for courtroom drama, did not appear.

Lark noted the news hawkers at full gawk. Before the afternoon waned, their broadsides would be all over the sooty city, their pockets bulging with coin.

Throat parched, head a-spin, Lark was finally returned to her cell. The verdict would likely be read on the morrow, the gaoler said, pending any other witnesses. Her pulse throbbed in her ears at the thought. So thick were her tears, she tripped over a chamber pot as the iron door slammed shut behind her. Sitting down hard on the cell bench, she groped for even a shard of hope.

Banished? Imprisoned? Hung? Transported to parts beyond the sea?

She could only hope and pray for *not proven,* akin to *not guilty.*

Meanwhile, the facts stayed hidden. Lark had not concocted the contents of the green bottle. Granny had. And she doubted Granny's remedy would have caused the symptoms Isla displayed at the last. Perhaps when combined with the other medicines and spirits she was taking, but not alone. Herbs were powerful but seldom so potent as to be fatal. Besides, Lark herself had been away at a birth when Isla met her demise.

There were many unaired details at play, and Lark knew they would remain so. 'Twas as Jillian said. Isla's powerful parents wanted a scapegoat, someone on whom to pin blame. They could not live with the taint of a daughter who had died from self-harm. Someone else would assume the responsibility, leaving their good name untarnished.

Her spirits were on the ground. She could not sink lower, weighted with the lies and half-truths Rhona had told. The court was all too aware of Isla's father's ability to sway both judge and jury simply by his appearing.

Lying down on the unfamiliar cot, she tried to block out the clanging of chains and the groans and epithets from the long cell row. Supper was eventually brought. Barely enough to keep a bird flitting, Granny would say. But in truth, she had no appetite. How odd to feel only half alive, to have hope lost like some misplaced, forgotten thing.

Lord, let the sighing of the prisoner come before Thee.

15

It's a complicated issue requiring careful analysis.

George Washington

On the day the verdict was to be read, the courtroom was nigh to bursting, the news hawkers foremost. The unsavory air rippled with tension. Lark sensed it immediately upon entering the packed chamber.

She sat with her back to the gawkers, wrists shackled. Was it true what was said about being branded on the thumbs with an *M* for murder? She'd never seen such, though some vague memory tugged at her. Once in the castle kitchen there'd been a scullery maid who'd kept her thumbs hidden. Some said she was a thief and had snitched a silver sauceboat. Cook had asked the laird to employ her, which he promptly did. What had become of her Lark couldn't recall.

Would Lark hide her thumbs too? 'Twas preferable to hanging. Or transportation. All she wanted was to flee the crowded courtroom and return to the castle, to her beloved isle. But her dismay soared amid gavel pounding and a fight that erupted in the gallery.

Rhona was brought back for questioning. Lark kept her head down, eyes on a crushed stem of rosemary at her feet. Its pungent smell had long faded. How her heart craved the solitude and sanctuary and fragrance of the castle garden. The comforting hum of the bees. Both seemed like heaven on earth.

Rhona was sobbing again. Oh, to shut one's ears to such a display. Did Rhona truly miss Isla? No doubt the horror of her mistress's final moments was a heavy weight to bear. But Lark had sensed no true affection between them in life, none other than an oft fractious mistress-servant relationship.

The jurors were whispering among themselves as Rhona was dismissed. She resumed her seat to Lark's far right on the front row. Lark lifted her head, her aching tooth throbbing along with her head. The judge was perusing court papers, the court clerk scribbling furiously.

"No other witnesses?" an official asked in

a loud voice, casting a baleful eye about the large chamber.

"Aye."

Lark stilled at a deeply resonant voice behind her. A startled hush descended, and then came the shuffling sound of a great many people getting to their feet. Yet no one had said, "All rise."

The deep-throated voice came again. "I call myself as a witness."

Lark looked over her shoulder, a wild tumult of emotion inside her. She struggled to stand, dizzy and queasy and disbelieving. Magnus was making his way to the front of the chamber. He had a presence that eclipsed that of anyone who'd entered, an undeniable vitality and intensity that made people stand when there was no formal call to do so. His longish hair, uncut during mourning, was worn loose, absent of his usual tie. Whiskers stubbled his jaw. Lean and lithe yet powerfully built, he looked ready to storm the courtroom, even tackle both judge and jurors.

His black armband, the only nod to mourning, was not lost on her.

She tasted freedom. Hope. Just a glimmer of each, yet . . .

"Ye kilt-wearing Jacobite!" The jeer was screamed from the gallery. Did someone in the crush of onlookers know his habit, his political leanings?

The judge looked in a fury. From the hurled insult or the fact that it was true? Lark tore her gaze from him to the laird, sensing all that was at stake.

The judge stared at Magnus. "A witness, you say? Your title?"

This almost made Lark smile. Magnus had the look of a bonny prince. But he was also angry and aggrieved, more so than she'd ever seen him.

"I am Magnus MacLeish. Laird of Kerrera. Husband of the deceased."

A murmur of shock washed over the chamber.

"Son of Wallace MacLeish, killed at Culloden," the judge said slowly.

"The same, aye," Magnus replied. Without acknowledging Lark, he moved in front of her and faced the jury. As if by standing between her and those who would condemn her, he aimed to shield her.

The subtle act swelled her heart and blurred her vision. She traced the beloved set of his shoulders and back through damp eyes, hardly hearing what he said, though the timbre of his voice touched her deeply.

She was cast back to their years of schooling in a cold castle turret. She, being a girl, had been left out of the debates between Magnus and his tutors. Had that prepared him for this moment? Was this what he did in Edinburgh, having studied the law?

"I beseech ye members of this jury . . ."

She swallowed and tried to focus. He was indeed arguing. On her behalf. Every word rang true, countering Rhona's lies and half-truths without calling them out. Nary a murmur was heard as he spoke. All were rapt. But not all were approving.

Rhona looked livid. The judge's face grew more florid. Even the court clerk, surely hardened by countless cases, stood transfixed, lips parted. Yet it was not just that Magnus was eloquent and compelling, even forceful. It was that he was kilted. And a widower, husband of the deceased. While some clapped at intervals, others looked murderous.

"Ye blethering Jacobite!" someone cried from the floor.

At this came several shouts in Magnus's favor — and then absolute mayhem. All around her erupted shoving, fighting, kicking, and biting.

Dropping to her knees, she took cover, crouching behind the bar. Her gaze swiveled from a stoic, now silent Magnus to the judge who'd lost control of the courtroom.

His call for order and repeated pounding of the gavel were snuffed beneath the brawling. Rhona fled out a near door, as did several other women who'd come as spectators, hungry for scandal.

Should she follow? Lark stood on trembling legs as Magnus moved toward her. A burly man, toppled by a blow to her left, was righted by Magnus, only to be kicked in the shin by another man. One lad threw a leather fire bucket at the jurors, dousing them with water. A bench overturned, and someone began pelting rotting neeps and tatties down on them from the gallery. One struck Lark's shoulder, a glancing pain.

An open door was to her right. Wanting to flee yet still shackled, Lark breathed in the unsettled air now tainted with . . . smoke?

"Fire!" someone screamed.

She was shoved viciously from behind, and then her world went black.

Who'd have thought a blow to the head would be a blessing in disguise?

"I'll not examine a patient I might well get the pestilence from. Besides, there's too much blood from the wound." The stern voice helped clear Lark's head. A physic? "See that she is bathed — with soap. And I insist on clean clothes for her."

"Very well, sir," came the obliging female voice. "A half hour then."

Lark was stripped. Scrubbed. Nigh scalded. The wound at the back of her head stung like fire and her tooth still ached, but she was deeply grateful for a bath. She gritted her teeth as the gaol matron cleaned her hair.

"These plain clothes will do. The Society of Friends oft visit here."

Lark regarded the olive-green cloth, the plain linen capelet, and the white cap. Weak-kneed, she sat in a simple shift and loose stays. Her parting with her filthy shawl was bittersweet. It seemed to belong to her former life, not her new, unknown self. Benumbed by all that had happened, she stared at white thread stockings and scuffed low-heeled buckled shoes. Even a simple linen apron.

The doctor came in and clucked his tongue at her sore head, applied a salve, pulled her troublesome tooth, declared her fit to transport, then left. The matron drew back Lark's hair so severely into a knot her scalp ached all the more.

Lark finally asked the hated question, afraid of the answer. "What does the physic mean by 'transport'?"

"The verdict was read once the courtroom

returned to order, but ye'd been knocked senseless and removed," the matron replied. "Ye've been found 'guilty in art and part' as an accessory to the crime. Ye'll soon be taken to a transport ship. I'm not sure where to."

Lark's belly gave a fierce, clawing clench as her mind grappled with the unwanted words. And then her thoughts swung to Magnus.

"What has happened to the laird of Kerrera? MacLeish?"

The matron gathered up Lark's soiled clothes. "The laird's been taken to the master's side of Glasgow Cross tolbooth."

"The master's side?"

"Aye. For indicted gentlemen. Yer on the common side."

"Indicted?" She searched the matron's expression and tone for some cruel jest. "For speaking in my defense?"

"Nay. For violating the Act of Proscription. His lairdship has been found guilty of wearing his plaid afore this. Two witnesses came forward to swear to such. Now he's liable to be transported to one of his majesty's plantations beyond the seas."

Transported? Banished.

Struck dumb, Lark watched her go out, the clink of the keys locking her in once again. How she hated that sound. What was left of her sheltered world — that sacred, inviolate haven made up of Magnus and Kerrera, croft and castle — lay in irretrievable ruins.

A stiff west wind, damp with salty spray, draped Magnus as he stood on the congested Glasgow pier along the banks of the River Clyde. He peered past the commanding customhouse and shipping office, a large sailcloth company and countless warehouses, to the towering masts of endless ships, each bound for separate ports.

Beside him stood his longtime confidant and ally, Richard Osbourne, one of the Tobacco Lords who traded with colonial America. His fortune was made in tobacco, sugar, horses, and slaves. Magnus could not make peace with the latter but was glad his influential friend stood beside him this day. Only the Almighty could have crossed their paths at such a time, allowing Magnus's letter to be carried to Osbourne's Glasgow residence with a holy haste.

"Here's what I discovered, having been denied my appeal that the lass in question be pardoned." Osbourne gestured to the nearest sloop. "Miss MacDougall's to be put aboard the *Neptune* with one hundred thirty other women convicts. As for yourself, I hope to secure a place aboard the *Bonaventure,* one of my frigates refitted to carry stores to the Sugar Islands."

Magnus withheld a wince. "So there's little more to be done for Lark MacDougall."

Osbourne sighed. "I did what I could to no avail, short of bribing the attending physic to declare her unfit for transport. Sadly, the jury was likely swayed by your late wife's father, so Miss MacDougall's conviction stands. She'll not be branded, but she'll be indentured." He cast a baleful eye on Magnus. "For the moment, I'm most concerned about you."

"Mayhap yer appeal of my case will go through." Magnus struck a hopeful tone though his spirits sagged. "Yer request that I leave tolbooth on a pass for two hours' time was granted this day."

"Aye, but the presiding judge you encountered for Miss MacDougall's trial is rabidly anti-Jacobite. And if he gets wind of what we're after, he might deny both requests."

"He's a kilt hater. I suspected as much. And pro-Hanoverian to boot."

"Aye on both counts." Respect rode Osbourne's features. " 'Twas bold of you to walk into an unknown courtroom and defend a condemned woman like you did."

"Mayhap foolhardy. But I could do nothing less. She's an islander like myself. Our family histories have been entwined for generations. And the truth of the matter is that she had nothing to do with my wife's death. I canna stand by when her very life is in jeopardy on my account. 'Tis a notorious miscarriage of justice."

"Aye, that it is. The whole affair is a flagrant violation of the biblical command to not bear false witness. The courts are nothing but bribes and perjury and more." He squinted into the glaring, sunlit water. "If you gain passage on the *Bonaventure* and arrive at my plantation in Jamaica as I hope, you can act as factor, something that may well suit you. At the end of your two-year term you can return to Scotland."

"There'll be naught to return to." The thought was so overwhelming Magnus could hardly speak. "I well ken what happens to Jacobite property seized and sold."

"True enough. 'Tis been the fate of many a Highlander and Lowlander too."

Magnus fixed his gaze upon a departing barge lying low in the river. "Tell me more about the voyage. What the *Bonaventure* is carrying. The date of departure."

"That depends on several factors. My

Jamaican plantation is in need of men and supplies. I'm keen on acquiring a few men skilled in agriculture and horticulture to make the voyage, and I've been given leave to carry a few male felons suited to the task. A special garden is being built on her quarterdeck. Room enough for pots of various vegetables, fruit, even herbs to use for food or physic in Virginia — my main estate — or Jamaica once there."

Magnus offered up a silent prayer before plunging ahead. "Miss MacDougall was the mistress of Kerrera Castle's stillroom like her grandmother before her. Keeper of the castle's bees too. Highly skilled. Why not arrange for a woman to oversee yer shipboard garden?"

"Why not, indeed." Osbourne looked at him intently, a wry smile tugging at his mouth. "Perhaps it's not too late. I shall try to have her transferred from the *Neptune* then. A female prisoner is far more manageable than a male. Perhaps the arrangement will benefit us both."

They fell silent as a commotion from behind made them turn. A coach was passing, a dozen women roped to the outside seats. A gaol turnkey sat atop the box, spewing tobacco and keeping an eye on his charges. One woman held a baby who was crying so piteously Magnus set his jaw. The coach lurched to a stop by a lighter bobbing at the edge of the pier, waiting to row the women over to a waiting ship.

Again Osbourne smiled rather wryly as he scrutinized the ship in question. "Could the *Neptune* be before our very eyes? Not to mention the lass in question?"

Stung by amazement, Magnus looked hard at the wagon. Lark was the sixth woman to step down. Nearly unrecognizable in Quaker garb, she glanced his way absently, then looked back again with wide-eyed surprise.

"Keep yer eyes down," the turnkey snapped. The women were marched across the dock then hauled into the lighter, a precarious business with each in manacles.

Lark looked to her shoes while Magnus stood riveted, overcome by a strange mix of fury and helplessness as she was rowed away across the expanse of churlish water.

A scowling sailor waited to pull them over the side of the enormous vessel. Shoulders bent, the women formed a line at an anvil to have the rivets knocked from their irons one by one. The jarring clank rippled over the water above the cries of gulls and shouts of the crew. Once the turnkey was paid his fee of a half crown a head, he returned to shore in the empty lighter.

"A miserable business," Osbourne concluded. "Even bound for fair Virginia."

16

True happiness consists not in the multitude of friends, but in the worth and choice.

Ben Jonson

As the hated manacles fell noisily from her wrists, Lark looked over the ship's rail to where Magnus stood beside an important-looking gentleman on the crowded quay. Her heart turned over. He'd looked no less stunned than she on seeing him in such plain clothes. Gone was his handsome Scots garb with its heather blues and grays, his sporran and sgian dubh, the kilt hose and brogues. What had been done to them? Why was he allowed out of the master's side of the tolbooth? Could it be because he'd been freed? Or was it simply because he had powerful friends?

The lack of details added to her angst. She might never see him again. 'Twas so undeserved, his gaoling. Banished for being clad in the garb of their people. Or did it have more to do with his untimely defense of her?

From the very beginning she'd tried not to rail at God. But as fear became commonplace and hope was lost, the future loomed large enough to entertain black doubts. She was innocent, not a convict to be condemned to a wild, unwanted land. All she held dear was on Kerrera. 'Twas the worst sort of sentence to leave all that was beloved. Why did the Lord allow such things? Had she not prayed hard enough? Trusted God enough? Was He punishing her?

The wailing at her side ended her painful ponderings. A baby, as bonny as his mother was sallow and frail, reached out to Lark with bare, plump arms. Lark took the wee fingers in her own, unsure of his mother's reaction. His damp smile was her reward, a welcome reprieve from his tears.

His mother turned dull eyes on Lark. "Ye've no babe o' yer own?"

"Nay."

"He favors ye, wee Larkin does."

Larkin, was it? Lark tried to smile despite the moment's misery, gazing over the babe's thatch of ginger hair to Magnus on the quay. He'd turned his back on her, and his stance, however unintended, rent her heart.

"Ye can hold him if ye like." Frail arms offered the babe to Lark.

She took the infant, going wide-eyed at his weight. A ruadh-headed handful he was. He gave a chortle of delight, and the knot of women looked relieved, spared of his fretfulness. His dimpled hand brushed Lark's flushed cheek, his bright eyes on her face.

"Yer a braw laddie," Lark crooned near his ear, nostrils stung with the smell of urine and soured milk.

She longed to give him a bath. Dress him in a clean shift. Amuse him somehow. Both he and his mother were missing a single plaything. How he'd love the coral beads. They'd fallen from her pocket when she'd readied to bathe, but the kindly gaol matron simply looked the other way, letting her keep them.

As she lost sight of Magnus on shore, her thoughts veered to the captain. What had become of him? By now he might've hanged. The hollowness inside her widened as rain began spattering down, causing even the babe to look up.

Her gaze roamed the strange ship. The quarterdeck was raised, a railing enclosing the officers. Far below was the cargo hold, the befouled orlop deck a horror. Long ago the captain had explained the parts of a ship to her when he'd procured the *Merry Lass*. Remembering, Lark bounced the babe on her hip as the women were led to a locked hatch and then farther below to a place where wide sleeping shelves hung from both sides of the hull.

She breathed in the sharp scent of wood shavings, refreshing after the rancid straw of the gaol cell. The stores in the hold on either side of their quarters was plain enough. Coffee and spices and tobacco mingled in the damp air. But she knew, too, that during their two or more months at sea the fresh newness would quickly wear off, the stink of the bilge unbearable.

For the moment, she felt sharp concern for the babe's mother. Droplets of sweat beaded the woman's brow, and when she reached for the ladder that led them past the hatch, a shaft of light called out a dull red rash splotching her neck and the tanned skin above her fraying bodice.

Gaol fever?

Granny believed such was spread by the bites of lice and fleas. Lark's own skin was nigh eaten up before her recent bath, and no hartshorn was to be had.

"Ye look bound for the sick berth, ye do,"

one of the women murmured to the babe's mother, taking a step back.

"She canna leave her bairn," another said, looking to wee Larkin who contentedly chewed on one of Lark's bonnet strings.

"He isna mine but my sister's," the woman confessed, wiping the sweat from her face with a begrimed sleeve. "She died in childbed. I'm his only kin."

"Who's his da?"

A shrug. "Some say he's a man o' some standing in Edinburgh. But she was one of them disorderly girls."

A dismayed murmur overshadowed them. "How've ye gotten nourishment for 'im?"

"He's right fond o' goat's milk."

"There's no goats here," clucked the oldest among them.

Lark sighed, knowing he'd soon need feeding. Chin shiny with drool, he smiled up at her, his pink gums sporting one pristine tooth. Her heart squeezed. Here he was, blooming like the heather in their soiled, sordid world, unaware of their grim circumstances.

He'd surely not live long in such brutish conditions. The pecking order soon came clear. With over one hundred women bound for the hold, a few vied for first place. Trinkets smuggled aboard were demanded or threatened or stolen by day's end. Never before had Lark heard such curses or bullying.

Coral beads secreted in her pocket, Lark kept to her shadowed corner, the babe with her while his ailing aunt slept. But Lark was still privy to the women's thieving and threats, their insults and abuses. Bett, deprived of a blanket by Nance, complained to the officers, only to be set upon in the darkness and beaten nearly senseless at midnight.

The next day the most troublesome of the convict women broke into the bulkhead and guzzled several bottles of port before they were discovered. This earned a dozen stripes from a cat-o'-nine-tails, and the voyage had not yet begun.

Lark looked on, dazed. Fighting the urge to scream, she weighed jumping overboard as fear gained another foothold. Would death not be preferable to this ongoing agony? This terrible wonder of what would befall them next?

Lord, what will become of us all after two months at sea?

She resisted a shudder, her homesickness fierce, her questions mounting. How was Granny? What about Magnus? Would he be released from the tolbooth and returned to

Kerrera? What of the captain? She'd lost all track of time. When was it she'd last seen him?

The present pressed in, the frenzied preparations on deck at a peak. Sailing was imminent. Lark waited for the telltale lurch of the ship, her last hope for a petition of clemency dissolving. The sick berth filled, and two women died of gaol fever by the third day. Braziers of herbs burned between decks, and even gunpowder was charged to dispel the miasma.

Would Larkin's aunt survive? The listless woman lay on her bunk, refusing so much as a sip of water. Though one of the other older women had offered to help tend Larkin, his aunt refused all but Lark.

Did she believe Lark a Quaker in her plain garb? A worthy guardian for her wee nephew?

The babe sat on Lark's lap, rosy cheeked and often babbling. His simplicity and innocence tugged at her. How content he was to just be held and sung to, satisfied with her portion of gruel or sips of water. She herself felt ravenous, starved for sunlight and clean air and solid ground. Her still-room and croft. Granny's quiet company. A place not sullied by coarse talk and curses.

Bereft of even the smallest trunk, all she

had were the borrowed Quaker clothes and the captain's coral beads. And a baby.

But even these could be taken, snatched away in the blink of an eye.

She fixed her eye on a roach crawling across a floorboard. Her whole being recoiled. How would she survive?

Lord, all I have is Ye. Make that enough.

A few well-placed words. More than a few gold guineas. Magnus knew something had been accomplished by Osbourne's glad expression as he faced him in his transport cell the next morn, iron bars between them.

"The appeal's gone through. Miss Mac-Dougall is to be transferred to the *Bonaventure* as an indenture."

Magnus leaned into the bars, almost light-headed with relief. "When will it happen?"

"In the forenoon. She's to leave the *Neptune* by lighter no later than ten o'clock. They're to sail soon after so the exchange must be quick."

His prayers had been answered — again. Few appeals were granted by the Scottish judiciary. At a time when women were still burned at the stake for petty theft, Lark's deliverance seemed nothing short of miraculous. Still, the tight timeline, the imminent sailing, begged further worry. More praying. But if it all came off . . .

"I owe ye," Magnus said.

"Nary a ha'pence I'll take, especially if she's as skilled as you say she is." Osbourne took a vial from his pocket and waved the smelling salts beneath his nose, then passed the vial to Magnus. "You'll have need of it till your own transfer tomorrow afternoon. The turnkey will deliver you to the docks no later than three o'clock."

"When do we sail?"

"Once the livestock pens on the foredeck are finished and stocked and the ship's watered." He reached for his pocket watch, a flash of ornate silver in the gloom. "I expect the ship shall depart Glasgow two days hence."

Even a crowded ship seemed preferable to gaol. In just a day their number increased, though a few female prisoners, like Larkin's aunt, were removed to the infirmary. Lark cajoled, bounced, sang, and begged milk from a steward, her back aching from toting the babe.

The next morn, a harried ship's surgeon faced her, expression doleful. "The wee laddie's kin is dead."

Lark sat on the edge of a sleeping platform as a hush descended on what now numbered nearly one hundred twenty convict women.

"God rest her soul," one said.

"Amen." Benumbed, Lark looked to the sleeping lad in her arms. "A prison ship is no place for a babe."

"Nay, but the law is all those six years and under be aboard whilst those older remain in their native land," the surgeon said.

"So yer saying the babe's banished too."

He wiped his hands on a rag dangling from his waist. "The woman's dying words were meant for ye. Said she bequeathed ye the babe and no other."

Larkin awoke and howled. Lark rearranged him, tucking his perspiring head beneath her trembling chin. 'Twas all she could do not to fall to pieces. However would she manage a needy bairn?

"Ye look every inch the laddie's mother," the woman nearest her said in consoling tones. "Yer hair's the same. Even has a dimple same as ye."

"Hoot!" another said. "She doesna have any milk —"

"Neither did his auntie. A milch goat'll do."

An argument erupted over the best nourishment, how to rear him and keep him clean and content. But all agreed Lark was the answer.

That night she huddled in her bunk, praying more than sleeping. Larkin's plump body curled into hers, a nugget of warmth in the bowels of a ship that seemed to lose every speck of heat once the sun set and take on the cold of the sea. He slept fitfully, having wet himself. She would have to beg some cloth.

The steward roused her at break of day with news she'd never in a hundred years thought to hear. Even he seemed flummoxed when he said, "Yer to come on deck for transfer to the *Bonaventure.*"

Transfer? "Why?"

He looked annoyed. "Orders."

Felons asked few questions, especially female ones. She carried a still-sleeping Larkin in a sort of sling about her back and shoulders, compliments of the ship's surgeon who'd seen West Indies mothers do the same. It eased her back and Larkin seemed to like it.

Without further explanation, into a lighter they went in the damp dawn, rowing across the harbor crowded with prison hulks, private merchant vessels, his majesty's warships, pilot boats, and the local fishing fleet.

Soon Larkin would awake and want to be fed. 'Twas a routine she dreaded, not knowing how the next batch of milk would be had. Her own stomach cramped with emptiness. The convict ship they'd just left seemed a child's toy compared to the behemoth looming ahead with its bow bearing the nautical figurehead of a mermaid.

Half a dozen men stared down at her from the gunwale. Soon she was raised in a boatswain's chair, reminding her of distressed livestock forced into canvas slings and hoisted on board. She felt just as ungainly with Larkin clutched to her bodice — a cow and a calf, truly.

"Ah, a Quaker miss," the mate said, handing her over the ship's side.

"I wasna told of a bairn," another said.

Would they send her back to the *Neptune* then? Heaven forbid. Glad of her modest garb, she was aware of the scrutiny of a great many men. Where were the female criminals? All she saw were sailors. Alarm spiked through her. Had there been some mistake? Nay, they'd called her by name.

She was led below to what she feared was the orlop, through an open hatch, past closed doors to a berth — all her own? One she'd share with wee Larkin. Once the door was closed, not locked, she took in her new surroundings.

Bethankit, Lord.

Her sense that she'd narrowly been delivered of something terrible swelled. Yet a tendril of anxiety took root. Why was she here aboard the *Bonaventure* instead?

Here, at the moment, consisted of four wooden walls, both a bunk and a hammock, a small table and chair, and a blessed porthole open to a breeze. No scent of bilge. No signs of cockroaches or rats. No one fighting for a sleeping platform or crust of bread. No one threatening to stick you with a straight pin in your sleep.

Silence. But for the sound of footsteps and creak of ropes above. And the babe's gentle breathing.

In minutes, a knock sounded and breakfast was brought. Porridge, still steaming. Toast with blackened crust. Tea.

She blinked as the tray was set down. It seemed ungrateful to ask for milk for the babe in the face of such bounty. Mightn't she spoon him some porridge and tea?

Larkin saved her the difficulty. Flushed and still perspiring from sleep, he awoke and stared at the strange steward and squawked.

"Sounds a bit like the captain's parrot, ye do." The man grinned. "But I ken 'tis milk yer wanting." He moved toward the open door. "And a private corner."

"Please — I'm not his mother. I canna

nurse . . ."

He swung back around, looking baffled. Truly, at first glance, their resemblance was uncanny.

"I've no experience with bairns, miss. What d'ye suggest?"

"Goat's milk?"

His eyes lit with satisfaction. "The bairn willna starve then. The last o' the livestock was loaded this morn. I did spy a nannie and kid among the bucks."

"I'll need a supply of cloth for clouts to keep him clean and dry."

This he might manage. A nod reassured her. "He's a braw lad, even if he's not yer own."

She smiled her thanks and stared at the tray. The porridge had ceased steaming. The tea was likely tepid. Best withhold any more questions or requests. She sat down at the tiny table, Larkin still close in his sling, and left nary a crumb, spooning her charge a tiny taste of tea now and again, his perplexed expression comical.

Time ticked on. Had the goat's milk been forgotten? The cloths? She'd used her apron as a last resort. Laying him down on the sleeping platform, she changed him, her cap now a clout.

He began to whimper and kick his feet,

not one to be distracted ere long.

"I left my baby lying here, lying here, lying here. I left my baby lying here to go and gather blueberries . . ." The Scots lullaby failed to soothe, and she was grateful for another knock. A piggin of goat's milk, still warm, brought by a red-faced cabin boy. He presented a horn spoon and scampered off quick as a squirrel.

"So, wee one, angels watch over ye." 'Twas something Granny had said to her in years gone by and now rolled easily from her tongue. But the ache the lullaby wrought remained, and she finished his feeding damp-eyed.

As she set him on the bunk, he gave a satisfied belch, bringing a needed chuckle from her. She took the coral beads from her pocket and dangled them before his snapping blue eyes, weighing the wisdom of using them as a plaything. Brittle, even fragile, they might succumb to the tiniest tooth.

He grabbed at the colorful beads and she drew back, expecting a scowl but gaining a gurgling laugh. Like sunshine he was to her merriment-starved soul.

They played the game till another knock sounded. The same cabin boy. But this time a sober summons.

17

Pity it is that thousands of my country people should be starving at home, when they may live here in peace and plenty.
Roderick Gordon, Scottish ship's surgeon

"I'm Richard Osbourne of Glasgow, and this is Captain Moodie who'll see you safely to Virginia."

The glare of sunlight on deck bespoke a sweltering three o'clock. All around them a great many sweating, harried sailors were preparing the ship to leave port.

At her silence, Osbourne said solemnly, "I hold yer indenture. For three years ye'll be in service, starting aboard this ship. Though with the babe . . ."

She hugged Larkin closer, like a child would a beloved doll. Would they send her back to the *Neptune,* encumbered as she was? A wild panic took hold, followed by a hundred unasked questions burning in her brain.

Behind her a shout rang out announcing another arrival. Had she lost her senses? Surely her mind was filling with fancies much like the wind-stiffened sails. She stood slack-jawed as Magnus stepped onto deck. Soon he stood before her. Silent. Equally overcome. She herself could not choke out the barest greeting.

He looked from her to Larkin. Befuddled. Transfixed. Knowing him as she did, sensing his surprise, she wondered if he was trying to reconcile the time since her arrest and a baby's birth.

"The bairn was given into my care by his aunt, who succumbed to gaol fever yesterday," she said above the rising wind lest it whip her words away.

"God rest her soul," Magnus said. He studied her, obviously noting she'd lost a stone or more since she'd left Kerrera, for he said, "Yer well?"

"As of this moment, aye." This she could barely squeeze past her throat as it tightened with emotion. "And ye?"

"Well enough." His eyes flashed wry relief. Here they were, he no freer than she, by the state of his convict clothing.

Osbourne shook his hand, conveying a

warm association, while the captain stood aloof. All looked at her as Larkin gave a shriek, his gaze and wee hands drawn above his head to a sail being raised. Magnus cracked a smile.

Osbourne chuckled. "We might turn the wee lad into a seaman, aye?"

His kind words assuaged her somewhat. "He's little trouble. Mostly he sleeps. He's partial to goat's milk."

Osbourne nodded. "I've a young son. Infants are fascinating creatures. And this one seems inordinately fond of you."

She nodded, still puzzling that out. Larkin seemed to have fixed his affection on her from first glance. Had his mother possessed red tresses? She'd never know with his aunt gone so fast, a host of questions unasked. She focused on the immediate present. "Am I to be the only woman aboard?"

The captain spoke when Osbourne was distracted by a cabin boy at his elbow. "The other female prisoners and indentures should arrive soon, as well as a few select male prisoners to round out the crew."

Select males with sailing expertise? Was Magnus now an indenture, same as she? What of Larkin? Born to a disorderly girl, with a convict aunt, was he a convict too? By the time they reached Virginia, if they did, he'd likely be crawling, a lap baby no longer.

Captain Moodie was regarding Larkin as if thinking the very same. No doubt he'd be the only infant on board.

She met Magnus's eyes and saw more than simple concern there. Oh, for a quiet corner to talk. He seemed a bit at odds with her again, much like when he'd left Kerrera long ago. Time and distance had driven a wedge between them once more. Or did he bear her a grudge over Isla? But surely he'd been behind her transfer to the *Bonaventure.* He had friends in high places, both in the city and in the country. And surely Providence was at play most of all. How else could they share the same ship?

One look at all the bobbing boats in so busy a harbor, as well as the hundreds of felons, bespoke the miraculous, lofty connections aside.

The Scotsman across from her was now a hero in homespun, a far cry from the kilted childhood laird she knew, but one who'd always had her best interests at heart.

For now, she'd take comfort in that and her belief that the Lord had a plan, come what may.

That night Magnus dined at the captain's

table with Richard Osbourne. Amid the wink of candles and myriad dishes that bespoke a ship still in port, Magnus listened more than he spoke, at least till called out by his hosts. Much needed learning. Even the drift of conversation eluded him.

"We struck the doldrums after Cabo Verde, going ten miles back again from where we'd started the day before," the captain said between bites of beef.

"A wretched business any time of year," Osbourne replied. "I well recall my black leather trunks turning white with mold one sailing. I even failed to free my razor from its case it rusted so fast."

Magnus's thoughts tripped down the companionway to Lark, whose accommodations he was unsure of. Small as an ant he felt aboard such a vessel. The ship was crawling with what appeared to be a crew of hundreds. There seemed little room left for even a dozen female convicts and no need for male convicts turned sailors. The term *convict* troubled him, yet he was one, was he not?

He held fast to the memory of Lark on deck, the sun making a fiery halo of her hair. The shock he'd felt at finding the babe bearing so sharp a resemblance to her still lingered. Anyone who didn't know better would think the braw lad her child. In his amazement, he'd not asked the lad's name.

Osbourne merely seemed bemused by the unexpected bairn while the captain was harder to read. But since Osbourne owned both ship and cargo, the captain was in his hire and did his bidding.

God be praised.

For now, he'd rest in the fact Lark was safely aboard. Granted, she'd lost the robust quality, that vibrant spark, she'd always had. Pale as parchment paper she was, shaved thin by lack of nourishment but not by some wasting disease, heaven forbid.

Did she feel as lost as he did? No longer mistress of the castle stillroom but now an indentured mother to boot. And he — in the humble garments that scratched his skin — no longer Kerrera's bereaved laird but a homeless criminal.

God be praised anyway.

As the sun set and the gulls circled the last day of July, there came twenty-seven women in brown serge, that lackluster convict color that seemed to flatter no one and call out every flaw. Larkin on her hip, Lark held herself apart as the manacles were struck from their wrists one by one, knowing a close association with these unknown women might prove fatal to her charge. When she pondered the babe, it seemed God had saved him for some special purpose. Not that these women intended harm, but some seemed bound for the infirmary with their coughing. She prayed none would see a rough coffin made by the ship's carpenter.

Kissing Larkin's brow, she murmured in his ear, "May ye be fruitful, wee one, and health, honesty, and happiness be yer gifts."

Then came the men, selected for their sea legs. She turned away, keeping her eyes down. She was vaguely aware Magnus kept to the quarterdeck, the officers' domain, which was elevated and enclosed with a railing. And off-limits to most, be it crew or convicts.

At daybreak, the *Bonaventure* set sail against a livid scarlet sky. Lark watched from her bull's-eye window, as the hatches were not yet open to allow women on deck. While Larkin slept in her bunk, she leaned into a post, wincing at the creak of timbers and shouted orders above as the ship heaved and shuddered and seemed more inclined to sink than sail.

More than the terrifying noise, the nose-curling smells, and the nauseating motion was the sickening sense of separation. From

Scotland. Granny. All she held dear. Never had she wished to leave it. Hugging the post to stay on her feet, she set her jaw so hard she feared her teeth would crack. For a few inexplicable seconds, Granny's presence seemed to hover.

Keep count of yer blessings.

Blessings, aye. Magnus. Health. The potted garden on deck that awaited her tending. The pocketed coral beads. And the babe now wedged against the bunk's far wall, safe from rolling.

A shout sounded and the hatches were finally opened. She enclosed a sleepy Larkin in the sling and began a sort of graceless dance to the rhythm of the ship, grabbing a handhold there, bending a knee here, taking a sudden step to the side or even back a step as she managed the tween deck and then the hatch.

Squinting at first, Larkin soon looked about in wide-eyed wonder. He had an endearing habit of burying his face in her bosom when a sailor came near, as if men were strange, untrustworthy creatures undeserving of a second look.

"Ye must be braw and brave as befits yer name," Lark said as he stared up at her. "A fierce warrior, aye."

High above them the sails filled and

stretched taut as the *Bonaventure* found her sea legs. The women in brown serge struggled to find theirs as they emerged through the hatch after Lark.

Saltwater tubs for washing awaited them, and instructions to hang their bedding to air on the yards and rigging, overseen by the ship's surgeon and a lieutenant. Matrons were chosen as mess captains who dispensed rations from the cook and then oversaw various tasks. A collective grumble went round as some were sent to milk the cows and goats in the bow while others cleaned poultry cages. Skilled needlewomen were set to mending and making shirts from stores of linen. Lark was led to the specially constructed plant cabin on the quarterdeck.

Full of milk, Larkin fell back asleep in the sling as Lark walked about her new domain behind the main mast. Even now Captain Moodie kept to the windward side, spyglass in hand.

She turned her attention to the bounty of plants on all sides of her. Tea trees. Two potted artichokes. Sage. Sorrel. Mint. Tarragon and chives. Currant trees and parsnips and bright-faced marigolds. Fragile hyssop and pennyroyal beside hardy balm and sprawling mint, all in good health. Two of the hives she'd seen earlier were situated among the pots, bees zigzagging hither and yon.

Her fingers brushed a velvety wand of lavender, its purple spires bending in the wind. A few plants already looked slightly spent. Pushing a finger through the soil, she gauged their thirst much as the *Bonaventure*'s navigator fixed the ship's position.

Magnus was nowhere to be seen. Nor was Osbourne. Had the owner of the *Bonaventure* stayed behind in Glasgow? If so, 'twas a loss. He seemed kind. Shrewd. A true Christian gentleman.

She moved toward a water cask and used a wooden dipper to water the plants in need, trying to get her bearings and take note of what was where.

"I hear you're skilled in botany." Lieutenant Blackburn, the ship's surgeon, stood behind her, his blue uniform a contrast to the common red and gray cloth of the enlisted seamen. His tricorne hat was tipped at a jaunty angle, his smile a rarity among the stern-faced sailors. "And are an apiarist."

She straightened, amused by the grand titles. "Simply the mistress of the stillroom and bee yard."

"A modest lass, aye? And an angel in disguise, given the bairn isna yer own."

She looked at him in surprise. News

spread like fever from masthead to stern, obviously. " 'Tis impossible to forsake a baby."

"He's a lucky lad." He knelt to inspect a mulberry plant. "These are flourishing and well on their way to producing silk. I've been experimenting in my cabin with cottonseed and cochineal beetles with less success."

"For scarlet dye, ye mean?"

"Aye. Perhaps you'd care to come below and have a look."

Heat inched up her neck at his scrutiny, her water dipper dangling from her hand. What could she say to this? Few could afford cochineal-dyed garments. She'd only seen them in shop windows in Edinburgh.

"The dye sets more firmly on woolens," she murmured, resuming her watering. "Or so I've heard."

He nodded, left, and then returned with a journal, quill, and ink. Sitting down on a sea chest, he made a desk of sorts. "We'll work together, you and I. Osbourne has given me charge of recording the health and progress of his unusual botanical garden you'll tend."

Relief riddled her. It was business then. She went about her new duties, a bit queasy from the ship's rolling. Several convict women had fled their assigned tasks at the forecastle and hugged the ship's rail, white-faced and sick. Seasoned sailors worked around them, every bit as busy as the bees in the buzzing hives.

She took a step toward a hardy mint as the ship careened. Fearing her feet were about to come from under her, she grabbed at the nearest anchor — Surgeon Blackburn's coat sleeve.

His reassuring chuckle eased her. "Mayhap you're better off without your shoes. There's a reason these sailors go barefoot."

She let go of him as the deck settled, her stomach with it. Dare she shed her shoes, stockings, and garters in front of him?

"I can turn my back if you like." He did so without her *aye,* the gesture gallant. "This ship is an alien world, you'll soon find, with its own unwritten rules."

The sun-soaked planks, worn smooth by salt water and scrubbing, warmed her bare soles. Already she felt less ungainly. Slipping or falling might harm Larkin. Better she be bare of foot than have an injured babe.

The surgeon turned a page. "Why don't you tell me the name and state of each plant to begin. Osbourne insists on a close accounting."

For an hour they worked. She shared names of the few plants he didn't know while he taught her the scientific names of the ones he did, explaining how they'd best protect them in a gale.

"Lord willing, we won't have one," he said with a good-natured wink, shutting the journal.

She bit her lip to still the questions raised by the scar across his stubbled jaw. With a last pointed glance, she got the gist of his sun-darkened features. Eyes like green glass. Tawny hair queued in back with a black ribbon. Powerful shoulders. 'Twas a face and form that lingered long after one quit looking. He moved with perfect balance, bespeaking years at sea much as his scar bespoke conflict. He was neither young nor old . . .

A shout went up from the forecastle. "All aback forward!"

She looked to the surgeon and he explained, "The head sails are pressed aback by the wind's sudden change."

There were a great many sails and a great many men aloft, but her gaze fixed on one. Something about his silhouette, the way he moved . . .

A different sort of wooziness swirled through her, as keenly felt as that of the retching women at the ship's rail.

Clad in trews — the cropped pants of sailors — and wearing a skullcap, Rory MacPherson was no longer the captain of the *Merry Lass* but a common jack-tar, as sailors were called. How had she missed him? Granted, there were upwards of two hundred souls aboard, and a dozen or more male prisoners had arrived late yesterday. Had he been among them?

What were the odds of the three of them sharing the same ship? Her gaze swung to the horde on deck. Magnus was still missing. Her stomach lurched anew though the deck stayed level. Had Magnus slipped away before they'd set sail like his friend Osbourne, much as the former captain had come aboard at the last? Had some deal been struck that he'd had no time to tell her about? Shouldn't she be glad for him, if so?

The thought punched her in the stomach. *Lord, nay.*

18

A great many who have been transported for a punishment have found pleasure, profit, and ease and would rather undergo any hardship than be forced back on their own country.
Roderick Gordon, Scottish ship's surgeon

His seafaring skills might have saved him from the hangman's noose on land, but his simmering resentment might earn him a hundred lashes at sea. Although the *Bonaventure* was as worthy a vessel as he'd ever seen, its crew was another matter.

Able to sum up a man at a glance, Rory took an instant dislike to Captain Moodie. Already the captain, reported to be a drunkard, had mishandled matters in the short time since they'd left Glasgow. It aggravated him like a saltwater rash, as did the presence of so many females.

Even the humblest cabin boy knew having

women aboard was cursed luck. He grimaced as he tied an overhand knot, gaze swinging wide as he finished. Aside from the wooden woman on the ship's bow, that comely figure of a mermaid, women passengers were a bad omen.

As for the Quaker miss below with her bairn slung about her, her prim hat hiding her hair and features, and the homely women in convict brown, he'd spared nary a glance. Yet his fellow jacks were plenty distracted.

He shimmied down the mast when the watch changed, past a knot of women picking oakum. Soon their hands would bleed and form black scars as they untwisted old rope to stuff into the ship's seams to make it watertight. He knew because he'd assigned his men the same when mutiny threatened. In the tolbooth he himself had picked two pounds a day to curry favor. Because of it he'd earned notice when a Tobacco Lord came looking for extra hands on the *Bonaventure*.

But any gratitude he'd felt then was short-lived. He railed against a God who allowed women to pick their fingers to pieces for the petty offense of stealing a bun to stay alive, though most were likely glad to be rid of the putrid tolbooth where gaol keepers drank down a gill of spirits each morn to steel themselves against the stench.

"MacPherson, man the pumps!"

The order was given by the captain's second-in-command, only slightly more agreeable than Captain Moodie himself. Rory nearly groaned aloud. Removing the reeking bilge water from the ship's hull was the equivalent of removing the tolbooth's stench.

Ignoring the wail of the baby, he strode to the hatch. Two months yet till he escaped the *Bonaventure.* Though he'd longed to traverse the Atlantic to the Scots stronghold in North Carolina, pumping bilge water was not how he'd envisioned doing it.

Magnus sat at the long dining table a second night, Captain Moodie at its head, his officers among them. The aroma of roast fowl mingled with that of the new tongue-and-groove paneling laid with linseed oil, a costly green baize rug at their feet.

Magnus's eyes roamed the great cabin elegantly fitted in brass and jewel-toned blues and greens, its grand curved window-panes spanning the width of the stern. His own berth was impoverished by comparison, the ship's mast running through it like an uninvited guest, taking up precious room.

Though not one of the officers, he was clearly someone, somehow retaining the respect and title due Kerrera's laird despite his convict status.

Since they'd sailed, he'd kept below deck, having been asked by the captain to organize his books and ledgers given the overhaul to his quarters, something Magnus was glad to do. And now this. Though he'd thought to dine alone in his berth, the captain's invitation stood.

To his left was the ship's surgeon, Blackburn, a Lowland Scot, and to his right sat the quartermaster, their royal-blue uniforms in stark contrast to his own garments. The steward had lent him a quality frock coat and cravat, reminding him of his Edinburgh-made suits of old, though this one hung a bit loosely.

Amid the creak of the ship's timbers and clink of utensils came a sort of recitation and review of their tumultuous naval world.

"England's had a frightful loss in the Bay of Cádiz," the first lieutenant intoned. "Eighteen ships foundered in January of this year alone, the foremost being the *Charm* with the loss of all but one of her crew."

"What of the *Nightingale* run down and sunk in the Atlantic ninety leagues off Vigo,

Spain, by a Dutch vessel?" another officer said.

"Not sunk but refloated and repaired. Her crew survived. But a close call, aye," the first lieutenant confirmed. "At present the Royal Navy is all agog about HMS *Mermaid,* driven ashore in a hurricane at Charles Town, South Carolina. All hands lost."

"I'd rather sink off the shores of British America than Spain," Surgeon Blackburn said. "I can speak English, at least."

A round of doleful chuckling.

"Why not talk of other matters?" the captain interjected. "Like the fair British nymphs on board?"

More laughter. Magnus put down his fork as the first lieutenant shot him a glance. "No doubt our Scottish guest isn't aware of how matters stand at sea."

"Let us waste no time in educating him, then," the quartermaster said with a wink.

" 'Tis no secret," the first lieutenant muttered. "Even the *Times* has reported that every officer is entitled by law to oblige the woman of his choice to serve him as mate for the duration of the voyage."

The captain poured himself more port. "Mayhap the laird will take advantage of a shipboard companion. No better way to navigate the open sea, aye?"

Magnus stayed silent, alarm widening inside him. Captain Moodie lit a fragrant Cuban cigar, clearly bemused.

"I suppose seniority must be observed," a lesser officer said dryly. "So what's your pleasure, Surgeon Blackburn?"

A slight pause. All eyes pinned the ship's surgeon.

"The Quaker miss."

Another officer snorted. "Surely you jest. There'll be precious little frolicking with a babe between you."

"The babe doesn't deter me," Blackburn replied around a bite of beef. "I first fixed my fancy on Miss MacDougall the moment the rivet was knocked from her irons."

" 'Tis true she's the comeliest of them all, save for Mrs. Ravenhill."

"The society thief? From the master's side of tolbooth?"

The captain raised his glass. "I'll amuse Mrs. Ravenhill. At three and thirty, she's too aged for the likes of you — and far too wily."

"Watch your pockets, sir," a junior officer warned to a burst of spirit-sated laughter.

Names and crimes and attributes were soon bandied about, the comeliest mentioned by name. Polly Nicolson, guilty of thieving Irish linen. Phoebe Edgar, drunkenness. Ann Barlow, forger. Rose Randall, a double felony. All sentenced to the *Bonaventure* as indentures bound for British America.

"What of the Quaker miss?" A lieutenant directed the question to the captain. "Little is known in her regard except that she hails from the western isles, a former stillroom mistress."

Moodie held his smoking cigar aloft. "Osbourne said precious little about her, only that she's his indenture and is needed to oversee the plant cabin and was thus transferred from the *Neptune*."

Magnus marveled, eyes on the dripping candelabra. Could these men be aware of so little, these sailors who knew far-flung continents better than their own home ports? Shipping in and out year round, they lacked both time and interest regarding the landlocked scandals of the day.

They seemed to know little of him as well. Osbourne's being a man of few words was a boon to both him and Lark. Only once had Captain Moodie made reference to the absurdity of being kilted as a crime, then let it rest.

No one seemed aware that he was mourning a wife whose maid and kindred had made Lark the scapegoat, or that his own defense of her was more shocking than his being kilted.

"We shall invite the chosen ladies to dine with us on the morrow." The captain stood, ending the meal, to a murmur of masculine affirmation.

Peevish. Cross. Lark well understood wee Larkin's foul mood. The presence of the former captain of the *Merry Lass* and the laird's marked absence lent to her own loose ends. She paced the tiny square of space in her berth to soothe the baby as much as herself, singing an ancient lullaby as she went. To no avail.

Was his belly turned by all the rolling? Mayhap he was hungry, as he'd spit up his milk.

Abandoning the sling, she held him chest to chest, his head tucked beneath her chin, his warm tears wetting her bodice.

"Blow the wind, blow. Swift and low. Blow the wind o'er the ocean. Breakers rolling to the coastline, bringing ships to harbor, gulls against the morning sunlight, flying off to freedom . . ."

A rap on the door made her pause. The ship's steward thrust open the door, issuing an invitation over Larkin's fretting. "You're invited to the captain's table, eight o'clock tonight. But you'll have to leave the babe behind."

"That I canna do," she replied straight-away. Thus far she'd only given him over to whoever was nearest to use the necessary in the bowsprit, then took him right back again.

"Captain Moodie is disinclined to dine with only officers," the steward said, darkening as if loath to relay her refusal.

"Why am I even asked," she said a bit testily, worn down by Larkin's crying, "being a common criminal?"

Glowering now, the steward fairly shouted, "Captain's orders!" He shut the door with a decisive bang.

Lark resumed her pacing, another mystery now added to Magnus's disappearance and Rory's discovery.

Mrs. Ravenhill seemed to fill the entire berth with her beribboned, flounced attire as much as with her fragrance. Lark recognized its blend at once, drawn to the perfume bottle of cobalt-blue glass in her hand.

Rosemary. Pennyroyal. Marjoram.

"A worthy blend for the captain's table. As for your prim dress, you must instead wear this from my own wardrobe." She held up a gown overlapping one arm. "I promised the captain we would look our best as his guests."

With Larkin lying on his back in the bunk, absorbed in his toes, Lark was free to admire the offering. " 'Tis kind of ye."

"Kind?" Amusement flashed across Mrs. Ravenhill's lightly lined face. "I've been called many things but seldom kind. Shrewd, perhaps. Even canny, as you Scots say. 'Tis our chance to ingratiate ourselves to the captain and his officers, perchance curry a few favors."

The flowery words rolled over Lark, who was now besotted by the lovely dress. Was she so starved for a bit of beauty and elegance she overlooked the implications of this surprising invitation?

"You'll want to wear your hair up, hence the pins. I'll see about paste gems."

"No need. I have a coral necklace," Lark murmured, eyes still on the gown. "How many of us will attend?"

"Ten or so. 'Twill be a bit crowded in the captain's quarters. I've even coerced him into a bit of dancing on deck."

Lark looked to Larkin, who was finally quiet and content. Even the prospect of a little merriment failed to quell her angst over his care. Was she being overly cautious? Afraid someone might harm him? Why did she feel so strongly about a babe not her own?

"Jane Spencer raised half a dozen of her own children before being sent to the poorhouse," Mrs. Ravenhill reassured her. "You needn't spend a second fretting. The captain expects us by eight o'clock."

19

A gaudy dress and gentle air may slightly
touch the heart, but 'tis innocence and
modesty that polishes the dart.

Robert Burns

A disgruntled meow sounded outside his
closed door.

Ignoring it, Magnus tied his stock, securing it with a buckle at the back of his neck,
then shrugged on his borrowed dress coat.
Glad he was that he'd always tended to his
own dressing. Though he missed his manservant, he missed Nonesuch more. There
were no dogs aboard, just cats to keep the
rats at bay. These shipboard felines were
canny creatures, sensitive to weather. The
Bonaventure had a black cat that occupied
the captain's quarters, growing skittish and
nervy before a storm, so the cabin boy said.

He felt nearly as skittish, just as wary of a
storm below deck, if only an emotional one,

as he headed into this third supper at the captain's table. Given a hearty greeting by the officers when he arrived a bit before eight o'clock, he knew the women were not far behind.

Would Lark come? What of the bairn?

Mrs. Ravenhill, the Bond Street thief, entered first, sumptuous in silk brocade. The captain greeted her as the other women followed, none in brown serge but bedecked in their finest, whether begged, borrowed, or mayhap stolen. A clearly reluctant Lark brought up the rear. She hovered in the open doorway, looking like a kelpie she was so slender. And in that unusual gown, a tad peacockish, jarringly unlike the Lark he knew. He swallowed down a strangled protest.

Wheest! Could ye not look so douce?

Clad in dark blue silk, her waist tied with a white sash, she wore a necklace of what looked to be coral about her slender throat. She made a discreet sweep of the room, lingering longest on him, as Mrs. Ravenhill managed introductions. To Magnus's knowledge, no one here knew of his and Lark's tie. He'd not end the ruse now.

Wine was promptly served, a coveted collection from the Canary Islands. He stood beside a bookcase while the ship's surgeon maneuvered to stand by Lark across the room. Having declared his intent the previous evening, Blackburn now moved in.

Blackburn and Lark had been together on deck in the plant cabin, perusing greenery, watering, and scribbling in a journal. Magnus's prayers that the surgeon's interest in her was merely work related resurfaced. But Blackburn's bald-faced statement the previous night removed all doubt.

I first fixed my fancy on Miss MacDougall the moment the rivet was knocked from her irons.

Something rare and disagreeable twisted inside him, settling in his gut like a rancid meal.

"I've been wanting to meet the laird," Mrs. Ravenhill was saying, diverting Magnus's attention from Blackburn. "I've met a few London noblemen but few Scottish ones."

Vivacious, witty, and pretty in a hard sort of way, Mrs. Ravenhill sipped her wine with a gloved hand. She extended the other for him to kiss. He uttered something in Gaelic about it being his pleasure, to which she laughed uncomprehendingly.

"You must become acquainted with Miss MacDougall, as bonny a lass as ever set sail, aye?" she said in her lighthearted way.

Lark moved toward him then, the ship's surgeon not far behind. "The pleasure is mine," Magnus said in English. When she stood across from him, he said in Gaelic, "Pretend ye've ne'er set eyes on me." Being a Lowlander, Blackburn would not understand their Gaelic.

She touched the coral beads at her throat a bit self-consciously and bent her knees in a curtsy. "Pleased to meet ye, sir." In Gaelic, she murmured, "I feared ye'd stayed behind in Glasgow with Osbourne."

He smiled politely, even stiffly, as if they'd simply exchanged pleasantries.

"How delightful!" Mrs. Ravenhill exclaimed at their unintelligible exchange. "Your native language must be quite a boon to you, especially when you chance upon a fellow Scot."

"Indeed," Magnus said. He uttered a few final words in Gaelic, meant for Lark alone. "Play coy, aye? For yer own protection. And as the evening progresses, act as if yer besotted with me though we've just met."

At this, her wide-eyed surprise gave way to an amused, agreeable smile, and she took her place between Magnus and Surgeon Blackburn at table.

Lark placed her serviette in her lap, awaiting the first course as the captain told a story of once being marooned in the Caribbean. Whatever these men of the sea were made of, they were not dull.

Her joy and relief at sitting to Magnus's right cast a golden glow over the evening. Any fretting over Larkin was pushed to the back of her mind, at least briefly.

Play coy . . . act besotted.

So he wanted her to pretend? Why? She dared not ask him outright, not even in Gaelic. Something more was afoot, truly. And that was why Magnus's quiet words came cloaked in a veiled warning. The long glittering table with its polished candelabra and china did seem a lure, all the convict women playing dress-up, herself included. But to what end?

In English, Magnus said offhandedly, "Tell me about yer bairn. I'm unused to seeing ye without him."

She smiled around a sip from her goblet. "Larkin's a wee braw lad who has completely won my heart. He's not above six months, his aunt said, God rest her."

"An orphan but for you," Blackburn said, leaning in.

She looked down at the steam rising from a bowl of consommé set before her. "Sadly so."

"Nay, happily," Magnus returned, his gaze intense in the shimmering haze of candlelight. "Yer a born mother. He seems very content."

" 'Tis a God-made circumstance," she said with conviction. "Mayhap a baby is less trouble than a husband."

Both men chuckled and returned to their supper, allowing her a look at the women interwoven with the officers about the finely laid table.

Something *was* afoot. Something more than dinner and dancing. She hardly needed Magnus to tell her so. Beyond the finely lacquered ceiling of the dining room came the trill of a fiddle on the quarterdeck above.

"D'ye dance, yer lairdship?" She nearly smiled at the silly question when she well knew the answer.

"Betimes," Magnus said. "And ye, Miss MacDougall? I've heard it said Quakers disdain such amusements."

"Some do. But a jig and a reel are hard to resist." She looked to her right. "And ye, Surgeon Blackburn?"

"Depending on the partner, aye. I'll be glad to lead out with you. After the captain and his lady, of course."

The pairing was no surprise. Of all the women on board, Mrs. Ravenhill was first lady of the ship, every bit as much as James Moodie was its captain. In their short acquaintance, Mrs. Ravenhill had not missed a step, polished as the paste gems winking on her flawless bosom. Despite her whispered-about reputation, she was amiable. Interesting. As lovely as she was shrewd. Lark tried to look past the fact that the woman's silks and laces might be stolen or that her renowned brother was a highwayman who'd escaped when she'd been caught.

"Yer gown reminds me of midsummer," Magnus told her between courses, eyes down. "Scotia's bluebells."

"Oh aye," she murmured. Could he hear the lament in her voice? "Where I once lived, there was a wee loch rimmed with them like blue lace."

"Yer a Highland lass then?"

"Nay, the western isles." Fearful of steering too near the truth, she changed course. "Where are ye bound for, sir?"

"The West Indies."

"Not Virginia Colony?"

"Nay." Magnus toyed with his meat, looking as dangerously close to despair as she felt. And then he righted himself, stabbing a bite of beef and chewing resolutely.

She stifled her own dismay, lowering her

eyes with a sweep of her lashes in the surgeon's direction. "And ye, Surgeon Blackburn? Where are ye bound for next?"

"I'm unsure. I may well shun the sea. Try my hand at farming in the colonies."

"Oh? Surely the plant cabin is a fine start." She set down her fork and took a bracing sip of wine. Its sourness nearly made her sputter.

The ship's surgeon leaned in, so close the lace of her upraised sleeve draped across his own coat sleeve. "Are you all right, Miss MacDougall?"

"Not to worry." She smiled. "The fare is bountiful. Delicious. I'm simply unused to such rich food after . . ." She hated to even mention the tolbooth as it stirred so many dark memories.

"I'm glad to hear you're not indisposed. Though I'd be happy to attend you should the need arise . . . no matter the hour."

Lark sensed Magnus's resistance at the surgeon's words. She knew him too well to miss such. It lay about him like a winter cloak, cold and forbidding. Could Surgeon Blackburn sense it too?

Magnus forked a last bite of beef, as aggravated by Lark as the lieutenant. Did she have to be so charming? So attentive?

Surgeon Blackburn was thoroughly besotted. Did she not see how he kept looking at her? He was ignoring the woman to his right, who seemed not to mind, absorbed as she was in the clutches of another fawning officer. As for the attentive doctor, his Lowland Scots aggravated like a burr.

By meal's end, the captain had consumed such a quantity of spirits Magnus doubted he could stand without listing, much less climb the ladder to the quarterdeck, where music now wafted on a warm southwest wind.

But up they all went.

Newly bereaved widowers did not dance, did they?

Aye, they did, if only to prevent any ill-trickit doings on board. Yet Surgeon Blackburn soon claimed Lark for a reel while Magnus was left to look on, standing with the two fiddlers on the small platform in front of the foremast, where the halyard and ropes were secured.

The open sea was so vast. His gaze swept skyward where stars winked like angelic candles overhead, breaking up the blackness, moonlight falling to the deck's sand-scattered surface.

Did the surgeon have to be so able a

dancer? So attentive? Magnus was cast back to the tenants' ball when Lark had danced in Isla's stead, her surefootedness and grace winning admiring glances both then and now. Once he'd been her laird but no longer. His responsibility for her, his protective reach, had ended. Though indentured, she was perhaps freer than she'd ever been, now well beyond his and Kerrera's keeping.

He looked to his shoe buckles, grappling with their new standing. What if she was fond of Blackburn? She could do worse. Yet a lonesome life in some coastal town with a husband at sea who was free to take a female mate whenever he pleased . . . Lark deserved better. For all they knew, Blackburn already had a wife. But what sort of future awaited her with Larkin? She was now tied to the bairn in inexplicable ways. How would she fulfill her indenture chasing after a lad not her own?

"Are ye not going to dance?" Scarlet-cheeked, Lark stood to his right, her Gaelic coming in winded, indignant bursts as a jig was stepped.

He fisted his hands behind his back. "In truth, I have no heart for dancing."

"How can I act the besotted miss if ye willna play along?" Her high spirits fell away. "Yer in mourning. Missing Kerrera.

As I am."

"Dinna look so aflocht. We've only just met."

She sighed and forced a smile at the same time, eyes on the circling dancers. "Is it true what ye said? About the West Indies?"

"I'm now a prisoner of the Crown, ye ken. Not even Osbourne could change that. I go where I'm told, at least two years hence."

"But my laird ye'll always be," she answered softly but firmly. "No matter where we are, nor how much time passes. Nor what the Crown says."

His voice gentled. "And ye'll always be my Lark."

Her poignant expression told him she'd heard his Gaelic despite the rousing music, despite her not looking at him. He said no more, facing into the wind as the night wore on and she partnered with every officer present, including the captain.

Should he warn her? Tell her the officers' intent?

Indecision warred inside him. He was not used to asking questions but providing answers. And though he knew Lark, he did not know where her heart would lead her in the face of their ever-shifting circumstances.

20

The devil's boots don't creak.

Scottish proverb

When half a dozen women spilled onto the quarterdeck from the officers' quarters instead of through the usual hatch at daybreak, Lark's suspicions were confirmed. She'd come the usual way, the warm weight of Larkin in his sling testing her balance as the ship heaved, emerging into a world of mist where white-capped waves sprayed salty water at every turn. Little stayed dry on such a day.

She breakfasted, feeding Larkin first. Milk drunk he was, gulping the fresh offering from a bottle fashioned from a cow's horn with an occasional appreciative burp.

"And how's yer wee charge this morn?" asked the ship's carpenter with a gap-toothed grin.

"Bonny and bright-eyed," she answered,

as proud as a new mother. Never had there been eyes so hugely blue or a grin so wide and heart-stopping. Her smile slipped as she took in Larkin's every roll and dimple. His fair skin was splotched pink from the glare of sun on water, despite his linen bonnet with its short brim.

"I've made a play-pretty for 'im," the aged man said, dangling a shell rattle from a leather loop with a piece of teething coral attached. Larkin lunged for it as the sailor added, "It ain't gold nor silver, but it'll do. Fitted with a whistle too."

Though it would take time for the babe to discover the whistle, the orange coral end had already found his open mouth with its sole tiny tooth.

"Gnawin' on it like a baby beaver, he is. 'Tis a hard bit o' coral that won't break. I'll make a toy soldier next, mayhap a pony." He went away whistling to Lark's high praise and Larkin's chewing.

She kissed the babe's damp brow, thankful, wishing they could sit in the shade of a sail to escape the strengthening sun. She left the yawning women behind as she walked to the fenced quarterdeck and plant cabin. Surgeon Blackburn stood, back to her, reminding her of their reel last night.

She'd excused herself from the after-supper frolic shortly after Magnus did, ready to return to Larkin. She found him sleeping, his caretaker dozing too.

Would a second summons to dine be forthcoming? Their shipboard supper remained a riddle, though her fellow convicts held a clue — the select few who had emerged from the officers' quarters, Mrs. Ravenhill leading. Was this what Surgeon Blackburn expected of her? A night in his hammock? Heat burned her face and neck like a saltwater rash when he swung round to face her.

"Miss MacDougall." His politeness was intact despite any disappointment over the previous eve.

"Good morning, sir. A fair day, aye?"

"Indeed." He looked beyond the green square of plants to the purling blue sea. "Cat's paws."

No cat was in sight. She studied the water, puzzling out his meaning.

"Light, variable winds on calm waters, producing small waves resembling —"

"Cat's paws," she finished. "The waves do look like them."

"The sea has a language all its own." He came closer, examining the rattle Larkin fisted. "Orange coral. Not quite so comely as the beads you wore last night at supper."

"Larkin doesna seem to mind."

He chuckled, surprising her by lifting the babe from his sling so that the fabric lay limp about her. "He's becoming something of a barnacle, attached so."

It was her turn to smile. In the surgeon's strong arms, Larkin stiffened before bringing the rattle down on the man's broad chest with a musical clatter of shells. "You're a Highland Scot, surely, striking a Lowlander so." His gaze met Lark's. "Try tending the plants unencumbered for one morn, at least."

Not wasting time, she turned away and began to do just that. Blackburn was not far behind, no doubt for Larkin's sake.

The tea trees seemed slightly wilted, being wind-whipped, while the parsley and mint were flourishing. An ominous brown edged the rosemary while the marigolds were a colorful riot. She stroked the lamb's ears, the velvety leaves soft as Larkin's skin. The bees buzzed contentedly, one of the most reassuring sounds she knew.

Casting a glance over her shoulder, she felt a tendril of pleasure. The babe, clad in his white bonnet and gown, looked like spilled milk against the surgeon's dark blue uniform. Besotted with his rattle, Larkin chewed fiercely, eyes fixed on Lark nevertheless.

"Surgeon Blackburn, sir. Yer needed in the infirmary. A jack is down with a fever."

Handing Larkin over, he disappeared below deck. Lark resumed her work, if it could be called that. Other than watering and watching, staking and pruning, what more could be done? 'Twas a chancy endeavor and not all the plants would survive. And if there came a gale . . .

The sails snapped as the wind stiffened. She looked aloft to where she'd spied Rory MacPherson. In sailor's trews and cap and even pigtailed, he in no way resembled the captain of the *Merry Lass.* But he was somewhere on this great ship, though their chance of doing more than exchanging a fleeting glance was slim.

The laird was nowhere on deck that she could see. But with so large a crew and so many nooks and crannies, he might be right beneath her very nose.

The morning glare was fierce, and she blinked into its brightness. Day three at sea. Why did it seem weeks already? 'Twould be September when they made landfall, Lord willing. Already Scotland seemed faded, a tattered dream. No longer could she recall the exact hue of the bluebell-rimmed loch she'd mentioned to Magnus, nor the musky smell of the peat fire or the hearty taste of oatcakes. Too many new sights and sounds had elbowed their way in, lapping over her heartfelt memories like cat's-paw waves, erasing what had come before.

Here there was just wind and wood, salt spray and sail. Larkin was her world, and she his. With her hands and heart full, her sorrow was halved. For now.

Lark returned to the captain's table a second time. And a third. Magnus was always there, seated to one side of her at supper since the arrangement did not alter. Surgeon Blackburn was on her right.

It slowly dawned on her that she was now one of the select few while the rest of the convict women were left on the orlop deck, in the hold at night and picking oakum by day. In close quarters, it didn't take her long to sense their distress.

"We must help them," she told Surgeon Blackburn. "Make a salve."

His brow arched. "What have you in mind?"

"Dried comfrey. Yarrow and rosemary. Oil."

"Come down to my makeshift apothecary. I believe I have what's required." He shrugged. "But does it truly matter when they must continue oakum picking?"

She had no answer. If the women continued their brutal task, their hands would not heal, nor even scar. "Might ye speak with the captain? Have them do something else, at least for a time?"

Silent, he studied her in the sun's harsh light. The squint lines about his eyes were pronounced, his eyes intense. At night, her own eyes burned from the water's glare, but it seemed of no consequence compared to torn and bleeding hands.

They went below. Though his cabin was not as grand as the captain's, hers was a mouse hole in comparison. The surgeon's included not only a sleeping berth where his hammock was suspended but a second chamber lined with shelves containing jar after jar of herbs and simples, many that she recognized. A seaworthy apothecary.

The fragrance alone made her close her eyes and take a deep, delighted breath when his back was turned, yet he clearly sensed her mood straightaway.

"This place makes you smile. Why is that?"

She traced the design on a green glass bottle. " 'Tis the stillroom's fragrance."

"Your castle stillroom."

Her smile faded. Any thought of the stillroom was now tainted. Gone was that joyous feeling, that sense of place, of belonging. Her banishment had seen to that.

"I apologize." He cleared his throat. "I shouldn't have mentioned it. Something happened there, I take it, that explains why you are here."

She nodded, shifting a sleeping Larkin to ease the knot of the sling digging into her shoulder. " 'Twas unexpected, terrible —"

"Think no more of it. Nothing matters but here and now." Reaching out, he stilled the words on her lips, his fingers cool and smelling of camphor. "Let the past go, Lark."

He was so near. Never had he called her by her given name. She didn't even know his, other than Blackburn. Yet she knew his particular scent, that pleasurable melding of soap and sandalwood. In the closed space of his quarters it was like a lure. She returned her attention to the assortment of jars and vials and bottles, cleverly arranged behind a shelf made secure in stormy seas. She leaned past him, reaching for what she thought was comfrey, only to find it was foxglove instead, she was so aflocht.

"I could talk to the captain. Ask a reprieve for the women." He reached for a mortar and pestle and set it on a table. "No doubt his response will be that the ship must be watertight and the work continue. Still, I will ask . . . for you."

The last two words were said with such intent there was no mistaking the underlying meaning. He wanted something in return. From her.

"Thank ye, sir," she murmured.

"Alick, if you will."

Alick . . . Blackburn. Knowing it made him seem less a stranger, not simply a surgeon.

He ground the herbs she'd selected with a practiced ease. "I've been wanting to consult you about a particularly stubborn fever suffered by the master's mate."

She kept perusing jars for something more that might benefit the salve, listening as he described the mate's ailment.

"Of course, it could be the ague, a malarial fever that's rampant in certain southern ports, particularly British America." At her wince, he added, "Like as not, 'tis a simple shipboard fever."

She shared what remedies she knew, adding, "Rest and plenty to drink — and I dinna mean spirits. Fresh water will do."

He nodded, brow creased in concentration. "Our water stores will soon turn brackish and we'll all be drinking bumboo."

"Bumboo?"

"Rum water mixed with sugar and a bit of nutmeg."

"Sounds little better than brackish." She reached for a jar of something she couldn't place, uncorked the lid, and sniffed. "As for the master's mate, is he unable to perform his duties?"

"Aye, though he's hardly missed. Magnus MacLeish is more than capable of accomplishing anything the captain gives him. Moodie is in no hurry to lift the quarantine, I assure you."

Though she smiled at his wry humor, she was cast back to the castle with a pang. Magnus had ever been a hand with accounts and ledgers. In his study, he seemed the king of Kerrera, at least in her eyes.

"You seem fond of MacLeish." He passed her the mortar and pestle. "Rather, he seems fond of you."

She paused, added another ingredient, and ground the herbs with renewed vigor. "No more than a laird can be with a simple Scots lass."

"The MacDougalls have rich roots. Noble roots, aye?"

"Once upon a time, mayhap. But I am proof of how far they have fallen," she replied with little emotion. "What of the

Lowlander Blackburn?"

"We've no Brooch of Lorn to boast about."

She shrugged off her melancholy. It came at odd times, when she least expected it. 'Twas particularly thick now with the sights and scents of her former life swirling around her here in this makeshift apothecary. "Some sort of binding oil is needed next."

"Beeswax pastilles?" Sitting on his haunches, he began rummaging beneath the table. The pastilles appeared and she mixed them with the crushed herbs.

Cocooned in his sling, Larkin began mewling like a kitten, a reminder he'd soon need feeding. She worked quickly, praying the salve would be a comfort to the convict women, body and soul.

"We must try it first," he said once she was done mixing. "Give me your hand."

She offered him her left, her right hand busy patting Larkin's backside. Into her palm the ship's surgeon placed a dab of salve, massaging it in slow circles. She nearly sighed as he worked his way to her fingers and the sunburnt skin on the back of her hand, his touch sure yet gentle as befitting a physic. After a fussy night with Larkin, she was nearly lulled to sleep.

Her lashes came down and her eyes

closed. The sore-handed women would be helped.

At the brush of Blackburn's lips on her extended fingers, her eyes flew open.

He let go slowly, his voice as dulcet as his touch. "A lady's hands, aye?"

Hardly. She had no illusions about that, sun-speckled and callused as she was. Avoiding his eyes, she shunned his words, his nearness. Her gaze cut to the open door leading to his sleeping quarters. The dangling hammock adorned with a land-worthy coverlet. Full bookcases. A fetching painting of a lighthouse. Her comfort-starved heart craved a closer look.

And then Larkin howled, breaking the spell.

"I must go." She took a step back.

Blackburn was rubbing some of the salve into his own hands now, releasing another fragrant wave that marked this defining moment. Something had changed between them. Some thawing. Some door cracked open, some invitation issued. Or was she woolgathering?

"Leave the salve to set here where it's cooler till you're ready to dispense it."

"Thank ye." Turning on her heel, she hurriedly left the cabin as Larkin's cries reached fever pitch.

21

He threatens many that hath injured one.

Ben Jonson

"So yer aboard. I could hardly believe my eyes when I first saw Lark and now ye."

Facing Rory MacPherson across a mountainous coil of rope, Magnus nodded, struck by the odd irony of it all. Not long ago he'd confronted the captain of the *Merry Lass* in the Thistle, warning him against involving Lark in any free trading, and yet 'twas through his own and Isla's tangled circumstance that brought Lark low. A humbling moment, to be sure. He nearly squirmed as it came clear.

The former captain was looking at him as though fully realizing this too, his hardened expression adding another layer to Magnus's angst.

"Three unfortunate souls we are," Magnus finally said. "Though Providence might say otherwise, working all things together for our good, aye?"

"I've long stopped believing in Providence," MacPherson spat back, reseating his hat after raking a hand through his windblown hair. "More the devil."

"Yer indentured to Richard Osbourne now?"

"Osbourne and Virginia Colony, aye, though I'll make my way soon as I can to the Scots strongholds in North Carolina. And ye?"

"The West Indies."

MacPherson's stubbled jaw seemed to clench. "I'm most concerned about Lark, but I canna speak with her, me confined to the forecastle and her keeping to the quarterdeck like some officer's mistress."

"She's no man's mistress," Magnus said.

" 'Tis clear the Lowlander Blackburn fancies her."

This Magnus couldn't deny. "Their work brings them together."

"Watching o'er the plants and the like? Such a hapless endeavor. What's to happen come a gale?"

What indeed. Every pot would be moved below deck, likely. Magnus crossed his arms. "Yer at home here at least, be it fair or foul."

MacPherson gave a heave of his shoulders, looking past Magnus. A look over his own shoulder centered on Lark, at work in the plant cabin once again. She seemed a bit bow-shouldered of late, as if the weight of the babe was too much for her, thin as she'd become.

"The bairn will ne'er see landfall," MacPherson muttered.

Magnus almost scoffed. He'd never seen so robust an infant. Despite the babe's somewhat burdensome beginnings, he was thriving. Content. That Lark doted on him was plain to see.

"And I've heard the master's mate is some better, but the first lieutenant is nigh dead of the ague."

True enough. Surgeon Blackburn bemoaned that no remedy helped him. He wasted away in the sick bay while Magnus quietly assumed his duties too.

"No time to blether." With that, MacPherson snorted and strode away.

Magnus stepped onto the raised quarterdeck. For once, Lark was alone in the plant cabin. Other than sitting beside each other at the captain's table, they rarely crossed paths. While the other officers had made mates of the women invited to dine and dance by the second evening, there had been no such pairing for Lark and Black-burn.

His prayers for her, no more than a breath betimes, seemed unceasing. And as he breathed those prayers, he'd decided to continue playing the besotted suitor, at least in Blackburn's presence, matching the surgeon look for look, word for word. Clearly lovelorn, the Lowlander had begun to send a few barbed glances his way.

To her credit, Lark held maddeningly aloof yet was thoroughly charming.

How much longer would they play this game before Blackburn tired of it and chose another? Wearied of waiting, Magnus longed for the surgeon's hopes to have an end. Granted, the fairest of the women were taken, appearing for supper around the captain's table bedecked with some new bauble or trinket in return for their keep, while Lark continued to wear the colorful necklace of coral beads.

A gift from whom? Not Blackburn, surely. Magnus had a gift of his own for Larkin. In one hand was the miniature box bed he'd asked the ship's carpenter to make, with its cleverly sewn awning from an old sail, its mattress filled with downy goose feathers. No longer could he stand by as Lark grew more stoop-shouldered while trying to manage the task Osbourne assigned her, tailor made as it was. But Magnus feared something more weighted her than the babe, some grief unspoken that extended beyond her loss of kin and country.

She startled slightly when she saw him, and he heard the babe's fretting. "What have ye there?" Her face brightened. "Something for wee Larkin?"

"Who else could fit in so small a space?"

The tiny bed was a well-constructed marvel, each end crowned with a wooden finial fashioned into a removable toy. A thistle. A unicorn. A soldier and eagle.

Magnus positioned the bed in a patch of shade out of harm's way, reached for Larkin, and extricated him from the sling, a great many sailors looking on aloft. Kneeling, Magnus sat him square in the middle of the box bed while a smiling Lark dug the coral rattle from her pocket. Her quiet delight was Magnus's own. He'd not seen her so pleased since the night of the tenants' ball when they'd feasted and danced to their hearts' content.

As for Larkin, he blinked and looked down, surveying his new territory with surprised interest. The small awning that shaded him was well beyond his reach, but he wasted no time in wresting the toy unicorn from its perch and gumming it gustily.

"Fit for a prince," Lark said, stooping so that her linen skirts swirled around her. She lay the coral rattle down beside Larkin, then smoothed a curl of red atop his head. She must have forgotten his cap below.

Having little or no experience with infants, Magnus studied the bairn like the extraordinary specimen he was. "Does he eat much?"

"A great quantity of milk. But lately that seems not to fill him up, so I share my porridge and raisins."

"Try the hardtack."

"The ship's biscuits? I doubt even a babe would take to that."

"He'll soon grow into the hammock Archie is fashioning to hang from a crossbeam."

"The ship's carpenter? A wee hammock?"

"Best keep that a secret. No cause to spoil an auld man's surprise."

The sun beat down on a remarkably calm sea, warming their backs and Larkin's canvas awning. For once he did not reach for Lark but seemed content with his new arrangement.

"What have we here?" Surgeon Blackburn was behind them, eyes on the miniature box bed.

Magnus stood to his full height while Lark began removing Larkin's sling from around her neck.

"The ship's carpenter is quite clever," Magnus replied. "And Miss MacDougall's back is spared."

"Indeed."

Lark got to her feet, gaze swinging from the babe to Blackburn, whose expression seemed unusually grave.

He rubbed his jaw. "I regret to tell you that the master's mate is dead of a fever. Captain Moodie asks that the laird perform the burial at sea."

"Of course," Magnus replied without hesitation while Lark murmured condolences. Hadn't the poor man been on the mend?

"Once the women have finished sewing him into sailcloth, we'll have the service," Blackburn told them before walking away.

How strange that even the weather shifted, the sky now clad in somber shades of gray. A black pennant was flown on the main mast and the sails adjusted so that the ship was motionless for a time. Everyone to a man stood on deck. Even Larkin, back in his sling, stayed quiet as Magnus read from the Psalms.

"Which made heaven, and earth, the sea, and all that therein is: which keepeth truth for ever."

A prayer was said, and the body, stitched into sailcloth, was sent into the sea.

Lark shivered more from the surrounding pall of melancholy than the weather. Sailors were notoriously superstitious. Even Surgeon Blackburn seemed agitated. She could only guess the gist of the crew's thoughts. Would that it had been one of the convicts and not so important a personage as the master's mate.

Immediately the captain called for a meeting with Magnus. Watching, she prayed rather than stewed as the men went below. Slowly the great ship resumed its routine — Rory aloft, Lark tending to the plant cabin, the "unchosen few," as they were called derisively, back to their tasks. The most unfortunate resumed picking oakum on the forecastle, their task no easier despite the salve that would only be of benefit if they were allowed a rest. But Surgeon Blackburn's request on Lark's behalf had fallen on deaf ears.

Unable to stand the women's predicament any longer, Lark finished watering the plants, placed Larkin in his box bed close at hand, and joined them. A sailor who'd neglected his watch was among them, spared the cat-o'-nine-tails but sentenced to this. His callused hands were soon bleeding.

The women stared listlessly as Lark took a seat on a crate without a word and picked up some frayed rope. 'Twas old. Stiff. Soiled with grease and rust. She began picking at it with her fingernails, trying to separate the strands. The fibers bit into her skin, burning and itching after a mere quarter of an hour.

"Yer one of the chosen few," the woman to her right said through blackened teeth. "Why stoop so low?"

"If I canna help ye with the salve, I shall try to lighten the load this way," Lark replied, already wanting to abandon it.

" 'Tis no' just my bloody fingers," another said, holding up her red-stained hands for all to see. " 'Tis the ague settlin' in and swellin' me joints, makin' them stiff as a ship's timbers."

The sailor glowered at his wad of picked rope. "I'd as soon suffer a whipping."

Larkin cooed beneath his awning, waving his toy unicorn about. Lark focused on the endearing sound, not her reddened fingers, determined to pick her share of the tarred rope.

The sun shifted, drenching them in yellow

heat. Beads of sweat stood out on her brow, trickled down her neck, and stained her bodice. She kept to her task, only looking up when the sun hid behind a cloud. Nay, a man.

Surgeon Blackburn stood over her, blocking the melting warmth. "You're needed on the quarterdeck, Miss MacDougall." Though his voice stayed smooth, she sensed his surprise, his consternation, at finding her thus employed.

She finished picking apart the piece she was working on before getting to her feet then fetching Larkin from the box bed. Balancing the babe on one hip, she followed Blackburn across the smooth deck and up the steps to the plant cabin.

He turned and faced her beneath the main mast, well away from the officer of the watch. "Lark . . . your hands."

She looked down. Already they were beginning to crack and bleed.

"Why would you do such a thing?"

She nearly sighed. "Have ye not seen someone suffer and want to relieve it? Is it not in the heart of a physic — a surgeon — to do just that?"

"Aye, 'tis the nature of my calling — and yours. But it grieves me to see you doing so when there is no reason for it."

"There is a call, beyond our work. 'And as ye would that men should do to you, do ye also to them likewise.' "

"Your fellow oakum pickers have little appreciation of it."

"That, too, is no matter. 'Whatsoever ye do, do it heartily, as to the Lord, and not unto men.' "

He rubbed his jaw. "And will you continue to preach to me instead of having an honest conversation?"

"Scripture is nothing if not honest. 'Tis truth."

He crossed his arms. "As a vicar's son, I was raised on it. And like youth, I've left it all behind." He regarded Larkin with studied intent, the disgust she'd sensed thrusting to the surface. "No doubt you have a ready Scripture for your charge, who is said to be no more than the son of a common harlot."

Stung, she smoothed Larkin's flame of hair where it tufted on top. "That he may be, through no fault of his own. 'Pure religion and undefiled before God and the Father is this, to visit the fatherless and widows in their affliction, and to keep himself unspotted from the world.' "

They regarded each other in a sort of deadlocked exasperation. Why did she sense this tiny tempest was about more than oakum and Larkin? Frustration and longing roiled beneath Blackburn's heated words much like the sea roiled against the ship's immense frame.

"No doubt your Scripture-spouting laird agrees with you." The words were tinted a jealous green. "Somehow he always manages to bend things in his favor, including you."

She dropped her gaze to Larkin gnawing on his toy, his chin shiny with drool. "Please, Alick." If he found her disagreeable, might he make trouble for Magnus? Even separate her from the babe? "I dinna mean to rile ye. Ye are my friend and fellow physic, are ye not?"

"I would be more, Lark . . ." He moved nearer, his voice so low it was nearly lost beneath the rush of wind and sea. "If you were willing."

Nay. Double nay. Prickles of heat climbed to her face. She tucked a few wayward wisps into her Quaker cap only to have them pull free again. Larkin dropped his toy and she was only too glad to retrieve it. By the time she'd straightened, Blackburn had moved away, disappearing through the hatch leading to his quarters. But the ill feeling remained.

22

Honor's a good brooch to wear in a man's hat at all times.

Ben Jonson

Dinner round the captain's table was becoming . . . tedious. A gauntlet of innuendo and romantic tension that bordered on bawdy. Magnus stayed quiet unless questioned, acutely aware of both Lark and the surgeon. Sparse with her smiles, she kept her eyes down demurely, taking tiny bites and avoiding a second glass of spirits. Tonight her mood seemed pensive, even reflective, candlelight flickering over her face and catching every emotion.

They'd been at sea a fortnight. Six weeks remained of their journey — if they stayed on course and escaped any storms, enemy warships, or privateers.

"Hurricane season is upon us," Captain Moodie said, eyes on the cabin boy replenishing his glass. The captain lifted his goblet with the slight tremor of his hand that Magnus was becoming familiar with.

"August and September are dismal seasons at sea," Mrs. Ravenhill lamented. "I pray we are soon safely in port."

"We'll be in several ports after Virginia." Moodie sent a look in Magnus's direction. "Osbourne's Jamaican plantation is truly a sight to behold. Sugarcane as far as the eye can see, literally from one end of the island to the other. Rum and molasses abound though sugar is currently king."

"Glad I am of it," another woman said. "We simply must have sugar to sweeten our tea and cake."

"Sugar has surpassed grain as the most valuable European import," the second mate remarked. "More Africans are needed, which is why more sailors are captaining Guineamen in future."

"Guineamen?" Lark asked.

"Indeed. The Guineamen are among the handsomest ships, modeled after the frigates and rather more ornamented."

"But not the slave cargo. That comes with no fine trappings." Magnus stood, looking down at Lark. "Would ye care to take a turn with me on deck, Miss MacDougall? Yer quite pale."

She pushed away from the table. "Some fresh air will do me good." The fine fabric of her borrowed dress made a little rustle as she thanked the captain for his hospitality and moved toward the door ahead of Magnus.

Once on deck, Lark took a long breath, clearing her senses of spirits and smoke. Her sorest hand clutched the ship's rail while the other rested on her stomach as the wind rolled over and around her, stirring her skirts and unraveling her carefully pinned hair.

Beside her, Magnus rested his hands on the railing, staring out at the sea like she'd seen him do so many times on Kerrera's ragged shore. Moonlight turned him just as craggy, calling out every line, few though there were in the silvery light. Bereft of all merriment, he looked ages old. After all he'd lost, would he ever smile again? It tugged hard at her, his somberness. They were hurtling toward the unknown without a clue as to it being a bane or a blessing. Soon they'd be separated, mayhap for good.

Her eyes smarted. Her arms felt empty without Larkin. The old woman, Jane, was keeping him again. It seemed to please her to be trusted with Lark's treasure. In Lark's pocket was a bun and sweetmeat from the captain's table, a small way of thanking her.

Swallowing, near tears for a tangle of reasons, she ironed out the wrinkles in her voice. " 'Twas bold of ye to leave the captain's table like ye did."

"And take ye with me, ye mean." He turned and leaned his back against the rail, arms crossed. "I've just made an enemy of Blackburn, no doubt."

Lord, let there be no trouble between them.

"He's not a bad man," she said quietly.

"Nay. Skilled. Smitten. And very married."

Her stomach dropped. "What?"

"To a Bristol lass. He's also a father to half a dozen, so the captain tells me, not all of them at home." He looked up at the crow's nest. "I'm sorry to bring such sore news, especially if yer fond of him."

Fond? "I counted him a fellow healer. No more." Now Surgeon Blackburn seemed a deceitful stranger. She felt a trifle betrayed yet relieved all the same. "I'm weary of the captain's table. All the crass talk, the spirits and the smoke . . ."

"We could eat here, on deck. Most do, barring foul weather. Ye, me, and Larkin."

"Let's," she said softly, already picturing it. A picnic, like of old, on some sunny spot of ground when all was in flower. "I've almost forgotten what month it is. Here, on the sea, everything is the same. There are no seasons."

" 'Tis almost time for the blooming haeddre."

"Once I found some white heather when I rowed to Lismore. It covered a cove like snow, then turned a coppery gold on the glens and hills."

"Ye ken what's said about it? 'Tis lucky, white heather."

"Mayhap I should have picked some, but I thought it too lovely. Too sacred. If I'd done so, mayhap we'd be spared of all this."

"Nay, Lark." His tone was one she knew too well. No superstitious talk. No looking back.

"I wonder if heather grows in America."

"There's some in yer plant cabin, aye?"

"Two pots." She nearly sighed. "Neither are blooming."

"Homesick for native soil, like us."

"So yer homesick too?" She searched his face for some sign of it.

"I'll not lie. Some things I miss. Others, nay."

What *didn't* he miss? She could think of nothing but the tax men, the Philistines, the wrenching poverty and want across the island in late winter. "I worry about Granny. If I'll ever see her again."

He ran a hand across the railing. "Even the chest of specie I gave her canna replace yer company nor grant her another three years till yer free."

A chest of coin? So he'd done what he could. Granny would not starve. But who would care for Granny when she grew ill and bed bound?

As if sensing her angst, he said quietly, eyes on the sea, "Scripture speaks to every situation we find ourselves in. Here's a verse to cling to, one to keep ye afloat when worry swamps ye: 'And even to your old age I am he; and even to hoar hairs will I carry you: I have made, and I will bear; even I will carry, and will deliver you.'"

She nodded. Only lately had she begun to measure every circumstance in the light of Scripture. It helped anchor her, helped hedge out the rootlessness she felt so keenly. "Listening to ye I feel I'm back in kirk."

"Mayhap in the new world I'll become a preacher." He smiled, lifting the gloom. "A man can be what he wants there, aye?"

She studied him, trying to grasp all that he was or had been. Laird. Jacobite. Barrister. Indenture. 'Twas too much for her head and heart to hold.

"I'm missing Larkin," she said suddenly, hoping he didn't mind her abruptness or her honesty. Betimes the babe solaced her like nothing else could. Even their cramped berth seemed a haven of sorts, away from the prying eyes and ears of the ship.

Taking her elbow, Magnus walked her to the hatch. She took a last look about, spying the shadowed form of who she thought was Rory before going below to the tween deck and her quarters.

Her wee man was waiting for her, as wide-eyed and smiling as if it was morn. He gave a little shriek from his bunk as the door shut, rousing a sleeping Jane in the chair beside him. She quickly made off to the forecastle with her treats.

Dropping to one knee, Lark knelt at eye level to her charge, nose pressed to his. His throaty chuckle melted her, as did his soft hands that fingered her face. She kissed his dimpled cheek and chin, then drew a surprise from her pocket. She held it within easy reach, smiling as he took the stick of black treacle. He turned it over in his plump hands.

" 'Tis hardened molasses," she told him, grateful to the cabin boy for the offering.

Larkin mouthed it, expression shifting from curiosity to delight. She rested her head upon the linen bedding beside him. His outstretched legs were tangled in his nightshirt, bare feet peeking out, his milky, sugary scent a solace.

Her thoughts spun to the married surgeon before circling back to Kerrera and Magnus, then veering yet again to the floating bees and heather in pots that refused to flower.

Granny. The castle stillroom. Isla's passing. The past filled her thoughts to the brim. Was there a Scripture for that? For bittersweet memories? Or only a verse for the future?

Take no thought for the morrow.

23

The soul becomes dyed with the colour of its thoughts.

Marcus Aurelius

It was laundry day on deck, the few hours save the Sabbath that the convict women were spared picking oakum. Fires smoked across the waist of the ship, overriding the stench of the ballast — countless boiling kettles overseen by all but Mrs. Ravenhill, who had other more refined tasks like mending and patching officers' clothes.

By noon the deck bore a slippery, soapy sheen, the rails and rigging adorned with drying garments. Lark washed Larkin's clouts in salt water while he napped in his box bed in the shade. Glad she was he'd not be walking till they landed. Would Osbourne's plantation be fit for a baby? Would Larkin be counted an indenture same as she?

She went to the quarterdeck to judge the state of the bees, dismayed to find a few already dead or dying. Some flew about as if dazed, a worrisome sign. A dozen or so flowering pots from the plant cabin had been cloistered around the straw skeps. Was that even necessary? One skep seemed almost idle, another furiously active. Though they'd surely perish by too much handling and mismanagement, she wondered if they might be better below deck.

She replenished their water, unsure if doing so mattered, before returning to a sleeping Larkin and the plants. Surgeon Blackburn was there, writing in his journal. She'd not seen him since leaving the captain's table abruptly with the laird the night before.

"Good day, Miss MacDougall."

"Good day, sir."

Avoiding his gaze, she checked on Larkin again and found him sweating beneath his awning, so she removed his cap. He dreamed on, his damp hair a riot of ginger wisps in the heat.

"Feels like the merciless Virginia sun," he remarked, looking decidedly overwarm in his uniform.

She'd pushed back her own sleeves, her Quaker cap doing little to shield sunburn.

The sea was blue glass, the sails mostly idle, little wind to cool them. Would they soon encounter the doldrums so hated by sailors, their ship becalmed for days, even weeks?

She felt Blackburn's eyes on her, following her as she moved among the plants. A few needling words begged saying.

Tell me, sir, about yer wife and bairns.

Biting her tongue, she maneuvered around him, watering, pruning, even praying.

He looked up from his scribbling. "One of the tea trees is listless."

"So I see," she replied. And not only the tea tree. One too many plants bore curled or limp leaves and brown edges. Some seemed nearly scorched on deck after the cooler Scottish climate. The sweet gale was long past hope, so she tossed the deadened stalks overboard, saving the precious pot and dirt. Amid all the water, her whole being hungered for solid ground, much like these long-suffering plants.

"There's a storm coming."

She ceased watering, eyes on the flat sea.

"Ring around the sun, rain before day is done."

"Ring around the moon, rain before noon." She well knew a halo around the moon bespoke a storm. "Moonbroch."

"Aye." His perennially serious expression

of late grew pained. "We'll be in the teeth of a gale by dusk."

Lark looked up and spied the sun's strange ring. A shiver shot through her. No sooner had she finished her morning round of watering and tending than the wind began to pick up, blowing her skirts sideways.

The afternoon wore on, the wind keener, and the sailors all around her grew more watchful, even wary.

"Trim the sails!" The boatswain gave the order and several sailors began furling the canvas, Rory among them, one hundred feet high in the rigging.

"Take the plants below." At Blackburn's stern order, several seamen obeyed with alarming haste, removing the pots around her and hauling them out of sight to a more secure location.

What of Osbourne's precious bees? These were removed with more care, even hardened seamen chary of being stung. She let go a breath of relief.

In rough seas, if the water sloshed into the ship, the straw skeps would fall to pieces with no clooming or waterproofing — not even a hackle, the humblest of straw roofs. Below they might survive.

Mrs. Ravenhill appeared, helping the women gather the partially dried laundry.

Lark went to Larkin, who was awake now as if stirred by the activity all around them. He reached for her, expression pensive as a pelting rain began to slash sideways, borne on the surly wind.

Magnus and the captain were at the stern. Magnus's very presence bolstered her, yet it couldn't allay her rising queasiness. Reared on Kerrera, she knew the sea's many moods and she'd learned to respect them, safely ashore with her stomach settled.

But here in the midst of so much angry water . . .

She'd seen storms break a ship apart, dashing it to pieces on Kerrera's coast while she stood by helplessly from her croft's rain-spattered window. Many a ship stayed afloat but were caught in the deep trough between waves, the hulls slammed mercilessly by walls of water till the storm's end.

Mrs. Ravenhill touched her arm. "Being London reared, I know little of the sea." Her cultured voice belied her convict status. "You're an islander, born and bred to the coast. What does this storm mean?"

Shifting Larkin to her other hip, Lark weighed her answer. The bald truth? "Best go below to yer hammock. Keep to the stern where there's less rolling." This she knew from Rory and the *Merry Lass.* "Mayhap the captain's quarters."

"With a bucket, I fear." Her fair skin, mottled by smallpox scars and the sun, paled even as Lark's own stomach somersaulted.

Lark fixed her gaze on the waves, no longer blue but an unpolished pewter. "Pray."

A thin smile. "Prayer has never been my forte."

"It may well be, come the storm's clearing."

Mrs. Ravenhill moved away as the deck tilted, her feet taking little dance-like steps to keep her upright.

Lark looked to Larkin who gnawed on his fist, his other hand clutching her bodice. She nearly missed Magnus's sudden appearance to her left, Larkin's box bed in hand.

"Go below, Lark. To yer hammock. Pay no mind to the plants and bees lest ye be knocked about." His voice was snatched by the wind, and together they sought the hatch, his hand on her elbow to steady her. "I'll be in the captain's quarters. He feels we'll likely be swept off course."

He opened the door to her cabin and placed the box bed in a corner, tied it down, and moved a candlestick and a few other belongings for safekeeping into a chest. The hammock swung invitingly, and Larkin gave a yawn.

"Remember," Magnus said at the last with a reassuring smile, "that even the wind and the waves obey Him."

Somehow she slept, Larkin wedged into the hammock with her along with the extra blanket Blackburn had given her early on. All around them roared the chaos of the sea, the terrible straining of the ship's timbers. Every creak and groan brought a wince. And then came the rush of moving water, an odd sound as it cascaded down the hatch and companionway, sliding beneath her door to slosh against the cabin wall.

Lord, have mercy.

She shifted, legs cramped from lying too long. Larkin's cheek rounded like an orchard apple against her linen-clad breast, his lashes a sweep of ginger fringe. Perched above the water, hammock swinging but slightly, she eyed the pouch hanging from a peg near the door. In it she'd stored ship's biscuits and molasses sticks, beset with the ongoing quest to feed him. If he awoke hungry, there'd be no goat's milk. For all she knew the livestock would wash overboard. Even the crew secured themselves with ropes on deck to guard against the storm, but the helpless animals . . . She shivered again in the dampness, struck by a darker thought.

What if the ship foundered and they all drowned?

Overcome, she squeezed her eyes shut. Lost at sea. Kerrera's kirkyard held bodies washed ashore, unknown and unmourned. Magnus bore the cost of burial. Here, in the uncharted Atlantic, countless miles from land, they'd simply succumb to the deep. And the deep would deny her many a hope. A husband. A home. Babes of her own. Yet mightn't the depths also be kind? Spare her a strange land with its strange ways and servitude?

Larkin grew blurred. She turned her face to the hammock to catch her tears before they dampened him. The ship rolled anew and she drew in a quick breath, expecting the violent motion to swing the hammock toward the wall like a pendulum and spill them out. She clutched Larkin tighter, riveted by the rush of pouring water, the force of it flinging open the door.

On its heels came Magnus, wind whipped. His black hair was torn from its usual tie and plastered to his corded neck, shirt and breeches soaked. Shoeless. Hatless. She'd never seen him so unkempt.

One hand closed over the knotted end of her hammock where it hung from the ceiling. His other hand held a small lantern aloft, its flame flickering. He hung it from a beam as the ship pitched the other way, nearly flinging him into the wall.

Larkin awoke with a sharp cry. Water trickled from the ceiling, spattering her as she tried to shield him. To no avail.

"D'ye need to be lashed in?" Magnus shouted.

"Nay." Lashed in to the hammock and likely drowned? She smoothed Larkin's damp hair with a trembling hand as he squirmed uncomfortably. "Have ye been on deck?"

"Aye, bailing. All but the captain and some of the women." He ran a hand over his dripping features. "One man overboard. And the stern's sprung a leak."

She mulled the loss and the implications of *leak,* and her mind lurched along with the struggling ship. Larkin cried louder, and she gestured to the pouch and flask along the wall, miraculously still dangling.

Magnus brought them with some effort. Hanging onto the hammock, he watched as she fumbled in the pouch for both a biscuit and a sweet. Larkin finally quieted when she gave each into his hands.

"I'd milk the goat if I could," he told her wryly.

She nearly smiled. Another groan of the timbers erupted and they tipped sideways again.

Magnus stared at the dripping ceiling. "Pray the waves dinna pitchpoll her."

End over end? If so, the *Bonaventure* would capsize and all would be lost. But at the moment, Larkin's clout had simply overflowed, wetting her lap. Yet it hardly mattered, damp as they were. Shutting her eyes, she uttered another silent, prayerful plea.

"Lark, listen to me." Magnus had worked his way to the head of the hammock, his mouth near her ear as he strove to be heard above the storm's fury. "Ye need to ken I'll make this right with ye. In time. 'Twas my fault, what happened with Isla. I shouldna have wed her." His face contorted as a rivulet of water from above spattered him. He shook it off before leaning in to her again. "Ye were my choice. From the first. I told my father so, long before battle. Before Culloden. But he naysayed the match."

Ye were my choice.

She forgot the storm. Larkin's fretting. Her own rolling innards and urine-soaked lap. Even the imminent peril of capsizing. Was he jesting? Or was she simply dreaming? She looked at him, stunned and a bit shy. His heart seemed to be in his eyes. The storm had stripped away all pretense, all distance, paring them down to a few impassioned, soul-stirring words.

He naysayed the match.

Tears blinded her. If Magnus had had his way, there'd have been no crime. No conviction or banishment or indenture. No *Bonaventure.* No facing such a storm.

But the former laird, forceful and unbending, had had his customary, iron-willed way.

"Ye need to ken, Lark. I'll not let it go unsaid any longer." He let go of the hammock after another long, hard look at her, then made his way to the open door and disappeared.

She stared after him, unseeing. Her heart felt too big for her chest. Did he tell her such because he believed they would perish? Did he think it would comfort her at the last?

So Magnus had gone to his father about making her his bride. The sweetness of it was as sharp as her surprise. Never had he acted besotted. Never had he spoken about love.

Yet . . . there *had* been some fine feeling.

'Twas almost too tenuous to pin down, this bond, muted by circumstances, stretched thin by absence. Yet still there, if only fragile as spiders' webbing. She'd not allowed herself to think of it — till now.

Who was to pinpoint a time when childish affection turned more tender? When a mundane look became more? Had her simple croft existence blinded her to the possibilities at the castle? Did it even matter?

The years of sweeping aside her feelings, of confining them to a tiny corner of her mind and heart, began to shift. Dare she admit her own heart?

She wiped her face, unsure if the damp was from the storm or her tears. Larkin howled despite another biscuit, and then, with another heave of the ship, emptied his stomach across her wet bodice. She followed suit, leaning over the hammock and missing the bailing bucket. The lantern Magnus had hung up went black as another onslaught of water came from above — and below.

Despite her misery and their bleak future, not even a raging storm could dim the awe and honor she felt at being once wanted. Or deny the overwhelming evidence that always, always, something had come between them. This time a roaring, fearsome storm.

24

I find as I grow older that I love those most whom I loved first.

Thomas Jefferson

He'd told her. Unburdened his heart. Spoken the words that had lodged in his soul for so long he couldn't mark the beginning of them. His confrontation with his father stood tall in his memory. He'd faced Kerrera's formidable laird in the castle library that afternoon long ago, shutting the door behind him to make sure no servants overheard the intimate exchange.

"Ye look deep in thought," his father said, rising from the ancient mahogany desk that separated them. As a lad Magnus had played beneath that desk, fascinated and half afraid of the desk's massive legs carved into the likeness of lions.

Now he stood before it, hands fisted behind his back, fully kilted as was his father. Once again, fear tried to take root deep inside him. He had his mother's blessing, at least. And Saundra's. Saundra loved Lark like a sister. But now, face-to-face with the one whose judgment mattered most, he sensed a fight. Had they already told his father whom he wanted as his wife?

" 'Tis time to take a bride," Magnus stated. Between each word was woven a prayer. He'd asked God's blessing first. "I have decided to wed none other than Lark."

"Lark. A MacDougall?"

"Aye." Magnus countered the stern resistance in his father's tone. "None fairer than she."

"And ye would make her a MacLeish?"

"With yer blessing." Or without it.

Their eyes locked. The battle had begun. If silence was a weapon, Magnus knew its power. He moved not a muscle besides.

His father rubbed his jaw, the whiskered stubble silvered, his weathered face a map of wrinkles. "She has no dower to speak of."

"That matters little to me."

"I would have grandchildren from a worthier line."

"She descends from Somerled himself. Aside from that, I would have the mother of my children be Lark and none else."

His father turned his back and stared out

a tall, rain-smeared window. "Ye disappoint me, Magnus. Mayhap I erred educating the girl alongside ye. I ne'er thought it would cause ye to lower yer sights."

Magnus had expected a fiery outburst. An impassioned denial. Not this. Wallace Mac-Leish seemed tired. Worn. Full of regrets.

"I am growing auld and have seen many things. Betimes I ken I will not live to see many more. Let yer father have his way, aye? Allow me to make so weighty a decision as one who knows ye best. A decision that will benefit us both — and Kerrera — for generations to come. Ye are my only heir. The future of the island rests on yer shoulders, remember. Let me die proud."

Magnus studied his father carefully. He had in mind a wealthy bride, no doubt, one whose fortune would profit more than them. Magnus turned away, letting the unwelcome words hang in the winter air.

They had been at an impasse over this bride business till spring. Then, leaving Edinburgh and Parliament Square amid the turbulent talk of impending war, Magnus returned home for an extended stay. There'd been precious little time to speak with Lark, to declare his intentions, to determine if she was willing. Swept up in the Jacobite cause, he'd traveled to Culloden alongside his father, proudly if a bit reluctantly, in Cameron of Lochliel's large regiment. All were hungry and exhausted from days of hard riding and incessant rain. Soon they would come face-to-face with the English who seemed intent on denying the Scots even the right to breathe.

There amid the sulphurous yellow smoke of battle, the desperate wail of bagpipes, the furious clash of swords and Lochaber axes and grapeshot, his fallen father had grabbed at Magnus's leine with a bloodied hand. "Magnus . . . promise me . . ." His words came hard, all life ebbing out of him.

Magnus knelt in the slick grass of Drumossie Moor, tearing his plaid free to bind the gaping chest wound. "Dinna speak, Father. Save yer strength."

All around them fled those in full retreat, the very ground shaking beneath them.

He stared in horror as the old, umber-colored eyes closed then reopened with effort. "Promise me ye'll marry none . . . but the daughter of Erskine-Shand." With a low groan he let go of Magnus's shirt, leaving a scarlet stain. "My son . . . promise me."

Though his entire being screamed *nay,* Magnus ground his back teeth and uttered the binding word he had no wish to say. "Aye."

A final nod and then — nothing. Torn with anguish, he'd carried his father's lifeless body off the field, past writhing men who lay wounded, frantic horses, and overpowering smoke. How had he himself emerged with only three balls through his garments in so vicious a battle, with so many dead?

For months after, both waking and sleeping, he recalled the binding, irreversible moment, caught in an ominous stranglehold of memories. Equally memorable was the day he'd told Lark he was to marry Isla. That had cut just as deep.

And now this heartfelt confession on a beleaguered ship in the teeth of a storm. Never would he forget the look on Lark's face when he'd confessed his hopes of years before. Wanting to make her his bride, mistress not of the stillroom but of Kerrera Castle. Thunderstruck she was. Not even working the pumps or bailing with buckets in a gale could subdue her image. Not even the guns that had been jettisoned and the valuable cargo thrown overboard. Lark's lovely, stunned face stayed foremost.

His reverie ended as the sea washed across the deck, slamming into them and sweeping away everything not lashed down. 'Twould almost be comical if it wasn't so perilous, all of them slipping and sliding and wrestling with wind and water. Exhaustion benumbed him. Tethered about the waist like every other man in sight gave him little security when the gray waves climbed to mountainous walls on all sides. 'Twas blowing forty knots or better, the wind shoving him about at every turn. Sea and sky turned from foamy gray to black as daylight eroded. Airborne spray blinded him, leaving a salty, stinging aftermath.

Gathered around the capstan was the captain and second mate with Surgeon Blackburn. All a sodden mass of blue, their tarred hats streaming water, their hemp lifelines lashed to stanchions.

Throughout the storm, Blackburn seemed to shadow him. Or was it only his overwrought imagination? Shrugging off the concern, Magnus resumed his frantic bailing in the gathering gloom of night. The sea seemed to spread itself out and away from the *Bonaventure* as if gathering for another assault. How much more could the vessel stand? Each swell seemed more violent than the last.

He braced himself as the ship rose and crashed downwards. More seawater poured across the deck, sweeping Magnus off his feet. He braced for the tight tug of his lifeline, but it never came. Toward the foredecks he went on a foamy, iron-fisted wave, senses stung as salt water flooded his eyes and nose. But 'twas his shoulder, shoved against the lanyard, that screamed with pain. He fought for a hold on something — anything — as frantic seconds ticked by toward a greater danger.

Lord, help Thou me.

On the knife's edge of washing overboard, he collided with the anchor chain. Dazed, torn with pain, he held on to the rusted metal as the ship plunged into a trough then rose again with a shudder.

Sick, completely spent, he opened his eyes to find Rory a stone's throw away.

"Yer lifeline's been cut!" the former captain shouted.

The rope's hemp end lay between them like a dividing line. Cut? Magnus's head swirled with the implications. Did someone mean to send him overboard? Aye. He felt it to his sodden shoes.

Dropping to one knee near him, Rory hung his head, his face the color of sailcloth. Blood soaked the trews of one leg, his torn pants revealing a terrible gash.

"Go below!" Magnus shouted, pulling himself upright.

Rory looked up at him and then to the

boiling cauldron that was the sea. No matter that the foamy spray washed the wound clean, it bubbled up again and again like a scarlet spring, just like his father's that fatal day at Culloden.

Magnus fought his way forward to where Rory now lay, then all but dragged him to the hatch. They couldn't waste another man. Not with one already overboard and his own close call.

Rory's weight was formidable, Magnus's own shoulder anguished as he lifted him. But it was go below or die, the both of them.

At last the sea was spent. An almost eerie calm ensued. A warm breeze caressed Lark's face as she sat on the storm-washed deck near the ship's rail the next day, Larkin on her lap. A porpoise made a graceful leap into the water, now a settled cerulean blue without even a hint of a lacy wave. The calls of sailors and the ship's carpenter as they repaired the *Bonaventure* and its tattered sails sounded at her back, punctuated with sawing and hammering.

Her stomach had finally settled as well. Larkin was dry, full of goat's milk and porridge. More than a few plants had perished, drowned in the storm below deck, and all but two hives. Overnight her duties had lightened, but all seemed of small consequence given they'd survived one of the most harrowing happenings of their lives.

Rory limped about, making her wonder why. Magnus's shoulder was set in a sling pulled tight to his chest. Had he broken it or merely dislodged it? The black crepe ribbon on his forearm stayed intact.

She lowered her chin and kissed Larkin's sun-warmed head. His little cap had disappeared, mayhap washed away. She would make another, having begged needle and thread. His bedding was airing, his wee wooden box bed beside her. No one seemed to mind that she sat on the quarterdeck with what remained of the plant cabin. After a busy morning cleaning up straw skeps and returning plants back to their place, mayhap this was her due.

"Allow me to escort you to the captain's table tonight for a small celebration of our having survived the storm." Blackburn stood near her, casting her in shade.

Would he never cease trying to sway her? Her response was quiet, a *nay* tucked within.

"And how would yer wife feel about that, I wonder?"

A tight smile touched his surprised expression. "Very well then. I shall ask another."

No sooner had he left than Rory appeared, speaking to her through the ornate railing that separated the quarterdeck from the main. "He's a bad one, Blackburn."

"And how goes it with ye?" she asked, unwilling to discuss the surgeon's faults.

He winced. "Glad the gale is o'er."

"I pray we'll not repeat it." Even the thought made her shudder. " 'Tis a miracle we didna founder."

"Yer and the laird's prayers likely kept us afloat."

She'd not naysay that. Only an outright miracle had kept them from the bottom of the sea. Her gaze traveled to his bandaged leg. "I'll pray for yer wound."

He shrugged. "Ye'd best pray for the laird. His lifeline was cut clean through. Someone wanted him overboard."

Her gaze fastened on his haggard face. "Who?"

"Yer doting surgeon, no doubt. He's fixed his eye on ye and the laird is in his way."

"The laird is in mourning. And Surgeon Blackburn is very married."

He snorted. "There's neither one much observed aboard ship." He released his grip on the railing, limping back to light duties given his injury.

Blackburn had likely set Magnus's shoulder. But had the surgeon meant to kill him? Or had the rope been cut another way? Magnus was respected here in this strange floating kingdom. Even liked. She was not ignorant of the nods and deferential treatment given him. Despite the MacLeish temper that sometimes flared, he had an easy, affable way with people. A natural dignity and kindness just as he'd had on Kerrera. And here he remained more laird than indenture, no matter what British law had to say. Pondering it, Lark kept her eyes on the cavorting dolphins, her fingers worrying a crease in Larkin's gown.

By nightfall 'twas whispered the rope that tethered Magnus to deck had indeed been cut in the worst of the storm. Knowing it gnawed at her. Casting blame was not her way, but the fear remained.

Be his defense, Lord. Please.

That night she ate a simple supper on deck as the setting sun painted the sky a jolly pink. Larkin had sprouted a new tooth, his lower gum now bearing two tiny pearls. She tickled and made over him, his belly laugh a delight.

Laughter lifted from the captain's quarters below, reminding her she'd missed a bounteous supper. When the officers and their ladies finished dining, they fanned onto the deck, Mrs. Ravenhill and Captain Moodie leading. All began to walk about.

Lark had purposely positioned herself in a corner, nearly hidden. She tried not to gawk at Mrs. Ravenhill's colorful gown. Seven officers paired with their chosen partners, all but Surgeon Blackburn, still missing a mate, as they were called. Magnus hadn't joined them but had eaten on deck with the crew, as had she and the other convict women. The fare coming out of the galley kitchen was a far cry from that of the captain's table, but she was free of any matchmaking seamen.

Pressing her back against a crate, she breathed in the unmistakable odor of rum and perfume in the warm breeze. Her senses filled with the party's exaggerated speech and movements, their boundless laughter. When a sailor brought out a fiddle, Lark pressed her hand to her mouth to keep from laughing as a tipsy officer bowed to his partner and then tripped over a coiled rope. Larkin let out a shriek as the fiddle screeched and began a reel. Sitting him on her lap facing her, she clapped his dimpled hands as the moon rose and silvered his smile with gentle light. Soon they were both yawning, still recovering from their sleepless night in the storm.

She went below and gave him a bath. A kindly sailor had brought her a partial tub of rainwater warmed by the sun. Larkin splashed, tasted, blew bubbles. She ran a soapy cloth over him, smiling at his antics then frowning at the beginnings of a saltwater rash. A bit of salve would end the aggravation, surely. After drying him off, she applied both salve and clout, then eased him into a linen nightshirt made from one of her clean petticoats.

"Ah, wee one, ye've stolen my heart completely, both now and forevermore."

Taking a comb, she swept his damp hair into a little russet wave atop his head before bundling him in a blanket against the damp and coaxing him to sleep with a lullaby.

Hours later, having traded the hammock for the narrow bunk, she came awake, Larkin's even breathing preferable to the ship's incessant creak and the call of the watch. The sound of the sea was a whisper tonight as if worn out from the recent storm. She kissed the back of Larkin's head, breathing in his beloved baby scent. Gradually she drifted, caught in the after-terrors of the gale and feeling queasy all over again before the solace of Larkin's warmth reminded her all was well . . .

Had the door come open? She pushed up

on one elbow, blinking at a sliver of candle-light and a silhouette. The door closed. The light snuffed.

Fear sank cold claws into her, raising gooseflesh. "Who is there?"

Silence. Shadows.

She waited for the answer but only heard the scrape of a chair across the planked floor, as if it was being positioned against the door. Sitting up abruptly, she bruised her head on the bunk's low oak ceiling. Pain yanked her fully awake. Cradling Larkin, she pressed her back against the ship's side.

"I beg ye — leave!"

In answer, cold fingers grazed her bare arm before shackling her wrist, causing her to spill Larkin. He rolled onto the bunk, snatched from sleep, the thud of his skull against the bunk's hard edge making him cry out.

"Quiet!" Blackburn hovered, so close she smelled sour port.

Recoiling, she tried to shove him away. Uttering an oath, he tore at her nightgown with a quick hand. The rip of fabric collided with Larkin's cry.

"Stop!" She wanted to scream, but shock jellied her voice to a quaver and it was lost beneath Larkin's startled howling. With the babe behind her, she tried to fight off her attacker, but he was far stronger than she, fueled by spirits and fury.

When he'd pushed past the limp hammock and climbed into the bunk, the cabin door slammed open. In breathless seconds, the ship's surgeon was pulled away from her and sent sprawling into the nearest wall. The thwack of it signaled the frightful disturbance was done. Clutching her torn nightgown with one hand, Lark groped for Larkin with the other.

Through the darkness came Magnus's winded voice. "Lark?"

Before she could answer, the second mate was in back of him, lantern held aloft. The seasoned officer surveyed the scene in grim disgust, toeing Blackburn's inert form with his boot.

"Collapsed, more from an excess of spirits than yer pummeling, likely," he said to Magnus before glancing Lark's way. "My apologies to ye and the babe, Miss Mac-Dougall."

Magnus reached for Larkin while Lark tried to gather what remained of her modesty and composure. In mere moments, Blackburn was hauled away.

Magnus began pacing while Larkin, mayhap taken by the novelty of a man carrying him, began to quiet. Shaking, Lark sat on the bunk's rough edge, arms wrapped round herself, staring at the floor planks polished yellow-gold by the lantern light. Queasiness climbed her throat and soured her mouth. To think she'd once been flattered by Blackburn's attention. Her gaze lifted to Magnus, Larkin now fingering his shadowed stubble of a beard.

One arm dangled uselessly at his side. His hurt shoulder. She stood, noticing the sling on the floor along with his crepe armband. Picking them up, she knew the short scuffle had cost him dearly.

A question seemed to hang between them. "He didna —" Magnus left off, coming to a sudden standstill, his eyes asking the rest.

She swallowed, looking to her bare feet rather than meeting his compassionate gaze. "Ye came in before he could cause such harm."

"Glad I am of that." He resumed his pacing. "Larkin's howling woke me. Betimes I ken ye were given the babe for yer own protection as well as his."

She'd oft thought it too. "Just when I think yer lairdly duties are done, something new arises."

"Mayhap. But we'll soon be parted."

He needn't have said it. The day loomed like a thorn in her heart. Their lives were no longer their own. Years of servitude stretched before them both. Bleak. Barren.

"I fear for ye when we're parted. Who will look after ye?" He was a handbreadth away now. In his intent gaze was a blaze of regret and something else that shook her completely. Something so raw yet so heartfelt it caused her stomach to flip. Reaching out, he touched her cheek, not quickly or carelessly but gently and lingeringly, as if wanting to mark her skin's softness in memory and make the most of this very rare, private moment.

Larkin was drooping now, as if lulled by Magnus's former motion. Lark took him back, laid him on the bunk, and tucked the blanket around him, praying the bump to his head was of no consequence.

She turned back to Magnus, noting pain skitter across his face as he fisted the hand of his injured arm. "Let me tend ye," she said. "I'll not let Blackburn touch ye."

He stood patiently as her fingers explored his shoulder. Still tender. Still out of socket. She gripped his elbow as gently as she could and then placed a hand on his thick forearm with a whispered warning. A circular crank gave way to a satisfying if painful pop as the shoulder slid back into place. He set his jaw against a groan. Next, she knotted the sling to hold his arm in position, with a silent prayer for hasty healing.

"Are ye still able to keep the captain's ledgers?" she asked, standing back reluctantly.

He nodded, his eyes holding hers. "Aye. He's in a bad way, shaking as he does. But the palsy hasn't affected his mind. Nor his courtship with Mrs. Ravenhill."

His sudden wink lent him a roguish air. She gave him a sleepy smile, the events of the last two days catching up with her. Five weeks of the voyage remained. Never had time moved so slowly or been so fraught with danger.

She bent again, her fingers closing over the crepe mourning band. Now it brought back not only his loss but his heartfelt declaration. Tears pooled in her eyes. When she went to tie it on, he stopped her.

"Nay, Lark." Taking the crepe from her hand, he fisted it. "God knows 'tis mostly a trapping. What's past is past. Leave it be."

She said nothing, melancholy overshadowing her relief to have escaped Blackburn.

He paused at the door. "I'll ask to be moved nearer ye for yer safekeeping."

"Will the captain allow it?"

"He's agreeable to most anything I suggest."

She opened her mouth to thank him, but he went out and shut the door firmly behind him, leaving the lantern and its comforting light behind.

25

Give me but one hour of Scotland,
Let me see it ere I die.

William Edmondstoune Aytoun

Years later, what would she remember? The gale that nearly sent them to the bottom of the sea? Their eventual landing in British America? Or Surgeon Blackburn's brutal lashing?

At seven bells — half past eleven in the morn — all mustered on deck to hear the offense and resulting punishment read aloud by the captain. The charges were weighty. Drunkenness and lewd conduct unbefitting an officer. Beside the captain stood the boatswain's mate holding the whip with its nine tails of knotted, waxed rope. Flogging Blackburn barebacked before the eyes of the entire ship after he'd been bound to a grating seemed harsh, when nothing happened except that she'd had a terrible fright and Larkin had bruised his brow. But had Blackburn had his way . . .

Lark looked away as the first of a dozen lashes was struck, hard enough to scar bare skin. She wanted to plug her ears. Turn her back. All she could do was avert her gaze and focus on Larkin as he played with the coral rattle, unaware of the grisly scene. When it was done, Blackburn would be taken below and salt rubbed into his wounds, a severe mercy to allay infection.

'Twas as much a punishment as a warning. The sailors' sober faces bespoke it. But what irony. Were not most of the officers guilty of drunkenness and lewd conduct, having taken shipboard mistresses and indulging at the captain's table? Sighing, she shut any sordid thoughts away, glad to escape to the plant cabin where a young lieutenant replaced Blackburn in his duties there.

Time passed. The air turned cooler as summer waned. Days became a succession of watches. Blessedly, nothing extraordinary happened till land was finally sighted.

Lark stood at the taffrail as the green edge of a new continent beckoned. Speechless, she stared, finding it immensely moving. Hard-won. Terrifying.

She craved land. Yet the wistful yearning,

honed after eight long weeks at sea, was tempered by a keen sadness. The *Bonaventure* would dock, then sail on to the British sugar islands, the laird still aboard.

After the incident with Surgeon Blackburn, Magnus stayed busy with the captain's ledgers and correspondence, eating with the crew on deck. Often he would send her a long, lingering look. Occasionally he would seek her out and speak with her or hold Larkin, but this was so rare it seemed almost remarkable when he did so. Eyes were everywhere. Never had they another private moment. Betimes it seemed she'd dreamed his revelation that stormy night of once wanting her as his bride. Such seemed to have little bearing on the present. What had he said to her below decks?

"What's past is past. Leave it be."

Soon they would say goodbye. Stern with her heart, she rehearsed a cool farewell in her head, not wanting to make a spectacle of herself once the time came.

Their port was Hampton, Virginia. British America.

Now she stood on deck, Larkin in her arms, staring at the fringe of green coast. Their entrance into the harbor was almost leisurely, this new land, so unlike Scotland, unfolding before her riveted gaze. She could not help but make comparisons despite the check in her spirit not to do so. Nothing compared with her beloved country, the land she knew best. Virginia meant a host of inconsolable things. An unfair verdict. Servitude. Irreparable loss. How would she ever look at it without this sick sinking in her stomach? This sense of taint and loathing? Her tangled thoughts gave her no rest as they sailed toward the unwelcome shore.

But any further ruminations were short-lived. Once they'd docked, the on-deck sale of convicts unfolded with haste, shackling them further to this new place. Before her very eyes, frowning, quarrelsome masters purchased contracts in exchange for years of labor or a possible sale to another planter. She herself was bound to Richard Osbourne's Royal Hundred. 'Twas an odd name to her Scots ears.

The sweet scent of tobacco hung in the salt air, along with that of coffee, rum, molasses, and exotic spices. Though the sun played hide-and-seek with wispy clouds, it steamed on deck, dampening her bodice and sending itchy trickles of sweat down her temples.

Virginia was naught but a bake oven. Tidewater, they called the surrounding land. Countless vessels rode at anchor.

There were more Africans than whites. Her whole being rebelled at the difference.

Osbourne's colonial factor stood before her. He looked from her to a babbling Larkin, whose fat fist was in his mouth, face ruddy beneath his humble bonnet. Did this man not like children? His scowl told her nay.

Might he take the babe away from her? Did he have the right?

She swallowed hard. Fear had a terrible taste. Rarely had she known it on Kerrera. But since leaving Scotland . . .

The factor finally spoke. "I pray to heaven you're not one of the sorners so common on these shores."

Anger stiffened her spine. She was not a shirker, a shiftless vagabond who avoided work, no better than a beggar.

"Your son is the image of you," he said.

She held her tongue, long past explaining Larkin's beginnings.

His clipped British tone was dismissive. "Though he survived the voyage, he'll not likely survive the seasoning."

The seasoning?

He looked down at the documents given him by the captain. She tried not to stare at his gentlemanly garments, his ribbed waistcoat stretched taut over a middle rounded by ham and biscuits, his tobacco-brown features pitted with smallpox scars. They lent him a hard air along with his hard words.

"Your term of service is three years hence in exchange for sufficient meat, drink, apparel, lodging, and all other necessaries befitting a servant bound to Richard Osbourne or his heirs at Royal Hundred."

He thrust the papers toward her with a bit of lead to write her name or mark the more common *X*. Shifting Larkin to her left hip, she signed her full name. Boldly. Proudly.

His brow lifted in surprise, but he said nothing. Again he riffled through his papers. "In the list of rebel prisoners imported by Captain James Moodie is Magnus MacLeish, transported for adhering to the Stuart cause and violating the Dress Act, becoming factor to the West Indies plantation of Richard Osbourne in Jamaica."

Lark stared at the papers. A bottomless sense of loss began poking holes in her composure. She looked toward Magnus, where he stood talking with Captain Moodie. She saw no sign of Rory.

A wagon waited on the dock below, quickly filling with the remaining straw skeps and contents of the plant cabin, all secured for travel. The factor gestured in irritation for her to start walking. Four other convict women followed her down the sun-soaked gangplank, their scant possessions with them. But 'twas no simple task gaining one's land legs after so long at sea. The earth seemed to sway and send her into a spin, making her grip Larkin all the harder lest she spill him onto the dirty wharf.

A burly man, black as printer's ink, helped them into a second wagon, its bed filled with sweet-smelling straw. Noisy gulls circled, drawing her notice to the cloudless September sky. Her gaze shifted to the *Bon-aventure*'s deck, mostly empty now.

Magnus came toward her and took a seat beside the factor, atop the wagon box that held the bees and plants. Would her breath always catch in anticipation now that he'd unburdened himself about his former feelings for her? Why was he going with them?

Both wagons rolled away, dodging cargo and sailors, slaves and roustabouts. Shops along the King Street wharf were as many as ships. Taverns and storehouses and shipfitters abounded. A rutted road led inland, pushing past fences and ditches to the surrounding countryside.

Lark sat in a sort of trance as they bumped along, Larkin in her lap, her senses shifting from the azure of the ocean to endless emerald fields made bright with blue lobelia and red cardinal flowers. These she recognized. The rest, nay. Nary a stem bent nor a leaf stirred, the heavy air was so still. 'Twas almost too much to take in. She inhaled a sticky breath. No pesky midges like in Scotland, but an abundance of long-legged mosquitoes and persistent horseflies.

Her fellow convicts, all oakum pickers, were quiet. One nodded off like Larkin, lulled by the wagon's motion. Magnus's voice floated on the air, but mostly the factor did the talking. She caught little except a mention of the *Bonaventure*. Watering and provisioning the ship took time. Days, mayhap. Likely their departure for Jamaica wasn't imminent. Some of the officers had left the ship soon after docking. Magnus was coming with them when he didn't have to, to Royal Hundred, the plantation that had made Osbourne a Tobacco Lord.

Hope began building inside her. Since he'd professed his former feelings, she'd sensed a new sort of bond between them, something fresh and even more heartfelt.

All of a sudden, he looked back at her as if confirming it. This was no careless glance. She met his gaze, all else falling away, and was overcome by his attention and the force of feeling behind it, as if he'd reached out and touched her. She held his look till he faced forward again, wanting to impart all that she could not say.

I feel like a girl again when ye look my way. Not an indentured spinster with a babe not my own. More a princess or a queen.

With effort she returned to looking at the landscape, her thoughts still firmly anchored to him. A gate crafted of brick and scrolling ironwork led to a lane of trees she had no name for, thick and majestic and stretching to the sky. At its end was a house the rival of any she'd seen in Scotland, a masterpiece of Flemish bond brickwork and a mansard roof crowned with a cupola. She fixed her eye on the idle weathervane atop it as they rumbled past the circular drive and welcoming porch to more fence and field. Up close she could see that Royal Hundred possessed a rich if somewhat neglected grandeur.

Beyond them stretched a wide river, blue as watered silk. She wondered its name. Wondered why they'd come to what looked like a village of wooden huts, dark children running hither and yon. The burly black man set the brake and got down, then helped the women down and pointed to their lodging. In moments, the factor bid Lark join them in the wagon holding the bees and plants. Magnus helped her up onto the seat, and they took yet another lane, looping to the back of the mansion house.

Here she felt less out of place. A walled garden. A glass hothouse. Small, well-kept outbuildings running the length of the lawn, connected by crisscrossed shell paths, herbs and flowers between.

"You'll lodge here," the factor said, gesturing to a cottage the size of Granny's croft, but of brick rather than stone, a chimney at both ends. "The stillroom is to one side."

A double purpose then. Magnus eyed it approvingly, she thought. Pleasure rose up to sweeten their strange surroundings.

They began unloading the wagon, avoiding the stirring bees. She pushed open the door to her new dwelling. Clean. Spare. It smelled damp, walls holding the tang of a vinegar wash.

She eased a sleeping Larkin onto the bed's woven coverlet and passed through a connecting door to the stillroom. Overcome, she shut her eyes, savoring the cool shadows and scents of a great many beloved herbs and simples, like old friends. They crowded the rafters, dried bouquets of lavender and everlastings, all faded but lovely.

"Ye fancy it?" Magnus's voice sounded at the room's threshold.

She turned toward him. "I do."

"Wait till ye see the bee garden." He sounded satisfied. Even relieved.

Excitement carried her to a window. The great house cast a tall shadow over the rear lawn at what she guessed was four o'clock. "If Osbourne doesna live here, who does?"

"The mansion stays empty till he comes. There's a housekeeper who will oversee you, according to Osbourne. Yer here to solely keep the stillroom and tend the bees. Not a poor position for ye and wee Larkin."

Nay, not poor. Providential. Yet he dashed her fragile contentment when he said, "Take care with the factor, Granger. He's a hard man and he's unwell."

His words were punctuated with a distant coughing fit as the wagon rumbled away.

"Are American factors like Scottish ones, like yer Mr. Chandler?"

He ran both hands through hair in need of trimming. "More or less. Granger deals mostly with the indentures and enslaved. Field hands. He lives elsewhere. Ye'll likely see little of him and more of Mistress Flowerdew."

"Flowerdew?" Lark brightened. "Ye jest."

"Nay," he replied with a wink. "Let's hope Royal Hundred's housekeeper is as bonny as her name."

The castle's servants flashed to mind but

seemed from another world. Was he remembering them too? The fleeting thought toppled when he closed the distance between them and took her hands. She stared down at their entwined fingers, moved by a more distant memory of holding hands and running across the island as children, young and free.

His fingers tightened about hers ever so slightly. "We've not much time, ye ken. I'll not be so foolish as to wait three more years with what weighs on my mind and heart."

She looked up at him, more than a wee bit shooglie. There were no words for the way he made her feel. He even spoke what was on her own mind and heart. Bending his head, he brought her hands to his lips and slowly kissed them. She leaned in slightly, wanting to bury her face in his wealth of hair, unkempt yet clean and still carrying a hint of the sea.

He looked up but didn't release her. They were so close she could feel the warmth of his breath when he pressed his bewhiskered cheek to hers and whispered in her ear, "Promise me ye'll wait, Lark . . . or mayhap I'd best ask if waiting is what ye want."

Her voice wavered with emotion when she answered. "Waiting isna what I want, but wait I will, no matter how long."

He seemed on the verge of saying something else, something that had her holding her breath, when he let go of her hands and stepped back. "For now, 'tis enough."

26

A house without a dog, a cat, or a little child is a house without joy or laughter.

Scottish proverb

Mistress Flowerdew pressed a hand to her heart. "A real, living laird?"

"Aye, a banished one," Magnus said apologetically.

The housekeeper darted a look at Larkin next. "And an infant?" Her rapturous expression bespoke much. "If you but knew the sameness — the mundaneness — of keeping an empty house. All I have for company is a cat!"

Mistress Flowerdew was tiny and well-kept, her ruffled mobcap the biggest thing about her. She peered at Lark expectantly and then at Magnus. "The two of you must be married — and this is your son."

"Nay," Lark and Magnus said in unison.

Disappointment covered Mistress Flowerdew like a cloud. She looked at the sealed letter the factor had given her before he'd gone down the lane to what he called the quarters. "Perhaps I should read Mr. Osbourne's correspondence before leaping to conclusions."

They stood in the foyer of the grand house, front and back doors open to the drive and river. The housekeeper broke the seal and devoured the contents, seemingly as hungry for news as Lark was for supper. The teasing aroma of baking bread and roast meat made her stomach cramp. Larkin, now awake and fussy, banged an insistent fist on Lark's bodice, his sign for sustenance.

"Oh my! Mr. Osbourne writes that you're a personal friend and that I'm to lodge you right here till the ship sails to the Caribbean." She folded and pocketed the letter. "We shall maintain you in true Virginia fashion then, beginning with your rooms." Taking hold of a small bell on a side table, she rang it, the merry tinkle calling a young housemaid. "I'll have refreshments served on the riverfront portico immediately. Dinner is at eight o'clock."

Magnus nodded and smiled. "I am a personal friend of Richard Osbourne just as Mistress MacDougall is a friend to me.

Mayhap we can all dine together, yerself included."

Appearing flattered and flustered, Mistress Flowerdew curtsied. "As you wish, your lairdship. I'll even have Cook concoct something special for the babe."

Magnus had bathed and shaved. The water in the copper hip tub was cool and clear as a loch. Clad in a suit of broadcloth from his bedchamber's wardrobe, he stood before the second-floor window, Lark's cottage and attached stillroom below. This bird's-eye view of the walled and kitchen gardens, the dovecote, and other dependencies was eye-opening, even jolting. Flanking the house were fields as far as the eye could see. Here everything seemed almost new whereas his beloved Alba stood centuries old.

On the voyage to Virginia he'd read from the captain's small library on American agronomy, riveted by the fact colonial soil was so hospitable when his rocky isle was not. Though the Virginia coast lacked the grandeur and majestic awe of Scotland's western islands, it had a compelling charm, a lush freshness that surely must have wooed those first settlers a century or more before.

And here Lark would make her home.

He needed to see her at Royal Hundred. Needed to ascertain if she was safe before he left, counting the days till they were reunited.

Osbourne's vast plantation comprised eight thousand acres, half of which were under cultivation. Magnus's mind spun. He thought in hectares, not acres, but knew his host's holdings were vast. Tobacco was king and had made Osbourne a Tobacco Lord, yet he complained of his factor and overseers and the toll tobacco was taking on both his land and slave labor.

Magnus hadn't yet told Lark that Rory MacPherson was bound to one of Osbourne's smaller farms a few miles distant to toil as a field hand. Likely she'd find out soon enough.

Lord, if it pleases Ye, let me stay.

He had no wish to see the sugar islands, not as an indenture. Captain Moodie had warned him of both disease and the harsh climate cutting down his fellow countrymen within mere months. He'd not court fear, but it was a concern. Many failed to survive the seasoning, though some eventually thrived. Which would his lot be?

He smoothed a finely tailored coat sleeve then touched the soft linen of his stock. Lark lacked proper clothing. Could he presume on Royal Hundred's hospitality and secure something suitable for her to wear to supper?

What did he have to lose?

"I realized," Mistress Flowerdew said, arms full of garments, "that being ship bound for so long, you're in need of a clean gown and underpinnings."

Fresh from her bath, Lark felt her remaining weariness wash away. "Bethankit. I brought little with me and all is soiled."

Taking the offering, Lark noticed Mistress Flowerdew's perplexed expression. "Pardon, Miss MacDougall, but my English ears have a sore time of it with your Scots speech."

" 'Tis understandable, yer confusion, as I oft speak so fast."

"Indeed, my dear. I'm a tad deaf besides." She peered over Lark's shoulder to Larkin sitting atop the bed. "Might you need a hand with the babe while you're dressing?"

Lark sensed the older woman's lonesomeness, the hollowness of being a spinster. "Oh aye," she replied, setting the garments aside to scoop Larkin up. He smiled his toothy smile, flipping her heart over, and went to Mistress Flowerdew like a lamb.

"We shall walk about the garden, Master Larkin and I. He might enjoy the pineapple fountain."

Lark almost chuckled at the comical picture they made, he so stout and the housekeeper so tiny. "Careful, he's a tub," she warned.

"Indeed. Soon he'll be toddling about and in need of a pudding cap and leading strings."

They went out, leaving Lark the luxury of managing her borrowed stays and stockings, shift and petticoats. Where had Mistress Flowerdew gotten such garments on short notice? And the shoes! Calamanco slippers with shiny gilt buckles. She'd only seen the like in Edinburgh's shop windows or adorning fine ladies like Isla.

She shut her mind to the dark thought and selected one of the prettiest dresses. Made of India printed cotton, it was both colorful and comfortable. She pinned up her damp hair, covering it with a lace-edged pinner and surveying the gaunt woman before the small, cracked oval looking glass.

The Glasgow tolbooth and the ship had remade her. A small woman she was not. Never had she been called dainty. But this was the closest she'd come to turning sideways and disappearing.

Dismayed, she left the cottage and made her way up the shell walk in her slightly cramped shoes, her eyes everywhere at once. They lingered on the bee garden in back of the herb garden near the reflective glass orangery Mistress Flowerdew had pointed out so proudly.

Beyond this was the service yard, the kitchen and laundry, salt house, smoke-house, and scullery, all cleverly concealed behind a high boxwood hedge. Tonight, at least, she felt less like an indenture and more a guest, thanks to Osbourne's letter of introduction and Mistress Flowerdew's hospitality.

A maid met her at the riverfront door and led her to the dining room, where the factor and Magnus were already gathered along with the housekeeper. Larkin sat at her feet on a plush carpet, playing with a collection of silver spoons.

Dinner was nothing short of an astonishment. Salted ham, baked shad in pastry, peanut soup, sweet potatoes and sweet corn, turnip greens and creamed celery with pecans. Meringues with cherry sauce were served for dessert, at which Larkin clapped his hands between bites. These Virginians had mastered the culinary arts. Lark was only familiar with the fish. All else was so foreign she felt like an Egyptian. By meal's end she was as stuffed and drowsy as Larkin, who kept nodding off in her lap.

Coffee was served, and Lark sipped the bracing brew as Magnus and Granger discussed Royal Hundred. The factor was indeed a hard man as Magnus had said. She tried to see past his hardness to the root cause beneath.

"You must be anxious to learn more about the gardens and plantation's workings," Mistress Flowerdew told her. "But only after you've rested."

"Tomorrow morn," Lark said as the lengthy supper came to a blessed end. "Will ye show me about? Or is there someone else?" She prayed it wouldn't be the factor.

"I shall gladly show you. Sadly, Royal Hundred has seen a spate of ill fortune. We've had the usual summer fevers and then a spring scourge of smallpox taking both a housemaid and the gardener."

"I'm sorry," Lark murmured as they rose from the table and said good night.

The evening air was cooled by a westerly breeze. Once in her cottage, she put a sleeping Larkin in his box bed and left the door open, sitting just outside on a wooden bench in sore need of paint. There Magnus joined her as the factor rode away and one by one the lights in the mansion went out.

The leaves were stirring in the breeze, and

the coo of doves made a sort of haunting night song as the moon rose. She looked toward the river, darkened to deep blue in the gloaming. The enchanting scene matched her mood. Magnus was just a breath away. Would he take her hand again?

For the moment his attention was on something just ahead. Together they stared, transfixed. Between them and the river was a twinkling like countless fallen stars. Tiny winks of white light first here then there, never ending.

"Glowworms?" Magnus said. "Like the ones in Kerrera's hedge?"

"Nay. These are . . ." She stood and began a slow walk toward the nameless river. "Winged."

He followed, his low chuckle as much a delight as the magical lights. He'd not been merry in ages.

They came to a stop, surrounded by the otherworldly, blinking creatures who seemed neither aware nor afraid of them. Cupping his hands, Magnus captured one. She peered down as he half opened his fingers. A yellow flash.

"A fanciful insect," he mused. "A winged beetle."

"I've ne'er seen such."

He released it and it flashed again in

flight. "Peculiar to the colonies, mayhap."

" 'Tis like a flash of lightning," she marveled as it winged away. "I thought we might be stung."

He smiled in the gathering darkness. "Like yer bees."

Side by side now, they looked out over the wide river, shoulders touching.

"What is it named?" she asked in awe.

"The James if yer English," he answered. "The Powhatan if yer Indian."

Her eyes rounded. "Are there Indians near?"

"Nay. Not to my knowledge. Once this was their land before they were driven west."

She couldn't imagine such. It sounded mournful. Fearsome. Yet hadn't they themselves just experienced the same? "When will ye leave?"

"By week's end."

"Ye could have stayed in Hampton harbor till then."

"Royal Hundred holds more appeal." He looked at her intently before turning back to the river. "I wanted to see ye here, make a picture in my mind of where ye'd work and lay yer head."

"I wish I could do the same. See where ye'll be in the sugar islands."

"I'll pen it in a letter. Tell it to ye in word

pictures."

She narrowed her gaze to the twinkling all around them. "Is it true what the factor said about yer contract? That yer term of service is but two years?"

"That's the way of it, aye, in the Caribbean. Conditions are harsh. Ye heard Granger at supper. That we outlanders run a frightful risk venturing there."

The darkness inside her deepened, though she was used to his plain speaking.

"But if not for Osbourne — and Providence — I'd be in Marshalsea by now."

She shuddered. Marshalsea Prison meant certain death. At least the Caribbean, whatever its dangers, was free of bars.

"Will ye go back to Kerrera? In time?"

He turned toward her, the shadows masking his features but not his beloved scent. Sandalwood. Fresh linen. The taint of the sea was no more. His voice was remarkably even when he said, "There might be precious little to return to. The Crown will seize my holdings and transfer them to someone else. Our headright grants us land here once our service ends. A solid fifty acres."

She stifled the urge to turn up her nose. Virginia land held little appeal. "And what is fifty acres to a man who once owned an island?"

Her hasty reply wounded him, she knew.

"If I live to see it, 'twill be a bonny beginning."

His quiet words rebuked her. Tears choked her apology, swelling her throat. All this change, the fierce pull between the old and new, their near parting . . .

"Yer weary, Lark." He took her by the elbow, his touch on her ruffled sleeve gentle. "A good night's sleep is what's needed."

Her needs went far beyond sleep. She craved Kerrera's wild coast. The simplicity of porridge and strong tea and bannocks. Granny's peaceful company. The cry of gulls and the purple haze of heather in the glens. 'Twas worse than a death, this separation. A death was final, complete. The land went on living, always calling them home . . .

Didn't his longing for Alba go bone deep too? Or, having left Kerrera behind years before in Edinburgh, did he now weather the change better?

"If Virginia is to be our home, I want to embrace it, but —" She trod carefully, trying to sort through the tumult of her feelings. "Betimes it seems traitorous to do so, to take to this new land and new people that have been thrust upon us. Being fond of Virginia makes me feel I'm being unfaithful to Scotland somehow."

"Yet God has seen us here and promises to turn things in our favor no matter how dark. If He promises to bring good from all this, should we not look for the good too?"

How simply he explained things. And how truthfully. "Aye."

"And since He has miraculously placed us together, I feel we must make the best of it." The warmth in his tone lifted her sagging spirits. "With ye by my side, Virginia seems a sort of sanctuary to me, ye ken. Almost paradise. At least this night."

This night was theirs, aye. Her heart brimmed with a great many things. On the tip of her tongue was the simplest of questions.

Do ye truly still feel the same as of auld?

She wanted to be sure, to tighten the tie between them that distance would soon test. His gentle hold on her arm was telling.

With his free hand he touched her cheek in that beguiling way that left her weak-kneed. "What is in that head and heart of yers, Lark?"

Reaching up, she covered his hand with her own. "Both are full of a place that's home to us and wee Larkin. Our own abode, one of beauty and peace with a garden and bees and yer sheep. I'll make oatcakes and tea and ye'll hang yer hat by the door, and we'll shut the world away. 'Tis as real to me as if I was standing on the threshold."

"Hold tight to that then. I'll do the same. Mayhap the Lord has given ye a vision to weather our time apart."

She nodded, having thought the same. Cling to it she would.

A sudden cry from the cottage cut through the twilight. With a hasty, reluctant good night, she brushed his clean-shaven cheek with a fleeting kiss before hurrying across the lawn to Larkin, who was no doubt wide awake and wondering about his strange surroundings.

27

No one is without difficulties, whether in high or low life, and every person knows best where their own shoe pinches.

Abigail Adams

The featherbed made a downy nest, soft and warm. A linen sheet was hardly needed. Sometime in the cicada-laden night a smirr of rain chased the heat away. Toward dawn a cock crowed. Lark lay staring at the cracked plaster ceiling, putting down the urge to kindle a fire and fill the teakettle. Ingrained in her since she was no bigger than a kelpie was this comforting ritual. 'Twas early morn when she most missed Granny and her old life, before the day's business took hold. Betimes her head still spun with all the changes in her life since summer. It all harkened back to a betrothal announcement, then a bottle left on a shelf . . .

She pushed back the distant past to savor the memory of the night before. And the vision, as Magnus had called it, the secret revelation of her very soul. Not just a home but *their* home. She couldn't say if it would be in Virginia or Scotland. But it was home, and it was so vivid and lovely it seemed she could reach out and touch it.

Her stomach gave a low rumble. She'd forgotten to ask the housekeeper about breakfast. She didn't expect to partake of it in the mansion's dining room. Her workday was about to begin. Next to her, Larkin made his usual morning noises in his box bed, merry sounds that chased away the worries of a new day. Rolling over, she peered down at him, his wide smile lighting up their odd world. She chattered to him as she dressed, exchanging a nightgown for a plain but bright blue-striped petticoat and jacket that Mistress Flowerdew had given her per the terms of her contract.

She gathered Larkin up in her arms and traced the shell path to the kitchen house in the service area behind the hedge.

"Mornin', Mistress MacDougall," a stout woman said, a bright red kerchief wrapped round her ebony head. "You and Master Larkin's up with the cock's crow." She left the hearth where half a dozen items sizzled and simmered, wiping hardened hands on her grease-spackled apron. "I'm Sally, boss o' the kitchen house. Flowerdew tol' me 'bout you."

Flowerdew? No "Mistress"? The omission made Lark smile. "Ye served us a fine supper."

"That I did, with a little help from my man, Cleve. Now let me greet this here baby who looks like he might o' rolled off that big ship." Her brows shot up as she took him from Lark. "Mercy, is your back broke? You need fattenin' up yo'self." Patting a bench, she bade Lark sit at the table.

Steaming coffee that was half cream, eggs, grits pooling with butter, and salted ham crowded Lark's end of the table, which seemed to groan at the addition of biscuits. Sally sat opposite her, Larkin on her lap, and began feeding him a bit of this and a bit of that, chuckling at the faces he made. Lark wanted to make a face or two herself. Whatever these Virginians boasted, grits was not porridge. Indian corn or maize, they called it. But the abundance continued to astound her, and afraid of seeming ungrateful, she ate heartily, as did Larkin, which seemed to please the cook.

"I expect you be back at the big house for supper tonight, least till the Scotsman leaves," Sally said. She went to a churn and lifted the lid, Larkin balanced on one ample hip. "It's good for us to be doin' for folks. Osbourne stays gone so much this house is full o' ghosts."

"I ken little about him," Lark said between bites. "Except that he seems kind."

"Kind he is. And mournful sad, least when he comes here. Once upon a time he wed a Carter from downriver. The both of them turned Royal Hundred into a place fit for royalty, the rooms and table always full to burstin'. And then yella fever took the mistress in three days, their unborn babe with her. The master closed Royal Hundred down and sent us to the other farms for a year or better. House and gardens got overgrown. Things fell to pieces."

Would the same happen to Kerrera Castle? "A woeful loss."

"Happens," Sally said with a resigned sigh. She poured Larkin's milk into an earthenware cup. "And then the master up and took hisself another bride, this one from England. She wants to come here now, acrost the ocean."

"I hope never to cross the ocean again," Lark murmured, thinking of Blackburn. Yet she would see Kerrera again, wouldn't she? Three years more. How could she ever call

Virginia home when Scotland had her heart?

Sally set Larkin on her aproned lap with an ease that bespoke a familiarity with children as much as with the kitchen.

"Yer good with him."

"I have me some grandbabies in the quarters. Try to see them when I can. They gonna be moon-eyed over this little rascal with hair red as a brick."

Larkin drank the fresh milk, his chin glistening with cream. He clapped his hands when Sally went too slow to suit him, which elicited a throaty chuckle from her.

"He's lively as can be," Sally said approvingly. "Powerful smart. I'll watch o'er him for a spell till you learn yer way around."

Thanking her, Lark left the comfort of the kitchen house and stepped into the rising heat. Bent on the bee skeps, she crossed into the kitchen garden where the hives were kept. The two that had survived the ocean crossing were among the eight swarms Royal Hundred already had in place. All were different varieties of bees, each making a quantity of unique honey. Built into the bricked wall were the more protective bee boles to shelter the skeps, much like the ones in the stone wall at the castle.

'Twas almost time for the honey harvest. By a fortnight's end she'd don the protec-

tive garments she'd seen in the stillroom —
the long smock and veil made of willow —
and begin. Each season here would bring
different tasks, the same as in Scotland. The
time would come when she must smoke the
bees by burning sulphur beneath them,
carefully cutting out the beeswax and gathering the honey. The hives would be bundled
and kept under cover all winter till spring,
when she'd line the inside of the skeps with
lemon balm, planting thyme, and borage in
abundance in the bee garden's upturned
soil.

Here was her life's work for the next three
years — the garden that was part apothecary, part culinary, part perfumery. She
walked about, memorizing beds. One overflowed with tansy, parsley, madder, walnut,
and woad, the best plants for dyes. The
favored culinary herbs lived near the kitchen
doorway — wild clary, sage, rosemary, mint,
and thyme. The medicinal patch, crowned
with feverfew, angelica, and valerian, was a
stone's throw from the orangery. Colorful
butterflies hovered in the bee balm, a lovely,
spirit-lifting sight.

"You look at home in the garden." Mistress Flowerdew stood beneath an arbor
overhung with a fragrant flowering vine.

" 'Tis all I've ever known." Lark smiled.

"When is Mr. Osbourne expected?"

"Late spring or early summer in the new year. By then we shall all have Royal Hundred restored to its former glory."

A formidable task. Lark's gaze roamed the weedy paths, dependencies in need of painting, tumbled-down fences, and shutters askew.

"The laird is out riding with Mr. Granger. There are some farming matters to discuss that might stand his lairdship in good stead in the sugar islands." She bent and picked several sprigs of mint. "You'll join us for supper again, of course. I want to hear all about how you and the babe came to be here. The tale is exciting, no doubt." She returned to the house, linen skirts swirling as she walked.

Kneeling, Lark began to weed a bed of lavender, her stomach knotted. How to explain Isla's death? Tolbooth? A convict ship? Would it not be better left unsaid?

Lord, grant me the words.

Leaning in, palms biting into the oyster-shell walk, she let the lavender's timeless sight and scent soothe her. She'd prepare a tincture of lavender. Sew it into the hem of Larkin's garments. Make lavender soap. Gather bunches to hang upside down from the rafters.

The late summer season was waning. She must harvest carefully, not only the lavender but a hundred other things vying for her attention. And tend the bees. Always the bees.

And Larkin.

How was she to prepare for Richard Osbourne and his family, and manage the still-room and Larkin too?

Och, to have a helpmate — a husband — and a home of her own. Then these precious hours would be hers alone to spend with Larkin and do as the day bade.

Heaven help thou me.

The clink of cutlery and rumble of thunder were the only sounds heard for several tense moments as Mistress Flowerdew digested their tale.

"You were arrested, then, for wearing a kilt? Pardon me, your lairdship, but are there not more serious crimes for the king to be concerned with?"

"Apparently not," Magnus answered, forking a bite of fowl.

The factor, Mr. Granger, was absent. Indisposed. Relieved, Lark found dinner far more pleasant with just the four of them, including Larkin who sat upon the carpet playing with an empty snuff box. The tale of their coming to America unspooled with considerable finesse as Magnus skirted the sordid details sure to raise their housekeeper's eyebrows.

Lark added truthful embellishments when she could. "I confess to the babe not being mine. Larkin's kindred perished before we set sail, so I gladly took him, though I ken little about babies, having none of my own."

"Not yet, you mean," Mistress Flowerdew said. "No doubt you'll have a long line of suitors once word spreads that Royal Hundred has a new stillroom mistress."

"I shall be too busy for courting," Lark said softly, not daring a look at Magnus. She took up a spoon to sample a fluted glass of quince compote. "And the terms of my contract say I canna wed."

"Mr. Osbourne has allowed it before," the housekeeper returned. "So long as you and your groom remain at Royal Hundred and fulfill the contract terms."

Magnus regarded Lark through the haze of candlelight. She gave him a self-conscious smile. Was he thinking of their heartfelt talk since his confession aboard the *Bonaventure*? Her gaze fell to the dripping wax coating the silver candelabra like white icing. The perfume from the bayberry candles was heady, another Virginia oddity. Bayberry bushes grew by the sea and gave a smoke-less light, unlike their beeswax candles on Kerrera.

"And you, your lairdship? Is there a Lady MacLeish?"

The amiable question hung in the air. No mention had yet been made of Isla.

"Once there was," he said in that low tone laced with resignation and regret. "I'm recently bereaved."

The housekeeper's lined face clouded. "My sympathies, sir. I recall Mr. Osbourne saying what a support you were to him in the loss of his first wife, my dear niece. I never imagined you would share the same fate."

So, Mistress Flowerdew had a personal connection to Royal Hundred, beyond her position as housekeeper? Another piece of their colonial puzzle fell into place.

As if sensing their surprise, she continued, "I am the spinster in the Flowerdew family whose position here as housekeeper keeps me from the poorhouse. Mr. Osbourne's benevolent bent makes me quite devoted to his happiness and those in his employ."

"He is a man who pays more than lip service to his faith," Magnus said.

"Indeed, a rarity. I'm anxious to meet his new wife and son when they arrive."

"How long will they stay?" Lark asked.

"A year, perhaps. His bride is very curious about British America and has family in Philadelphia. She'll remain here at Royal Hundred while he conducts his colonial business. He may venture to Jamaica. There was a recent uprising among the slaves at Trelawny Hall. The overseers are too harsh, I fear." Lifting a hand, she summoned a servant to serve coffee. "Mr. Osbourne is a man of integrity who struggles with the matter of slavery. I'm sure he's made you aware of the difficulties you'll soon encounter."

"Aye, he has."

Did Magnus feel the weight of his responsibilities? If so, he gave no sign of it. Lark stirred sugar and cream into her cup, trying to develop a taste for Caribbean coffee over tea. How on earth did Magnus drink his coffee black?

Her gaze left the table and landed on Larkin, who'd abandoned the empty snuff box. He lay on his side, determination sketched across his round face, and finally rolled over on the rug before their very eyes. Delighted, Lark set down her cup and clapped her hands. He gave her a damp, lopsided grin. Forsaking his coffee, Magnus rose and scooped him up, tossing him high into the air till he'd gained a belly laugh.

Any mournfulness was pushed back. Magnus settled Larkin against his chest, where the babe began picking at the imported buttons of his linen waistcoat. He claimed their attention as Magnus sat down and fed him the rest of his pudding.

"Ye've won him over, ye have," Lark said, trying to paint an enduring picture of them in her head and heart — the babe appearing more interested in the man than the spoonful of dessert, and Magnus regarding him, a child not his own but who had a clear hold on his heart.

"Tomorrow I'll show you the quarters and dependencies," the housekeeper said as the last of the dishes were whisked away. "If you're not acquainted with the more practical aspects of plantation life, you'd best prepare yourself."

Prepare yourself.

The solemn words kept Lark awake as much as the tar-like coffee and the snippets of conversation that threaded through her dreams. Surely the plantation's quarters wouldn't be as humble and hunger-ridden as Kerrera in a lean year. Osbourne's Christian principles extended to his slaves, surely. Except Osbourne was an ocean away.

The next morn, she and Larkin again

breakfasted with Sally and Cleve in the kitchen. The stoop-shouldered Cleve was as quiet as his wife was talkative, but Lark found him amiable, his interest in Larkin unforced. He even sat the babe on his bony knee and amused him while she ate and Sally fried bacon.

"I'd leave the babe here iffen you visit the quarters. There's a late summer fever goin' round."

A pinprick of alarm prodded Lark more fully awake.

"We be glad to keep him." Sally pointed to a kitchen corner where she'd laid a quilt, with a wooden spoon and some kitchenware atop the diamond design. "Since he's not crawlin', he'll be content right there away from the heat o' the hearth."

Already the kitchen held a humid sheen, the late summer morn stifling. Thanking her, Lark situated Larkin on the quilt and placed a wooden spoon in his hand, listening for a parting cry that never came as she moved toward the mansion.

The Virginia residence was built in 1702, so a stone marker said. She liked the mansion's wide windows and the way the shell walk ran right up to the riverfront door, flowers and climbing vines on all sides.

Mistress Flowerdew greeted her, the

aroma of coffee lingering. "The laird was just amusing me with talk of Scottish breakfasts. Strong tea, porridge with a splash of whisky, and oatcakes."

Though full of biscuits, Lark hungered for the familiar. She followed the housekeeper into the foyer, where they perused family portraits on the paneled walls while waiting for the laird. Magnus didn't keep them long, and soon they were out the door and down the path to the quarters she'd spied coming to Royal Hundred.

From a distance, it did seem a village with rows of identical houses and garden patches. Small as Scotland's crofts, the log huts were daubed with mud, glazed windows keeping out insects in the summer and the wet in winter. But unlike Kerrera's stone cottages, these dwellings seemed flimsy.

Children of every color darted about like butterflies. Free of all but the simplest shifts or shirts or breeches, they went barefoot and bareheaded. A few drew near shyly, clearly curious about their coming.

"Some seventy or so souls live here. Most are married and these are their children. The elderly watch over the smallest till they come of age to work." The housekeeper gestured to a lane leading to yet another batch of log dwellings. "Down this row are the indentures, also field hands. Most labor long days in the tobacco and other crops no matter the season."

"And the Sabbath?" Magnus asked.

"All rest on the Sabbath. Mr. Granger issues passes between the farms for courting and visiting of kin for those with good behavior."

"Are these gardens theirs?" Lark lingered at a large patch fenced with split rails. She spied a few colorful squashes hiding among dwindling serpentine vines.

The housekeeper nodded. "These supplement the ration of meat and corn given them." She pointed to a far more substantial house in a copse of trees on a near rise. "The factor lives there. The overseers of the lesser farms dwell farther down the river. As factor, Mr. Granger manages them all."

They passed weavers, spinners, blacksmiths, tinsmiths, carpenters, and hostlers. Lark soon lost count. There was perpetual noise and activity in this part of the quarters as craftsmen and artisans toiled without even acknowledging them or looking up. Magnus was especially interested in the joiners and brick men. Lark found the spinning house intriguing, the telltale sheen of the Virginia heat on the dark skin of the spinners a constant reminder of just where they were.

Was it this warm in all the thirteen colonies? Or just here?

Magnus stepped to an open door of an end house while Mistress Flowerdew spoke with a white-haired woman at the next. Lark joined Magnus, a bit shy about intruding. But the place yawned empty, pallets on the dirt floor. A crude table and chairs sat before a fireless hearth.

Magnus leaned into the door frame. "I ne'er thought I'd see the day when a mere Scots croft seemed more castle."

Her heart squeezed. There was a telling poverty here, and a wariness, a wall, as if someone had knelt down in the dirt and drawn a line. Though she was indentured, she wasn't enslaved. All she'd ever known were the castle servants, who were able to come and go as they wished outside of work. But this . . .

The thought of a long winter spent in such spare surroundings bespoke a terrible kind of hardship. "Are Virginia winters cold, d'ye ken?" she murmured.

He looked at her, the depth of concern in his gaze making her own eyes smart. "I'll pray 'twill be an easy winter for all."

She forced a smile, though the coming season, brightened by her favorite holiday, would be nothing like in Scotland. 'Twas an occasion that she and Magnus had rarely spent apart. He'd always enjoyed New Year's at Kerrera.

They returned to the mansion and formal gardens, silent and deep in thought.

Toward afternoon, at work among the bees, she heard a horse beyond the yew hedge near the stables. Magnus was in the service yard talking with the rider. When he'd ridden off in a storm of Virginia dust, Magnus walked toward her and said, "We sail tomorrow."

Tomorrow. The word sank like a stone inside her. Shifting Larkin to her other hip, she simply nodded, then returned to the stillroom where she lay Larkin in his box bed for a nap. Keeping the connecting door open between them, she set about finishing the soap she and Sally had started making yesterday. The frothy mix had cooled and hardened in large wooden frames on the stillroom's worktable. Today she'd cut the soap into bars to cure, transforming a simple cupboard into a fragrant bower. Lavender and wintergreen made a fine toilet soap, silky and with a good lather, but Sally preferred sassafras, something unknown to Lark.

" 'Tis good to see the stillroom busy

361

again." Mistress Flowerdew stood in the doorway. Closing her eyes, she breathed in the delightful fragrance. "Did I show you the bagnio — the bathhouse — next to the laundry? Soon you'll have it in use again, though Dr. Meakes — the physic who treats the servants — may take you to task. He believes bathing destroys the body's natural defenses and makes one prone to disease."

"A common mindset." Lark had mistaken the bagnio for a privy — a necessary, the housekeeper called it.

"By now you likely know the laird is leaving soon." Even Mistress Flowerdew looked downcast. "This evening there's an invitation to Mount Brilliant, the seat of the Calverts. I hoped you and his lairdship might accompany me."

"Well . . ." Lark swallowed. Weary and soap-spackled, she'd envisioned a quiet evening with Larkin and Magnus. As for an invitation, a proper dress . . .

"I shall lend you another gown. And the bagnio is at your disposal. I'll send one of the maids to help you dress." She started away, clearly delighted. "Larkin will be kept by Sally. We shan't be out too late."

28

George Washington danced upwards of three hours without once sitting down.
General Nathanael Greene

In the span of a few hours, they walked to the waterfront where a shallop awaited instead of a carriage. Their hosts lived on the other side of the James, a mile or more downriver. Stepping into the waiting boat with six oars, an awning, and both coxswain and bargeman in livery, Lark felt she'd fallen into a fairy tale.

Seated across from Mistress Flowerdew and beside Magnus, she arranged her embroidered skirts. The airy lavender lustring was a perfect pairing for the sultry Virginia eve. Thanks to the help of a housemaid, her hair was powdered, her stays breathlessly tight, her throat circled with a genteel velvet ribbon and cameo.

Mistress Flowerdew looked triumphant.

"You'll be something of a célèbre tonight," she said to Magnus, "you and Miss Mac-Dougall."

"Surely yer neighbors are acquainted with the Scots who make up so much of Virginia's economy."

"The Scots merchants, you mean. A far cry from a landed, titled laird like yourself. You remain one of the gentry, no matter what King George may say."

Magnus chuckled and reached up to adjust his stock. "Kilt-less and castle-less yet still welcome."

"Yes, indeed. I daresay you'll find none of the middling sort present tonight. Only the top tier of Virginia society, including the new French dancing master from Williamsburg."

Lights lit up Mount Brilliant like a beacon. The slope of lawn leading to the dock was illuminated by several servants holding lanterns who accompanied them up the hill to the mansion. Virginians had a penchant for brick, this house bearing countless diamond-glass windowpanes and soaring columns.

They passed from porch to foyer and through an arched doorway to a ballroom of creamy woodwork and English wallpaper, elegant and airy but for the crush of guests.

Music spilled from a raised dais at one end of the long room. Supper smells, seafood foremost, rode the humid air.

Lark pressed a lavender-lined handkerchief to her upper lip. So many candles, the lights calling out the flash of jewels and sheen of colorful dresses. Their hosts greeted them warmly as a minuet signaled the ball's beginning. She curtsied and Magnus bowed again and again as other couples greeted them in turn.

Taking her arm, Magnus led Lark out to join the gathering dancers, those of the highest rank going first. Though she preferred the country dances, the minuet was measured and artful, and Magnus had always been a splendid partner. Though his father might have been against their marriage, he'd had few qualms about her being educated alongside his son, and that had included an itinerant dancing master. Her lovely gown gave her extra confidence amid the whispering behind fans. They were creating quite a stir.

"The laird and his lady," someone said.

Being Scottish, they did everything a wee bit differently, and that included dancing. But the attention was approving, even admiring, and she felt the delight of it to her toes.

Soon she was singled out by other gentlemen of all ages and stations, though all had one thing in common — a love of dancing. She forgot the fierce heat. The odd mingling of accents. Her humble station. Larkin's well-being. Even Magnus's impending departure.

Suppertime found them full of Virginia's remarkable fare — and syllabub, a frothy concoction that Virginians seemed as fond of as dancing. One cup left her light-headed so she declined more. Magnus claimed her for one reel, then a jig. Throat parched, she wanted to drink from the garden fountain.

How they snuck away from the crowded ballroom after hours of dancing was no small feat. The gentle pressure of his hand on her lace sleeve led to a night dazzling with stars and the perfume of late-blooming roses beyond the ballroom's French doors. Sitting down on a wrought-iron bench near the fountain's splash, Magnus at her side, she watched the melee of swirling dancers in a way she hadn't been able to inside.

"These Virginians dance till dawn," he mused.

"They seem not to mind the close quarters."

"Their stamina is staggering." He ran a finger around his stock as if wanting to untie it altogether. "Mayhap they have Scots blood."

She smiled and shut her eyes as the breeze strengthened, stirring both her hair and her gown's hem. Oh, to slow time or wind it backwards. What she would give to hold on to the few precious moments left to them before parting.

"Ye promise to pen me a letter?"

Her eyes opened. So he was thinking of the morrow too. Her voice lifted above the music. "Long ago I used to write to ye, after ye'd gone to Edinburgh."

His buckled shoe kicked at a pebble in the grass. "I still have yer letters. All nine or so."

Oh? "Yet ye wrote but once."

"I owe ye a belated apology." He angled his head toward her, arms crossed. "Yer letters were so prettily written yet so full of Kerrera, each felt like a thorn to me."

"Ye missed the island."

"Aye." He hesitated. "And ye."

She fingered the borrowed cameo at her throat, her heart so full her mind was empty.

He continued, "I have them now, in my trunk. Tied with blue silk ribbon, yer favorite color."

Regret pummeled her. She'd saved his very first letter to her in the family Bible at the croft. As for the second, she'd fed his few penned lines to the croft fire as if doing so could ease her angst. It hadn't. "If ye've kept them, ye dinna need me to pen another."

He took her teasing with a flash of a smile. "I would have the penned musings of Lark the woman, not Lark the girl."

"Lark the tattie bogle, ye mean." She smoothed a crease in her lustring.

"Yer no scarecrow, Lark. Not in that gown. Whatever tolbooth and the *Bonaventure* stole, it wasna yer womanliness."

The night turned warmer. She looked to her lap as his thoughtful words seared her memory and took a bold breath. "Write to me first. Then I'll have something to remember ye by, come what may."

"As soon as I land, then."

She nodded. "Before ye go, I want to give ye a kit of Jesuit's bark and some things to take for fever and the like."

"Yer prayers are more effective."

"Ye'll have both. And a letter in time."

Just how long was the distance from Virginia to the sugar islands?

As if reading her mind, he said, "A month's sailing to Jamaica."

She bit her lip. "So very far."

"Closer than Kerrera. From what I've

been told, 'tis a different world. Hectares of sugarcane, mills for refining it. Coffee, indigo, rice. Slaves and indentures. I ken little else."

It sounded harsh. As different from Virginia as Virginia was from Scotland.

Inside the ballroom, a reel gave way to an allemande but she felt in no mood to dance. Weary to the bone she was.

Lark looked up. The moon foretold midnight. Morning came too soon.

Before she could stifle a yawn, a fast-moving Mistress Flowerdew rushed down the mansion steps into the garden, skirts a-swirl. "There you are! 'Tis after midnight and the shallop awaits."

Bypassing the house, they took a path through the garden down to the river, where the lantern-lit vessel waited to return them to Royal Hundred. Their night of enchantment was over.

How long had he been standing there?

Lark paused in her morning's work, taking a moment to rock a fretful Larkin in the chair near an open window, when a dark silhouette at the door caught her eye.

Hat in hand, Magnus regarded her as if unwilling to intrude. The memories they'd made the last few nights would carry her through the coming days. These were a gift.

He cleared his throat. "Goodbye for noo. See ye efter."

The simple Scots farewell had come at last. Even Larkin quieted. Twisting on her lap, he sat up and reached out plump arms toward the deeply grounded voice.

Her heart tore in two.

Tossing his hat and knapsack aside, Magnus strode in and caught up Larkin in a bearish embrace. He buried his face in the lad's downy shoulder, his coal-black hair a startling contrast to Larkin's stark red.

Lark stood awkwardly, biting her lip till her tears retreated, and passed into the still-room where the medicine kit she'd made him waited. Her heart, so bruised since leaving Kerrera, broke anew. So fragile she felt. Life was fragile. Only God knew if she'd see him again.

Chin firming, she took Larkin back while Magnus untied his knapsack and put her bundle inside. When he looked over at her in thanks, his blue eyes glistened like the sea about Kerrera on a clear day. Her forced composure shattered anew. Tears wet her face, the ache in her throat building toward a cry. Sob she would not. She'd not leave him with anything less than a gladsome goodbye, be it a tad tearstained. He deserved a better parting.

"Slàinte, Magnus." She lay a hand on his sleeve, her other arm full of Larkin.

He put his arms around them both. His Gaelic came soft. *"Is thu mannsachd."*

Thou art my most beloved.

He set Larkin down so that his arms were for her alone. She closed her eyes. She'd come home. All her years-long yearnings were quelled in that instant.

She stayed standing while her senses were reeling, immersed in sandalwood and clean linen and the marvel of his mouth meeting hers. Their first kiss. Kisses. Till she was breathless and astir and all thought of anything but the two of them had taken wing.

And then he was gone, her last look at him a tear-washed blur.

That evening, she found the locket. The MacLeish heirloom. It lay on the stillroom table, previously unseen, busy as she'd been with the bees. It was heart-shaped. Transparent. Yellow-gold and crowned with tiny diamonds. His mother had worn it and then his sister.

She picked it up gently, having only viewed it at arm's length before. Inside was a lock of dark hair. Magnus's own? She melted like candle wax.

Afraid she'd somehow mar the heirloom by wearing it as she worked, she kept it close by pocketing it. Even its slight weight brought her joy.

Of all the things he'd left behind in Scotland, the locket had not been one of them. 'Twas a tie to Kerrera. His family. The past.

And now her.

29

The Great Hall . . . and everything in it is
superbly fine. . . . The front has the sea,
shipping, town and a great part of the
island in prospect, and the constant sea-
breeze renders it most agreeable.

Janet Schaw, St. Olives Plantation,
St. Kitts, 1774

Montego Bay, Jamaica
At first glance, the warm turquoise waters
and lush, lyrical landscape were all Magnus
saw. When his head cleared, other things
tugged at his attention. The comingling of
cocoa and coffee, sugarcane and spirits, a
potent blend in the sultry sea air. The
mishmash of languages and shades of skin,
from coal black to cinnamon to tobacco.
Slavers lay at anchor in the bustling harbor,
their contents a great many stoop-
shouldered, emaciated men, women, and
children bought and sold before his eyes.

His gut churned as his wary gaze landed on raucous parrots and agile monkeys in cages. Odd yellow and orange fruits. Coconuts. Plantains.

Hawkers shouted their wares as he inhaled meat-tinged smoke. The captain's pointed finger and explanations were so plentiful they failed to find anchor in Magnus's swirling brain.

Relief filled him as the wagon sent from Trelawny Hall to collect him left behind the colorful melee. His sole trunk had been thrown in back with a dull thud. The rutted road raised a fine red dust as it hugged the coastline. White sand glittered like diamonds. Other islands had black sand, even pink, but this creamy coastline stretched on as far as he could see, full of picturesque inlets and coves and beaches.

The Jamaican driver was mostly silent, his few words nonsensical to Magnus's untrained ear. Pidgin or Patois, Osbourne had called it. How would he as Trelawny Hall's factor expect to communicate here?

Osbourne had told him the former factor had died. Being hated by the indentures and slaves who often broke tools and equipment in retaliation, who shirked work by developing a system that let them avoid detection by those in charge, had surely lent to his demise. Trelawny Hall had tumbled from its standing as king of the sugar island plantations in terms of exports under the former factor's tenure. Magnus's charge was to regain its standing.

Was Osbourne's placement of him here a slur on their friendship? Or more a demonstration of faith in Magnus's abilities? Owing Osbourne a great debt for extracting him and Lark from tolbooth, he'd not shirk his duties, whatever they might be.

Even before they'd rolled past the plantation's wrought-iron gates, his spirit grew more troubled as the facts he'd been told resurfaced. Slave uprisings were commonplace. Overseers must always watch their backs. Some had been poisoned by their own household staff, others ambushed in the fields as they made their rounds. This was always followed by a swift hanging, but the unrest still roiled. Or so he'd been told by the *Bonaventure*'s crew while coming here.

Osbourne had told him the worst offenders among the Ashanti, the Africans known for their superior strength who formed the bulk of the plantation's labor. On the stormy ship's passage, he'd committed the unique names to memory. Kwasi. Gaddo. Kenu. Okoto. Manu.

Osbourne's longtime housekeeper and her husband, both Jamaicans by the names of Naria and Rojay, met him on the long, palm-fronted porch. Would he truly live in this place with its sweeping view of both the mist-shrouded Blue Mountains and a sheltered cove?

He'd expected a thatched roof hut, not this. The house was built on a foundation of solid stone, and the upper floors were timber, able to withstand both hurricanes and earthquakes. Window shutters and wide shades blocked the sun. The colonnaded loggia ran the length of the house on all sides.

"You, sir, are don dada, the chief of Trelawny Hall," Naria said with a wide, flashing smile, her flamboyant dress as bright as the parrot he spied on a near sea grape tree. "Your overseers live in the huts."

His bedchamber sat at the end of a cool, shadowed hall, a Spartan bower of mosquito netting and shuttered windows. His office was gained through a connecting door that reminded him of Lark's quarters and the stillroom at Royal Hundred. The territorial view gave him pause. The dwelling overlooked cane fields and the mill Osbourne had described in detail, made of imported British stone.

Field hands, much like those in Virginia, toiled in the two o'clock sun, their skin a-glisten. He didn't know their language, their customs. Their hearts.

If he'd ever missed Scotland before, he missed it fiercely now. Here he was naught but an outlander. A foreigner. Another factor to be despised and feared.

When a sudden shower snuffed the sun and drummed on the tiled roof, he wondered at the fickle weather. Ignorant as a schoolboy he was, and at the helm of a sprawling sugar empire he was expected to resurrect and return to its former glory.

Lord, help Thou me.

Within a fortnight Magnus grew used to Trelawny Hall's house servants moving about on whispering feet, the sudden tropical squalls, the rhythmic speech of the people around him. The damp linen of his garments seemed a second skin in the steamy heat as he rode his gelding mile after mile, familiarizing himself with Osbourne's overseers and operations.

At night, by the light of two tapers, the whine of insects outside the netting around him, he penned Lark a letter.

Dearest Lark,

I write this to you in a midnight room no less cool than midday. Though the calendar says we have been parted but a month, it seems an age. You and wee Larkin hover in my thoughts. When I left he was on the verge of crawling out of his box bed. Soon he will walk or run away from you and you'll be hard-pressed to catch him. I wonder with some pains if he'll remember me.

I covet your prayers. The enslaved here are of a warlike tribe, startlingly strong people from Africa's Ivory Coast. They live in squalor made worse by careless, cruel overseers.

Tomorrow I meet with the foremost troublemakers of the Ashanti themselves, whom I confess to liking better than their white masters. I would sooner whip an overseer than a slave.

I do not mean to weary you with plantation talk. Just pray.

How goes it with the bees? Your colonial garden? Mistress Flowerdew? What new words does Larkin ken?

I beseech you to write as often as you are able.

Yours entire,
Magnus

Lark broke the indigo seal. 'Twas her first letter from Magnus on this side of the Atlantic. She brought the fine vellum to her nose, imagining it carried a hint of exotic spices and trade winds.

"Slow ye doon."

Granny's cautionary words echoed in her thoughts. Savor the letter she would. It seemed he'd been gone an age. Time and distance did strange things.

She purposed to answer his penned questions one by one. By day's end, she'd fashioned a reply in her head, so tired by the time she inked her quill that she misspelled letters only to cross them out and try again.

All the hives are harvested. Mistress Flowerdew had a spell of the gout but found some relief with the elm leaf tea I gave her. Larkin calls me Mim. He says "ball" and "cat." I keep your locket near at hand . . .

She folded the letter. Pondered all she kept tamped down like a hogshead of turmoil but could not pen.

I have survived my first fever. Larkin swallowed a button, and I was beside myself till it came out. Mr. Granger chides me for visiting the quarters too often and taking remedies and small conveniences there, which he says will spoil the Africans and make them unfit for work. I spoke back and said that so long as he allows them to live lowly as beggars, I will try to allay their miseries when I can. Sally cautions me and tells me he may complain to Osbourne to have me sent elsewhere, but secretly she supports me and says the people are glad of my coming.

The heat continues to be my greatest foe. Often I feel too weak for the work and long for a bracing headwind and Scottish sunset. For you.

But it is not to be.

He felt a wee bit like the biblical Joseph. Sold into slavery by his kinsmen, then placed in a position of authority in a strange land. But 'twas the prophet Isaiah who held him captive and gave him courage.

And if thou draw out thy soul to the hungry, and satisfy the afflicted soul; then shall thy light rise in obscurity, and thy darkness be as the noon day: And the Lord shall guide thee continually, and satisfy thy soul in drought, and make fat thy bones: and thou shalt be like a watered garden, and like a spring of water, whose waters fail not.

His mindset as a laird did not alter though he'd lost his Scottish holdings. Though Jamaica was more like Hades to him — affliction and hunger abounding in this strange land in far more profound, soul-tearing ways than on Kerrera — he grappled with what could be done.

He assembled Osbourne's overseers, a hardened trio who made the excise men in Alba seem like saints. One had his whip at his thigh, which prompted Magnus to say, "There'll be no more use of the whip until any quarrels are brought to me straightaway. If I hear of ye breaking the new mandate, 'twill be yer own back that's striped." He paused to let the words find purchase, unsurprised by the flare of ire and indignation in their eyes. "Any incident of insubordination is to be brought to me first for a fair hearing, aye?"

Their grudging grunts were belated.

He plunged ahead regardless. "There are two matters that need mending. The first concerns the weekly ration of the workers." He refused to call them slaves. "A peck of corn, a pint of salt, and a pound of meat is akin to starvation. 'Tis an outright disgrace. Ye'll oversee a tripling of the rations and assign a rotation where a number of workers have days to cook for their fellows in the fields, each getting a turn. The fare will be supplemented with ample quantity of fresh produce sold in Montego Bay."

"Triple rations? Are you daft, sir?" the oldest of the three said. "You'll bankrupt Osbourne —"

"Nay. 'Twill simply ensure the laborers are fit for the work and reduce the sick and infirm, thus helping quell the ongoing threat of uprising." He went to a window and lowered a shade where the afternoon sun slanted blindingly across the ledgers on his desk. "Ye'll also set about repairing their dwellings, many of which are in poor condition, and ye'll spare no expense doing so."

"But there are countless huts. Will you have us refurbish them all?" said the youngest, a florid-faced Dutchman with a thick accent.

"Every one of them, aye, beginning today. Enlist those whom ye will to assist ye. I'll keep a close tally of expenses. D'ye have questions?"

A sore silence. Hats in hand, they eyed each other, and then the eldest spoke again.

"I say it cannot be done — should not be done. Our tasks are many, yet you heap more on our backs, all for an ungrateful, shiftless lot of slaves who require the whip to do the slightest task. What if we refuse you? Object to do as you bid?"

"Refuse?" Magnus looked toward the open door where three Negro men waited. "Then ye'll be replaced by the Ashanti themselves — Kwasi, Gaddo, and Yaw."

A curse split the stunned silence.

Magnus stared at the offender. "And ye'll keep a clean tongue in yer head, at least in my company. Good day to ye."

Where had Osbourne gotten these men? Granted, the work of an overseer was arduous and unenviable, but would their lot not be made better by improving the lots of the workers?

The overseers trudged out. The three Ashanti took their places, their dark eyes never settling as they assessed a place they'd never been — this inner sanctum, a chamber considered too grand for slaves.

Rojay, Magnus's manservant, stood to his left, facing the Africans. All were understandably wary. Their dealings with Europeans had been dark from their first point of capture on the Ivory Coast. Their ingrained, justified guardedness might never lessen.

But he would stay true to Scripture and attempt to satisfy the afflicted souls in his keeping, no matter the cost or consequence.

"How do you say 'welcome' in Ashanti Twi?" he asked Rojay.

The older man hesitated, his sweat-dampened features lined with surprise. *"Akwaaba."*

"Akwaaba," Magnus repeated, wanting to meet the men's eyes though they would not look at him. Would they ever? "Today I call ye here to tell ye of coming changes. From this day forward ye will have more to eat. Better huts to lodge in."

He paused to allow Rojay to translate. The words were oddly melodic.

He continued slowly. "Today is the day we find other ways to benefit yer people and this plantation. Every sennight we will meet here and ye'll bring word of what is happening in the homes ye live in and the fields where ye labor — any and all injustices, sickness, and unrest. Anything that might be made better by coming to me. If I do not know of these things I cannot fix them. Yer to be my eyes and ears since I cannot be everywhere at once all the time. Only Almighty God has that power."

Rojay translated in short bursts, sometimes grappling for a word not easily had in

Twi. Listening, Magnus felt at sea. Mightn't it be better if he tried to learn their language? Could he? No doubt he'd be among the first white men in Jamaica to do so. Or even want to.

He trod carefully, saying little else. No need to overwhelm them with too many words. Too many changes. They spoke among themselves, their gestures and intonations fascinating and wholly unfamiliar.

'Twas said there were ten Africans for every white man in Jamaica. Yet he felt more comfortable in the presence of these men than he had the overseers.

The Ashanti filed out, backs straight, their tall, underfed frames a wonder of muscle and sinew, their faces masks of composure. Magnus's gaze lingered longest on Kwasi's back, crisscrossed with a horror of scars from a whipping scarcely healed. They'd all been branded with Osbourne's mark.

How would it be to own a man? A fellow human being? A body, if not a soul? To embed one's name in another's skin till death? That side of Osbourne was unknown to him.

At the end of the veranda, the tallest of the Africans turned back and gave Magnus a lingering look before disappearing from sight. He had said something to Rojay at the last. Something that escaped Magnus completely.

The slight smile touching the translator's mouth was mirrored in his eyes. "They call you *Adofo.*"

"Adofo?" Magnus echoed.

Rojay nodded slowly. "In Ashanti, it means 'the special one from God.' "

30

Dark and sour humours, especially those which have a spice of malevolence in them, are vastly disagreeable. Such men have no music in their souls.

Abigail Adams

'Twas November. In Scotland, the seasons were more muted. In Virginia, autumn seemed all aflame. Everywhere Lark looked was a burst of color, even in the fading garden. Sally had finally harvested the last of the vegetables. Larkin grew plumper on roasted pumpkin and boiled squash and delicious mincemeat tarts.

"You no longer a scarecrow yo'self," Sally told Lark as she served her another piece of cushaw pie with cream. "Gettin' plumper by the day."

"Not so peely-wally?" Lark replied with a smile, Larkin on her lap.

"None o' that neither, whatever it is."

Sally chuckled as the babe tried to grab Lark's spoon. "He's goin' throw hisself a fit lest you share that pie."

Lark fed him the pie. "Am I wrong to want to keep him wee?"

"Naw. A lap baby's easier than one with legs. Pert soon he'll be runnin' to the quarters."

"He's fond of the other children. They're good to him, toting him around and making much of his hair."

" 'Tis a mess o' curls, all right. Bright as the noonday sun. Yours is a bit lighter since you in the garden so much." Sally set down a kettle of greens. "Don't the sun ever shine in Scotland?"

Lark regarded her through a ray of light dancing with dust motes. Would her homesickness never lessen? Did Magnus feel the same? "The sun isna so strong, nor so warm there. Scotland's a land of clouds and mist, mostly."

"Well, you goin' to be more Virginian when you is through. And yo' man, he'll be more Jamaican."

"Nay," Lark said. "Scots to the bone, the both of us, as is wee Larkin." Flushing, she added, "And the laird is not mine, truly."

Not yet.

"Now whatever made me think that, I

wonder?" Sally winked. "You just mention his name night and day."

Did she? They talked often of her former life, she and Sally. Stifling a sigh, Lark spoke what she'd mulled in her mind countless times. "Jamaica is too far for courting."

"But not letter writin'. Flowerdew tol' me you send posts right regular — and done got a reply all the way from Jamaica."

"Just once." There, she had voiced it. "I fear he's ill."

" 'Tis the seasoning, likely," Sally muttered. "He'll either get well or die, and nothin' you can do but pray."

Magnus had the kit she'd given him from the stillroom — the Jesuit's bark and ample herbs and simples — to sustain him. But she was not there to dispense them if he was too ill to fend for himself. This was a new worry, added to her hogshead of angst. Was there a physic to be had in Jamaica?

She looked to Larkin, a reason for praise. Here he sat, a wingless cherub, the picture of health, thriving like a hardy Scottish thistle in Virginia's rich soil.

She left the kitchen, Larkin in arm. Situating him on a quilt with a wooden spoon and playthings, she surveyed what needed doing. There were never enough hands for the work. With the former gardener felled by the pox and an advertisement for a replacement just posted in the *Virginia Gazette,* her days were longer even as daylight grew shorter.

Dropping to her knees in the pleasure garden, the formal beds hedged by tall yew, she began uprooting stubborn weeds even as new worries sprouted in her mind. When she was most tired, most overwhelmed by the work, she fretted most. *Lord, forgive me.* The distance, the unknown, chafed like never before.

Was Magnus lying there, friendless and far from home, too sick to hold a quill and pen a letter? Had he gotten her replies? Had he done the unthinkable and died? Was he even now buried in fine Jamaican sand? Her thoughts swerved to Granny, who could neither read nor write. Lark had not penned her a single sentence, yet the very thought pained her so. Mayhap a letter should be sent to Kerrera's reverend, a man of letters who could reassure Granny she was all right.

Pondering it, she sat back on her heels as a shadow snuffed the sun. A tall, uncommonly lean shadow.

The captain stood over her as in days of old. Rory MacPherson.

Her backside collided with the soil even as her mouth made an *O* of astonishment.

He looked over his shoulder as if certain of being followed. "I heard ye were at the main house. I'm at one of Osbourne's smaller farms. In the fields. Brutal, back-breaking work."

She believed it. He wasn't made for land but for sea. Even his cheekbones were sharper, his frame hollowed out when it had been so solid before.

His hopeful glance at the kitchen house reminded her Sally and Cleve had gone to the quarters. "Are ye . . . hungert?"

"Always. Barely enough to keep a bird alive."

She stood, shaking the soil from her skirt. In minutes, she'd returned with some corn cakes. He made a face but took them. While he ate, she drew water from the well and gave him a drink too, wishing for a little sweet milk. Or ale. He was partial to the latter, or once was at the Thistle.

"Cursed country." The epithet spilled from his lips like bread crumbs. "How goes it for ye?"

" 'Tis not Scotland."

"Nay. And for Scotland I'm bound. But first Cape Fear in Carolina. A few of us are set on making our escape."

"But Mr. Granger — ye ken what's done to runaways."

"Only if they're caught." He finished drinking and swiped the water from his chin with the back of his hand. "The overseers are worthless. And the factor ye mention isna in the fields much as he's ailing."

This she knew. Granger's wife was oft at the stillroom door, seeking a remedy. And Mistress Flowerdew fretted, secretly confiding she hoped both the factor and his wife would move on.

His eyes pinned her. "Will ye run with us?"

"With a bairn?" She got back on her knees and began pulling weeds with a vengeance. "And break my contract?"

His eyes flashed. "An unjust indenture, based on a crime ye didna commit."

"Be that as it may, I'm here and here I'll stay." She wouldn't say she had more to eat in British America than she'd had in Scotland, or that Mistress Flowerdew, nigh starved for company, spoiled her and Larkin by having them to the house and giving them privileges. Rory knew no such niceties in the fields.

"Yer waiting for the laird to return, no doubt." He dropped to his haunches, gaze on the chain she wore, the heirloom locket now hidden beneath her bodice where once she'd worn the coral beads. She'd placed the beads in a stillroom cupboard, unsure of what to do with them. "Ye'd as soon resurrect the dead. The sugar islands devour outlanders like us. The laird's done."

He'd spoken her greatest fear aside from losing Larkin. All her carefully constructed hopes flew away like startled sparrows.

He spat into the dirt again. "Leave the bairn behind. He's not yers —"

"Aye, he is. I couldna love him more if I'd borne him." Even now her heart squeezed as she looked at him babbling and cooing across the grass. "He calls me *Mim* as he canna say *mither*. I'll not tell him any different."

He shrugged her sentiment aside. "There'll be other bairns. Blood kin. And a husband if ye were not so stubborn."

Bidding him wait, she retrieved the coral beads from the stillroom cupboard. His brow raised when she returned them. "They're yers and may make yer journey better. I can wear them no longer. My heart belongs to another." She braced herself for any questions, but he simply pocketed the necklace without a murmur of displeasure.

A door banged shut and he shot to his feet. "Star Farm. Send word to me there by month's end and we'll arrange to meet should ye change yer mind."

November's end? Star Farm was unknown

to her, though she'd heard it produced Osbourne's best tobacco.

Rory vanished behind the hedge and she let out a long sigh. She continued her work through the afternoon, finishing with the bees.

Late in the day Larkin gave a loud mewl — his restless cry upon rousing from his nap — and Sally rounded the corner, making a beeline toward the stillroom to fetch the babe. He quieted when he saw Lark, reaching out his arms to her. Lark took him, thanking the woman. The day was almost done. At nearly six o'clock, Sally needed to mind supper.

Lark kissed the babe's soft brow. Clad in a linen shirt and clout with pilchard, he gave a sleepy smile as she took him to see the new pony in the stables. Brushing aside one of many autumn cobwebs, she passed several shadowed stalls, breathing in pungent hay and horse droppings. Simple, earthy smells that reminded her of Scotland.

Larkin squirmed in her arms, only settling when a groom set him atop the pony's bare back. Pleased as punch he was, making them laugh. Soon he'd need a quilted pudding cap stuffed with horsehair to protect his head when he toddled and fell. Mistress Flowerdew had recently shown her a milliner's advertisement that read, "Thin Bone and Packthread stays for Children of three Months old and upwards." How she hated to put him in stays.

Mistress Flowerdew talked of taking her to shop at the capital, Williamsburg, less than five miles distant. Would the housekeeper feel differently if she knew of Lark's convict status and Larkin's own dubious birth? Was she not being forthcoming by keeping silent?

That evening the two of them did their usual handwork in the mansion's sitting room, where the housekeeper worked on embroidery while Lark sewed a handkerchief.

"I have something that needs saying," Lark began, hating the dread arising in her like indigestion. "Ye've been so kind. I dinna want any secrets between us."

She took a deep breath and the story poured forth — Isla, tolbooth, Osbourne's timely intervention, Larkin's sad beginnings. To her credit, the housekeeper's expression remained unchanged. She didn't miss a stitch.

" 'Tis the stuff of novels!" she exclaimed when Lark finished. "Mr. Osbourne simply said in his letter you'd been falsely accused by powerful people anxious to place blame.

He didn't give details. The laird's offense is laughable, as I've said from the very beginning. Kilt wearing, indeed! As for the babe, 'tis no accident but the highest workings of Providence that Larkin came to be in your hands. The Almighty takes special care of widows and orphans and the fatherless. That includes us three." She put away her handwork. "Now, shall we have a dish of tea?"

No more was said about the past. Lark felt a burden lift like a slate wiped clean. The lovely porcelain tea set appeared, the cozy room suffused with the fragrance of souchong. Though the housekeeper took her tea plain, she remembered Lark liked otherwise. Silver sugar tongs and a small jug of cream sat on the tea table. Truly, tea was the cup that cheered.

"Only the finest, though I do favor Caribbean coffee," Mistress Flowerdew said.

At this, Lark's thoughts spun south again. She offered up another silent petition on Magnus's behalf. What could she do but pray, as Sally said?

"Why don't we go to Williamsburg next market day?" Mistress Flowerdew said. "I'm in need of some things that only town can offer. I daresay 'tis naught but a speck compared to your Edinburgh and Glasgow. But the Virginia capital has a charm all its own, and an outing will do us good."

At their feet, Larkin waved two silver spoons and smiled up at them as if understanding every word.

"We shall leave you, sir, at home with Sally. But we'll bring you back a special play-pretty from one of the shops."

He gave a gurgling shout and they laughed, savoring the coveted tea.

Williamsburg, a new venture, awaited.

The woman who nursed him was not Lark. Dark as midnight she was, but oddly blue-eyed. A mulatto? He'd never seen her till now. She'd come in on the heels of the fever. Never had he been so sick. Sick enough to want to die and end the misery of each agonizing moment. Overnight his life had shrunk to sweat-stained bedding, a basin to retch in, and four walls.

But still he dreamed, stabbed by discontent and longing. Lark hovered, nearer than she'd ever been before. He breathed in her sweet, stillroom-laced scent. Felt the brush of her brilliant hair across his bare arm and chest as she cooled him with cloths. The few times he'd forced his eyes open she'd disappeared, the blue-eyed woman in her wake.

But 'twas Lark he wanted.

This strange woman — she chanted over him — put amulets beneath his bed. Once he'd grabbed her wrist in a feeble attempt to ward away more ill. "No witchery," he spat out through a throat dry as late autumn leaves. "Only Scripture."

She'd recoiled. Did she even understand his garbled words? After that, Naria and Rojay were at his side.

Time ticked on, he with it. A drenching rain forced stray drops through the ceiling and mosquito netting about his bed. Not chill Scottish rain but hot and unrefreshing. Or was he fancying that too?

Lord, let me die.

He was brought low by more than physical illness. He was sickened by affliction. Starvation. Cruelty. The melee around him. Little difference could be made in so vast a sea of suffering, surely. And he was sickened by separation. Unfulfilled longing. Miscarried dreams. He even missed Nonesuch with a keen ache.

Hope deferred maketh the heart sick.

Scotland seemed like paradise, its superstitions small and harmless. Here, a strange man in a strange land, he was in a fight. For more than his life.

At last a British voice broke through the blackness. "Yellow fever, no doubt. If he's lived this long it likely won't kill him. Scots are a hardy breed. Absolute devils in battle. The colonies have become a dumping ground for them . . ."

He was bled. Dosed with something vile. Then he slept. Dreamed. This time 'twas Larkin close at hand, a warm, weighty armful, just like he'd been at the last. How it had twisted his stoic heart to bid them farewell at Royal Hundred. If he saw the lad again, he'd be a babe no longer.

And Lark? Always Lark . . .

31

Wherever you travel . . . your ears are constantly astonished at the number of colonels, majors, and captains that you hear mentioned. . . . The whole country seems a retreat of heroes.

Edward Kimber, English traveler to America, 1745

"Williamsburg has less than two thousand residents, but the crowds swell during Publick Times when the courts are in session," Mistress Flowerdew said as their handsome carriage glided over leaf-littered dust that was ankle-deep, already earning them curious glances. " 'Tis lively as ever today."

Truly, the streets teemed with people. A fair unfolded on several acres with puppet shows, fiddling contests, foot races, and pig chases playing out before their eyes. Here there were more blacks than whites, of all castes, and a great many men in uniform.

Lark stared, transfixed by a copper-skinned people resplendent in furs and feathers beneath a sprawling oak tree.

"Indians. Cherokee, perhaps," Mistress Flowerdew explained. "Governor Dinwiddie tries to maintain friendly relations. They're feted at the Governor's Palace and entertained at the theatre. Soon it will be his majesty's birthday with fireworks on Palace Street and a ball."

Never before had Lark seen fireworks. Would they flare like muskets? Like the blue lights the smugglers used in free trading?

Their carriage slowed before what looked to be a tavern, where a line of slaves stood on the steps, heads bowed. A group of well-dressed men gathered, some clutching handbills and newspapers. The auctioneer's voice overrode the crowd's raucousness.

Lark tore her gaze away and fixed it on the far more comfortable millinery sign just ahead. Out of the open shop door spilled several young women in head-turning dresses and hats, ribbons aflutter in the Williamsburg wind.

"Solomon in all his glory was not arrayed like one of these," Mistress Flowerdew murmured. "Virginians do love their finery."

"So I see," Lark replied, smoothing her striped skirt. She had on her own beribboned straw hat, a posy of tiny violets at the crown to match the purple sash about her waist. Not the first fashion but as pretty and turned out as she could be.

Into the shop next door — labeled "Trevor Greenhow, Merchant" — they went. Its shelves abounded with earthenware, iron skillets, soap, chocolate, coffee, saddletrees, and far more.

"What do you buy?" came the customary merchant's greeting.

"Seed for spring planting," Mistress Flowerdew returned. "Royal Hundred's gardens must look their best, keeping in mind the Osbournes' arrival and a great many guests to follow."

They spent a pleasant hour choosing seed. French artichokes. White wonder cucumbers. Lettuces and broad beans. Melons. Around the vegetables would go China pinks, foxgloves, and peonies. The formal garden was another matter entirely. Another gardener had been hired at last and was on his way to Royal Hundred.

They went to the millinery shop next, this one advertising a variety of toys.

"I wonder if Larkin would like a puppet or Bartholomew doll?" Mistress Flowerdew mused. "Or something more befitting a lad?"

Here were rocking horses and rattles, whistles and tin drums, stilts and wooden hoops. Maple fifes. A bowling set. Marbles. They settled on a toy ship complete with miniature captain in blue and a lead anchor. Lark staunched the memory of the *Merry Lass.*

She smiled as the toy was purchased and packaged, anticipating Larkin's delight. A visit to the printing office secured sealing wax and paper. She'd pen another letter to Magnus this very night. And one to Granny.

"Now to pay a call to the widow Ramsay, a longtime friend."

Across Market Square sat a large house the color of a deep red oak leaf. Lark hadn't seen its equal in all of Williamsburg other than the Governor's Palace. A liveried servant let them in and led them through a foyer with a sweeping staircase to a rear garden where several ladies gathered.

"Frances, is that you?" A bewigged woman came forward, hands outstretched. "What perfect timing!"

All eyes were on them as introductions were made. Names pelted Lark like raindrops. Only one found purchase, that of Theodosia Ramsay, their hostess's dark-haired daughter-in-law who looked to be the same age as Lark.

"You must be prepared to hear the name of Ramsay frequently," Mistress Flowerdew said to feminine laughter. She gestured to Lark with a gloved hand. "And this is Miss MacDougall of the western Scottish isles, born of an ancient, powerful clan."

Lark stood a bit straighter but was hard-pressed to suppress a smile. Though of little consequence now, her family history did ring true. Had all that been in Richard Osbourne's letter about her? These Virginians did like their titles.

"Royal Hundred is all the better for her presence," Mistress Flowerdew finished with a gracious smile.

"You'll be quite at home when you come to town, then. Our royal governor is a Scot, as are many of Williamsburg's townspeople," Theodosia said. "Please join us for refreshments in the garden. Some lemon syllabub, perhaps? Cook has also baked some delicious apple custard tarts."

They slowly moved toward a linen-clad table, late-season chrysanthemums and bittersweet making a center bouquet. Chairs were scattered about, and Theodosia gestured for Lark to take a seat beside her.

"I've seen you before," the young woman said, studying Lark over the ethereal froth of her syllabub glass. " 'Twas at the Mount

Brilliant ball. You were with a very handsome Scotsman I assumed to be your husband."

"The laird Magnus MacLeish." Another pang. Without thinking, Lark touched the locket now secreted in her pocket and drew Theodosia's eye. "An islander like myself. And a longtime friend."

"I think you are too modest. That very night I said to my husband 'twas clear the laird adores you. Surely there is more to your story. Is he not here?"

"In the West Indies. He is factor for Richard Osbourne at present. He's also in mourning for his late wife."

"Oh? My deepest sympathies. Though I must mention that mourning never lasts long, at least here in the colonies." Her features clouded. "My brother is in the Caribbean — Barbados — in hopes of curing a lung condition."

"I pray he fares well," Lark said, surprised consumption was as much a scourge here as in Britain.

"Amen. Let that be our prayer. Do you ride?" Theodosia asked with an arch of dark brows.

"Seldom," Lark confessed. "Is it true ye Virginians are as fond of horses as dancing?"

Theodosia laughed. "Indeed. When we are not dancing we are on horseback. My husband keeps a fine stable here. Perhaps I shall ride out to Royal Hundred."

"Then ye shall see the bee garden and orangery."

"And take tea. Mistress Flowerdew sets a lovely table."

Lark took a drink of the foamy syllabub. Sweet yet lemony tart. Since the ball she'd wished for more.

"And who have we here?" A masculine voice cut through the feminine chatter. "A fair Virginian I don't know?"

Smiling, Theodosia set down her syllabub and motioned the gentleman nearer. "You admired Miss MacDougall at the Mount Brilliant ball, along with the laird."

Lark turned and stood. Could this ponderous, impeccably dressed man be Theodosia's husband? Lark had no memory of him in the sea of strangers who had swelled the ballroom that night.

"Ah yes." He kissed her hand. "I am Prentice Ramsay, cousin to Richard Osbourne. And a great-nephew to Mistress Flowerdew." He gave a wink. "Tarry in Virginia long enough and you'll soon be related to everyone too."

His easy manner won her over. She smiled

as he spoke with each lady present and then turned back to the house, syllabub in hand.

"My husband wears many hats," Theodosia said, "but his role as the colony's attorney general is foremost. He learned the law in London."

"The laird is also a lawyer," Lark said, never missing a chance to speak well of him. "Formerly in the Court of Session in Edinburgh." Not even banishment could change that, could it?

"Oh? Perhaps he might be of service here rather than the West Indies. Virginia has need of a great many qualified men."

"I shall write to the laird and tell him." A spark of hope kindled. "Thank ye."

"Then I shall tell my husband," Theodosia said. "And please, call me Thea."

32

Do not anticipate trouble, or worry about what may never happen. Keep in the sunlight.

Benjamin Franklin

Lark moved the candle nearer till golden light spilled onto the page. She paused, gaze lifting from the Bible to Larkin as he lay sleeping in his box bed, clutching a rag doll Sally had made him, the gentle rise and fall of his chest reassuring.

Her eyes returned to the Psalms.

The LORD is nigh unto them that are of a broken heart; and saveth such as be of a contrite spirit. Many are the afflictions of the righteous; but the LORD delivereth him out of them all. He keepeth all his bones: not one of them is broken.

She had asked the Lord for a special Scripture then landed on this. It seemed a promise, the words rife with hope. *Saveth. Delivereth. Keepeth.* She prayed that for Magnus. But nary another letter came. The delay chafed and sent her nearly running when the post arrived. Even Mistress Flowerdew began to look disappointed. But the lack of letters did not stop Lark from writing. She penned half a dozen to his one, overflowing with news of Virginia, even Theodosia Ramsay's inquiry about him.

Now that fall had taken hold, Lark spent more time in the stillroom than the garden. Soon the cupboards were full of more than soap, with tonics aplenty to see them through the coming winter. Her visits to the quarters increased. In turn, the people came to her, seeking this or that for some ailment or another when the factor and overseer weren't watching. A doctor was sent for if matters turned dire.

She'd not seen Rory again. As the time ticked closer to month's end, she wondered, Had his plans to flee changed? Would she know if he got safely away? His desire to see the Scots stronghold in North Carolina she understood. But would it improve his lot? Would he not still be bound? An indenture on the run? If he dared return to Scotland he'd run the risk of being caught and put to death.

Betimes she felt almost guilty at Royal Hundred. She was bound, aye, yet treated as more of an equal by Mistress Flowerdew. Even Sally deferred to her, helping care for Larkin as if Lark was a member of the Osbourne household. Kinfolk. Her work seemed almost child's play compared to a field hand.

Blessings abounded. Plentiful meals. An adequate dwelling. Work she favored. The gardens both here and in Williamsburg were an endless delight. Though she hated to confess it, even the castle's gardens paled in comparison. Her grudging acceptance of Virginia was giving way. She'd not dwell on the loss of her beloved homeland, her tarnished heritage, or Granny. Nor Magnus. She couldn't lose Magnus. The heart words he'd spoken before leaving warmed her whenever she pondered them.

The next morning found her cutting flowers for the house. Mistress Flowerdew was fond of fresh bouquets in both the mansion foyer and her personal sitting room. Lark brought the blooms into the stillroom to arrange them in a vase she'd gotten from the pantry. Once finished, she made her way to the house, smiling at Larkin's chortling as Cleve sat with him beneath a pecan tree.

Mornings held a special joy as the plantation slowly came awake, the day unblemished, the wide river a serene blue. Up the back steps she went, calling a greeting.

Mistress Flowerdew was in the foyer, holding a note. She waved it at Lark, eyes alight. Had Magnus written at last?

"We're to have afternoon visitors. Theodosia Ramsay and a certain gentleman."

Lark set the blooms on a foyer table. "Tea, then?"

"Yes, and Mr. Ramsay wants to make the acquaintance of Royal Hundred's new gardener."

"Theodosia's husband?"

"Nay, his barrister brother and an avid horticulturist."

"The Ramsays have no end."

The housekeeper laughed, seeming years younger. "I'd best prepare Mr. Munro. As for you . . ." She looked at Lark's workaday attire. "An afternoon gown might be more suitable. Let's have a look, shall we?"

They proceeded to an upstairs bedchamber, the only room undisturbed by renovations. Great progress was being made in repainting and wallpapering all around them, but this room remained untouched.

"Before Felicity died she bequeathed her wardrobe to me to do as I wished. I sent most of her garments to the poorhouse. I've borrowed a fichu here and a sash there and have remade a few of her gowns to wear. But I daresay her youthful taste suits you far better."

Soon Lark ran work-worn hands over the skirt of her chintz gown. Celestial blue, the color was called. Her ankle-length white petticoat drew attention to her shoes, also celestial blue, with ivory-colored rosettes. Hardly the stuff of the stillroom.

Her hands gave her away. She wore mitts that Mistress Flowerdew said were in fashion, though Lark refused to powder and pomade her hair, simply coiling it at the nape of her neck and affixing it with pins and fresh flowers.

By afternoon, while Larkin napped, Lark kept busy in the stillroom in anticipation of their guests. A look out the window told her Mr. Munro had tidied himself as well in weskit and breeches, no dirt or leather apron in evidence.

She felt she'd swallowed a swarm of butterflies. But why? Because she felt out of her depth in Virginia society? In Scotland she knew who she was, her place. Here . . .

She went into the garden and spoke with Mr. Munro, whose affable Scots set her at ease. Osbourne had secured the very best. Mr. Munro had been plucked from a Highland estate near Aberdeen because he'd heard Virginia gardens were the finest in the colonies.

"I had to set my aging eyes on the black-eyed Susans, the goldenrod, and the fall-blooming asters," he'd said of the American botanicals. " 'Tis a privilege to prepare Royal Hundred in advance of the Osbournes' arrival."

And not only the Osbournes. At half past two, the decisive clip of horse hooves sounded on the driveway. A merry exchange of voices could be heard in the mansion's foyer through the open riverfront door. In minutes, Mistress Flowerdew led their guests down the bricked steps and into the formal garden. Though Mr. Munro had only been there a sennight, his capable hand was in evidence everywhere.

Lark's gladness to see Theodosia again was tempered by the sight of her companion. Behind her came a tall figure in navy broadcloth. His cocked hat was held in his right hand, angled artfully over his heart. He gave a little bow as they made introductions.

Trevor Ramsay was nothing like his brother, Prentice, though nonetheless powerfully built. This man was so tall Lark had to tilt her chin to look up at him.

"My brother-in-law has just returned from London as his legal studies are at an end there," Theodosia said. "He's happy to be back home in Williamsburg."

He was studying Lark, a lively light in his gray eyes. "Have we not met before, Miss MacDougall?"

"Only if ye've been to the Isle of Kerrera," she returned with a smile. "Though I was once in Edinburgh and Glasgow."

"I'm told you ken, as the Scots say, a great deal about gardening and stillrooms."

"Not as much as Mr. Munro," Lark said as the two men shook hands. "And I've yet to be thoroughly schooled in yer colonial gardens. They are as different from Scotland's as homespun and silk."

"Or bannocks and biscuits," he said with a wink.

They laughed and began to look about. Theodosia fell into step with Mistress Flowerdew, and Lark expected Trevor Ramsay to partner with Mr. Munro, but he did not.

"Shall we?" he asked her, extending an arm.

She rested her fingers on his coat sleeve, and they took a bricked path past a dry fountain whose basin was filled with colorful autumn leaves. Beyond this stretched the part of the garden that was the most beautiful in late fall and nearest to the river.

"So tell me, what have you found to your liking in Virginia?" he asked.

"Other than sweet potatoes and hoecake?" At his amusement, she said, "Virginia's jasmine I find intoxicating, and the tuberoses are the largest I've ever seen, particularly the apothecary rose."

"You've not yet witnessed the flowering dogwood and redbud in spring."

"Nay. I've only just arrived, sir, in September."

"Please, call me Trevor." He paused to examine a daylily. "And I would dispense with Miss MacDougall as well."

She swallowed. Was an exchange of first names so soon a colonial custom? "Then ye may call me Lark."

"Lark?" His eyes met hers with unabashed pleasure. "You belong in a garden then. I am wearied of so many Marthas and Janes and Theodosias."

Theodosia cast a look over her shoulder at his teasing. "Don't think I am deaf and cannot hear you, Trevor. Your time in England did not take away your roguishness, I see."

"Nay," he said. "Those staid London courtrooms only amplified it."

415

"Beware, Lark," Theodosia said. "Trevor is quite a charmer."

"I shall set Royal Hundred's bees upon him if he grows too knavish," Lark returned with a smile, gesturing to the skeps.

"Bees?" His eyes found hers again. "Surely you jest. Mistress of the stillroom and the swarms too? I intend to have bee boles at my new property on South England Street in Williamsburg. Perhaps I can have a swarm of yours to start."

"Not all survived the crossing. There was a frightful storm — several of the bee skeps were lost," she lamented. "A good many plants perished. But yer welcome to take cuttings and such come spring, if Mistress Flowerdew permits."

"If you'd like to tour the orangery, sir," Mr. Munro said, "Miss MacDougall and I can show you what did survive. Fruit scions might be of particular interest to you in regard to your future orchard."

Mr. Munro led them down another path bordered by a neatly trimmed yew hedge leading to the glass house. The orangery door was open, beckoning. 'Twas a favorite place of hers, smelling fresh, even exotic, and hosting the estate's most prized and delicate botanicals.

Delight took the edge off Lark's awkwardness. She held back while Mr. Munro began the tour, Mr. Ramsay — Trevor — rapt.

"Come, ladies, let us go to the arbor while the men speak their Latin and conspire," the housekeeper said. "We must catch up on any unmasculine gossip."

Lark heard a cry and started toward the stillroom, only to see Sally dart in and whisk the wide-awake Larkin away. To the kitchen, likely, to have milk and gingerbread, a favorite. Lark felt more at home in Royal Hundred's humble kitchen than in the waiting elegant bower smothered with trumpet honeysuckle and wisteria. Thankfully, tea with Mistress Flowerdew had become so commonplace she'd learned the etiquette well enough, though 'twas a far cry from Granny and the croft with its cracked treenware. What would her grandmother think of her now? If Virginia's colonial governor began life as a humble Scots merchant, why shouldn't she be comfortable at this refined tea table?

Beyond the arbor's deep shade, the southern sun mimicked summer. Indian summer, Mistress Flowerdew called it. 'Twas four o'clock in the afternoon.

Lark watched as Mistress Flowerdew poured steaming water into a silver teapot and let the tea leaves steep for the customary three minutes.

"I'm growing quite fond of cups with handles," Theodosia said. "No more burning one's hands and spilling tea on one's skirts. I've ordered an entire set of Wedgwood from England and expect it any day now."

Mistress Flowerdew smiled. "What news do you bring from Williamsburg?"

"The very best." Theodosia looked to Lark. "There's to be a fete in the governor's new ballroom the first of December."

"A winter's ball?" Lark mused, envisioning it. Mistress Flowerdew had taken her past the Governor's Palace earlier, as the royal residence was just down the street.

"No doubt the governor will be happy to meet a fellow Scot. A variety of guests shall attend, including the emperor of the Cherokee Nation with his empress and their son the young prince. Governor Dinwiddie even asked my husband about the laird. He remembers him from the Mount Brilliant ball. I explained he was in the sugar islands." She took a sip of tea. "I suppose you've heard from him?"

"Nay." Lark read the questions in her eyes, ones she herself couldn't answer. Fighting melancholy, she changed course, suspecting Theodosia enjoyed talk of fashion. "What shall ye wear to the ball?"

"Something in blue, the very hue of your gown. The milliner is already at work. You must come into town and see her progress when I have a fitting."

"I'd love to." Summoning enthusiasm wasn't hard, though would she herself even attend? "Kerrera Castle — the laird's ancestral home — hosted many a ball." As a child, she'd simply pressed her nose to a glass window of the Great Hall while sitting atop her father's shoulders. But once she'd come of age, she'd been a guest, if only in the shadows.

"A Scottish fete!" Theodosia came alive. "I suppose the castle is ancient and majestic."

"Ages auld, and majestic indeed." Lark felt a wistful pleasure take hold. "All the ladies wore their finery, and many a tiara and gemstone were seen."

"I can only imagine it, having never been outside these colonies. But you have had the good fortune of being both places. I wonder what you'll think of this colonial ball?"

"I'm sure she'll find it most agreeable," Mistress Flowerdew said with her usual enthusiasm. "A chance to meet more of Williamsburg's residents. A shame the laird can't join us."

"Perhaps the Osbournes will host a fete when they return to Royal Hundred. To become reacquainted with society all at once instead of a chance meeting in town or at church."

"A splendid idea! I shall write Mistress Osbourne and inquire. The great parlor is being redone in verdigris at her request. 'Tis large enough for dancing."

"Have you heard the minuet might be going out of fashion?" Theodosia asked as the housekeeper poured more tea.

Their chatter died down when Trevor reappeared, stooping a bit as he stepped beneath the arbor. He took a seat beside Theodosia across from Lark, eyeing the now tepid teakettle.

"It matters not whether it's warm or cold," he said at Mistress Flowerdew's insistence the water be reheated. "I'm not a fussy sort."

Lark smiled. He had an endearing way about him, an easy grace she found in few men. Theodosia was right. Trevor Ramsay *was* charming.

"So," he began, holding a teacup that looked ridiculously small in his large hands, "I thought I overheard talk of a ball. Will you attend?"

The question was meant for Lark. She met his eyes, a bit unnerved by the intensity of his gaze. "I never thought to be invited to a royal governor's ball."

"I plan to," he replied, taking a drink, "if only to reacquaint myself with town life. I've been away for so long I don't know who's who in Williamsburg of late."

They turned to other subjects, circling round once again to a place rarely out of Lark's thoughts. The sugar islands. Theodosia's kinfolk had just returned from there.

"Your ailing brother found them utterly forgettable, and of no help to his condition," Trevor said. "The Caribbean gives the appearance of unspoiled beauty. A pretty gloss covering the ills of slavery."

"Now, Trevor," Theodosia interjected, setting down her cup, "there are nearly thirty souls enslaved at Ramsay House. No doubt there are nearly as many laboring to build your fine townhouse. Don't bore our hosts with any double-minded talk."

"What of Miss MacDougall?" he said, looking again at Lark. "What are your Scots feelings on the subject? I know of enslaved Africans in Scotland, though not so many as here."

"None on the Isle of Kerrera," she said quietly. "I stand on Scripture. Does the

New Testament not say that God 'hath made of one blood all nations of men for to dwell on all the face of the earth, and hath determined the times before appointed, and the bounds of their habitation'? Can it be any clearer?"

They lapsed into a thoughtful silence till Mistress Flowerdew asked Trevor, "What is in store for you now that you've returned from London's Inns of Court?"

"Rumor has it that I'll be appointed to a post by the royal governor. But for the moment I'm most interested in ground being broken for my home and the garden and orchard that need planting."

"Perhaps you can borrow Mr. Blair's Williamsburg gardener as we did," Theodosia told him. "I highly recommend him."

"Mayhap." He leaned back, done with his tea. "I'm pondering what to call the place. There's only one Ramsay House, after all."

"And now there shall be two," his sister-in-law said as a cool breeze lifted the lace edges of her kerchief. "We'll lodge you as long as you like, though thankfully you'll only be moving across town once you do go." She looked at the timepiece attached to her bodice, bringing an end to a memorable tea. "How quickly time passes in the company of friends. Thank you for the lovely afternoon."

"Till the Sabbath," Trevor said, putting on his cocked hat. "I bid you gracious ladies good day."

33

Be slow in choosing a friend, but slower in changing him.

Scottish proverb

By the Sabbath the weather took an abrupt turn, closing the curtain on a colorful fall. Snow began swirling down — huge, white flakes that reminded Lark of lace. By the time they reached Bruton Parish Church, all of Williamsburg was dressed in white. The bells pealed in the snowy stillness and were heard for miles.

Mistress Flowerdew had given Lark a cloak in dove gray, cape trimmed with ribbon, the muff of the same. When Lark had protested such finery, she'd received a fine scolding. "You shan't go to church and freeze to death!"

Larkin had remained home with Sally, snug by the fire.

Now Lark huddled beside Mistress Flowerdew near the back of the church, noting the Osbournes' box pew was conspicuously empty. The Ramsays sat at the front, Trevor's broad shoulders a striking counterpoint to Theodosia's slender, sloping carriage and Prentice's fleshed-out form. The widow Ramsay sat between her sons, her graying head covered in a large calash.

Though the church was beautiful, hallowed, 'twas cold as a tomb, their combined breaths pluming like white feathers. The brazier of coals beneath her feet warmed only those. Yet she was glad of the cold. How weary she'd grown of the oppressive Virginia heat.

She took a discreet look about. These Anglicans were a far cry from her Scots-Presbyterian roots. How did Magnus worship in the islands? Was it not the Sabbath everywhere? Lark took a childish, whimsical comfort in the fact they shared the Sabbath, at least. On Kerrera they honored the day quietly. No telling what these Virginians did. Till now she'd spent the Sabbath simply reading Scripture at Royal Hundred, till Mistress Flowerdew begged her company today.

Her gaze lifted to the rosette windows letting in snow-glaring light. Governor Dinwiddie arrived to sit on his canopied chair at the front. Next came the government officials, mostly burgesses, Mistress Flowerdew whispered to her. They took their assigned places and the service began, the beadle casting a wary eye over the congregants, especially the William and Mary students in the gallery.

Lark followed Mistress Flowerdew's lead, reading from the prayer book after the minister. In two hours the sermon was done. Her extremities were numb, and the ancient woman in the pew ahead of them snored softly. A benediction was said, and all filed past the liveried footman at the entry.

"Your cheeks are red as the Hawthorn berries by the church's tower door," said a voice behind her. Trevor Ramsay.

She stepped into a corner of the vestibule, firming her chin to keep her teeth from chattering, and buried her hands deeper in the borrowed muff. "Good morning, sir."

"Sir? Didn't we dispense with that at Royal Hundred? Must I call you Miss Mac-Dougall? Lark is far more fetching."

"As ye wish, Trevor." She smiled up at him, admiring his handsome fulled cloak while people pressed past.

Theodosia came down the flagstone aisle at last. "Come with us, Lark. You and

426

Mistress Flowerdew must warm up before riding home."

Trevor winked. "My sister-in-law wants to parade her latest acquisition from London before you."

"Nay, I do not," Theodosia protested. "I am not proud, Trevor. Just cold." She looked about for Prentice, who was deep in conversation with several burgesses. "My husband seems determined to turn me into an ice sculpture."

"Let us go, then," Trevor said, escorting them to a waiting coach. He stepped aside to help his mother and Mistress Flowerdew into the Osbourne conveyance. "My brother can walk. Heaven knows some exercise will do him good."

Lark nearly laughed. Truly, the ponderous Prentice could benefit from a brisk if brief walk. Ramsay House was not far.

Down Palace Street they went, going slowly in the slippery snow. In a quarter of an hour they alighted and were escorted up the slick steps and into the foyer like before, the enormous window on the landing framing a leaden sky. To their right was the dining room, door open.

"And what is your pleasure, Lark?" Theodosia asked as a servant removed her wraps. "Tea or cocoa?"

"Coal," Trevor said with a wry smile. He took Lark's elbow and guided her into the dining room toward a papered, paneled wall.

Lark blinked. Tried to puzzle out the odd contraption before her, though the delicious heat emanating from it gave a telling clue.

" 'Tis a warming machine," he told her. "Designed by a clever Londoner named Buzaglo."

Taking her gloved hand, he placed it lightly on the stove's ceramic face. Her fingers thawed. She smiled, taking in the embellishments and scrolling design, an artistic marvel from tip to top. " 'Tis like an enormous three-tiered cake."

"Aye, 'one of the most elegant warming machines that ever was seen in this or any other kingdom,' says the papers. I'm considering ordering one for the orangery I hope to have built."

"Complete with lemon trees like Royal Hundred's? Mr. Munro said you are especially fond of those."

"Don't forget the oranges." He let go of her hand as Theodosia invited them toward a cluster of chairs.

"Where is Mistress Flowerdew?" Lark asked. "And Mistress Ramsay?"

"In the small parlor," she replied, motioning a servant to set down a tray.

"My mother has pronounced the warming machine extravagant," Trevor told her, taking a chair. "Youthful vanity."

"Oh?" Lark moved her feet nearer the warmth. "I confess I am quite smitten."

"As I am," he said with a wink, holding her gaze. She looked away, rattled, glad for her friend's presence.

"Have some chocolate, Lark, to further warm you." Theodosia poured then passed her a delicate cup.

Lark took a careful sip. Never had she sampled cocoa. She tasted vanilla, sugar, and spice. Rich and creamy and satisfying on such a day.

" 'Tis new to you," Trevor said. "Like syllabub."

"Indeed. And like syllabub, I hope cocoa will be a dear friend."

He chuckled, taking a drink from his own cup. " 'Tis reputed to be a digestive aid and of benefit for lung ailments, especially nourishing for the sick."

"Mayhap I should keep some in the stillroom. Surely 'tis good for body *and* soul."

"At least in the snow and cold." Trevor balanced his cup and saucer on one knee. "Thankfully, Virginia's winters are brief."

"Nonsense," Theodosia said, taking a chair nearest the warming machine. "Two years ago, we didn't see the ground till April. I felt I was in the arctic. Every gardener in Williamsburg was apoplectic!"

"I was in London, remember," Trevor said, gaze shifting to Lark. "When the snow melts you'll have to see the progress of my property. I'd like your opinion of the layout of the physic and bee gardens."

"Of course." Lark smiled at him over the rim of her cup.

"Any word on when the Osbournes are due?" Theodosia asked. "I'm anxious to meet the new mistress of Royal Hundred. The former, God rest her, was also a dear friend."

The lament in her tone tugged at Lark. "Mr. Osbourne's last letter spoke of a spring sailing."

"Any news from the laird?" Theodosia asked, pouring more chocolate.

At Lark's simple nay, Theodosia and Trevor exchanged glances. Instantly she felt a qualm. Did they know something she didn't?

A noise in the foyer was followed by Prentice Ramsay's entry. Face reddened with cold, he greeted them heartily and took a cup of cocoa from his wife's hand.

" 'Tis snowing harder," he remarked, obviously not minding his bracing walk.

Lark's gaze strayed to the windows clad in heavy brocade and wooden Venetian blinds. All were covered but the one nearest the door, showcasing a blindingly white world.

Her cup was empty. She craved the still-room's scent. Her humble hearth. Larkin. "We must be away then."

"Away? Surely there's no need to hurry on so stormy a day," Prentice said. "We have room aplenty should you and Mistress Flowerdew need to stay the night."

"Kind of ye, but I am missing my wee lad." The quiet words tumbled out before she'd given them thought. To her knowledge no mention had yet been made of Larkin. "He's at home in a servant's keeping."

All eyes pinned her, their shocked silence begging explanation.

"You have a child?" Theodosia finally said with something more akin to envy than surprise.

The Ramsays had no children, Lark remembered. "His aunt placed him in my care before she died. His mother passed away before that. And his father's whereabouts are unknown."

"Orphaned, then," Prentice said. "Like so many, including my dear wife."

Theodosia's lovely face darkened. "My mother died of a brief illness when I was a girl. Then the year before Prentice and I were wed, my father and two sisters were taken. Their deaths were such a shock 'tis still talked about in town. They were struck by lightning during a summer storm."

"I'm so sorry," Lark murmured, though the words seemed woefully inadequate.

"We've helped raise Theodosia's younger brothers," Prentice said, moving nearer the stove. "At the moment, they are enrolled at the Grammar School at the College of William and Mary on the outskirts of town."

"How old is your" — Theodosia mulled the word — "son?"

"Not yet a year."

"A baby? How delightful! And what is his name?"

"Larkin. It means fierce or warrior in Gaelic. But ye may call him Laurence, the English way, if ye'd rather."

Theodosia's eyes widened. "How extraordinary to learn his name mirrors yours."

"He's by far the bonniest lad I've ever seen," Lark said, craving his company. "A redheaded handful."

"Nothing like a child to enliven a home," Trevor remarked.

"Providence does have a sense of humor," Prentice said.

They lifted their chocolate cups in a sort

of toast to Larkin at Trevor's invitation. And then the merriment was broken by Mistress Flowerdew's voice and the click of a door closing.

"Come, Lark," she called. " 'Tis time for us to be away."

"Only if you'll let me escort you." Trevor stood and followed Lark into the foyer. "If your coach should break down or some mishap occur, you'll need an able hand."

"Very well." Mistress Flowerdew stepped toward the door opened by a liveried servant, snow blowing in on a gust of wind. "But you must stay the night at Royal Hundred, Trevor Ramsay. Something tells me the storm is here to stay."

"Come, my little prince, and meet yer company." Lark bent over Larkin, who lay on the bed of their cottage as she changed both his clout and his clothes. "Ye must look yer best. And act yer best too."

He squirmed as she pulled the linen leine over his head, freshly washed and smelling of the dried lavender she'd sewn into the hem. She wished she'd had time to give him a bath. He smelled of wood smoke from the kitchen, though Sally had fed him, his mood content.

He smiled up at her, making his baby

noises as she tickled him, calling forth his gurgling laugh. Taking up a blanket, she wrapped him snugly before heading out the door to the mansion, mindful of the slippery walk. Cleve waited just outside the cottage door with a lantern, lighting her way through the still swirling snow. Sally was likely preparing supper even on the Sabbath.

Up the steps into the big house she went, Larkin in arm. What would Trevor think of him? The Ramsays' shock that afternoon left her feeling she'd been keeping Larkin a secret. But in truth, her short acquaintance with them hadn't called for sharing so personal a matter.

She'd dressed Larkin as snugly as she could in a knitted cap and stockings yet still fretted he wasn't warm enough. Her mother's heart wouldn't rest, yet she felt all the pride and pleasure of presenting her first-born to a guest. The fact their guest was Trevor Ramsay, a person she was becoming aware of as a man of some standing at least in Virginia, made the occasion more memorable.

"There you are," Mistress Flowerdew exclaimed with all the warmth Lark found endearing. "No doubt Master Larkin thought we'd forgotten all about him, spending so long a Sabbath in town."

Trevor stood by the hearth, hands behind his back, eyes on the lad she carried. Larkin's hair strayed in bright wisps beyond his cap, and his alert blue eyes fixed on the sole man in the room. Immediately the babe reached out plump arms to him.

Surprised, Lark handed him over. "He doesna always take so kindly to strangers. He was terrified of the sailors aboard ship. But ye, sir," she added with a pleased smile, "are no sailor."

"He has a fascination for buttons," Trevor replied as Larkin began examining his silver-threaded waistcoat. "A stout fellow. And pure Scots from the look of him." He shot a glance at Lark. "I still find it remarkable he shares your coloring. He could well be your son. And your eyes are the same shade of blue."

"Remarkable, indeed, though many Scots have such coloring," Mistress Flowerdew said. "Master Larkin has brought a great deal of joy to this echoing house. And I hope he'll soon have a playmate once the Osbournes arrive with their young son, Master William."

"Soon your young man will be ready for Grammar School at William and Mary as I was." Trevor took a chair, Larkin on one knee. "There are a number of students, even

Indian youth, who board there."

"A few years yet till he's eight and ready to cut the leading strings." Mistress Flowerdew took a chair opposite Trevor, leaving the seat nearest him to Lark. "I shan't like to part with him just yet."

Lark sat, feet to the crackling wood fire, finding the marble hearth far less cozy than the Ramsays' coal stove. Seeing Larkin happily settled on Trevor's lap unleashed an avalanche of memories. Magnus kissing Larkin's unfurrowed brow. Magnus tickling him and tossing him in the air. Larkin reaching for Magnus at the last. Babies needed fathers. Other than Cleve in the kitchen, Larkin rarely saw another man.

"This makes me think of a family of my own." Trevor's candidness turned him grave. "When one considers there are no children at Ramsay House after seven years . . ."

"I still pray for an heir," Mistress Flowerdew said. "You'll make a fine father, Trevor, if our stout Scotsman is any indication."

Truly, Larkin seemed as at ease as Lark had ever seen him, now besotted with the chain that led to Trevor's timepiece.

"He takes in everything. And I mean everything," Lark said, remembering the swallowed button. "And he's quite fond of

Royal Hundred's fare, especially peach preserves and biscuits."

"He has a healthy appetite then." Trevor took his timepiece from his pocket and planted it in Larkin's hand. "No maladies to speak of?"

"A cold and cough soon after we arrived but nothing of consequence."

"I've cautioned Lark to keep away from the quarters this winter," the housekeeper said. "Fevers and the like spread like wildfire among the servants."

Trevor nodded knowingly. " 'Tis the same at Ramsay House. The doctor is often sent for when Mother and Thea cannot manage on their own." His eyes found Lark's. "I suppose your hands are full with tonics and the like in the stillroom."

"Betimes. I told the overseer any sickness was bound to be reduced if the quarters were improved and the people given ample bedding, clothing, and food."

"And did he take your recommendations?"

"Nay." Could he hear the regret in her tone? The frustration? " 'Tis especially hard on the wee ones. And there are so many of them. With winter here, I'm especially concerned."

"Lark has secured a large quantity of

osnaburg to make winter garments for the children. And the spinning house is weaving extra coverlets, of which I wholeheartedly approve. Lark has all the makings of a fine plantation mistress."

"Ye flatter me. 'Tis only what any charitable person would do," Lark said with a slight smile. Was Mistress Flowerdew trying to do a little matchmaking? Not with one of the most eligible bachelors in all Virginia Colony, surely. And not when her heart was so firmly anchored to Magnus. "I ken I'm better suited to a Scottish island than a Virginia plantation. I miss it with all my heart."

Tiring of the watch, Larkin struggled to be free. With an ease that surprised her, Trevor stood him on the carpet, holding on to his hands to keep him upright. Apparently pleased with his newfound accomplishment, Larkin laughed and revealed his latest tooth.

"Will you go back, then?" Though Trevor kept his eyes on Larkin, Lark sensed an undercurrent of dismay. "To Scotland?"

"Did ye not miss Virginia when ye were in London?" she asked gently.

His features relaxed. "Aye. Being native born to America, 'tis my home. Like Scotland is yours." Leaning forward in his chair, he began to walk Larkin over to Lark.

"Whoever would have thought a barrister could be so good with children?" Mistress Flowerdew commented before leaving the room to see about supper.

The compliment made Trevor seem as proud as Larkin. "We legal men are not all bewigged and dour."

Once again, Lark's thoughts cut to Magnus, as much a barrister as Trevor Ramsay. All that was no more. Had his banishment stripped him of his legal standing? Would he ever again don his judicial robes and resume his position in Edinburgh's Court of Session?

She took Larkin in her arms, softening when he burrowed his face in her bodice then lifted his face and gave her a wet kiss on the chin.

"Ye imp." She hugged him nearer, aware of Trevor's eyes on them. "I wonder what sort of future he'll have here."

"He'll be a Virginian, if you stay," Trevor said. "As his guardian, you have the choice."

"We're here for three years hence at least. Mr. Osbourne holds my indenture, ye see."

Trevor looked less surprised than when he'd learned about Larkin. He merely nodded. "Indentures are coming into the colonies in droves and have for a hundred years or better. Not only from Great Britain but all of Europe."

She'd lost track of all those indentured aboard the *Bonaventure* but Magnus and Rory MacPherson. Had the former captain and free trader run? If he was caught, the penalty would be severe. In the hands of Factor Granger, harsher still.

"Let us have supper, shall we?" Mistress Flowerdew reappeared and opened a hall door that led to the dining room.

Once again, Trevor surprised her by plucking Larkin off the carpet, where he'd been hugging Lark's knees, as if he weighed no more than a feather. Larkin peered over one wide shoulder before Lark went into the dining room ahead of them.

Mistress Flowerdew had spared nothing for their Sabbath supper. The best plates and crystal shone, and the pleasant scent of beeswax bespoke the best light. Lark helped situate Larkin in the walnut infant chair rescued from the attic. When he grabbed at the fine linen tablecloth, she handed him a silver spoon to fist instead.

Trevor took Magnus's chair. The accompanying pang was so acute it felt almost physical. Would she ever get over missing him? Waiting and wanting to hear from him?

"This is how I envision family life," Trevor

remarked, eyeing the fine papered walls and paneling. "No children shut away in separate rooms but all present and accounted for."

Lark smiled. Which colonial belle had he set his cap for? Mistress Flowerdew said his arrival back in Virginia had caused quite a stir.

He said grace, and thoughts of Magnus again intruded, his resonant Scots overriding Trevor's melodious Virginia dialect even in memory.

She looked to a window, the panes blurred by snow. Trevor Ramsay might be snowbound at Royal Hundred for days.

34

The true measure of a man is how he treats someone who can do him absolutely no good.

Samuel Johnson

Around noon the next day came Factor Granger, tromping through snow that nearly reached the ankles of his high black boots. Lark shuddered and turned away from the stillroom window, squinting at the glare, as he passed by the glass and cut across the service yard to the mansion.

Though Royal Hundred's six chimneys all belched smoke, she'd not seen Mistress Flowerdew nor Trevor this morning. Was he a late riser? After supper, he'd asked use of the Osbournes' library. Before she'd tucked Larkin into his box bed beside her, she'd taken a last look at the mansion house and saw a sole light upstairs. No doubt their guest had read into the wee small hours.

She dressed Larkin warmly, donned her own scarlet cape, and trudged to the kitchen where Sally and Cleve huddled near the snapping fire. A copper teakettle puffed steam beside a small pot of porridge.

Their glum faces stole Lark's appetite. Not even Larkin's merry, nonsensical chatter put a dint in their demeanor, usually as steady as the Virginia sun.

"Sit a spell," Sally said, taking the kettle from the fire. "I expect you be called to the big house 'fore long."

Lark sat down hard on a crude chair, Larkin on her lap. "What has happened?"

"Runaways," Cleve said. "And no way to track 'em in this snow, not even with dogs."

So Rory had gotten away. Lark sat very still, letting the fact sink in with all its mournful implications. "Why would Granger report runaways to Mistress Flowerdew?"

"For all his high and mighty ways, he can't read nor write. Least here lately. It's left to Flowerdew to tell Osbourne. Pen him a letter."

"It ain't like he's never learned," Cleve explained. "Something in his head gets letters and figures backwards ever since he first took sick."

"What do ye think ails him?" Lark asked,

443

genuinely interested despite Granger's harsh reputation.

"Don't know what to call it." Sally shook her head and poured tea into cups. "Ever so often he seizes, freezes up. Frightful how it comes on all a sudden and leaves him wrecked. Can't even walk for a spell after. Then time passes and he gets around again."

'Twas what Mistress Granger, his wife, had said when seeking out Lark in the still-room. Pondering it, she fed Larkin spoon-fuls of porridge laced with honey. Granger was brusque, argumentative even, and he offended Mistress Flowerdew's sensibilities. Their infrequent meetings were fraught with peril. Though the housekeeper spoke ill of few, she did complain about the factor.

Cleve began humming a tune as if to cut the tension in the kitchen, reminding Lark of the Watts hymnal she'd found in a still-room cupboard. She'd given it to the only literate slave she knew, Royal Hundred's blacksmith, Josiah. As musical as he was skilled at the forge, the industrious Josiah seemed grateful. She'd lost count of all the times the singing from the quarters drew her, the blend of voices like some heavenly choir.

"Ye needn't any printed music as yers is divine," she'd told him as she'd offered the

444

hymnal. "But mayhap this will be of use to ye in some way."

Emotion glazed his dark eyes and he took the gift almost reverently, making her glad she'd offered it. "We want to thank you for the help you give," he said, eyes on his hands. "The coverlets and stockings you bring. Our children don't suffer as much from the cold."

Glad she was to help, though such seemed a tiny golden thread of relief in a dark tapestry of needs. But she'd done what she could.

Sally was studying her as if privy to her thoughts. "I suspect Granger's goin' to make trouble for you now that he's stirred up about the runaways too. Told Cleve just yesterday he don't like you goin' to the quarters."

What could she say to this? Mistress Flowerdew had no qualms about her visits. Yet she knew she acted in a manner no usual indenture would. Should she fear doing what she thought was right? What she felt prompted to do? Would the Lord not hold her accountable if she bowed to fear and ignored His compassionate leading to help where and when she could?

Be mine defense.

She sipped her tea, pondering this news,

445

the hot liquid stealing to the benumbed parts of her. Looking toward the frosted window glass, she envisioned what she wished she could see. Scotland. Spring. Bees and birdsong. A letter from Magnus.

Within a quarter of an hour, a housemaid came to summon Lark. Her terseness betokened something dire. Without a word, Sally reached for Larkin, leaving Lark to walk the just cleared path to the mansion alone, a few snowflakes sifting down.

Raised voices greeted her from Osbourne's paneled study off the foyer, Granger's foremost. No sooner had Lark wiped the soles of her shoes on an entry mat than he stormed past her, the stench of his unwashed garments leaving a sour smell. Her dread eased only a bit at the slamming of the back door behind him.

Mistress Flowerdew stood in the open study doorway, her face a strange mingling of ire and distress.

"Yer upset," Lark said. "What has happened?"

"I fear Mr. Granger's illness has scrambled his mind in the extreme. He lays part blame at your door for the latest runaways at Star Farm. Someone saw a Scots indenture, a former sea captain named MacPherson, talking to you not long ago in the garden.

This man is one who got away."

"He said he planned to run, but I wasna sure I believed him. He told me to come to Star Farm by month's end if I wanted to go with him."

"Why would you?"

"He's a fellow islander. From Kerrera. The laird knows him too. But I have no wish to break the covenant with Mr. Osbourne, nor leave Royal Hundred."

Nodding, Mistress Flowerdew took a steadying breath. "Let us forget the overseer's outburst. His quarrel with you likely stems from your latest interference, as he calls it, in the quarters, more than this flimsy association with a runaway." She backtracked into the study, a paper in hand. "Please sit down, my dear. I have other unfortunate news."

Lark's heart seemed to skitter to a stop. Magnus. At last?

"Mr. Granger communicates occasionally with an overseer at Trelawny Hall in Jamaica, a distant relation. Since Granger's illness, I have to pen his replies and manage his correspondence as his wife is not literate."

Lark waited. Would she not hurry and tell all the rest?

The housekeeper began reading from the

Jamaican overseer's post, voice wavering.

"The Scots laird and factor, Magnus MacLeish, lies gravely ill with yellow fever. He is not expected to recover. I have sent word to Osbourne about a possible replacement, one who is not averse to enslaving Africans and the conditions in which we must keep them. MacLeish has plans in place not only to teach select slaves to read and cipher but to place them in positions of authority here. 'Tis no surprise these chosen Africans warm to his outrageous plan. As they are lords over their own people, I suspect much mayhem to follow. Even so, there is to be a better harvest this year, due to the Scot's management. MacLeish is a force to be reckoned with, even half-dead. By your receipt of this letter, he will likely be buried . . ."

Mistress Flowerdew's voice trailed off wearily.

Long moments passed before Lark said, "No more?"

With a shake of her head, Mistress Flowerdew folded up the letter. The room grew colder and grievously still. Lark herself felt turned to stone.

Nay, Magnus, ye canna leave me yet.

What had he said to her at the last?

Goodbye for noo. See ye after.

She fixed her gaze on the fire, the anguish of the unknown welling inside her.

"The Lord preserves whom He will," Mistress Flowerdew murmured before they fell into another sore silence. "We pray the laird is among them."

So lost was she in the misery of the moment, Lark startled at Trevor's voice. She'd all but forgotten he was snowbound with them.

"May I intrude?" He filled the doorway, a book in hand, impeccably dressed and no worse for the weather.

"I'm afraid we've had rather an unpleasant visit from the factor, Mr. Granger," Mistress Flowerdew said.

"I overheard something about indentured runaways."

"Indeed." She nearly grimaced. "I fear Mr. Granger was shouting and I apologize."

"No, please. I would have come down sooner but thought I might aggravate the situation further."

He entered the room and took a chair. They sat in a sort of triangle, Lark and Mistress Flowerdew on a brocade settee across from him.

"Several indentures from Star Farm have

gone missing," Mistress Flowerdew said. "Of course, Mr. Granger is upset about the lack of labor and breaking of covenants, a definite loss to the plantation. Normally he'd send trackers and dogs after them, but with this snow the runaways are likely gone for good."

"What is this mention of Lark and the runaways?"

At Mistress Flowerdew's hesitation, Lark briefly explained her tie to Captain Mac-Pherson.

"But that is of small consequence," the housekeeper said. "Word has come that the laird, Magnus MacLeish, has been gravely ill with yellow fever and might not recover."

Hearing it again was just as much a trial as the first time. Could it be?

"I'm sorry to learn of this," Trevor said quietly, staring down at the book he held.

"Is it true what they say," Lark began with difficulty, "that those who want to die quickly go to the West Indies?"

Their eyes met, and she read his answer before he said a word.

"Few survive the debilitating fevers and diseases and climate, not to mention the dangers."

"The laird strikes me as a man who isn't hindered by much," Mistress Flowerdew

450

rushed to reassure her. "Besides, he's a man of faith, is he not? I recall what George Whitefield, the great evangelist, once said, that as believers we are invincible until our work is done."

Mulling this, Lark committed it to memory, praying that even as they spoke Magnus was on his feet, the sickness far behind him.

2 December, 1752

Dearest Lark,

I have heard the sorrowful news about the laird. I so want to cheer you now that the snow has melted and the way to town is clear. Might you come to Ramsay House for tea around our cozy warming machine on your next free day?

And do bundle up the babe and bring him with you. Trevor says he is the most splendid little fellow he's ever seen.

Yours,
Thea

The prospect of warmth and fine tea wooed her. Weary of the cold stillroom, her mind worn to a melancholy rut over Magnus, Lark was only too glad to flee Royal Hundred. Yet something else marred the day just as she and Larkin pulled away from the service yard in the carriage. Mr. Granger appeared and stared after them as they rumbled over the hard winter's drive to Williamsburg.

She tried to tuck any dark thoughts away and focus on Larkin. He sat on her lap, amusing himself with a tassel on the window shade. A brazier warmed her feet, but by the time they reached town the coals were tepid at best.

Theodosia was waiting at a front window as a servant hurried out the front door to the mounting block. Would she always feel surprise at being entertained by the likes of Mistress Ramsay? But Theodosia herself was not a society woman, Mistress Flowerdew confided, preferring the comforts of home and a few close friends.

Theodosia embraced her warmly beneath the magnificent stairwell window before taking Larkin from her, her face lit with delight as he smiled shyly then buried his face in her shoulder. Though Theodosia was barren, she hadn't let it sour her, unlike Isla.

"Dear Trevor did not exaggerate. He's truly beautiful — or what is it you Scots say?"

"Braw." Lark smiled. "Bonny."

"He has a penchant for silver spoons and hat boxes, or so Trevor told me."

They passed through the dining room door to the warming machine, which was stoked full of an endless supply of coal. Coal was luxuriously warm. Toys decorated the carpet at their feet, so many and so well made that Lark's eyes went wide.

"These are from Bellhaven, my family's plantation where I was raised," Theodosia said. "My little brothers have no use for them now that they're in Grammar School at the college."

She set Larkin down on the rug with a grace that reminded Lark that Theodosia was the oldest of ten children. Together they watched as Larkin picked up a toy drum then set it down in favor of a wooden soldier.

"Ye spoil him. Soon he'll be asking to come visit ye," Lark teased. "He's begun saying a few words."

"No doubt he'll like our refreshments. I asked Cook to make some almond macaroons."

The tea service was brought in and set between them on a cherry tea table with a decorative piecrust edge. Theodosia served, leaning down to give Larkin a macaroon. He took it readily, letting go of the toy to examine the tasty offering.

"Say thank ye," Lark told him with a

smile. "Or 'bethankit' as we Scots say."

He babbled a nonsensical word, waving a wee hand and the sweet in his endearing way.

Theodosia returned to her tea with a lingering smile. "How do you manage, Lark? A baby and your duties in the still-room and garden too?"

"Little is done in the winter but dispensing tonics and readying for spring. Sally — Royal Hundred's cook — is a blessed help. She is fond of Larkin and sees her grandchildren in the quarters but little."

"I can only imagine. We have such a busy household even without children of our own."

"What is yer day made up of? Ye are far more than a pretty gentlewoman, Mistress Flowerdew tells me."

"Pretty gentlewoman, indeed! I start the day in the kitchen, deciding what recipes to have for dinner and then supper. I measure out sugar and spices that are kept in a locked cupboard. Sadly, some of the servants have been soundly whipped for stealing. I keep a close tally on accounts. Entertaining and social obligations never end. Last year we went through twenty-seven thousand pounds of pork, nineteen beeves, one hundred fifty gallons of brandy, five hundred bushels of wheat, and one hundred pounds of flour for our guests. No doubt Richard Osbourne will do the same when he's in residence."

Aghast, Lark stared at her, then remembered the prosperous Ramsays had a great many servants. Still, managing and supervising them and an abundance of guests was no small task. "I've heard yer an accomplished embroiderer."

Theodosia smiled over the rim of her teacup. " 'Tis as scandalous for a woman not to know how to use a needle as it is for a man not to know how to use a weapon. Petit point is my specialty, mostly chair seats and fire screens for practical purposes."

"I was taught the same at the castle," Lark said, sampling a macaroon. "But mostly linen samplers worked with wool and silk thread, though once I completed a stomacher for a tenants' ball."

"Which brings me to the real reason for our meeting. The laird. You've received no more word of him, other than secondhand about his illness?"

"Nothing more, nay." Lark fixed her attention on Larkin's head, his curls a red halo. "His last letter was some time ago." And perused so many times it was coming apart at the seams, the ink smudged from one too many emotional readings.

"Once you told me there was naught between you and his lairdship but friendship. I want to make certain of that before I say more."

Lark leaned back in her chair, a bit overwarm from the hot tea and sitting so close to the warming machine. "I've known the laird my whole life. And until recently there's been no talk of the future."

"Until recently?" Theodosia leaned forward with interest.

"Before the laird left we spoke of our hopes for the future." Lark looked to her lap, tripping over her words if only because sharing her treasured feelings seemed to open a door better left closed. Besides, Theodosia was a new friend, the future uncertain. If Magnus succumbed to yellow fever, there would be no future. She focused on Theodosia's rapt expression, trying to stay atop her fractured feelings.

"I only met him briefly but 'twas enough to make a lasting impression. He's an uncommon man and I'm truly sorry for his loss. And yours, if so." Theodosia returned her teacup to its saucer. "I wouldn't want to intrude on your grief but feel 'tis time to mention my brother-in-law."

Trevor? Lark saw the hesitation in her

eyes, the worry of mishandling a fragile situation.

"Trevor has become quite fond of you." She studied Lark as if gauging her reaction. "There are other young women who look his way, but he seems to have eyes only for you."

'Twas no surprise. Had she not sensed his interest? Even when she'd been forthcoming about her indenture? Still, she balked, at least in her innermost thoughts. "Surely a man of Trevor Ramsay's standing wouldna seek a lass such as I, not even in forward-thinking America."

" 'Tis precisely his standing that allows him the freedom to choose. He has no need of any dowry. And he can redeem your contract in a breath. I doubt even Mr. Osbourne would object to the match."

"But I remain a stillroom mistress. A low-born Scot."

Theodosia's smile was wry. "Say what you will about yourself. Your deportment, fine bearing, civility, and speech belie your humble station. Your family history and schooling alongside the laird makes you not only suitable but far more interesting than these Virginia belles. Not only that, you share Trevor's interests. Gardens. Beekeeping. Babies."

At that, she handed Larkin another macaroon. He'd pulled himself up, holding on to Theodosia's skirt, and was eyeing the tea table.

"He's quite taken with Master Larkin. Think of the advantages the new attorney general of Virginia Colony could give him as a stepfather."

Was she serious? Marriage into the powerful Ramsay clan? No more worries or woes over Mr. Granger and what he might do. A new home of her own in Williamsburg, a town as charming and current as Kerrera Island was rustic and remote. But also instant social standing, something she cared nary a fig about. And they were a slaveholding family like so many wealthy Virginians.

Her prolonged silence set Theodosia to talking again, crafting a persuasive case of which her barrister husband would be proud. "You must meet the Gilliams. They arrived on Virginia's shores as indentures in the seventeenth century, and through a combination of industry and clever marriages now find themselves in the top tier of society here. Their home, Weston Manor, is not far."

"I should like to meet them," Lark said, finishing her macaroon and finding it delicious. "Almond with a hint of rosewater?"

"You have a discriminating palate, another fine attribute."

"Where is Trevor today?"

"At the capital." Theodosia seemed pleased at the inquiry. "When he's not there he's at his property on South England Street supervising construction of his new house. We seldom see him these days."

Finished with her tea, Lark bent and reached for a jack-in-the-box, showing Larkin how to turn the crank so that a jester popped up.

"You can expect Trevor to come calling soon," Theodosia announced with a soft, satisfied smile. "He rather enjoyed being snowbound with you at Royal Hundred."

35

A day to come seems longer than a year that's gone.

Scottish proverb

"You are doing too much," the physic warned.

"There is much to be done," Magnus replied.

His work began at four o'clock in the morn and did not let up till nearly midnight. Already a fortnight had been lost due to illness. The three overseers kept their distance in fear of catching the fever but 'twas simple enough to ken they hoped he wouldn't recover. The Africans waited to see if he would die or survive as they prepared the fields for planting. He still felt like death, but the needs before him were unrelenting.

Turning his horse away from Trelawny Hall's colonnaded loggia, he rode toward yet another new windmill that marred the landscape. He finally dismounted and turned loose his horse to graze on the lush Guinea grass the livestock favored. He then took up a hoe while one gang of Ashanti men regarded him with unveiled astonishment. Did they think the fever had burned his brain? He worked with determined intensity alongside them, digging trenches and laying cane end to end. By sunset they'd planted two acres as other gangs fanned out around them and did the same.

"If I am to understand ye — and ken this plantation — then I am to be one of ye," he explained, knowing that without Rojay the words were lost to them. Yet perhaps they understood simply by his actions. Confusion cleared from their expressions as he finished speaking and took up his implement again.

How else was he to master this unsavory operation if he did not learn it like they did, from planting to harvest, using the broad curved machetes for cutting? Even though he was bleeding from the cane's sharp edges, back nearly broken from the work, sugar was but one crop in an endless succession of harvests. There was cocoa and coffee and indigo too.

He penned Osbourne a letter that evening from a chair on the loggia, a lap desk on his knees. A cooling coastal wind ruffled the paper's edges and dried his ink nearly as fast as he formed the words. Weighing his thoughts, he looked out on a series of sandy, turquoise coves shimmering in the setting sun.

Care shall be taken that the Negroes shall have an abundance of food and every other assistance. I consider their preservation and comfort to be the first object on every well-regulated estate, their houses put into repair . . .

Though the overseers had implemented the changes, they grumbled and called him a sorner behind his back.

"What means this, sir?" Rojay had asked, ever faithful.

"Sorner?" The word sat sourly in Magnus's mouth. "Worthless vagabond. One who shirks work."

"I think *they* are that," Rojay replied before he showed the trio into Magnus's study for another meeting.

The overseers gave an accounting of the improvements and a report on runaways, which had decreased markedly in Magnus's short tenure, even with the removal of the mantraps, the slave catchers at the plantation's edges. Then came a litany of petty grievances.

"There's no cure for their deceit," one said, face shiny from the evening's heat. "Continually the worst of the slaves break tools to retaliate for some perceived slight or another. They even have a system where they sleep or shirk work, using hand signals or speaking their language to warn when we are near."

"Then bring any sorners to me," Magnus said, dismissing them.

They'd moved off the porch, a simmering resentment in their wake.

Dismissing the memory, he resumed his letter writing, still weak from the lingering effects of the fever. A dish of freshly cut, sugared lemons and limes were near at hand, a luxury. Beside these were a stack of ledgers to review that he'd gotten from plantation clerks.

He reached for his quill again, inked the tip, and penned the name at the forefront of his every thought.

7 December, 1752

Dearest Lark,
I am on my feet again, having turned yellow from fever. Such did not set well

with my Scots coloring, to be sure. As you were not here to nurse me back to health, my recovery was slow.

But I will not speak to you of hardships. I ken you have your own. I'll speak to you of the small pleasures to be had even in the midst of Hades. For one, there are butterflies here big as my hand. Swallowtail, they are called. They would do well in your garden alongside your bees. The flowers here are just as large, though I do not know their names. I tried drying one that was red and one yellow to send to you, but they stay limp and damp in this tropical heat.

I am surrounded by a sea of Africans. As many as thirty slave ships arrive daily in Montego Bay, a grievous number, even as we export as many ships overfull of sugar and rum. The Ashanti are a remarkable people of greater faculties than the white men who oversee them. I am of a mind to make managers of them, these Africans, if they are willing.

Lest you think I am starving here, I oft wish I could sit down at table with you. I wonder what you would make of the curious Caribbean fare. There are plantains, not unlike the Virginia sweet potato. And stew peas and rice, even salt fish aplenty. I am partial to the jerked meat cooked over green pimento wood, and bammy, a bread. Alas, nary a bannock in sight.

As I go about this strange country I imagine how you and Larkin are. Those last days in Virginia retain their sweetness. I pray they will stay so till we meet again.

Yours entire,
Magnus

The slave quarters were most brutal in winter. Lark could almost not bear to go and dispense the needed tonics, pushing another cartload of coverlets and stockings besides. A few chimneys puffed smoke, but with Mr. Granger rationing firewood as an unnecessary expense, how warm could the people be? Still they sang, prayed, labored. They died and were born in an endless cycle of poverty and want, though some remained remarkably rich in spirit.

Josiah was one of those shining souls seemingly undaunted by the injustice around him. He preached to his fellows, encouraged them, strove to better their lot when he could. Now he held the Watts hymnal she'd brought him alongside his Bible. Somehow Granger hadn't stopped their singing and sharing the Word. Lark sent up a bethankit for that.

"We heard Granger is against your comin' here, Miss MacDougall," he confided. "We pray you stay strong. We pray for your boy to stay strong too."

It struck her then how a marriage to Trevor Ramsay might somehow help. If Magnus had passed — *Lord, nay* — mightn't she as Lark Ramsay do more than simple Lark MacDougall? Sway Trevor to enact legislation in the slaves' favor? Was that worthy grounds for marrying him, coupled with her desire for Larkin's well-being — even if she didn't love him? Might she learn to love him?

She went away as burdened as if she still carried the load of quilts and stockings she'd just dispensed. She was unsure of Trevor and his stance on slavery. She knew his politics yet was unsure of his religion, his true heart. All of this turned her own heart to Magnus, though she had no idea if he even lived. Theodosia seemed to expect the worst, even spoke of him in the past tense. Not knowing his fate grieved her mightily, but what could she do?

Her steps were slow, her whole being weary, but she was more wearied in mind than body. The cold day gathered round her as the sun dipped to the west in a puddle of golden light demanding her notice, its beauty solacing her a bit.

"Mistress MacDougall." The voice, loud and firm, even grating, stopped her cold. "I would have a word with you."

Behind her, the factor had gotten off his horse. A patch of snowy ground was between them, not yet melted beneath the canopy of oaks above. She turned warily. No smile of greeting was lighting Granger's harsh features. Or hers.

Would he take her to task about the runaways? Her visits to the quarters?

"I have spoken to the parish about your infant. It falls to them to take the child and assume responsibility for him." He fingered the whip in his gloved hand, looking smug. "Indentures are to be served without the encumbrance of children. I have given testimony that the child is interfering with your work."

"Interfering?" Fury stiffened her voice. "Mistress Flowerdew says quite the opposite."

"But Mistress Flowerdew is merely the housekeeper. Granted, Osbourne gave her charge of you for some inexplicable reason. But I remain the factor and supervise all other indentures and their covenants. You

467

are in violation of yours."

"So ye would take my child from me? 'Twill be by force. I'll not give him up to ye or the parish or anyone else. Mr. Osbourne had no objection to my having him when we left the Glasgow docks."

"But Osbourne is not here." He paused, and then a cold smile made his sallow, distorted face more grotesque. "Female indentures have little voice in these matters. If I say the child is keeping you from your work, then the child is keeping you from your work. Period."

She turned away from him, walking with such haste her cape flew out behind her on the scantest wind. Thankfully, Larkin was not here but with Mistress Flowerdew in the mansion. She had requested Lark not take him to the quarters. Fearing illness — or Granger?

"How were the coverlets and stockings received?" the housekeeper asked when Lark entered her private sitting room.

"Well enough," she replied breathlessly. But the visit to the quarters had left her mind. Granger filled it to overflowing, adding another layer of misery atop her heartache over Magnus. "The factor stopped me on the way back. He —" Misery nearly choked her. She looked to Larkin sitting on

468

the housekeeper's lap, contentedly chewing on a toy. Would he be taken from her? Given over to the parish poorhouse? Did that mean she could not see him?

"I'm afraid he's been by here too."

Lark stared at her, waiting for the words she had no wish to hear.

"No doubt he told you the same thing he told me. His threat about the babe, I mean."

"Can he do such? Take Larkin away?"

Her prolonged pause only spiked Lark's alarm. "Mr. Granger is a man who is not in his right mind and is capable of doing great harm. But we are going to counter it, you and I."

"But we women have little say in matters. I dinna ken where to begin. If the laird were here —"

"We shall turn to Trevor Ramsay. Studying law at the Middle Temple in the Inns of Court in London counts for something. He may well advocate for you and wee Larkin. Factor Granger dare not stand up to that."

"How do we contact him? Shall I send a note to Williamsburg? Or go there myself?"

"Neither." Mistress Flowerdew bounced Larkin on her lap when he began to fret. "Providentially, he's sent a note round saying he would like to call tomorrow afternoon."

■ ■ ■ ■

The candlelight flickered on the paper, the glistening ink slow to dry in the cold. Shrugging her shawl closer, Lark dipped the quill into the ink pot again.

Dearest Magnus,

Word has come that you have been unwell. I pray night and day that nothing shall take you down nor disturb the good work you have started there. I continue to believe that you are alive and well and that it is only your letters that miscarry. I have received no word from you since your one post, dated soon after your arrival in Jamaica.

I ask that you pray for me and Larkin. The overseer here is bent on removing the babe from my care. I believe it is in his power to do so but am yet unsure. Indentures have few rights and Osbourne is an ocean away. Granger has even spoken of selling my contract to another. If I am to lose Larkin I cannot bear knowing he may go to the parish poorhouse and receive little loving care. 'Twill likely be the end of him, and me.

I am sorry to burden you with this but

470

have always looked to you as laird and counselor. Though you are far away, you remain close in spirit. I cannot accept that you are gone from me forever.

Yours,
Lark

She paid the post and the letter was carried away. Benumbed, she spent precious time rocking Larkin, who slept against her with the warm weight she'd come to treasure, oblivious to all that swirled around them.

Am I to lose everything, Lord? Scotland, Magnus, and now the babe?

Twilight drew a curtain on the melancholy day. Sally brought supper when Lark failed to appear at the kitchen house. But Lark had no heart to eat.

"I been prayin'," Sally told her as she set down the tray. "I told Josiah in the quarters what Granger wants done. He's prayin' too." She darted a fretful glance at the door as if suspecting the factor hovered outside. "That babe is yours and ain't deservin' o' no poorhouse. And you done nothin' that calls for sellin' you to another plantation."

Lark placed a spoon in Larkin's fist and watched as he began feeding himself his supper with a clumsy hand. "Pray that Mr.

Ramsay is able to turn things in our favor, though colonial law regarding indentures might be set in stone."

Sally went away more mournful than Lark had ever seen her. The stillroom clock ticked on. Mistress Flowerdew was expecting them as usual. Her cozy sitting room had become a haven of acceptance and comfort. Did that rile Granger too?

Trevor Ramsay arrived at two o'clock the following afternoon. He came into the mansion foyer whistling a low tune and unintentionally lifting Lark's spirits. Mistress Flowerdew took his cloak and gloves, her expression a stew of worry and relief. "Welcome back to Royal Hundred."

"Dear Lark." His eyes met hers across the expanse of polished foyer.

His lack of formality and his unexpected tenderness distracted her from her own distressing circumstances, if only momentarily.

They passed into the sitting room where Larkin gave a little shout at the sight of the tall man in his finely tailored winter's suit. In a gesture that made the moment sweeter, Trevor picked Larkin up and sat him on his knee, giving over his timepiece to play with.

He eyed both Lark and the housekeeper. "You seem uncommonly worried. Surely my visit isn't the reason for that."

"Heavens, no," Mistress Flowerdew assured him. "We simply find ourselves amid distressing circumstances that coincide with your visit. Perhaps that barrister brain of yours can be of help."

"Of course. What is the trouble?"

"New concerns with the factor here, Mr. Granger. He is a man of many schemes. Of late he seems bent on selling Lark's contract to another plantation and removing her from Royal Hundred. His resentment of her interest in the quarters knows no bounds. He's even spoken with the parish about giving them charge of Larkin. This would make for a more profitable sale of Lark's contract. Few are willing to take on an indenture saddled with a child."

Lark listened to the bare facts, the fragile life she'd constructed in Virginia about to shatter like window glass. But what did it matter if Magnus was gone? She was on the edge again of the unknown, trying to pray her way through a great many ill-scrappit feelings. Fear. Sorrow. Anger. Helplessness. Resignation.

She looked to Trevor entreatingly. His calm blunted her rising bewilderment. Uppermost was her panic over losing Larkin, nearly as huge a hole as Magnus's loss. The both of them would send her into an abyss she would never recover from. This she *knew.*

"Indentures do have rights, including the right to protest ill treatment from someone like Mr. Granger." He looked at Larkin. "The babe I'm less sure of. I'll have to consult the burgesses and parish vestrymen in the capital. See what can be done."

"With your good name, your family's standing, I'm sure something will turn in our favor," Mistress Flowerdew said, pulling the bell cord. "If you'll excuse me, I'll oversee refreshments."

Trevor studied Lark, alone with her but for Larkin. Though her hands were folded sedately in her lap, Lark's unease soared beneath his close scrutiny. Could affection be felt so early? Love at first sight was not something she believed in. The love she sought grew with time and loving-kindness, shared circumstances and bedrock beliefs, stoked into a steady blaze that could not be put out. Or so her practical self said. What had she with Trevor Ramsay on such short acquaintance?

Dunderheed.

The slur curled in her mind like black smoke, a taunting hiss.

Here she sat with one of the most eligible

suitors in Virginia, who was looking at her with something more than friendship in his countenance, mayhap offering her the moon, and she was . . .

Unmoved.

She cleared her throat and forced a smile. "I shall leave the matter in yer capable hands. And I thank ye for helping us."

Larkin tired of the pocket watch and reached for her with a yawn. She took him, settling him on her lap and rocking him back and forth in the finely wrought Chippendale chair. Rain smeared the windowpane behind Trevor's fair head, reminding her once again of Scotland. Home.

"Lark, your safety and comfort are of utmost concern to me." His voice was cool and unconcerned, a hue and a cry from how she herself felt. "This may sound premature, but you needn't waste any time wondering what might befall you and the babe."

She nodded and attempted to turn his attention away from her and back to the present. "Tell me how it goes with yer property on South England Street."

At this he came alive, describing the construction thus far and in future. A solid sandstone foundation. A cornerstone with his initials and the date. A dry brick well in the cellar to keep ice and food fresh. The approach lined with elms. Ninety acres of woodland, gardens, and orchards. He seemed especially proud of the ordered pine paneling and walnut doors with heavy brass locks. She herself was taken with the plan for a second-floor gallery that overlooked the foyer.

" 'Twill be second to the Governor's Palace in grandeur," he said.

"Will ye have an orangery, Trevor? Bees?"

"If you like, Lark." A faint flush crept into his fair features, and he looked down at the carpet as if contemplating its swirling design.

"I should like that very much, but it isna for me to decide."

His chuckle made her feel cornered. Flustered. Theodosia had told her of his intentions. Must she herself now thwart them? Beyond the sitting room she heard the clatter of crockery. Larkin finally slept and she ceased her rocking, wondering why Mistress Flowerdew was taking so long.

"You make a fetching picture," he remarked.

"Larkin means the world to me."

"That I see. 'Tis a trait that commends you, having taken in an orphan that would have a very dour outcome otherwise. Have you chosen godparents? Considered having him baptized?"

"I would follow Scots-Presbyterian tradition."

"Would you consider becoming Anglican?"

Anglican was so very . . . English. All she knew of his religion she'd found within the ornate walls of Bruton Parish Church, so different from the simple stone kirk on Kerrera. Yet she recalled something an officer had said aboard the *Bonaventure,* that many colonial Anglicans — the gentry mostly — were shallow as a puddle in their faith and congregated mostly for social reasons, their souls growing fat and proud on fancy colonial trappings. But could she trust the judgment of a profane seaman?

"I ken little of yer faith, being new to America," she admitted.

He gave a slight shrug. " 'Tis of little consequence. A private matter, mostly."

Of little consequence? Her knowing about Anglicanism, or faith in general? She opened her mouth to question him, but the maid came in with Mistress Flowerdew and refreshments were served. They passed another pleasant hour with the housekeeper before he departed, his lingering look promising a speedy response about the matter with Granger.

The post rider passed him on the drive, and she waited alongside Mistress Flowerdew in the open doorway for fresh news, again on tenterhooks.

Lord, please. Just one line. A simple *I am well* would suffice.

But there was only a post for the new gardener, Mr. Munro, from Philadelphia.

Despite her best efforts, Lark's spirits sank to her soles.

36

Never draw your dirk when a blow will do it.

Scottish proverb

I continue to believe that you are alive and well and that it is only your letters that miscarry. I have received no word from you since your one post, dated soon after your arrival in Jamaica.

He stared at the words upon a second reading, calculating, mentally tracking time. 'Twould soon be January. Lark should have heard from him by now. He looked up from the creased paper, flummoxed beyond all reason. Did nothing make it out of this accursed place? Not even a post? Folding the paper, he pocketed it, weighing his actions, schooling his reaction.

Reining his horse round, he left the noisy sugar mill and returned to Trelawny Hall, his priorities shifting. This time he'd not just pen her a letter but would track it as discreetly as circumstances allowed. Never had he written so quickly, his quill so ink-laden. His angry scrawl was not directed at Lark but at her predicament. By now, for all he knew, Larkin had been taken to the poorhouse and she herself transferred to another plantation. At least at Royal Hundred he knew where she was, could envision her going about her daily tasks under the motherly eye of Mistress Flowerdew. He somehow, mayhap blindly, trusted Osbourne's influence to protect her, even across an ocean.

But now . . .

Feigning indifference he was far from feeling, Magnus let the letter dry, then sealed it before calling the houseboy. The lad came hastily on bare feet and took the post and coin from Magnus's outstretched hand as usual. Off he went, down the palm-lined lane toward the dusty main road. What he did once he was off Trelawny's grounds had always been a mystery. Till now.

Magnus followed, cutting through the grounds so that the greenery hid him. The lad veered left down a row of tall, wide-reaching guango trees to the overseers' quarters with a quick look over his shoulder.

Magnus's suspicion flared. He walked uphill, keeping to the line of trees, then paused outside the offices where much of the plantation's business was transacted by plantation clerks, their bobbing heads bent over their work. Each sennight their ledgers were given to him for review.

'Twas now the forenoon, the heat climbing to sticky heights. He breathed in a heavy breath, accustomed to feeling draped in a warm, wet blanket. Stepping into the hall, he saw the lad pass into the overseers' office. Low voices rumbled. Through a crack in the door Magnus watched and listened. His letter to Lark passed into the eldest overseer's tanned hands. The man dug in his pocket and flipped the lad a coin. At that, the lad scampered back outside. Once he was gone, the overseer broke Magnus's seal and tore open the post. Magnus sensed his glee. His greed. The overseer took the money Magnus always included in his letters for Lark's benefit and pocketed it.

Magnus set his jaw. Fury flared like a hot coal inside him. With a push at the door, he stepped into the unkempt room. Paper littered the floor. Were his past letters to Lark among them?

The overseer was slow to look up. When he did Magnus was rewarded by stark surprise. Fear. It flashed over the man's lined face, followed by the stain of guilt. There was no need for any talk. The stolen letter fluttered to the cluttered desk as Magnus crossed the room in three strides and took the overseer by the throat.

In response, the overseer tried to shove Magnus backwards, but it did little good. Magnus's hold on the man's collar tightened, twisted, till the purple hue in his sun-creased features caused him to gasp for air.

Several bookkeepers gathered at the door in time to see Magnus give the surly overseer a sound thrashing, sending him somersaulting over his desk at the finish. He lay on the floor as if unconscious, lip bloodied, clothing rumpled. Reaching over, Magnus reclaimed the money from his pocket.

"Yer services are no longer needed as of this morn," Magnus said, breathing hard through clenched teeth. "If I see ye anywhere on this plantation, I'll set the authorities on ye after I give ye another drubbing. As it is, I could have ye punished for mail theft, which I suspect is only the beginning of yer offenses." Kicking aside a scattering of papers, he turned to the stunned onlookers. "I'll return in an hour. This pigsty should be clean and well swept, with no sign of Mr. Talbot. He's been replaced."

He took back his letter to Lark and strode past the onlookers, out of the offices, and toward Trelawny Hall. Once there, he called the houseboy to him. The lad appeared in the doorway of Magnus's study, head down, clearly suspecting something amiss.

"I've no quarrel with ye," Magnus told him gently. "I ken ye simply did as ye were told by the man."

"That I did, sir." His dark eyes filled with tears. "He told me to bring him your every post, that he would see them mailed and to think no more of it."

"Aye, we'll now think no more of it. Go back to yer tasks. And if, in future, something seems amiss, come to me first."

He penned another letter to Lark, stuffed the money within, and set out to Montego Bay himself to assure the letter was posted without delay.

God help her, he could do but little so far away.

Lark smiled tentatively at the churchwarden, glad Trevor was near. Larkin sat on her lap, the picture of health and contentment. Or so she hoped. In the churchwarden's hands was the letter of complaint against her filed by Granger. Neglect of duties. Preoccupation with the child, whom he called a word

Lark would not utter. Then in an odd about-face, Granger cast a cloud on the truth of her story, saying she attempted to pass off the child as an orphan when he was indeed her own. The proof was in their shared coloring, their red hair.

"Truly remarkable, the resemblance," the churchwarden said. "Sadly, if this child was born of you 'twould be easier to have him remain with you. Given he's an orphan who fell into your hands quite by accident makes him more a case for the parish poorhouse."

Lark nearly cringed. "I dinna believe in accidents, Mr. Wellinghurst. More divine instance. The Almighty cares very much for children. I believe He delivers the poor and fatherless and them that have none to help them, as Scripture says."

"Indeed. And amen," he replied, perusing the paper.

Reaching up, Larkin touched her cheek with a wee hand. She smiled down at him, caressing a lock of hair that covered one brilliantly blue eye.

"Each case is unique," Trevor said. "The law is not as inflexible as it would seem. I have a written statement here from Royal Hundred's housekeeper, who is the aunt of Richard Osbourne's deceased wife."

"Mistress Flowerdew?" The churchwarden

took the paper and read it silently. "What begs weighing is Richard Osbourne's opinion."

"Osbourne took Miss MacDougall on board the *Bonaventure* knowing the babe was in her care. That must speak to the surety of her indenture."

" 'Tis an unusual arrangement, indeed. Children are usually bound out in such cases, apprenticed to masters when they come of age, once the poorhouse releases them."

"If they live long enough to reach their majority," Trevor replied. "I know the state of the parish poorhouses in Virginia. Many have shut down because of inadequacies and outright failure. They're no place for a young child, given they're overrun with vagrants and criminals, more like gaol."

"Aye, mostly because of Publick Times when the general assembly meets and the town turns into a fair attracting all manner of indigent and idle. But what else do we have as a remedy? Those destitute cannot become the care of his majesty's government."

"In Miss MacDougall's case, I ask you to make an exception. Allow her to remain at Royal Hundred per the terms of her contract and continue as the caregiver of her adopted son. Wait till Osbourne arrives and resolves the matter himself."

Lark listened, softening toward Trevor for his defense of her. She was yet unsure what to make of the churchwarden. Sally said Granger had him in his pocket, whatever that meant.

At his silence, Trevor pressed the matter. "If you cannot ensure that this happens, I have no choice but to appeal to a higher power and take the matter to court."

The churchwarden frowned and studied Lark. "You could place the babe with a family in town. Such has been done before. Then at the age of seven or so, the child is apprenticed."

Apprenticed? At so young an age? At seven she had been running free on the moors and beaches of Kerrera. Would Larkin's earliest memories be of work?

"What if I became the child's godparent or guardian?" Trevor said with a confidence born of authority. "Take it upon myself to ensure he has a proper education when the time comes at the Grammar School, avoiding apprenticeship altogether. I'm certainly capable of maintaining him prior to that."

"There is still the matter of his caregiver."

"What if he was adopted?"

Lark's brows arched. The churchwarden

486

asked the question she couldn't. "By whom?"

"Someone who is childless. Able to give an orphan all that an indentured caretaker cannot."

Theodosia?

Though Trevor didn't look at her or name a particular person, Lark knew. She vehemently wished his words back. Suddenly she was cast in the role of one who would hold on to Larkin selfishly when faced with giving him up to a childless, more financially capable friend. Her heart, so sore over Magnus, wrung all over again at this latest complication.

Larkin began fretting and Lark dug in her indispensable for something to amuse him. In the flurry of the morning she'd left his toy in the coach. She began to bounce him gently on her knees in an effort to distract him.

"Let us have time away to think on the matter further," the churchwarden said. "We shall meet again once I've looked into it more thoroughly."

Trevor nodded, shaking hands with the man amicably. To Lark, he said quietly, "Let's retire to Nicholson Street. My sister-in-law will be quite contrary if I don't bring you to see her for a brief visit, at least."

They exchanged the drafty Bruton Parish Church for the coal-stoked warmth of Ramsay House. Lark's spirits lifted at Theodosia's delighted greeting, and then her mind veered to Trevor's proposal. Would Theodosia be a fitting mother for Larkin? She gave him over to Theodosia's open arms with a sudden reluctance.

"Ah, Master Larkin, you are looking especially fine this winter's morn," Theodosia said, peeking at him admiringly beneath his cap. "Did you make his garments yourself, Lark? If so, they are well-wrought indeed."

"I am a passable seamstress at best, though Mistress Flowerdew kindly gave over the lace for trimming." Lark forced a smile as a servant took her cape and bonnet. " 'Tis cold of late. I aim to keep him as cozy as I can."

Larkin smiled coyly at Theodosia's adoring glances, sporting a new tooth. How he'd fussed till it poked through his tender gum. No amount of clove oil seemed to relieve him, only her rocking him all night.

"You must have tea. Warm up before returning to Royal Hundred," their hostess said as Trevor ushered them into the usual chamber.

The mantel was bedecked with greenery,

a festive medley of holly, ivy, mountain laurel, and mistletoe adorned with bright scarlet ribbon. Noticing Lark's admiration, Theodosia said, "You shall take part in 'the sticking of the church,' as we call it. Decorating it from the altar to the galleries and beyond. Reverend Dawson is even composing a special Christmas hymn for us to sing."

Distracted by all that had happened with the churchwarden, Lark said nothing as she took a seat near the stove.

"Come now, Lark, don't be so dull," Theodosia scolded good-naturedly. "Surely you Scots celebrate Christmas. Or are you as dour as those poker-faced New Englanders who frown on such?"

"Christmas is rather a quiet affair in Scotland, having been outlawed. But we on Kerrera celebrate in quiet ways."

"Then a lavish Virginia Christmas you shall have." Theodosia took a chair, trying to amuse Larkin, who had tired of being toted about. Screwing his face into a scowl, he let out a howl that snuffed their conversation. Theodosia reached to the right and pulled on a bell cord with a graceful move. A servant appeared, her dark face expressionless, eyes down.

"Come take him, Evie. We shall have a quiet hour."

Larkin howled louder as he left the room, his protests reaching a crescendo in the echoing entry hall. Would Evie take him to the far kitchen down the long servants' hall out back? Weary, Lark watched him go, craving the serenity and simple lines of their quarters. Nothing seemed better than their own crackling hearth's fire, just the two of them, if only for her to sort through the morning's events.

Trevor was watching her as if weighing her thoughts. But she always seemed to be his focus of late, especially with their case in his lap. Would he mention giving over Larkin to Theodosia here and now? She prayed not.

"Any word from the laird?" he asked, taking a sip from his steaming cup. At the shake of her head, he said, "A friend of mine is set to sail to Jamaica on business soon. I thought, if you liked, he might stop in at Trelawny Hall and inquire."

All weariness vanished. "How very thoughtful. Might ye ask yer friend to hand deliver a letter for me? I'm unsure of the post. I've heard nothing from the laird and wonder if my letters even reach him."

"Of course. I'm sure he'll not mind in the least." He looked to Theodosia. "What's this

I hear about carol singing on Saturday next?"

"Lark must come too. Perhaps you can escort her. We were so disappointed you didn't join us at the governor's holiday ball." She smiled at Lark invitingly. "We'd be happy to have you as our guest. I've just redecorated an upstairs bedchamber in painted chintz with new Axminster carpets. The carol singing goes quite late as we serenade all of Williamsburg. Then we make a bonfire on Palace Green. Last year it snowed and was quite magical."

"Rivers of punch and minced pies make me happiest," Trevor said. "But I'm not against some carol singing too."

"Mistress Flowerdew is invited also. And Master Larkin will be well tended by our servants."

Lark simply nodded in agreement, mind pinned to Magnus and the man soon en route from Virginia to Jamaica. How soon would she know about the laird's well-being? Time had slowed, and every delay was harder to take.

"What do you make of all this snow this winter, Lark?" Theodosia inquired. "Does Old Man Winter blow white in Scotland?"

At this Lark smiled. "I am not so deprived as all that. The sea in a swirling snow is a sight to behold."

Trevor chuckled and extended his cup for more tea. "Not one snowfall did we have in London while I was studying law there. Good to know you northerners weren't so needy."

" 'Tis a date, then," Theodosia exclaimed. "I shall ready the new bedchamber for your arrival, Lark. What a merry Christmastide we shall have!"

37

And fare thee weel, my only love, and fare thee weel awhile! And I will come again, my love, though it were ten thousand mile.

Robert Burns

Christmas was the farthest thing from Lark's mind. The next meeting with the churchwarden was foremost. But being a guest of the Ramsays came first. They bundled up and took the coach to Williamsburg — she, Larkin, and Mistress Flowerdew. A voluminous letter to Magnus was now sealed and tucked in her baggage, to be handed to the Jamaica-bound friend Trevor had mentioned. She prayed it would reach its destination. Or that some word was forthcoming from Jamaica.

As they pulled past Royal Hundred's scrolled wrought-iron gates, she looked back, chilled once more by the sight of Granger on his horse, watching them depart. A return of gout had kept him abed of late. His wife had gone to the apothecary in town this time instead of darkening Lark's door for a remedy. It must have helped, for today Granger was back on his feet, making the rounds on the plantation.

Had the runaways been caught? She rarely thought of Rory. Apart from Scotland, minus the *Merry Lass,* he had simply faded from her thoughts. Back then she'd been a naïve girl, enamored of the sea and the danger and a braw sea captain. But Isla's untimely death, the long ocean voyage and indenture, and Magnus's fate had turned her into a wary woman. She longed to recapture a bit of the childish spirit she found in Larkin. 'Twould make her a better mother. A better wife, if it came to that.

For the time being, she was ensconced in a bedchamber that resembled a silken garden with its fine floral fabrics and wallpaper and costly furnishings. Who would have imagined she'd sit to the right of Prentice at supper, arguably the most important man in Virginia Colony, second only to the royal governor himself? Who would have dreamed she'd walk about Williamsburg caroling, chilled to the bone? And quite pink-cheeked, throat tingling from singing, on the arm of Virginia's rising star, as the *Gazette* called him — the honorable Trevor Ramsay?

She mustn't let it go to her head.

Here on Palace Green they were amid a great many carolers, their breaths pluming in the crystalline winter air. Mulled cider was being passed about, merry faces illuminated by the leaping flames as the singers circled the bonfire. Trevor's fair features were ruddy from the cold, a woolen scarf wrapped round his neck. Lark's own fur muff was put to good use, and more than one lady remarked on her lovely matching cape and bonnet. Of pale mint silk trimmed with Canadian fox fur, it seemed fit for Queen Anne. Glad she was to be clad in the early Christmas gift Mistress Flowerdew had given her. Trevor said it went remarkably well with her bright hair. Truly, he'd not stopped looking at her all evening.

She peered down the street toward Ramsay House as people began to disperse. The big dwelling seemed to slumber. Somewhere within were a great many servants and Larkin. The truth was she missed him. Missed his damp, pearl-toothed grin. His sweet, lavender scent after a bath. The curls that wisped like red silk through her fingers. His sleepy weight as he lay in her lap. His gurgling laugh.

"You missed a note, Lark," Trevor teased as the caroling ended, obviously sensing her distraction.

"I'm wondering where wee Larkin is."

He smiled, extending ungloved hands toward the fire's heat. "He's tucked upstairs in your bedchamber, a servant watching over him. I warned Theodosia not to take him any farther."

She cast a glance about and found they were alone, the rest of the carolers slipping away to their homes. Silence reigned save for the crackle and snap of the now dwindling bonfire.

"Have ye any word from the churchwarden?" she asked tentatively, hating to spoil the festive evening with worrisome matters.

"Shush, Lark." He softened the rebuke with a smile. "We shall hear from him soon enough. What do your Scriptures say? 'Take no thought for tomorrow'?"

"*My* Scriptures, Trevor? Are they not yers too?"

He shrugged lightly in that familiar way she was coming to know. "I save Scripture for the Sabbath. For church, mostly. I've found the Bible to have little bearing on practical life."

"Oh?" Lark watched a burst of sparks swirl away into the night. "Because ye keep it so confined, mayhap."

"Confined? The Bible? I suppose so. Do you challenge me, Lark?"

"Do I?" She turned back to him. "As a native Scot, I would try to better understand ye native Virginians."

Again he gave that maddening shrug. "As my cousin Thomas Jefferson once said, question with boldness even the existence of a God, because, if there be one, He must approve more the homage of reason than that of blindfolded fear."

"Yet I do fear Him. He is holy and I am not. I am a sinner saved by grace. And I believe in Him with all my heart."

"As Creator of the universe, perhaps. Not as a personal, intimate being, surely."

"If He isna personal, He is worth very little to me," she said with more vehemence than the late hour called for. "Would a God give up His own beloved Son if He was impersonal and indifferent?"

"A pretty speech, to be sure." He turned toward her. "Let's not waste time with futile arguments and that which matters little. Not with the night on the wane."

Their little disagreement rolled past, his indifference unsettling. What he spoke of was beyond her ken. A highly trained mind he had, far beyond the reach of a stillroom maid, however well educated at Kerrera Castle. He was, after all, Anglican and American. She was Scots-Presbyterian born and bred. Matters of faith had always been heartfelt. The great Reformation had seen to that. Should she expect Trevor, raised in the faith of the Church of England, to be like her? Did his aloof faith truly matter?

He reached out a hand and touched a wisp of her hair that had slipped free of its pins. After a night of wind and caroling, she must look a fright. "I would speak of more important things."

What could possibly be more important than one's faith? She kept the thought close, wishing for a different sort of evening with a different sort of suitor.

"I'm preoccupied with the New Year. What it will bring."

For him, all seemed pleasantries.

"Yer thinking of the completion of Ramsay Manor. Planting yer gardens and orchards. Perhaps another appointment by the royal governor."

"All well and good, but not foremost in my mind nor my heart." He offered her an arm and they began a slow walk down Nicholson Street. "I want to be about the business of courting you, Lark. I would ask your father . . ."

"My father was lost at sea long ago."

"So Mistress Flowerdew told me. I have written to Osbourne instead, asking for his permission not only to court you but to wed you, if you are willing."

She turned her face toward him, the darkness denying her a look into his eyes. She regarded him, her thoughts and emotions in such a tangle she could not summon a single coherent word.

"I hope this means you are speechless with delight," he said, teasing in his tone.

"I . . ." She paused, not wanting to offend him. "I am —"

He silenced her with a kiss and slid a cold hand around her neck so that her face was tilted up to his. She tasted cider. Smoke. Safety. Security. All at once she was cast back to her first kiss in a sea cave and a captain who'd tried to claim her. She'd not responded then, nor did she now. Neither did she draw back, so stunned was she by Trevor's unexpected move. But he didn't seem to mind, nor even notice so passionless a kiss.

"Consider it, Lark. I shall court you. And if we wed, all your worries about Granger and his schemes, the babe, and the onerous contract you hold with Osbourne will blow away like chaff in the wind."

Kwasi sat on his horse like a prince, the sun shining off his composed, deeply etched features glistening with sweat, his regal bearing stoking Magnus's curiosity.

"Tell me of yer former life. In Africa," Magnus said by way of Rojay as the three of them looked out on sugarcane thrusting green shoots above the soil of hundreds of acres.

If the Ashanti seemed surprised by Magnus's query, he did not show it. "You are the first white man to ask that of me," he replied in his melodic cadence, the muscle in his jaw twitching.

Thoughtful seconds passed. The emotion the question wrought was felt in the silence, broken by a raucous parrot from a near palm.

"It was like this," Kwasi finally said. "I was a boy, out planting yams with my father not far from our village. I had seen white men seeking gold on our shores and had been warned to stay away from them. That final day, slave traders with dogs came upon us and seized us. They tied our hands with willow twigs and took us aboard a ship. We sailed to a place where men are sold. But first we were cleaned and rubbed with palm oil. The captain of a ship bought me, but my father was deemed unfit because he had a limp. More of my people were taken and we set sail."

"How long have ye been in captivity?" Magnus asked.

"I have lived longer here than in Africa. But it does not lessen my desire to return there."

"I wish that I could give ye yer freedom. The most I can do is make ye a manager of yer people here. But one day I believe ye will be free."

Kwasi's smile was bittersweet. "*Ebi Akyi wɔ bi.* Success follows patience."

Magnus repeated the Ashanti Twi slowly, capturing the pronunciation. He was learning the language rather quickly but not quickly enough to carry a conversation and dismiss a translator.

From their vantage point atop the hill where the largest mill was situated, the cane harvest had begun. Cutting and bundling in the fields was first, and then the cane was carted to the mill to be crushed, the work done by field gangs of both men and women. Each gang had a name, the youngest children and the sick and elderly given the lighter tasks of weeding and caring for livestock.

"More work is being done now. You should see a better harvest than ever before, now that the people are better fed," Kwasi said. "There is not so much sickness, not so much running away to join the maroons in the mountains."

"The poor yield of before was due mainly to slave exhaustion, not soil exhaustion," Magnus replied. "That and the overseers' refusal to rely on yer and other workers' judgment and knowledge in cane cultivation, always insisting on their own ineffective methods. Now we must find a better way to transport the hogsheads of sugar to the ships. And earlier too. The first sugar fetches the best prices."

The droghers, small boats used to carry the sugar, were haphazard at best. Recently a large quantity of cane had been lost when a boat capsized and two men drowned. But these were but a drop in the ongoing onslaught of sugarcane preoccupations and troubles. What with the weather, the pests, the diseases to the crops, the quality and quantity of sugar, the state of the sugar-making equipment, the fluctuating sugar market, and Osbourne's debts to merchants who sold their sugar, any profit was hard-won and oftentimes impossible to come by.

Was growing tobacco at Royal Hundred half as onerous?

Magnus's aim was to return to Virginia. Osbourne's recent letter had asked that of him, if only temporarily. Magnus was to leave Jamaica for the colony in spring, to give a report to Osbourne on the state of Trelawny Hall and sugar production so that Osbourne would not have to venture down to the plantation himself.

Spring was months away. In Magnus's absence, Kwasi would be in charge, a risk both to Trelawny Hall and to Kwasi himself. Magnus had sent the other overseers to manage outlying fields of cocoa and coffee.

For now, he parted with Kwasi and Rojay and went on to the nearest village of wattle huts with their wood rafters, each surrounded by colorful, sweet-smelling gardens. There he met with a surgeon to examine the bairns. Of late, the dreaded kissing bugs were a bane, as were yaws and worms. If they were caught early, the prognosis was good. But someone akin to Lark was needed to distill and dispense the required tonics, always in short shrift here.

Gently, working alongside the physic, he sat each child upon his lap, all tugging his heart back to the time when Larkin had reached out his arms before Magnus had ridden away.

Little carried the ache of that fore or since.

38

Never marry for money, ye'll borrow it cheaper.

Scottish proverb

She had only to say aye and end the matter. Here they sat again with the churchwarden, listening to new particulars in her and Larkin's case. And she need only tell Trevor Ramsay she would wed him and the whole matter would end. Or so it seemed. Was he waiting on Richard Osbourne's reply and approval by post? If it was slowed by a sea voyage, they might not hear for another two months or more. Perhaps Osbourne would even wait till he came to Royal Hundred as planned to give them his aye or nay.

Bethankit for the delay.

She doubted Osbourne would care about Trevor's request to court her and mayhap marry her other than to give his blessing. Could anyone truly say nay to a Ramsay?

Could she?

She'd left Larkin with Theodosia at Ramsay House till the meeting at Bruton Parish was done. Yet it seemed to drag on, mired down by the ill health of Granger, who must appear to help resolve the matter. And he was too ill yet to join them.

The holidays had passed, and a new year had begun. Another spate of bad weather had kept them at Royal Hundred since Christmas. She'd not seen Trevor since their caroling and bonfire till today. Given that, he was in no mood to return her to the plantation in haste.

"Come with me to South England Street," he said when the futile meeting was over.

She obliged, her curiosity over the building of his new home stretched to the limits of her imagination. Kerrera Castle it was not, but the late winter sunlight revealed a sprawling, ambitious foundation, sure to become one of the finest homes in Williamsburg.

They walked across the acreage beyond the house's beginnings, the ground beneath her slippers hard and damp but holding the promise of spring. Here in Virginia even the weeds seemed to flourish in winter, warmth never far away. Williamsburg's riotous, colorful gardens had completely won her over.

"I'd not thought to see anything prettier than my island, but yer property holds great promise," she told him in the fragile winter's sunlight, burying her hands deeper in her fur muff.

He looked down at her with a smile. "Your Scottish climate is home to the hardiest of plants but lacks many of the fairest. I want these Virginia gardens to be yours as well, Lark. You know where I stand regarding our future."

"And I beg ye to reconsider," she said quietly, eyes on a barren dogwood tree. "Would it not be more advantageous for ye to marry a woman of standing? Of connections? With a dowry, at least? What will yer friends and acquaintances say of ye when word of yer suit is made known?"

"I care very little for the opinions of others and, being a Ramsay, have no need of the things you mention. Your beauty and character are enough. And I'm baffled by the fact that you tread so cautiously, especially given the case against you. Has it something to do with my person? Some trait or attribute you find disagreeable?"

Pity lanced her. Here was the catch of Virginia Colony looking as crestfallen as if she'd been the belle of Williamsburg and refused him. Yet she would be honest to the heart. "There's a Scots proverb my granny oft said: 'Fanned fires and forced love ne'er did weel.' "

He chuckled good-naturedly. "But love is as warm among cottars as courtiers, aye?"

She sighed, looking at the untilled ground before her and trying to imagine orchards, flowers, an orangery. "Ye have become a dear friend, Trevor."

He touched her cold cheek. "Perhaps friendship is the best foundation for marriage."

"If so, ye would make a bonny husband." Always Larkin leapt to mind. "And father."

"I would be both to you and the lad. Once I receive word from Osbourne, I would urge marrying without hesitation. The house won't be finished for a time, but my brother and Thea assure us we'd have a home with them until our own is done."

" 'Tis very gracious." Yet even as she pondered it, she did so for all the wrong reasons, large and small. A full table. The warming machine. Theodosia's friendship. Larkin's future.

And she hid the true reason for her ongoing reluctance.

"Mercy!" Sally said as she sampled a wooden spoonful from a black kettle over the hearth's fire. "Better eat up all this right fast lest you be put in charge of the kitchen house too."

At this Lark laughed and sneezed at once. "I misdoubt ye'll be replaced as cook. Yer Southern fare is a feast, even the simplest dishes."

Lark had taught her to make black bun and now Cullen skink, both Scottish favorites. Homesick, chilled by another snow, and nursing a cold, she dreamed of Granny's croft and the tiny window overlooking the sea. But 'twas futile to look back. Days past meant a time without Larkin. Without Sally and Cleve and Mistress Flowerdew. The Ramsays. The garden of her dreams. With effort, she turned her heart to spring.

"I sense you is pinin' for home," Sally said in her shrewdly observant way. "Yo' granny."

Lark nodded and dried her hands on her apron, looking toward Larkin as he played with Cleve. "I wrote Granny another letter, but she has to seek out the minister so that he might read it to her."

"So, she can't write back," Sally said. "Tell

you how she is and the like."

"For all I ken, she's gone . . ." She couldn't say *dead*. Or even *with the Lord in heaven*. She let the excruciating thought go.

"What you doin' now?" Sally asked as Lark donned a cape, tying the chin ribbons of her bonnet securely.

"I'm off to the quarters to deliver some needed tonics."

"Best look behind you while you is doin' it," Sally cautioned, her own eyes wandering to the window. "Any more word of Granger? He ain't been nosin' 'round here o' late."

"Glad I am of that. Word is he's ill again and keeping to his lodgings." She started for the door, basket in hand, and bent and kissed Larkin's brow. "I'll not be long."

He continued to play contentedly with some jelly molds Sally had lent him. Lark let herself out and walked through the service yard, bypassing the many dependencies, their respective sounds and smells comingling.

The gardens were already showing signs of life at the coaxing of Mr. Munro, who was a wonder with spade and shovel. New beds were in place, and piles of fertilizer awaited dispensing along with new shell walkways and botanicals. Of all the tasks that awaited her, she was most enthused about her bee garden, itching to turn over the loamy Virginia soil.

Before her the river spread a pearly blue-gray. She cut left through a copse of bare-branched trees she now knew as chestnut and oak. Smoke from a great many chimneys layered the chilly February air as she neared the quarters. In the distance, voices of children playing, punctuated with their laughter, lifted her spirits.

She preferred to come at dusk, an almost hallowed time when she heard the singing. Never had she experienced such music. Heaven seemed to come down when the slaves sang. There was no accounting for such beauty in a people so repressed. Mayhap God had gifted them with music to weather such a time well.

Now, in the forenoon, there was little music as field hands labored at plowing the distant fields for maize, or Indian corn, in former tobacco fields. Trevor had told her Virginia shipped large quantities of corn to the Caribbean for the workers there. She'd come to be nearly as fond of the grain as oats or even wheat, finding the pone, grits, hominy, and mush fine fare. Larkin clearly agreed.

"Mornin', Mistress MacDougall," the

greeting rang out from all sides as she walked the rutted way between dwellings.

Her smile was warm, for she was glad to see them. Children came from all directions to tug at her skirts. She tried to remember them when she visited, packing her pockets with some sort of treat. Last time it was sugar-coated nuts. Today it was tiny cinnamon and candied orange comfits. Sally had made a batch for Larkin to give to him over the long winter. Why not share the bounty with the quarters' children too?

"You be good now — and proper," one apron-waisted granny scolded as Lark handed out the comfits. Childish faces shone with delight. Pleasure welled up inside her, banishing her low mood of before. Surely giving was good medicine, as was a merry heart.

Pockets empty of all but a few treats, she moved in the direction of the blacksmith's dwelling. Josiah's wife, Nelly, was in need of one of her tonics for a complaint in her chest. No doubt the dismal living conditions worsened her cough. Lark could hear the familiar hacking the closer she drew. Their youngest child was in the doorway, about Larkin's age but already standing on bare feet.

Her heart squeezed. His clothing was

wanting, though he did drag a blanket after him. Was he not cold? One thumb was hooked in his mouth. She dug in her pocket, wishing for far more to give. Kneeling in the cracked doorway, Lark lay the comfit in her palm and offered it to him.

Across the room, Nelly watched her son's quiet delight, pleasure on her own face. "What you got today, Miss Lark?"

"A tonic for yer cough." She smiled as she came into the cabin, wanting to curl her nose at the smell of fatback and boiled turnips.

They visited awhile, Nelly's leanness necessitating an inquiry about what she was eating, if they had enough provisions. Lark learned much about the plantation from those who knew it best.

She moved on to a few more cabins, emptying her basket and assessing needs, before turning toward the mansion again. A sharp wind picked up from the river, ruffling the blue water till it frothed like fluted lace.

She mulled what remained to be done this day. Decocting a face wash for Mistress Flowerdew. Counting stores and taking inventory of the stillroom. Examining the bee skeps. Meanwhile, Royal Hundred was abuzz with new arrivals, mostly house servants and indentures, ahead of the Osbournes. Shipments of goods were arriving almost daily from England, including livery suits and silver-laced hats from London for the postilions and coachmen, as well as new garments for the housemaids and waiting men.

She shifted her basket to her other arm, eyes on the rocky path before her. Royal Hundred was no longer the sleepy plantation with an echoing mansion house. Spring was at hand, and with it a great many changes. Just that morning Sally had told her of the hiring of a French cook, not to displace her or Cleve but to help manage the Osbournes' future guests at table.

Her steps slowed as she mulled the many changes, and then a high whinny cut short her musings. There, blocking her meandering path, sat Granger atop his fine sorrel horse. She stopped. Wished him away. His eyes bore into her unblinkingly, his expression sullen. In one gloved hand was a whip. His other clutched the reins.

Wary to the bone, she waited, but he did not move. He bristled with ill will. It roiled between them in the damp air.

"You've been to the quarters again," he said, eyeing her empty basket.

She nodded. "So long as there is a need I

shall go."

He pushed his horse forward till he was within spitting distance. Truly, he looked capable of spitting, so strong was his ill will. She itched to take a step back, but cowardice was not to be borne.

"You look at me as if you've done nothing wrong," he said in a voice that raised gooseflesh on her arms. "Like the tart you are."

He slumped a bit in the saddle, pride and sheer will keeping him upright. He was a gravely ill man. His distorted face, struck with paralysis on the left side, made his words a bit slurred. A spasm of pity hit her before fury rushed in.

"I'll have you know that the ship's captain — the runaway of your acquaintance — has been caught and hung deservedly."

The captain killed? Shock cut through her, so swift it nearly sent her to her knees.

Oh, Rory. Though I didna agree with ye leaving, I kenned yer longing for a better life.

"I won't rest till I see you answer for your part in his fleeing." Granger shifted in the saddle, smug despite his infirmity. "Not only that, I have written Osbourne and met again with the churchwardens. Soon you'll be removed to another plantation, separated from your illegitimate son, incapable of meddling and squandering Osbourne's precious supplies —"

"A liar should have a good memory," she returned hotly, all sympathy fleeing. "Ye told the churchwardens my son is illegitimate, then turned round and said he was born of a prostitute, when in truth he was given me by his aunt out of desperation as she lay dying. I help the slaves here at Royal Hundred when the call and need arise, mainly because ye fail to supply them as a proper manager should. And now ye have the gall to waylay me on a wooded path like no proper gentleman would —"

"How dare ye!" He raised his whip with surprising ease, so quick she could not step back or even flinch. The leather descended with a painful snap, the tail end biting into her jaw like a stream of boiling water.

She stumbled backwards as he raised the whip again, nudging his nervy horse nearer. Would he beat her like she'd heard he whipped field hands accused of some oversight? Her hand went to her burning jaw and came away crimson.

"Mistress MacDougall?" The resonant voice rang out of the woods, and then the preacher-blacksmith stood between them. Josiah turned his back on her and faced Granger, a muscular, dark wall. "I beg ye, sir, to leave be!"

Granger tensed with renewed rage. Immediately Lark's fear for herself shifted. Defying a white man was a fatal offense. Granger raised his whip again and his face purpled, distorting his already grotesque features. This time his ire was for Josiah.

The whip came down again, but with a callused hand, the blacksmith grabbed the tail end like a child might a firefly, wrenching the whip from Granger's grasp.

"You filthy upstart —" Granger spat the words, spittle whitening his mouth. And then, in slow motion, he stiffened and clutched his own collar, as if the neck was too tight.

Stunned, Lark watched as the factor fell from his horse with a decided thud on the damp ground. For a long moment, neither she nor Josiah moved. Then, kneeling, Josiah carefully rolled the factor over, the abandoned whip on the thawing ground. Granger's wide, unseeing eyes stared upwards. Josiah tried to return him, shaking his shoulders and then his wide, jutting jaw as if to awaken him from a profound sleep.

"He's gone," Lark said, the sting of her injury helping her focus. "Ye can do no more here. If found like this ye might well be blamed for his demise. Please, return to yer work. I'll go to the mansion house and tell Mistress Flowerdew."

He stood and stepped back. Bowing his head, he said a silent prayer. She waited till he'd left them before she sent up a prayer herself. For protection. Peace. Granger's widow needed telling and the body laid out for burial.

Lark ran all the way back to the house on quavering legs. The riverfront door was open wide, housemaids beating and airing the rugs just outside. They saw her coming, eyes wide, attention drawn to her bloodied face and bodice. One ran to summon the housekeeper with a surprised exclamation that carried on the rising wind.

Lark waited on the back step, woozy. Sally had come out of the kitchen house, Larkin on her hip, her own eyes sharp. Amid her own revulsion, Lark felt a profound relief. No more Granger. No more lies. No more threats to Larkin or herself.

Oh Lord, let it be.

And yet, what if someone blamed her? Like they had at Isla's death? What if someone had seen her in the woods with Granger and accused her of lending to his collapse?

Mistress Flowerdew came with haste from the laundry, fairly flying across the service courtyard. "Merciful days . . ."

With gentle hands, she led Lark inside the mansion foyer to the safety and privacy of her sitting room. There the housekeeper examined her chin where the whip had cut deep. She went to a locked cupboard and opened it with a key from her chatelaine. The softest cloths and ointment were on hand, and a basin of warm water was soon brought.

"Tell me what has happened. I fear it involves Mr. Granger."

Lark spilled the tale, leaving out the blacksmith's part. He was but a passerby come to help her. No good would come of his involvement if told. "Mr. Granger struck me when I stood up to him. I fear 'twas the death of him."

"And he has none to blame but himself," the housekeeper replied resolutely.

Lark took a breath, her next words framed with disbelief. "What's more, he said the indentured runaway, the captain, was caught and hung."

Mistress Flowerdew nodded, her expression sorrowful. "I wanted to spare you that. I learnt of it a few days ago. Now, let us have no more trouble on account of that unhinged man."

No more was said. Chin salved and bandaged, Lark watched as Mistress Flower-dew went to fetch someone to summon the physic and authorities as well as stand watch over Granger himself. "But first his widow must be told." She returned to Lark. " 'Twill leave a scar, I fear. Mar your lovely face."

What was so small a scar? She'd seen ugly marks across the backs of Africans — and brands. Even her hardy Scots sensibilities were shaken by that. "I have little to complain of, truly."

"I urge you to rest here in my sitting room the remainder of the day. Let Sally tend to Larkin."

"Thank ye, but nay. Work keeps my mind from the worst."

She sought the solace of the bee garden the rest of the afternoon, attempting to return to her usual duties and quell any fears over being blamed for the factor's death. The news he'd brought about Rory wore a hole of sorrow in her. As she worked, or tried to, the sun broke through the clouds as if the Almighty Himself was trying to raise her limping spirits.

At six o'clock Trevor Ramsay rode up. A stable hand met him and led his horse away. Lark saw the familiar mount being taken to the stables. So the news had reached Williamsburg. Let Mistress Flowerdew tell their guest the particulars. Lark had no words. With a sigh, she dismissed a qualm about her unsightly chin, Larkin in arm. Though she was glad to see her friend, her whole being cried for word of Magnus. For Magnus himself.

Trevor opened the gate of the freshly painted white fence that hemmed in the bee garden. His face was drawn, even angry. Their eyes met over the slowly awakening beds of yarrow and hyssop, coneflower and asters.

"Lark, for heaven's sake . . ." His focus strayed to her throbbing chin, the bandage in place. "Thank God no worse harm came to you. If Granger was not bound for a coffin I'd call him out."

"The trouble with him is o'er, I hope."

"Most certainly. I'll meet with the churchwardens and burgesses and close the case tomorrow."

Tears stung her eyes. "I am sorry for his widow. But glad for the quarters and the people, all who came under his ill-trickit influence."

He grimaced, hat in hand. "Hell is made worse for his being there, if there is such a place."

She pondered that, the evening's chill overtaking them. Once Trevor had closed the distance between them, Larkin reached up and tugged at his waistcoat.

"You clever lad. 'Tis my pocket watch you're after, aye?"

Lark smiled. "Come inside and we shall have something warm to drink."

" 'Tis precisely what Mistress Flowerdew said when I arrived. Shall we?"

Together they walked arm in arm to the mansion house, Larkin held by Trevor and dangling the gleaming watch. The aroma of Darjeeling met them. But the housekeeper was absent, the maid said, called out to resolve a matter in the dairy.

They sat by the fire, Larkin on the settee between them, his bare toes peeking out from beneath his gown. Distracted by the events of the day, she'd changed his clout but forgotten to fully dress him. But the parlor was warm, her own color high.

"Tell me what happened after Granger collapsed," Trevor said once the maid had left the room.

She shared the details she'd been told. Of the sheriff's arrival and the body being taken away. The distress of Widow Granger. The lack of management left by the factor's absence.

"A new factor will be assigned in his stead." Trevor reached into his waistcoat and withdrew a post. "A bit of glad news amid the bad."

He opened the letter slowly. From Magnus by way of Trevor's friend who'd gone there? Nay. Osbourne's writing hand. Trevor's half smile seemed to confirm so. "Your contract holder states, 'I am not surprised that you have taken notice of Miss MacDougall's charms. I myself was not unaware of them when the laird introduced her to me in Glasgow. She is no common maid. This induced me to offer the indenture terms to begin with at the behest of Magnus Mac-Leish. And as such, she has my blessing should she agree to be courted by you or even wed, at which time you would redeem her contract and end the agreement between us. Legalities aside, am I to deny a Ramsay? I sense you would bar me from Virginia Colony, if so.' "

She smiled at the humor within. The way had been made. Permission granted.

If she was willing.

Trevor returned the letter to his pocket. "So now the courting can begin in earnest, perhaps."

Larkin let out a screech as if punctuating his words. They laughed, paying little attention to their tea. But for her stinging chin, she would have felt a glimmer of happiness, honored that such a man would count her worthy.

"Trevor, I am honored by your attentions. But they are misplaced." Gently, she tried to remind him of the truth of their situation, not wanting to lose his friendship, just remove any of his false hopes.

"I shall go slowly," he said. "I'll be away in Norfolk for a time, overseeing a shipment of stone for Ramsay Manor, as you call it. 'Twill give you time to recover. Consider my suit. Let any unsavory matters regarding Granger rest."

So, he would not give up despite her distancing words. Must she be more adamant?

"There's something else I must say before ye go away," Lark said. "Though 'tis hard for me to speak of such, I feel 'tis only fair. Ye see —" She grappled for the right words, her throat so constricted with emotion she felt she would choke. "My heart was captured long ago. I've only lately come to realize it. When I was a girl I didna ken what it was I felt, but now, as a woman . . ."

"You're thinking of the laird." Trevor looked at her a bit impatiently, like one who was about to correct a wayward child. "Lark, I doubt the laird lives. Perhaps 'tis only a childish hope that keeps him alive in your heart and thoughts."

Was that it? If so, she could hardly bear it. "I canna deny the way I feel. Mayhap one day my affections will turn or fade altogether if he is truly gone."

"That is my hope. Grieve for the laird but do not love him, for I truly believe he is no more." He brought her hand to his lips and kissed the back of it as if to solace her. As if he knew Magnus was gone for good. "Soon Osbourne and his family will dock, and Royal Hundred will return to life the way it was before tragedy struck and he left. 'Twill be a new beginning for many of us. A wedding would be a fine celebration for Tidewater Virginia."

39

Memory, of all the powers of the mind, is the most delicate and frail.

Ben Jonson

Was anything as lovely as a river ride in spring?

Lark sat in the shallop with Theodosia, two oarsmen in livery propelling them through the James current, which was smooth as blue glass in spring. She'd longed to bring Larkin out, but fear of a spill kept her from it. He remained on the bank with Mistress Flowerdew, crawling on the quilt she'd spread out. The housekeeper had declared the lovely March afternoon a holiday, something sorely needed, busy as they'd been. With Granger buried, Royal Hundred seemed and felt different. Or was it mostly because of spring and its many changes?

"I suppose you went out on the ocean

often, given you lived on an island," Theodosia said, trailing her fingers through the cold water.

"Nay. When my father passed, I shunned the sea. Ever since I've been more content on shore. And far safer. The Atlantic is nothing like this river."

"I understand. When my father and sisters were struck down, I feared storms and would go into my bedchamber, shut the door, and hide till they boomed and tore at the skies no longer." Beneath Theodosia's elaborate hat, her eyes glittered with emotion. "Not a day goes by that I don't think of the loss. But you must be the same."

Lark nodded, moved by the sadness in her friend's face. She missed them all unendingly. Granny. Her dear mother and father. Other kindred still living. And Magnus, always Magnus, whether living or dead. Would her every thought of him always be so tender? " 'Tis only right we remember those beloved."

She leaned over and peered at her own reflection in the water. A month had passed since Granger's death. Her chin was slow to heal. The water's dark surface reflected none of the redness nor what would soon be a scarlet scar. A lasting reminder of a disturbed man.

"Trevor was sorry he could not join us. The construction keeps him so preoccupied of late. I half expect to find him laying bricks himself in his zeal to finish. I suspect that is why he has been overtaken by a terrible, ongoing fever and cough since Christmas."

"I pray he soon mends." Lark had sent several remedies to Ramsay House to help in his recuperation but had not visited him. She wouldn't play the doting miss, especially after stating her true feelings. "Since the incident, we've kept to Royal Hundred ourselves."

"Yes, the *incident*." Theodosia grimaced. "A new factor has already come in Mr. Granger's stead, or so word is winging about Williamsburg."

"Oh aye, Mr. Murray hails from the northeast of Scotland and speaks Doric. But we converse well enough."

"Royal Hundred is becoming a Scots stronghold." Her smile returning, Theodosia gave a playful splash to the water with a mitted hand. "I may have to learn Gaelic."

"I'll gladly teach ye. I long to hear it spoken."

"Say a few memorable words."

Lark pursed her lips in thought. *"Triùir a thig gun iarraidh — gaol, eud, is eagal."*

Theodosia crossed her eyes comically. "I have absolutely no inkling what you just said."

"Indeed." Lark's laugh rippled over the water. "Three things come unbidden — love, jealousy, and fear."

Theodosia echoed it, mangling but a word or two.

"Well done," Lark said with a smile.

They quieted, each lost in thought, till a commotion on shore gave them pause. Lark looked back over her shoulder toward the oak where Larkin and Mistress Flowerdew were. The housekeeper had gotten to her feet and was waving something almost frantically in hand while Larkin crawled away in the grass, momentarily forgotten.

Lark's heart and stomach somersaulted. What was that she held? A paper? A post . . .

A letter.

The housekeeper's genteel English voice carried a beat of elation as it wafted to the drifting shallop. Even the oarsmen stopped their rowing. Was she dreaming? Or did her shouting — so unlike Mistress Flowerdew — mean Lark's long wait was over? She heard but a few words, yet they made her whole soul sing.

"Letter . . . Laird . . . Here."

Joy poured through her, so overwhelming

she shot up like a jack-in-the-box. The shallop rocked. Theodosia shrieked. The oarsmen snickered. In seconds, Lark lost her footing and went overboard with a resounding splash.

When she came up, Theodosia was laughing hysterically, motioning to Lark's straw hat that floated atop the water. Sputtering, treading water, Lark grabbed for it but it sailed out of her reach, borne on a warm Virginia wind. No matter. She turned toward shore, hope and fear waging for top place inside her. All her hopes and dreams were wrapped up in that letter. To have word that Magnus was dead or alive. At long last.

She fought her way to the sandy shore, encumbered by her heavy dress. But she hardly felt the cold that sent shivers over her in all directions, even forgetting to make her way up the bank at a ladylike pace. She all but seized the letter from the housekeeper's hands. As she looked down, dripping water onto the outer paper, Magnus's writing hand seemed to reach out to her in reassurance. She broke the seal and devoured the letter.

Dearest Lark,

I fear you must think me dead and gone due to my lack of letters. In truth, the post has been waylaid by someone bent on mischief.

I am as alive and hearty as ever, God be praised. Night and day I have asked the Lord to intervene, to hedge you behind and before and place His hand of blessing on your head and Larkin's.

I asked that He cast down any evil raised against you. I trust that He has done so, for He is a merciful, mighty Savior, our ever-present defense . . .

Suddenly weak-kneed, she sank down into the sand, all but kissing the paper she held. Tears streamed down her face alongside rivulets of river water. Bethankit. Overcome, she choked out a few words to Mistress Flowerdew, who hovered anxiously.

"The laird lives." Her heart was beating so loudly it caused a rush in her ears. A breathlessness. "His letters have simply miscarried."

Mistress Flowerdew closed her eyes in quiet thanks. Lark read on silently, hearing the slap of the paddles as the shallop neared the dock behind them.

I am pleased to tell you I will soon be on my way to Virginia. I am counting the hours till I behold your lovely face again. I long to take Larkin in my arms too. I will do all within my power to stay near you. Never again, Lord willing, shall we be parted.

Yours entire,
Magnus

"Why, Lark!" Behind her, on solid ground now, Theodosia observed her with a shrewd eye. "You have given away the state of your heart."

Slowly Lark turned, the letter dangling from her fingertips. "Glad I am to find the laird alive — and on his way back to us."

"Bethankit, indeed!" Mistress Flowerdew exclaimed. "When will he arrive?"

Lark looked back at the letter, missing that all-important detail. "He didna say."

"We in Williamsburg shall welcome him warmly whenever he makes an appearance, then," Theodosia said with a gracious smile. " 'Twill be interesting indeed to see what comes of his visit here."

"I pray 'twill be more than a visit," the housekeeper said. Her voice held subtle dismay and disgust whenever she mentioned the West Indies. "Perhaps Mr. Osbourne will see fit to keep him on hand here and not return him to Jamaica."

Lark folded the letter up. Heart overfull, she barely paid attention to the scene around her as one of the oarsmen handed over her limp hat. She took it, smiling wryly at its soaked state but hardly caring, equally unmindful of her thoroughly wet garments.

All that mattered was that Magnus was alive. His letter she would read and reread till it fell apart. As for his prayers for her, had they helped keep her safe that day in the woods when Granger had struck her and then fallen?

She and Theodosia began a slow walk to the house, Mistress Flowerdew and Larkin following. The skirt of her wet gown dragged across the grass and oyster-shell paths. She squinted at the sun, trying to remember the date when she'd last seen Magnus. Was he much changed?

"I wonder what the laird has to do here in Virginia," Theodosia was saying. "Whatever brings him, he's coming at a favorable time of year when all the gardens will be flowering and travel is most easy."

"Usually a month or more to sail from Jamaica, given unpredictable weather and currents and such," Mistress Flowerdew reminded them.

"If only 'twas as simple as crossing the James," she lamented. The horror of the hurricane had never left her. The thought of having to board a ship even to return to Scotland dampened her desire to see her homeland again. All that aside, the whole cry of her heart was simply Magnus.

Theodosia locked arms with her despite her sodden state. "I've never been on a ship, though many people come and go between the colonies and England, even Paris and the continent. Trevor has twice now."

"Trevor is brave," Lark said. "I wasna sure I would live to see Virginia."

"We aim to keep you here." Theodosia squeezed her hand. "And might I ask that you consider your future carefully? I'd like nothing better than to have you as my sister-in-law, and Master Larkin as my nephew."

"I should like a sister," Lark replied truthfully. Such seemed a luxury as she was an only child. She did not wish that for Larkin. "Or a daughter."

"You care for the laird very much." Theodosia was more serious than Lark had ever seen her. "Yet I can't help but wonder. Does he feel the same about you?"

"I believe he does," Lark replied, her joy undimmed.

He had cast off all the trappings of mourning. Life was not meant to be lived in hindsight, mired in the regrets and laments of the past. On the eve of his departure to Virginia, as the mosquitos whined in the netting about his bed, Magnus lay on his back and wondered, Had Lark received his letter? Was one from her even now on its way back to him? He found her posts especially dear. He looked toward the nightstand where a stack of them lay tied up with a bit of faded ribbon. He'd nigh memorized them, reading as much between the lines as the penned words themselves, trying to sift both thoughts and emotions.

He had to talk to her. Share his heart. Take her hands in his again. God forbid she'd gone somewhere else or lost Larkin. He'd go to the ends of the earth to find them both.

But first there was a precarious ship's journey from Montego Bay to Virginia to endure. His goal before he left Jamaica's shores was to have all three overseers in place and working together to manage the plantation in his absence. An onerous goal. After he'd pummeled the letter thief and sent him packing, another overseer had vanished of his own accord, leaving the one remaining man contrite and seeking his favor. Magnus had told him he'd be on a short tether, his tenure determined by how well he got on with Kwasi and the newest overseer, a fellow Scot, in his absence.

Virginia beckoned, a sort of oasis, Lark aside. And then? Would he return here to this hellish place, hot as a bake oven and writhing with snakes? The merciless cycle of sugarcane and cash crops never ceased. Perhaps one day it would become more peaceful and settled. But first the slavery must end.

Lord, help me reach Virginia and remain there if it pleases Thee.

40

I love thee, I love but thee, with a love that shall not die, till the sun grows cold and the stars grow old.

Shakespeare

Larkin had taken his first steps — and his first spill, a pudding cap firmly in place, compliments of Mistress Flowerdew. All wondered about his birthday. Was he yet a year old? How long ago it seemed that she'd first set eyes on him in Glasgow. Now, with a flaxen-haired toddler to mimic, Larkin seemed determined to catch up with the Osbournes' young son.

'Twas late April, the month made memorable with the Osbournes' arrival. At first all was a flurry as trunks were unpacked and Royal Hundred adjusted to a family in residence. Would Magnus soon raise the dust on the driveway in their wake?

Haste ye back, my love.

Might he reappear in broad daylight when all was abloom and abuzz? Or in the gloaming with its sweetly scented shadows as night tiptoed in? Even her humblest task turned fanciful. Romantic. But little time was left for wondering. Lark was busy from sunup to sundown. Angelica Osbourne, Royal Hundred's new mistress, wished to learn all aspects of plantation life alongside her husband, often peppering Lark with questions. Expecting again and a bit peely-wally, Angelica relied on the red raspberry leaves and gingerroot tea Lark gave her to quell any queasiness.

In the kitchen, Sally turned out an abundance of fine dishes alongside the French chef, while the British servants the Osbournes brought clashed with the American ones.

"Ain't just yo' bees stingin'," Sally said, fanning her perspiring face with her apron. "Some o' them high and mighty crumpet stuffers need to sail on home again."

But the Osbournes were a respected family whom everyone seemed to want to please. Soon all settled. But not Lark's emotions nor her ongoing anticipation. Would today be the day Magnus arrived? Never one to take pains with her appearance, she found herself peering into the cracked looking glass of her quarters far too often, re-tying her apron, repinning her pinner, and rereading his well-worn letter till she'd memorized every jot and tittle. She was in love. Totally, besottedly, unashamedly in love with the laird.

Lark fingered the MacLeish locket in her pocket as music from a pianoforte spilled from Royal Hundred's refurbished parlor. The Osbournes had invited their closest friends and kin for a musical evening a sen-night after their arrival. The Ramsays were there too, and Lark herself had been in-cluded but declined. She was not one of them nor ever would be, though she was glad of their kindness. She'd not seen Trevor but for church. He remained cordial but distant, as if waiting for her change of heart.

Listening to the lovely music but craving a quiet spot, she left the door to her quarters open to better hear Larkin if he awoke, and sought out the neglected bench along the outer stillroom wall. Half hidden by a hedge, she could still see servants hurrying to and fro between dependencies and the mansion. The May days stretched longer and longer, though they still held less daylight here than in Scotland at nearly eight o'clock.

Her own workday was done, though she'd yet to fulfill even a year of her three-year contract. Time ticked on, softening her harshest memories if not erasing them, blunting her homesickness and sharpening her hopes.

The fading sun weaving spokes of light through the hedge and warming her, she dozed, back to the wall, fingers folded around the locket in her pocket.

"Lark."

'Twas a voice from another life. Another world. Spoken in the language of her heart.

"Is thu mannsachd."

Thou art my most beloved.

Her eyes slowly opened. There, half hidden in the lengthening shadows, stood Magnus. Fireflies winked around him, akin to that first time when it was just the two of them locked in mutual wonderment on another warm Virginia eve. The flash of his smile was her complete undoing.

Joy surged through her. In the beat of a heart she stood. One hand clutched the beloved locket. She clasped it to her bodice, though what she wanted was *him.* Having stood too fast, she swayed. And then he gathered her up in his arms, her face pressed against the clean cloth of his shirt. She was held so tightly she melted into him, finding him much changed. Leaner and more muscled, no hint of the heather or sea about him. But his heart beat strong and sure beneath her cheek.

"Yer here," she whispered. "I nearly stopped hoping."

"Nay. Never stop hoping. 'Tis what keeps us." He released her just enough to look down at her, gently tracing the oval of her face with a careful finger, gaze on her scarred chin. "A new beauty mark?"

"If ye say so." She smiled. Nothing would mar the moment. "Pay it no mind."

He nodded, eyes still questioning. His gaze fell to the locket entwined in her hand. Carefully he pried it free before circling behind her in the velvety darkness. Cool fingers brushed her neck. Without any bumbling, he encircled her throat with the MacLeish heirloom, securing the clasp at the nape of her neck.

"For my bonny bride-to-be." His breath tickled her ear. "If ye'll have me."

If? Once again she faced him. His locket lay cool against her heated skin. His eyes darkened with desire. Years of unfulfilled longing charged the very air between them. Theirs had been a romance of restraint. Thwarted passion. Now, with choices before them, she could hardly breathe.

"Will ye have me, Lark?" His low question rent her heart.

In answer, she stood on tiptoe, pressing her mouth to his in a naïve kiss. His mouth smiled beneath her own. Though her eyes were closed, she could feel the curve of his lips as much as his hands when they took hers and placed them about his neck. Somehow he'd backed her against the warm stone wall, out of sight of any passersby. But they might have been back at Kerrera Castle, so lost was she in the nearness of him.

His own kiss laid to rest any questions. His mouth met hers softly and then thoroughly, so capably she didn't want him to stop. Nor did he want to, clearly. Within the intimacy of those endless kisses came a melding of thoughts and desires, hopes and dreams. A oneness that bespoke a coming union that time and distance could not alter.

"Tomorrow," he said, sounding a bit breathless. "I'll move heaven and earth to make it happen."

"The morrow canna come soon enough." What more could she offer but a heartfelt prayer? "Amen."

They stood in Royal Hundred's small parlor the next evening, she and Magnus facing each other beneath a wide window overlooking the formal garden. Bruton Parish's minister stood before them, *The Book of Common Prayer* in hand, seemingly unruffled by a hasty marriage license and wedding that had in fact been years in the making.

Behind them stood Mistress Flowerdew with Larkin, as well as Angelica, who'd insisted on a bouquet for Lark among May's finest flowers. The fragrance of roses and the gaily hued peonies and poppies sweetened the occasion, the petals to be pressed and dried in the stillroom. Lark drank in the solemn moment. She'd been kept up by a mix of elation and excitement as the light from Osbourne's study burned long into the night. He and Magnus had hammered out the details of a wedding, a covenant far more binding than indenture contracts.

"Almighty God, who at the beginning did create our first parents, Adam and Eve, and did sanctify and join them together in marriage, pour upon you the riches of His grace, sanctify and bless you, that ye may please Him both in body and soul, and live together in holy love unto your lives' end. Amen."

Holy and humbly wedded. Lark touched the locket about her neck as Magnus kissed her lightly, even teasingly. Flushed, she let him escort her into the dining room, where Sally and the French chef had conspired to make a remarkable wedding supper on short notice.

In the candlelight the white icing on both the bride's and groom's cakes shone. In Mistress Flowerdew's arms, Larkin was pointing to the fruit and sweetmeat pyramids atop the damask tablecloth. Lark had wanted little fuss. But now, beside her groom, she was seated and partook gladly of the marzipan hedgehog and sweet potato pudding, the oysters and ham and fish.

Looking at Magnus over the rim of her punch cup, she could hardly believe he was here. His handsome features were deeply bronzed by the Jamaican sun, almost startlingly unfamiliar as they were wreathed in an unending smile. In her borrowed dress of yellow taffeta, Lark hardly felt herself. 'Twas like a dream, all of them making merry as the day dwindled.

Mistress Flowerdew took Larkin for the night, but not before Magnus had held him and tossed him in the air then prayed a blessing over him. Only then did Magnus lead Lark upstairs to his room on the mansion's second floor.

She stood in the middle of the fine chamber fit for a laird, even a displaced one, and turned in a little circle atop the floral carpet to take in the box bed and fine Chippendale furnishings, the twin windows with Venetian blinds drawn. Outside the glass, a dove cooed a soft lament, waiting for its mate.

Magnus smiled down at her in the candlelight, hands busy untying his stock. "A far cry from the stillroom quarters. We can return there on the morrow with our wee lad if ye wish."

"Oh, Magnus, I have so many questions."

"And we have a lifetime together to answer them, aye?"

She sank onto a near loveseat, her skirts rustling. "Please tell me we shan't be separated again."

He got down on a knee, taking her hands in his, and kissed her slowly and tenderly. "Osbourne is a generous man. He asked me whose freedom I wanted as a wedding gift. It goes without saying whose I took."

"Ye redeemed my contract, when ye might have freed yerself."

"And now yer free to return to the West Indies with me. For the time left of my own two-year contract. Ye and Larkin."

Stunned, she smoothed back a strand of his charcoal hair that had escaped his queue and caught in the whiskered growth stippling his jaw. "But if ye'd redeemed yerself, we might stay here. Surely Virginia is a kinder master than Jamaica."

"Yet Jamaica is the greater need. The greater work. And I could not live with myself if I'd freed myself ahead of my bride."

She listened, their gazes locked, too moved to speak.

"One day, mayhap, we'll return home. To Scotland." Reaching out, he snuffed the candle flame a-dance in a warm draft. "Tonight, we shall put away all thought of the morrow. God has given us this day, this hour, aye?"

She nodded through her tears. Tears of joy, not sorrow. Truly, there was nothing she could possibly ask for other than Magnus and this very hallowed moment.

AUTHOR NOTE

Family genealogy has always been fascinating to me, so it was a true earthly delight to blow the dust off my own family heritage and dedicate this novel to my sixth great-grandfather, George Hume. He and my Scottish ancestors had a very colorful history living on the Scottish borders and being so close to England and its enemies back then. As a result, he was exiled to the American colonies for his role in the Jacobite Rebellion of 1715, settled in Virginia, and is credited with teaching surveying to George Washington from 1748 to 1750. I wish I could include all his exploits here but am happy to say he inspired this novel in countless ways.

I've always been thankful for those intrepid Scots, especially those who journeyed to America. After several trips to Scotland myself (which left me wishing my family had never left there), I've attempted to re-create what it might have been like forsaking such an epic place and coming to a new country against one's will. Yet since I am an American and more than two hundred years of history have severed my Scottish connection, I'm sure this novel is but a shadow of what that scenario was truly like. I'm also sure that a Scot would tell it differently. But I attempt to honor my Scots heritage and ancestors here with this fictional account and hope readers feel a sense of Scotland's majestic, heartrending history. Many of you share those rich Scottish roots. I like to think our ancestors may well have known each other!

This story was born while I was hiking on the Isle of Mull and descended a very steep cliff to enter a sea cave at low tide. Our guide told us this immense cave had been used by smugglers long ago. As we continued our hike, we climbed upwards to stone cottages, abandoned and crumbling, overlooking the sea. I thought of all the stories these places could tell in their time. The character of Lark came to mind right then, and later Magnus while I stayed at a castle on the coast. Edinburgh, which figures into this story briefly, is my favorite city, though Glasgow is fascinating too.

I relied on many sources while writing this

novel, primarily the Hume family history, letters, and other accounts of Scottish immigrants coming to America. My son also began beekeeping during this time, but I must confess I'm not an authority on bees, though I find them remarkable!

My hope is that you find this story meaningful and inspiring and can say, despite the valleys of life, "Yea, I have a goodly heritage" (Ps. 16:6).

ACKNOWLEDGMENTS

I'm always in awe of how the Lord gifts each of us with abilities. Though I sometimes wish I had chosen a different path than writing, I'm reminded by reading through childhood diaries that God gave me a love of words and books at a very early age and set me on the publishing path for a purpose. I'm eternally grateful.

Heartfelt thanks to Revell for helping bring this story of my heart and my heritage to the page. I also appreciate my savvy agent, Janet Grant, for being an important part of that process. And I want to thank readers for their encouragement, enthusiasm, and support of my novels. You are the reason I write and am able to continue to create stories that honor God and our amazing history.

Happy reading!

ABOUT THE AUTHOR

Laura Frantz is a Christy Award finalist and the ECPA bestselling author of several books, including *The Frontiersman's Daughter, Courting Morrow Little, The Colonel's Lady, The Mistress of Tall Acre, A Moonbow Night, The Lacemaker,* and the Ballantyne Legacy series. She is a devoted member of the Daughters of the American Revolution and the Colonial Williamsburg Foundation. Learn more at www.laurafrantz.net.